What Readers Are Saying about
The Bright Empires Series

"**His mastery of the art of description is beyond belief.** (I had to stop several times to jump up and down because I loved his style so much, seriously.) His level of attention to details like period mind-set and speech is a delight to behold (especially for die-hard background-first novelists like me)."

—Sir Emeth M.

"This is **a story that has it all**: mystery, history, damsels in distress, and a mind-bending meditation on the nature of reality. It is **equal parts** *Raiders of the Lost Ark*, *National Treasure*, **and** *Jumper*. Highly recommended!"

—Chad J.

"**Filled with descriptions that beguile all five senses** and all the beauty and charm of the language I have come to expect from Lawhead, this book is **a fascinating blend of fantasy and sci-fi.**"

—Jenelle S.

". . . a **hold-your-breath beginning to a new series**. This novel mixes ancient history, time travel, alternate realities, mystery, physics, and fantasy, to create a story so compelling that **I find myself recommending it to any who will listen.**"

—Sheila P.

"[A] sure winner for eager sci-fi readers . . . **The vivid imagery and witty lines help keep the reader on the edge of their seats.**"

—Jerry P.

"**Time travel and high adventure abound** in this brand new title from veteran author Stephen R. Lawhead."

—Ben H.

"**Imagine Narnia merged with Hitchhiker's Guide,** and you have a starting point for the adventures of Kit Livingstone."

—Rick M.

"Lawhead vividly describes the sights, sounds, and smells of the markets in Prague, the streets of Restoration England, and even the dry heat of Ancient Egypt . . . **The premise of ley line travel is fascinating yet mysterious,** with scientific definitions that are detailed without becoming too technical. The characters are personable and complex, and **it's easy to get caught up in their search for that elusive map.**"

—Malinda D.

". . . **an excellent, mysterious storyline** that draws the reader in."

—Kieran

THE
SPIRIT WELL

Other Books by Stephen R. Lawhead

The Bright Empires Series:
The Skin Map
The Bone House
The Spirit Well

King Raven Trilogy:
Hood
Scarlet
Tuck

Patrick, Son of Ireland

The Celtic Crusades:
The Iron Lance
The Black Rood
The Mystic Rose

Byzantium

Song of Albion Trilogy:
The Paradise War
The Silver Hand
The Endless Knot

The Pendragon Cycle:
Taliesin
Merlin
Arthur
Pendragon
Grail
Avalon

Empyrion I: The Search for Fierra
Empyrion II: The Siege of Dome

Dream Thief

The Dragon King Trilogy:
In the Hall of the Dragon King
The Warlords of Nin
The Sword and the Flame

A BRIGHT EMPIRES NOVEL

Quest the Third:

THE
SPIRIT WELL

STEPHEN R.
LAWHEAD

THOMAS NELSON
Since 1798

NASHVILLE   DALLAS   MEXICO CITY   RIO DE JANEIRO

Published in Nashville, Tennessee, by Thomas Nelson. Thomas Nelson is a registered trademark of Thomas Nelson, Inc.

Page design by Mandi Cofer.

Thomas Nelson, Inc., titles may be purchased in bulk for educational, business, fund-raising, or sales promotional use. For information, please e-mail SpecialMarkets@ThomasNelson.com.

Publisher's Note: This novel is a work of fiction. Names, characters, places, and incidents are either products of the author's imagination or used fictitiously. All characters are fictional, and any similarity to people living or dead is purely coincidental.

978-1-40168-787-8 (IE)

Library of Congress Cataloging-in-Publication Data

Lawhead, Steve.
    The spirit well / Stephen R. Lawhead.
        p. cm. -- (Bright empires ; Quest the 3rd)
    ISBN 978-1-59554-806-1 (jacketed hardcover)
I. Space and time--Fiction. 2. Time travel--Fiction. I. Title.
    PS3562.A865S75 2012
    813'.54--dc23

                                    2012018426

Printed in the United States of America

12 13 14 15 16 17 QG 6 5 4 3 2 I

In memory of Tiffany

*"The past and the present
are our means;
the future alone is our end."*

— BLAISE PASCAL

Contents

Important People

Anen—Friend of *Arthur Flinders-Petrie,* High Priest of the Temple of Amun in Egypt, 18th dynasty.

Archelaeus Burleigh, Earl of Sutherland—Nemesis of *Flinders-Petrie, Cosimo, Kit,* and all right-thinking people.

Arthur Flinders-Petrie—Also known as *The Man Who Is Map,* patriarch of his line. Begat *Benedict,* who begat *Charles,* who begat *Douglas.*

Friar Roger Bacon—An early philosopher, scientist, and theologian who worked and taught first at Paris and then Oxford from around 1240 to 1290; he has been called *Doctor Mirabilis* for his wonderful teaching.

Balthazar Bazalgette—The Lord High Alchemist at the Court of *Emperor Rudolf II* in Prague, friend and confidant of *Wilhelmina.*

Benedict Flinders-Petrie—The son of *Arthur* and *Xian-Li,* and father of *Charles.*

Burley Men—*Con, Dex, Mal,* and *Tav.* Lord *Burleigh's* henchmen. They keep a Stone Age cat called *Baby.*

Charles Flinders-Petrie—Son of *Benedict* and father of *Douglas,* he is grandson of *Arthur.*

Cosimo Christopher Livingstone, the Elder, aka Cosimo —A

Victorian gentleman who seeks to reunite the Skin Map and understand the key to the future.

Cosimo Christopher Livingstone, the Younger, aka Kit—*Cosimo's* great-grandson.

Dardok—The head of the River City Clan whom *Kit* first encounters in the Stone Age; also known as *Big Hunter*.

Douglas Flinders-Petrie—Son of *Charles*, and great-grandson of *Arthur*; he is quietly pursuing his own search for the Skin Map, one piece of which is in his possession.

Emperor Rudolf II—King of Bohemia and Hungary, Archduke of Austria and King of the Romans, he is also known as the Holy Roman Emperor and is quite mad.

Engelbert Stiffelbeam—A baker from Rosenheim in Germany, affectionately known as *Etzel*.

En-Ul—The elder statesman of the River City Clan.

Giles Standfast—*Sir Henry Fayth's* coachman and *Kit's* ally.

Gustavus Rosenkreuz—The Chief Assistant to the Lord High Alchemist and *Wilhelmina's* ally.

Lady Haven Fayth—*Sir Henry's* headstrong and mercurial niece.

Sir Henry Fayth, Lord Castlemain—Member of the Royal Society, staunch friend and ally of *Cosimo*. *Haven's* uncle.

Snipe—Feral child and malignant aide to *Douglas Flinders-Petrie*.

Turms—A king of Etruria, one of the Immortals, and a friend of *Arthur*; he oversees the birth of *Benedict Flinders-Petrie* when *Xian-Li's* pregnancy becomes problematic.

Wilhelmina Klug, aka Mina—In another life, a London baker and *Kit's* girlfriend. In this life, owns Prague's Grand Imperial Kaffeehaus with *Etzel*.

Dr. Thomas Young—Physician, scientist, a certified polymath with a keen interest in the archaeology of ancient Egypt, his astonishing breadth and depth of accomplishment led to his epithet: "The Last Man in the World to Know Everything."

Xian-Li—Wife of *Arthur Flinders-Petrie* and mother of *Benedict*; daughter of the tattooist *Wu Chen Hu* of Macao.

Previously

The phenomenon known as ley leaping or ley travel is an endeavour fraught with complication and error. Far from being an exact science, using ley lines to travel among, between, and across the various known dimensions of the multidimensional Omniverse is at best an art that can only be perfected through long apprenticeship, and even the most expert of explorers is likely to go astray—a fact that Kit Livingstone knows only too well. Using a ley line discovered by Wilhelmina, his former girlfriend, Kit has succeeded in eluding capture by Lord Archelaeus Burleigh, a ruthless and violent man determined to possess the fabled Skin Map at any cost.

In Kit's desperation to escape Burleigh's clutches, however, something has gone amiss; for although he landed in the right place, it seems to be entirely the wrong time. At least, the epoch in which Kit finds himself is definitely not the one Wilhelmina had in mind when she advised him to use that particular ley line for his getaway. Suffice it to say that for the time being, and perhaps the foreseeable future, Kit seems to be stuck in the Stone Age. Making the best of his predicament, Kit has stumbled upon a discovery that could prove important to the ongoing proceedings. It would appear that against all odds he has discovered the fabled Well of Souls or, as it is perhaps better known to readers of these pages, the Spirit Well.

Meanwhile, back in seventeenth-century Prague, Wilhelmina's enterprises go from strength to strength; her Grand Imperial Kaffeehaus is a rousing success and a boon to the city's population. Engelbert "Etzel" Stiffelbeam, Mina's business partner and a baker by trade, provides tasty pastries and invigorating coffee to a wildly appreciative public, as well as stalwart support to Wilhelmina. Her material welfare thus guaranteed, Mina now has time and money to spend in pursuit of the quest to find the scattered pieces of the Skin Map. To this end, she has formed a shaky alliance with the mercurial Lady Fayth against the same Lord Burleigh and his gang of base ruffians, the nefarious Burley Men. Yet, we ask ourselves, can Lady Fayth be trusted?

It should be remembered that Giles Standfast, the late Sir Henry Fayth's footman and driver, was sorely wounded in the attempt to flee Burleigh on the night Kit vanished and was taken to the Kaffeehaus for medical attention. The unfortunate Mr. Standfast has been returned to his home in England to convalesce. What lies in store for Giles remains to be seen, but it is expected that he will make a full recovery.

Half a world away in Egypt, Dr. Thomas Young and his new and enthusiastic assistant, Khefri, are deeply engrossed in their work. We last saw them beginning the task of cataloguing an astounding trove of treasure recovered from the sealed tomb of Anen, High Priest of Amun and brother-in-law to Pharaoh Amenhotep III. One of the items retrieved from the tomb was a portion of the Skin Map. Our Dr. Young, we may recall, is also in possession of a meticulously rendered copy of the map and, with Khefri's help, will endeavour to decipher its unique symbology. We wish them well, and hope they continue to occupy themselves to good effect.

Unbeknownst to the others, a rival questor has been quietly making progress in the search for the ultimate treasure—none other than Douglas Flinders-Petrie. For those who may be sensing difficulty with the expanding Flinders-Petrie line, there is a simple alphabetic mnemonic. The line begins with A for Arthur, followed by B for Benedict, C for Charles, and D for Douglas. The last in line, Douglas, the great-grandson of the intrepid Arthur, possesses a purloined section of the map and is diligently applying his considerable talents in learning how to read it. To this end, he has succeeded in locating and suborning an unsuspecting aide to the cause in the person of Friar Roger Bacon, a thirteenth-century scholar, philosopher, theologian, and scientist. Careful readers may recall the audacious assault on the British Museum by Douglas and his young associate, the surly and taciturn Snipe. The two forced entry into the venerable institution's Rare Book Room after opening hours and, following a brief search, made off with a prize volume plucked from the collection.

To allow a slight digression, it can now be reported that the book in question had long been part of a minor southern aristocrat's family library, which at the disposition of the deceased's estate had come to the museum along with his collection of Roman glass and Tudor silver. The volume was thought to be from the late 1500s; it was a small, neat, leather-bound tome handwritten by its author and entitled *Inconssensus Arcanus*, or *Forbidden Secrets*.

This particular work was prized not for its historic value, which was minimal, nor for its educational value, which was even less because it was wholly unreadable. The book was kept merely because all that could be deciphered in page after page of dense, cryptic text was the name Roger Bacon, who was none other than the famous professor of Oxford University in the early medieval period. Priest and scientist, the renowned "Doctor Mirabilis" was the author of many learned volumes, including the legendary *Opus Minus Alchemaie*.

Every page of the *Book of Forbidden Secrets*, as it is known, is filled with strange pictograms resembling the letters of an unknown alphabet, an alphabet serving a language no one on earth had ever heard spoken. A secret code? An occult language? Who could say? Douglas Flinders-Petrie had a fairly solid hunch that it was not a language, neither was it a code. Rather, it was, in his considered opinion, a wholly symbolic script devised by Friar Bacon sometime around the year 1250—the same symbology that had inspired his own great-grandfather, Arthur Flinders-Petrie, in the making of the Skin Map.

In short, it was Douglas' belief that the archaic manuscript was a catalogue of experiments and coordinates. The experiments detailed alchemical processes. The coordinates were those of ley line destinations. Ergo Roger Bacon, in addition to his other more highly lauded achievements, had also discovered ley travel.

More could be said about these matters, but one feels this is quite enough for now; in any event it is enough to be getting on with. So, keeping these details firmly in mind, we return to our tale in which Friday takes a holiday.

PART ONE

The Ghost Road

CHAPTER 1

In Which Friday Takes a Holiday

Cassandra Clarke dug bones for a living. She spent every summer of her professional life hunkered down in trenches of various depths with a trowel in one hand and a whisk broom in the other, excavating the skeletal remains of creatures long dead, many of which were known only to science and some known to no one at all. Although digging was in her blood—her mother was Alison Brett Clarke, palaeontologist of *Turkana Boy* renown—Cassandra did not plan to spend her entire life in plexiglas goggles with dust in her hair and a damp handkerchief over her nose. Her ambition was far greater than crating up fossils to be carefully catalogued and then locked away in some musty museum basement.

Her father—the astrophysicist J. Anthony Clarke III, whose theory on the origin of the universe through quantum fluctuations in a plasma field won him a Nobel Prize nomination—enjoyed telling people that his precocious daughter was born with her feet in the dirt and her head in the stars. Those who heard that quip assumed it was a reference to her parentage and the fact that she spent so much time scrabbling around in holes in the ground. True enough, but it was also a sly allusion to his beloved Cassie's penchant for fanciful invention.

As a child Cass ran a neighbourhood theatre company from a tent in the backyard; for two summers running she cajoled kids within a six-block radius of 8th Avenue and 15th Street into performing in a string of dramas she wrote, produced, and directed. Usually the plays involved beautiful princesses being menaced by either dinosaurs or aliens, sometimes both. Later she graduated to writing poetry and short stories for the school newspaper, and won a prize in junior high for a poem about a melancholy wildflower growing in a parking lot.

Despite these artistic leanings, she gravitated naturally to science. Blessed with her mother's patient persistence and her father's analytical proclivity, she excelled in her undergraduate studies and chose to follow her mother's lead into fossil hunting, spending her summers assisting in digs from China to Mexico, earning her spurs. Now, as a doctoral candidate, she was assigned as assistant director for a major Arizona excavation with career-consolidating potential.

Lately, however, the routine had begun to pall. Coprolites and Jurassic snails no longer held the fascination they once did, and the incessant backbiting and political manoeuvring endemic in upper-echelon academia—which she had always known and accepted as part of the scholastic landscape—was proving more and more of an irksome distraction. The further she travelled into darkest PhD territory, the more the fossilised remains of extinct creatures dwindled in fascination; she was rapidly specialising herself beyond caring about her subject. Whether or not the world learned what the latest new megasaurus ate for lunch sixty million years ago, what difference did it make? On bad days, which seemed to come fairly often of late, it all seemed so pointless.

More and more she found herself looking at the gorgeous Sedona sunsets and, irrationally, hankering for a clean canvas and a set of brushes—or seeing individual cacti as surrealist sculptures, or inwardly rhapsodising about the towering, wind-carved rocks of the canyons. In ways she could not fully describe, she felt she was being moved on to other things, perhaps another life beyond science. Still, she was not willing to throw in the trowel just yet. There was a tee-tering mountain of work to do, and she was up to her hips, almost literally, in unclassified fossils.

Using a dental pick, Cass teased a glassy curve of mineralised bone from the hard-packed brick-coloured earth. It came free and plopped into her hand—a black, leaf-shaped stub of stone so smooth it looked as if it had been polished: the tooth of a young Tarbosaurus, a thero-pod that streaked about the earth during the Cretaceous period and, until this very moment, had only ever been found in the Gobi desert. Cass had studied these creatures in detail, and now had the proof she needed to support the theory of a more far-flung population than previously recognised. There was a time when securing such a speci-men would have had her doing handsprings around the camp. Today, however, she merely tossed the fossil into a plastic bucket of other such treasures, paused, and straightened. Pressing a hand to the small of her aching back, she sighed, rubbed the sweat from the nape of her neck, and, shielding her eyes from the merciless afternoon sun, muttered, "Where's Friday?"

She made a quick scan of the surrounding terrain. The same bleak landscape met her gaze, unchanged in the twenty-one days since the dig season began, unchanged in eons: blood-red sun-scoured rocks, gnarled and withered creosote bushes, many-armed saguaro, scraggly yucca, choya, and assorted cacti by the carload. Of Friday—a Yavapai Indian who acted as gofer and scout for the excavating team—there was no sign. She turned to the west and glimpsed a faded red bandanna bobbing above a haze of purple sage as the work-shy fellow sloped off into the neighbouring canyon.

She glanced at her watch. It was nearing six o'clock; there was another good hour left before they would have to gather up their tools, load the vans, and head back into town.

"How's it going down there?"

Cass turned. The voice belonged to Joe Greenough, her colleague, team leader, and chief community liaison officer for the university field team. An affable chap in his early thirties, Joe coasted up with his hands in his pockets. "Anything interesting?" He peered down into the trench in which she stood.

"Same old, same old." She reached up a hand. "Here. Help a lady out."

"Any time." Grasping her hand, he held it and smiled, but made no effort to help her up.

"Today would be good," she told him. "Any time . . . *now*, perhaps?"

He put a hand under her arm and pulled as she scrambled up the side of the hole. "I hear there's a new invention called a ladder," he said, watching her dust off the seat of her cargo jeans. "Great for climbing. If you're ever in a town that sells 'em, you should get one."

"You know me," she said, moving off. "An old-fashioned girl to my fossilised bones. Don't hold with these newfangled contraptions."

"Hey!" he called. "Where you going?"

"After Friday. I'll be right back."

"I came to talk to you," he pointed out. "Not shout."

"What? You wearing cement shoes?"

"Cass, listen." He jogged after her. "Slow down a second. It's important."

"Then speed up." She kept her eye on the quickly disappearing Indian. It was strange how the indigenous folk could cover ground so quickly without appearing to expend any effort at all. "Friday's gone walkabout, and I don't want to lose him."

"It's about the dig." Joe paused, as if remembering what he had come to say.

"Yeah, with you so far," she said, giving him a sideways glance. She saw a cloud pass over his usually sunny features. "Gosh, it must be some kind of important if it has you at a loss for words."

"It's just . . ." He sighed. "There's no good way to say this."

"Then say it in a bad way," she urged. "Just say it already."

"There's trouble."

"Okay . . . and?" Before he could reply, she went on. "Don't tell me the department is cutting back on our grant money again." She stopped walking and turned to him. "I don't believe this! After all I've done to convince—"

"No, no," he said quickly. "The grant is fine. The committee is delighted with the results."

"Okay, then." She shrugged and started walking again.

"It's the Indians," he blurted.

"Native Americans."

"They're on the warpath."

"Why? What did you say to them *this* time?" She skirted a large prickly pear and stepped lightly over a fallen saguaro limb. The university's assurances and goodwill notwithstanding, the Arizona Native American Council had long ago decided to take a dim view of any archaeological activity in the region. So far, the project directors had been able to placate the ANAC by hiring local people to help with the dig and consult on indigenous culture—which was somewhat outside the remit of a palaeontology project, but helped keep the peace.

"Nothing to do with me," Joe protested. "Apparently there's a major celebration coming up—a holy day or something. The tribal elders are claiming the entire valley as a site of special cultural significance—a sacred landscape."

"Is it?"

"Who knows?" Joe shrugged. "Anyway, they have a state senator on their side. He's up for reelection soon, so he's got a bee in his bonnet. Senator Rodriguez—he's on the squawk box giving interviews about how we're all a bunch of cold, heartless scientists tearing up the countryside and defiling Indian burial grounds."

"This was *never* an Indian burial ground," Cass pointed out. "Anyway, we're not digging up the whole valley, only a few specific locations—the same ones we've been working for the past two years. Did you tell them that?"

Joe regarded her with a pitying expression. "You think logic and reason have anything to do with this? It's political, and it's gone septic."

"Well, that's just dandy," she huffed. "As if we didn't already have enough trouble with the Sedona Tourist Bureau and the New Agers. This isn't going to help one little bit."

"Tell me about it. I've arranged to speak to the editor over at the *Sedona Observer* tomorrow and put our case on record."

"Hold that thought," she said, and resumed her pursuit of the wayward Friday, who had passed from view behind a boulder at the foot of a washout.

"We have to stop digging until this is settled," he called after her. "Get Friday and his crew to help you tie things down and put a tarp over the trench."

"Can't hear you!" she replied.

Dodging a pumpkin-sized barrel cactus, she hurried on, leaving Greenough behind. Keeping an eye peeled for rattlesnakes—the constant bugaboo of desert digs—she clipped along, dodging the bristles, spines, and saw-toothed edges of the local flora, all of which seemed to have been designed to puncture, slash, tear, or otherwise discourage progress one way or another. Strange, she thought, how quiet it became, and how quickly.

The thought was no sooner through her head than she heard that rarest of desert sounds: thunder. The distant rumble, clear and present on the hot dry air, brought her up short.

She glanced up to see that the sky above the towering red-rock hills and canyons of the Verde Valley had grown dark with heavy, black, angry-looking clouds. Oblivious, with her head in the ground, she had failed to notice the fast-changing weather. The wind lifted, and Cassandra smelled rain. A thunderstorm in the desert was not unheard of, but rare enough to be fascinating and fragrant. The smell of washed desert air tinged with ozone was unlike anything else. It would be, she considered, less fascinating to be caught out in a lightning storm. She picked up her pace and called to the swiftly retreating figure ahead, "Friday!"

The echo of her cry came winging back to her from the surrounding canyon walls. Directly ahead rose a towering rock stack—a multibanded heap of the distinctive ruddy sandstone of the Sedona region. "Gotcha!" she muttered, certain that her quarry had ducked out of sight behind the massive wind-sculpted block of stone. She hurried on. The sky continued to lower; the mumbling, grumbling thunder grew louder and more insistent. The freshening wind sent dust devils spinning away through the sagebrush and mesquite.

As Cassandra rounded the base of the sandstone stack, she saw that it opened into one of the many feeder gullies of the larger system the locals called Secret Canyon. She thought she glimpsed a figure flitting through the shadows of the gulch some distance ahead. She shouted again, but received no answer; she sped on, moving deeper into the enormous crevice.

Her Yavapai colleague was in most significant ways the stereotypical red man: work-shy, taciturn to the point of monosyllabic, arrogant, furtive, given to odd moods. Habitually dressed in faded jeans with the cuffs stuffed into the tops of his scuffed cowboy boots, he wore his straight black hair scraped back into a single braid that fell down the back of his sun-bleached blue shirt, and bound the end with a leather strap decorated with a bit of red rag or a quail feather. In both dress and demeanour he presented an image so patently clichéd that Cass had come to believe that it was purposefully studied, and one he worked very hard to maintain. No one could have combined so many of these dime-novel qualities by accident.

Friday, she concluded, *wanted* to be seen as the quintessential Native American of popular romance. He chased it—to the point of standing outside the Walgreens on Main Street on the weekends dressed in a fringed deerskin vest and beaded moccasins, with two eagle feathers in his hair, posing for pictures with tourists for tips: Sedona's very own drugstore Indian. All he lacked was a fistful of cigars.

As to *why* he did it, she as yet had no clue. Why play a part so obviously derisory and beneath him? Why perpetrate a demeaning cliché that belonged to a backward, less enlightened time? Was it masochism, or some kind of elaborate joke? Cass could not begin to guess.

"Friday!" she shouted, still moving forward. "Come out! I know you're in here." She paused, then added, "You're not in trouble. I just want to talk to you."

The rock walls of undulating stone, layered in alternating bands of colour, rose sheer from the floor of the gulley, which upon closer inspection appeared unnaturally straight: a curious quality Cassandra noticed but put down to a trick of the uncertain light and oddly shaped stone walls. A sudden gust of wind sent loose pebbles falling from the heights above and, with them, the first drops of rain.

"Friday!"

The sound of her voice pinged along the sandstone walls, but there was no reply from the deepening shadows ahead. The sky grew dark and angry as a bruise, the low clouds churning. The air tingled with pent energy; it felt alive, as if lightning was about to strike.

With a hand flattened over her head to protect herself from the scattershot of pebbles, Cassandra raced on, taking the straight path through the canyon to avoid the loose debris from above. The wind shrieked a withering note, sending a sheet of rain down the length of the gulley, drenching everything in its path.

Cassandra was caught. The wind, funnelled by the canyon, surged over her, dashing cold water into her face. Blinded by the rain, she scooped water from her eyes and dived for whatever cover the overhanging ledges of stone could provide. A blast of icy wind slammed into her with the force of a jet engine, stealing the breath from her lungs and driving her along the canyon floor. She staggered forward, tripped, put out her hands to break her fall, and gritted her teeth . . . but the expected jolt did not come.

To her horror, the ground gave out beneath her, and she continued to tumble.

Between one step and the next she was airborne, plunging into an unseen void. The landing, when it came, was abrupt, but not the bone-breaking shock she instinctively feared. The ground on which she landed had an odd spongy granularity she could not have anticipated.

Her first thought was that she had somehow fallen through the roof of a kiva—one of the underground ritual houses favoured by the pueblo-dwelling natives of the past. These were often hidden, and the roofs were known to give way beneath the weight of unwary hikers. But whoever heard of a kiva hidden in a canyon floor?

Her second thought—an absurd possibility—was that a tornado had plucked her up and dropped her miles away. Did she not feel that she had been flying? How else to explain what she was now seeing? For stretching before her was a vast, arid plain of volcanic gravel without a single cactus or mesquite tree in sight. The towering red rocks of Sedona were gone, and in the far distance a band of black hills lined the horizon.

And that was all.

What had happened to Arizona?

Cass stared at the alien landscape, whirling in panicky pirouette like a dancer who had inexplicably lost her partner. Panic rising, she gulped air in a futile effort at forcing herself to remain calm. Two thoughts chased each other round and round in her spinning thoughts: *What happened? Where am I?*

Cass, the back of her hand pressed to her mouth to stifle the scream she felt gathering there, struggled heroically to make sense of this exceedingly strange turn of events, and was on the verge of collapsing on the path and gathering herself into a tight foetal position when a gruff and irritated voice startled her.

"What are you doing here?"

Distracted momentarily from her panic, she whirled to look behind her. "Friday!" Relief of an oily, queasy sort spread through her. "Thank God it's you. Didn't you hear me calling you?"

"No." He put his hand to her upper arm. "You must go back."

She looked around, the strangeness of the situation increasing by the second. "Where are we? What happened?"

"This is not for you." He started walking, pulling Cassandra with him.

She wrenched away from his grasp. "I'm not going anywhere until you tell me what happened," she insisted. She glared at him. "Well?"

An uncertain mixture of pique tinged with amusement squirmed across the Native American's sun-wrinkled features. "This is *Tsegihi*," he told her. "You do not belong here."

Cassandra frowned. If she had heard the word before, she could not place it. "I don't understand."

"You crossed the Coyote Bridge on the Ghost Road."

"There was no road, no bridge. I—"

"In the canyon." He made to take her arm again, but Cass stepped away. "We must go back before it is too late."

"Why?" She glanced around at the elaborately empty landscape. "What could happen?"

"Bad things."

Cassandra allowed the Indian to take her arm. He turned her

around and began walking along a path scratched in the pumice chips that covered the plain to a depth of several inches. The path stretched across the empty landscape in an absolutely straight line as far as she could see.

"Is this the Ghost Road? How did I get—" she began, but her next words were stolen by the wind that gusted out of nowhere, snatching her voice from the air as, between one step and the next, her feet left the ground.

CHAPTER 2

In Which the Secret Canyon Gives Up Its Secret

When Cassandra could see again, she was once more in Secret Canyon, sopping wet, her head throbbing with a headache so virulent she could not see straight. Hands on hips, bent low at the waist, she gulped air and fought down a queasy motion sickness.

Friday towered over her, frowning.

"What?" she demanded. "You might have warned me that was going to happen."

"You are weak," Friday replied, looking at the sky. The roiling black clouds were already dissipating as the storm sped off into the distance.

"And you are both stubborn and arrogant," she countered, wiping her face with both hands.

"We will go back to the dig now." He gave her a cursory glance and started walking. When she failed to follow, he stopped and looked back.

"I'm not taking a single step until I get some answers, mister."

"Okay," he sniffed. "You can stay here."

He started off again.

Cass watched him striding away and understood from the set of his shoulders that he would not be turning back a second time. She hastened after the lanky figure. "Listen," she said, falling into step beside him, "I want an explanation. You owe me that much at least."

"You followed me." He did not look at her, but kept walking. "I don't owe you anything."

"That place we were just at—where was that? How did we get there? What happened? Was it something to do with the storm?"

"You ask a lot of questions."

"Nothing like this has ever happened to me."

"It won't happen again."

"Hey!" she shouted. "I want to know what's going on. I mean to get to the bottom of this."

"You won't."

"Try me," she shot back.

"You don't know what you're asking."

"Then tell me. Make it simple so I'll understand."

"People will think you're crazy."

"So what?"

Friday turned his broad, weather-creased face to her. He was smiling. "You don't care if people think you're crazy?"

"Do I look like someone who cares?" she demanded. "Give it up. What happened back there?"

"I already told you."

"You said it was what—Zay-ghee-hee?"

"Tsegihi," he confirmed. "That's right."

"What does that mean?"

"In English?"

"If possible."

Friday nodded to himself. "You would say it is the Spirit World."

"That was no Spirit World. That was real."

"I said you wouldn't believe it." He strode on.

"Okay, I'm sorry." Cass hurried after him. "Continue, please. How did we get there?"

"I already told you."

"I know, I know—the Coyote Bridge on the Ghost Road."

He made no reply.

"But that is just a—what do you call it?—a myth, or a metaphor, or something."

"If you say so."

"No, tell me. I want to know. What is the Ghost Road?"

"It is the way the Medicine Folk use to cross from this world to the Spirit World."

"You mean literally, physically cross over."

"Yes."

"That's impossible."

"If you say so."

They had almost reached the mouth of the canyon. She could see the desert beyond and, judging from the long shadows cast by the saguaro and mesquite bushes, the afternoon was waning towards evening.

"Among my people, there are those who travel to the Spirit World to perform sacred duties." He paused, then added, "I am not one of them."

"So what are you then? A tourist?"

A faint smile touched his lips. "Maybe so."

"A tourist," she harrumphed. "I don't believe you."

"That is your choice."

"Okay, sorry. So you're a tourist in the Spirit World."

"We call one who travels the Ghost Roads a World Walker."

"Right, so how do you do it? This world walking—will you teach me?"

"No."

"Why not?"

"It is not for you."

Despite her repeated attempts to cajole, threaten, and otherwise bully him, Friday refused to tell her more. In the end she was forced to abandon the attempt and return to the dig to oversee the securing of the site.

On the ride back to town, Cassandra was preoccupied and distracted—behaviour that did not go unnoticed by her coworkers in the van.

"You're a quiet one today," declared Anita, one of the undergrads the dig relied on for donkeywork.

"Am I?" wondered Cass. "Sorry."

"Anything the matter?"

"I guess I'm just a little tired."

"Tell me about it. Mac had us wrestling bags of rubble all afternoon."

"Hmm." Cassandra gazed out the van window at the passing scenery, all red and gold and purple in the early evening light. "It really is a beautiful landscape," she said absently.

Anita gazed at her for a moment. "Are you *sure* you're all right?"

"Yeah, fine. Why shouldn't I be?"

"I thought Greenough might have got to you with this news about shutting down the dig."

"I suppose so . . ." She returned to her contemplation of the skyline with its monumental sandstone rock stacks.

A little while later the van convoy pulled into the motel parking lot.

"Hey, Cass—you going over to Red Rocks with us?" called Anita as the crew disembarked and headed off across the parking lot. Red Rocks served cheap tacos and fizzy beer and was the official digger watering hole.

"Yeah, later, I guess," replied Cassandra, walking away. "You guys go on without me."

She picked up her key from the front desk and meandered to her room. The King's Arms motel was a tired old fleapit, but it was inexpensive by Sedona standards. Moreover, it was about the only place in town halfway eager to cater to the diggers. The lobby smelled of damp dog ineffectively masked by Pine-Sol; the result was acrid. *This sucks*, she thought, not for the first time. To be a poor academic in a resort for wealthy tourists was, contrary to any expectations, no picnic. You couldn't turn around without being reminded that you didn't belong and, moreover, were just taking up space that could be better used by paying customers.

Once in her room, she threw herself down on the sagging bed and stared up at the ceiling, her thoughts whirling in unison with the creaky ceiling fan. She took her time showering and changing, and by the time she arrived at Red Rocks the party was in full swing. The worker bees were celebrating the fact that they had just received at least two, and maybe three, whole days off from the dig. Out of deference to the Native American sensitivities and a wish to avoid confrontation with Senator Rodriguez and thereby deny him a soapbox, Joe

Greenough had announced that they would suspend operations over the weekend. After a beer and a handful of nachos, Cassandra called it a night, made her excuses, and sneaked away. She walked back to the motel by herself, outwardly calm, inwardly a raging turmoil of half-formed thoughts and wild speculations.

She closed the door to her room, picked up the phone, dialled, and pressed the receiver to her ear while the dial tone rang again and again. When no one answered, she hung up and turned on the TV. She sat in bed watching mindless sitcoms for an hour or so, then picked up the phone again.

This time it was answered on the fourth ring. "Hello, this is Tony—speak to me."

"Dad?"

"Cassie? Is that you? What's wrong?"

"It's me. Does anything have to be wrong for a girl to call her father?"

"No, no—not at all, honey," he replied quickly. "It's just that— do you know what time it is?"

"Uh-um." Cass paused. "Is it late? Sorry, I forget about the time difference."

"No problem, sweetie. I'm glad you called. What's up?"

"Nothing. I'm sorry. Go back to sleep. Everything's fine. I'll call back another time."

"Cassandra," her father said in a tone of voice he used when he was serious. "What is it? I'm here to help."

She drew a deep breath. "Dad, ever have one of those days when the whole world turned upside down?"

"Of course, dear heart. That happened to me last Thursday."

Cass could hear him move across the room and settle into his big leather chair.

"So tell me about it. What's turned your world upside down?"

"Not just my world, Dad," Cass told him. "Everybody's world. In fact, the entire universe has come unhinged, or disconnected, or—I don't know what. It's just so weird. It's inexplicable."

"Well"—his laugh was a soothing sound, gentle and familiar—"you're going to have to try, or we're not going to get very far."

"That's just it. I don't know *how* to explain."

"Okay."

She could hear him putting on his scientist hat.

"Don't analyse anything, just start at the beginning. And don't skip anything. What are we dealing with?" At her pause, he added, "Don't think—just speak. Animal, vegetable, or mineral?"

"You know the vortexes?" she asked. "The famous Sedona Vortexes?"

"I'm familiar with the term—from what you've told me I assumed it was nothing but a racket hyped up by the locals to bring in the tourist trade—exploitative hooey."

"I suppose . . ." Cassandra sighed.

It was true; the Sedona Vortexes had been tarred with the tired old brush of New Age claptrap. Whatever the scientific legitimacy—if there was even a molecule of fact in the concept—the enterprise was now the hobbyhorse of aging hippies, earth goddess devotees, wannabe mystics, and assorted kooks, quacks, and fraudsters. Whether they existed or not, vortexes were grand for the Sedona economy: everything from Vortex Jeep Rides and Vortex Helicopter Tours to Vortex Psychic Readings and Vortex Energised Jewellery was to be had for a nifty price.

"Are we talking about the same thing?" her father asked.

"Yes, but something happened today—something really weird.

I guess you'd call it a natural phenomenon—but of an order I have never seen before."

"Excellent!" Before she could respond, he rushed on. "Now, where were you? What were you doing when you observed this phenomenon?"

She explained about her routine, the dig site, what she was doing, and went on to describe following Friday into the canyon. When it came to what happened next, she faltered.

"Yes, yes, go on," her father urged. "Don't think, just blurt it out."

"You know how all your buddies are always talking about those extra dimensions of the universe?"

"Mathematical dimensions, yes."

"Well, what if they weren't merely mathematical?" She took a breath and then plunged in. "Dad, I think I travelled to a different dimension."

This admission was met by silence on the other end of the line.

"Dad? Still there?"

"You mean . . ." he began, then paused and started again. "Exactly what *do* you mean?"

"Only that one second I was in the canyon being pelted by sand and wind and rain, and the next I was . . . Dad, I was standing on an alluvial pan of volcanic cinders—no canyon, no cacti, no nothing— only lines stretching to the horizon in every direction."

"Define *lines*," her father said after a moment.

"Lines—you know. Like someone had taken a snow shovel and dug a shallow trough through the cinders across the plain, but not arbitrary or haphazard. These lines were absolutely straight, and they went on for miles."

Again there was silence. Finally he said, "Was it hot today? I mean, hotter than usual? Are you drinking enough water out there?"

"Dad," Cassandra said, exasperation edging into her tone, "I am a seasoned pro—I don't get sunstroke. Okay? You think I was hallucinating?" Her voice rose higher. "It was not an hallucination or food poisoning or malaria. I'm not having my period. It was real. It happened."

"I wasn't judging you, Cass," he protested. "I'm on your side. But we have to examine every possibility. Rule things out."

"You're right," she sighed. "I'm sorry. It's just that the more I think about it, the more rattled I get. At the time it was weird enough, but now . . ."

"You said Friday was with you. You followed him and met him in this other dimension, and then what?"

"He said I shouldn't be there, and he brought me back."

"How did he do that?"

She paused to consider. "He turned us around, and we just started walking . . . the wind kicked up . . . some dust blew in my eyes, and everything got a little hazy . . . I felt the rush of wind on my face . . . and then it started to rain. When I looked up we were back in the canyon."

"The same canyon as before?" her father asked.

"Right. The same one—they call it Secret Canyon," she said, and paused. "That's all. That's what happened."

"Any physical symptoms? Anything at all?"

"I got a little seasick—queasy, dizzy, and a terrific headache. All that passed pretty quickly. Besides getting windblown and spattered from the rain, nothing else."

"Was Friday there too?"

"Yes, he brought me back, as I said," Cass confirmed. "I tried to get him to explain what happened, but he was very elusive about it.

He kept saying it wasn't for me—I took that to mean for white folk in general, not just myself in particular—and he used all these Native American names for things. He called it the Ghost Road and Coyote Bridge—things like that. He said we had visited the Spirit World."

"Extraordinary."

"You do believe me—don't you, Dad?"

"Of course I believe you, Cass," he said, his voice full of confidence and assurance. "What is more, I think this worthy of more extensive investigation. I think I'd better come out there."

"Dad, you don't really—"

"We need to test it, document it. I'll bring some instruments." He paused. "I wish your mother were here. She would be in her glory."

Cass could hear him thinking.

"Can you find this place again?"

"Sure, no problem. But, listen, I was thinking that—"

"Good. Don't do anything until I get there. Not a thing. I'll catch a flight out tomorrow afternoon. Can you get me a room where you're staying?"

"Yes, but—Dad, I'm not sure this is such a good idea—"

"It's settled then. I'll see you soon, sweetie. Now, don't mention this to anybody. Okay? You haven't, have you?"

"No—just you."

"Thing is, dear heart, the last thing we need is a bunch of amateurs and nutcases poking around, making things difficult. From what you tell me Sedona is full of those."

"Do you really think—?"

"Good-bye, Cassie. I've got some phone calls to make. Don't do a thing until I get there. Love you!"

Click. The line went dead.

"Love you too, Dad." She held the phone for a moment, then closed the cover and tossed it on the bedside table.

"Great," she muttered. Then thought, *Well, you dolt, what were you expecting? You wanted to be taken seriously—what did you think that would look like?*

CHAPTER 3

In Which Kit
Contemplates a Miracle

The cold seeped up through the frozen ground into the very marrow of his bones as Kit lay shivering in the snow. He had the feeling that he had been curled in a slowly chilling heap for days, if not longer—though it could only have been a few minutes at most. *Move,* he told himself, *or freeze where you lie.*

Slowly, slowly Kit rolled onto his side and looked around. His head ached and his muscles were stiff, and he was back: back in the forest clearing, back in the dead of winter, back in the prehistoric past. The sky was overcast and dark; silent snow sifted gently down from the low, heavy clouds, softening the contours of the Bone House. Constructed entirely of interlocked bones—great, curving mammoth tusks; the antlers, spines, and pelvises of elk, buffalo, antelope, and pigs; at least one rhino's skull; innumerable ribs and leg bones of lesser creatures; and who knew what else?—all intertwined in a crazy jigsaw pattern that formed a gently mounded dwelling that was somehow more than the sum of its disparate parts.

Set in the centre of a circular clearing deep in the forest, the odd igloo-shaped hut exerted an undeniable force—an earthy, primitive power like magnetism or gravity, subtle but palpable. The mere sight of the structure brought the vision back in all its splendour: he had seen the Spirit Well, and in some way he could not yet fathom, nor even begin to describe, he knew his life had changed.

He closed his eyes so that he could relive it all again from the beginning. First, he had been inside the Bone House, holding the ley lamp and feeling it grow warm in his hand as it became active; he saw again the little lights shining blue and bright in the weird half-light of the Bone House. Then, inexplicably, he had plunged through the snow-packed floor and into a realm of dazzling light and warmth, a realm of breathtaking clarity where even the smallest objects possessed an almost luminous radiance. His first impression was of a world of such beauty, peace, and harmony that it sent a pang of longing through his heart. Reeling from the almost intoxicating tranquillity, Kit had stumbled along a path lined with plants and trees of exquisite proportion in colours so vivid it made his eyes ache. Every leaf of every tree and plant seemed to shimmer with vitality, every blade of grass radiated the same energy of unquenchable life. Kit walked through this lush and verdant woodland garden in a state of rapt wonder, eventually reaching the edge of a lake unlike any he had ever seen before: an expanse of translucent crystalline fluid with a slightly viscous quality, like that of olive oil or syrup; it gave off a faintly milky glow, its smooth ripples shimmering with the restless energy of living light.

He remembered reaching out to touch that miraculous substance . . . and then . . . something had happened . . . What?

The creak of a nearby branch, cold and bending with snow, brought him back to the present reality of ice and cold and prowling predators; brushing clots of snow from his furs, he stood and shuffled forward, dropped to his hands and knees before the tunnel-like entrance of the bony hut, and crawled inside. The interior was sunk in gloom, but relatively warm—at least warmer than the clearing outside—due no doubt to the radiating presence of its sleeping occupant. On impulse, Kit reached out to the reclining form of En-Ul. The aged primitive was warm to the touch and stirred under his hand. The Old One was still alive, and still dreaming time.

The term was Kit's attempt to translate a concept that he could not exactly define—a sort of mystical meditation or prophetic journey that involved time in some way. Then again, maybe it was something else altogether.

Kit settled himself beside En-Ul and tried once more to reconstruct what had happened to him. After dropping through the floor of the Bone House and making the leap into the unknown, he had followed a sunlit, leafy trail through the paradise world as through a garden of delights, eventually discovering the Spirit Well. Something had happened there. At the mystical pool he had seen Arthur Flinders-Petrie and . . . something so incredible that even now it seemed to cast a magical glow over him—if he could only remember what it was.

Concentrate! he told himself. *What did you see?*

Pressing cold hands to his head, he squeezed his eyes shut, and into his mind came the image of his own feet on that otherworldly path . . . walking swiftly, almost running—away from the pool of light, retracing his steps . . . and then he felt himself falling, his foot catching something in the path—a vine maybe, or the root of a tree . . . falling hard, hitting his head . . .

Kit reached a hand to the back of his skull and felt a tender goose egg there. Yes! He had fallen and struck his head. Of course! That proved it was no dream. He *had* been there; he *had* witnessed a miracle. That was it! He had witnessed a miracle of rebirth, or resurrection.

Instantly, memory snapped sharp and focused once more; his mind filled with clear, precise images. He saw again the wondrous pool; a movement at its edge had warned him to take cover amongst the foliage. He withdrew into the shadows, and Arthur Flinders-Petrie had appeared at the edge of the pool carrying the body of a woman. The woman, clearly dead, had been restored to life by the vivifying waters of that extraordinary pool. Cradled in the arms of Arthur Flinders-Petrie, her corpse had been carried into the water, emerging a moment later fully alive. Kit had seen it with his own eyes, the same eyes that now misted at the thought that the beautiful world he had found was now lost again.

The memory of that wonder so fleetingly glimpsed and experienced filled him with a longing of such intensity he could hardly breathe. Kit slumped back, holding his throbbing head and feeling immensely sorry for himself until it occurred to him that what had been discovered once could be discovered again. Why not? The first time had been by accident; he had not even been searching. The Well of Souls had found *him*, so to speak. This time, he would find that miraculous pool and plunge himself into its living, healing water.

With that in mind, Kit fished the ley lamp from its place in the interior pouch he had sewn into his deerskin shirt. Wilhelmina's curious brass gizmo was dark now; the little row of holes that glowed bright blue in the presence of telluric activity were black and empty. From this Kit knew the ley portal that had opened to allow him to pass to the other world was no longer active. Just to be sure, he waved the device around the interior of the Bone House. The lamp remained a dark, cold, unlit lump of cast metal. The sense of loss sharpened at the realisation that he would not be able to return to the Spirit Well—at least not yet, not until the ley or portal opened once more. He stuffed the instrument back into the pouch; he would try again later. Resigning himself to waiting, Kit settled back and, listening to the slow, easy rhythm of the sleeping En-Ul, was soon dozing.

In his dreamy state Kit let his mind roam where it would, and it soon wandered to Wilhelmina. He wondered what she was doing. Was she still searching for him? Did she fear for his safety? As for himself, he had no such fears. He had found a place among the River City dwellers and, aside from the lack of a few obvious creature comforts, Kit was not only surviving but thriving. In fact, in ways he could not have predicted, he was content. He still wanted to go home, eventually, but for now it seemed right to stay. If this was meant to be, he could accept that.

Thinking of Wilhelmina tirelessly searching for him stirred in Kit a desire to somehow reassure her that he was safe and was content to wait, however long it might take. "I'm okay, Mina," he murmured as he nodded off. "Don't worry. Take your time. I'll be waiting for you."

Kit dozed on and off for a while. When he stirred again, it was darker inside the Bone House than before. He yawned and stretched and looked around, then saw that he was being watched.

"You are awake, En-Ul," he said aloud, holding in his mind the image of a man waking up.

The Ancient One gave the customary satisfied grunt that Kit associated with assent, and in his mind's eye Kit saw the clan sitting by a fire eating meat . . . followed by the image of an empty mouth opening wide.

"You are hungry?" asked Kit, rubbing his stomach in a panto-mime gesture for hunger. "Shall we go back to the camp?" He mimed walking with his fingers against his palm and then pointed in the vague direction of the gorge.

Again came the grunt of affirmation, and the old chieftain made to rise. Kit helped him sit up. "We can take it slow," he advised, form-ing a mental picture of this thought. "There is no hurry."

They sat in silence for a time, and then En-Ul moved to crawl out of the hut. Kit followed and emerged in the early twilight. A snow-softened hush lay upon the forest. He could hear the soft plop of clumps falling from the branches of the trees around them. The air was crisp and tasted of pine. Kit drew a deep breath into his lungs and exhaled, feeling the icy tang on the back of his tongue. En-Ul stood for a moment, gazing around, listening, then turned and began the trek back to the gorge and the safety of the rock ledge where the clan waited.

Night came upon them long before they reached the valley floor; Kit saw torchlight winking through the trees on the trail leading to the limestone escarpment, and they were soon greeted by members of River City Clan who had come out to welcome them. Once again Kit experienced the uncanny sixth sense of these primitive people; he thought of it as a sort of mental radio that allowed them to com-municate with one another instantaneously and over considerable distance. They might have had the vocal acuity of bright toddlers, but telepathically they were wizards.

Their looks, too, were highly deceptive. A casual observer might reasonably surmise that the typical River City Clan member was a shaggy, lumbering specimen, slow of foot and apprehension, a hulk-ing, ham-fisted brute utterly lacking all human refinements. In actual fact, they were agile and lithe, possessing a peculiar grace all their own. They could move through their forested world in complete silence and near invisibility; they knew how to avail themselves of every source of food on foot, wing, or root; they possessed the gentleness, patience, and long-suffering tolerance worthy of saints. They would never be mistaken for elegant; their stocky, muscular build, thick limbs, and broad bodies were not designed for dance, but for endurance. Shaggy they were, true, but in the months Kit had been with them he was no less hairy; in many ways life was simpler without scissors.

The clansmen were glad to see them; with much patting and pawing and grunts of satisfaction, the two sojourners were gathered back into the fold. To Kit it felt like a genuine homecoming; he had a place among these people, yes, but in light of his experience at the Well of Souls, he could not help thinking it was something more—that he had some more definite purpose here. What that purpose might be eluded him at the moment, but the feeling was real and inescapable.

The words of Sir Henry came back to him: *No such thing as coincidence.*

Despite all that had happened to him, or maybe because of it, Kit could accept that at face value, thinking, *I am meant to be here.* Now all he had to do was figure out why.

The welcome concluded, the greeting party led them back to the winter quarters. The soft flutter of the burning brands and the soft squeak of snow beneath feet swaddled in bearskin were the only sounds to mark their passing. They moved along the river's edge, now iced over, the snow-covered humps of stones creating a lumpy field; they trooped up the narrow passage along the wall of the gorge to the generous rock ledge that was the clan's winter home. By the time they tumbled into camp once more, Kit was chilled all the way through.

A wide, flat space on the lip of the ledge had been given over to a sizeable campfire, which was kept burning day and night. Sleeping mats made of bundles of dried grass overspread with pelts and furs lay scattered around the perimeter of the fire, and at the back of the ledge two hollows—one for food and one for water—allowed the clansmen to keep ready supplies close at hand.

Kit threaded his way among the well-wishers and stood as close to the campfire as he dared until the flames warmed him once more. Strips of venison from the haunch of a deer were sizzling on wooden skewers, filling the air with the aroma of roasting meat; the skewers were passed hand to hand. After all had eaten their fill, River City settled in for the night. Kit sat up for a long time, watching the fire and thinking about what he had experienced in the Bone House and what it meant. Then, tired at last, he squeezed a place in amongst the scattered bodies and slept to the slow tick of smouldering embers.

It snowed throughout the night and was still snowing the next morning when En-Ul rose and stood before the clan as they huddled around the fire. Kit, like the others, noticed at once—it was not a common action—and all looked in hushed expectation of what the Ancient One would do. Standing before his people, En-Ul looked around and then gave a grunt. Into Kit's mind came the image of a dimly flickering light and a hand. The hand was red and dripping with blood. Then he saw animals—whole herds of deer and antelope and great ruddy-haired, slow-moving mastodons—all in motion on a great plain of tall grass.

The image faded and, to Kit's surprise, the hunters of the clan all rose as one and began swaying back and forth, grunting their approval. Kit watched, hoping for some other sign, but nothing more was forthcoming. Dardok—the one Kit thought of as Big Hunter, the clan leader—rose and took up his spear; he lofted it and gave a low, rumbling call, like that of a bull elk or buffalo. The other hunters acclaimed this by lofting their own spears and repeating the bull roar. Then they left the rock shelter, descending down the narrow passage leading to the valley floor. Dardok was the last to leave, and as he turned to go, En-Ul made a clicking sound in his throat. Dardok paused, something passed between Old Chieftain and Big Hunter, and Kit found himself the object of scrutiny. Dardok gave a grunt of assent, and En-Ul reached out and rested a hand on Kit's head.

At the touch, Kit felt a sudden surge of warmth spread through him, and in his mind's eye he saw himself walking with the hunters. Dardok regarded him expectantly. By this Kit knew he was meant to accompany them on their expedition. Dardok stooped and gathered some embers from the fire, placing them in a vessel made from a hollowed-out bit of wood. He covered the embers with ash to preserve them, then picked up his spear and left the rock ledge.

Kit followed Big Hunter down the path to the frozen river and into a day bleached white as bone.

CHAPTER 4

In Which Confession Is Good for the Soul

Wilhelmina came to the conclusion that Kit had made good his escape from Burleigh's murderous clutches, but that something had gone haywire in the leap. Consequently, he had not ended up at the agreed-upon destination. In short, Kit was now lost somewhere in space and time. Fortunately she had thought to retrieve the Skin Map from him before he fled; otherwise that would be lost too. The scrap of human parchment, almost translucent with age, had been recovered by Kit and Thomas Young from the tomb of Anen, High Priest of the Temple of Amun, during the Eighteenth Dynasty. After examining it—she could make nothing of the obscure squiggly symbols scattered across its surface—Mina had wrapped it in a bit of clean linen and hidden it in the iron strongbox bolted to the inside of the clothes chest at the foot of her bed.

Probably, I should have locked Kit in the strongbox as well, she thought sulkily. His disappearance had caused Wilhelmina no end of concern, and now it was causing her sleepless nights as well. What had happened to Kit? She had given him explicit instructions—where to go, what to do—and the River Ley, as she called it, was tried and true. She knew this because she had personally explored it numerous times and found it wholly reliable, boring even. Never had she experienced the slightest difficulty when traversing it. Added to that, the River Ley led to a very stable part of the world—a place she called simply Mill Valley—for the old grain mill in its deep limestone gorge. It was a peaceable, rustic place that, from all that Mina could tell, was inhabited by gentle souls who tended their flocks of geese and sheep and were scrupulous about minding their own business. What could possibly have gone wrong?

Of course, knowing Kit, almost anything was possible. She could not begin to guess what he might have done. True, he had fled Prague on the run, chased by Burleigh and his gang. No doubt that had complicated matters somewhat, but she had covered for him on her end and taken care to arrange a fail-safe hiding place. Trust Kit Livingstone to bollix things up big time.

Even given the fraught situation surrounding his disappearance, she should still have been able to locate him when the heat died down. The fact that after repeated attempts in numerous time periods she had not been able to locate him—and she did keep trying, faithfully, whenever she had a spare moment—was deeply worrying. If Kit had been wounded or worse, killed, she would doubtless have found his body on the trail when she searched the ley on the other side. Dead or injured, his body might have been dragged off somewhere by a wild animal; but there would have been signs of that, and in numerous searches she had turned up nothing to indicate a mauling or a struggle of any kind. Added to this, she had Giles' eyewitness testimony that Kit got clean away, which she had no reason to doubt—all the more because her sources indicated that Burleigh, for all his trying, had not been able to find Kit alive or dead either. The current report that Kit, in a frantic attempt to escape capture, had leapt into the river and tried to swim to freedom was merely a ruse concocted to hide the fact that he had escaped via Mina's ley line. And just supposing Kit had panicked and done something so harebrained as jumping into the river and getting himself drowned, his soggy corpse would have fetched up downstream. Just to be sure, she had made discreet inquiries with the local officials in the towns and villages all along the Moldau. No one had found so much as a washed-up shoe.

So now, weeks later, frustrated and perturbed, Wilhelmina was at the end of her expertise. She had one last recourse. If that did not succeed, there was no hope. In the meantime she applied herself to learning the subtleties of the new and improved ley lamp—the upgraded version of the one she had slipped to Kit to aid his escape. The new model, like the first, had been supplied by her friend and co-conspirator Gustavus Rosenkreuz, a young alchemist in the emperor's court. Rudolf II maintained a cabal of palace alchemists charged with the duty of lifting the veil on various mysteries of the universe, chief among them immortality and how to achieve it. This august and imposing work was led by Herr Doctor Bazalgette, one of the emperor's favourites, and Gustavus was his much put-upon personal assistant.

Naturally, such blindingly arcane labour necessitated regular refreshment, which the alchemists took at the Grand Imperial; the weirdly cloaked-and-hatted coterie maintained a ready presence in the Kaffeehaus, and Wilhelmina made certain they always had a good table and the best of Etzel's sweet pastries. Through Gustavus she supplied the alchemists with the "bitter earth"—spent coffee grounds—that they valued so highly for their obscure experiments. By way of reciprocation, if not revenge for his neglect at the hands of his superiors, young Rosenkreuz supplied her with useful information and, happily, another illicit copy of Burleigh's latest ley-finding instrument. If his lordship ever found out that Mina had a spy inside the palace—the same person, in fact, seconded to fashion the earl's special devices for him—the full extent of Wilhelmina's deception would be revealed and her life would be forfeit. She shuddered to think what the Earl of Sutherland would do if he ever found out she possessed copies of his gizmos. Whatever form it took, she had no doubt his revenge would be complete, and deeply unpleasant.

One bright day in early winter, a month or so after Kit's disappearance, Wilhelmina pulled on her coat and shawl and took the mule and wagon out into the countryside to experiment with the new and improved ley lamp. Despite repeated efforts, she had yet to discover the extent of its alleged enhancements. She did not doubt improvements had been made; according to Rosenkreuz, Lord Burleigh's investment in the new device had been considerable. Everything from the rare elements that powered the lamp—including gold, platinum, and other precious metals, and more exotic earths like radium, lithium, phosphorus, and some even the alchemists had never seen—had been obtained by the earl at great expense. Presumably, the increased benefit was thought to be worth the high price paid to realise it. The improvements were there, waiting to be discovered. Mina just did not know what they were.

Upon reaching the River Ley, she turned the mule onto the narrow path that ran between a double row of beech trees, arrow straight—its end, if there was one, lost in the shadowed distance. She tethered the mule and fitted the sturdy animal with a nosebag so it could eat while she was gone. Then, tying her shawl more tightly around her shoulders, she pulled the new ley lamp from her skirt pocket. The basic size and shape was much the same as the original—the one she had sent away with Kit: made of brass, burnished with a swirling filigree of swooping lines connecting tiny holes. It was bluntly rounded, like a water-smoothed river stone, and big enough to fit comfortably in the palm of the hand but, unlike a stone, heavier for its size. The new version had more holes and a series of small nubby protrusions—for grip? Controls of some sort? Wilhelmina could not say.

She began walking at a slow, steady pace, holding the lamp comfortably before her. She had taken but a few steps when, as expected, the little row of holes along the curved side began to glow with the distinctive indigo light. This, Mina knew, indicated the presence of a ley. She felt the small hairs on the nape of her neck prickle to the energy around her. Not wishing to make a jump just yet, she stopped in the path.

While she waited for the energy to dissipate, she found herself thinking about Etzel back at the Kaffeehaus and what a patient, understanding man he was—a random thought, for no apparent reason. The new ley lamp flickered to life. A heretofore unrecognised row of tiny holes lit up with a pale yellowish glow. On closer examination, Mina saw that the series of holes in the brass carapace ran completely around the perimeter of the instrument. The light was weak, and would have been almost imperceptible in stronger sunlight, but in amongst the trees she could make it out well enough.

Even as the thought passed through her mind, the little yellow lights faded and died.

She stared at the thing, resisting the urge to shake it gently, and instead began walking again to see if that would bring them back. It did not. Motion, then, was not the trigger. She then began to try out various combinations in walking, touching, and direction as they occurred to her. This went on for a fair amount of time, but produced no result at all; the perimeter holes resisted any attempt on her part to coax them back into life.

Finally frustration got the better of her and, fed up, she turned around and started back to retrieve the mule and wagon. "Gus," she muttered aloud, "what have you given me?"

At the mention of the alchemist's name, the yellow lights sparked with a faint gleam. The effect was so quick and so definite she did not fail to discern the connection. She stopped and took a deep breath, clearing her mind of all thought. Then, very deliberately, she brought the image of Kit to mind and held it.

The pale yellow glow faded and the tiny holes went dark.

"That's it!" cried Wilhelmina. "It works on sound."

Gazing at the device, she raised it before her face and, speaking slowly and clearly, said, "Kit."

But the holes remained unlit. "Kit," she said again, but to no avail.

"Bother," she grumped. "Just when I thought . . ."

On a sudden inspiration, she brought an image of Etzel to mind once more—Etzel as she had last seen him working in the kitchen. Immediately, the row of lights took on the looked-for gleam.

Wilhelmina stared at the instrument in amazement. "Not sound, but *thought*," she whispered. Still holding Etzel's pleasant round face before her mind's eye, she turned in the general direction of the city, and the row of lights grew gently brighter, with those pointed more directly towards the city taking on a deeper, warmer hue. Then, as a test, she switched the mental image back to Kit, and the little lights immediately dimmed and went out.

"I am gobsmacked." She raised the ley lamp and pressed it to her lips. "You clever little thing."

She tried the same small experiment a few more times, and each time obtained the same result: the lights winked on when thinking of Etzel—whom she knew to be in Prague—and blinked off the moment she shifted her attention to Kit. For a more difficult trial, she thought of Thomas Young, the archaeologist she had sought out to help Kit excavate the tomb containing the Skin Map. Again, the yellow lights came up, fainter this time; the marginally brighter area shifted along the perimeter, pointing vaguely towards the southeast. *Directional signs . . . nice touch,* she thought.

Instantly, the lights went out.

"Now what?" She stared at the gizmo. What had she done to make it behave that way? She decided to try again and consciously drew up the image of Dr. Young once more; the lights flicked on, as intense as before. Then, on a whim, she dismissed the doctor and thought instead about Giles. Again the little lights flickered slightly, then glowed, but the ring around the edge moved, the brighter lights indicating a different direction. "In-bloody-credible," Wilhelmina murmured, shaking her head in wonder.

She tested this theory a few more times to be certain—each test with a different person—and it did seem to be the case that whenever she thought of someone she knew, whether in a separate dimension or not, the device reacted. But as soon as the mental link with the desired object of her attention was broken, the lights faded—as if, connection severed, the line went dead.

Head swimming with the implications of her discovery, she stood in the narrow gap between the trees gazing at the device, only stirring from her contemplation when she heard the rooks calling in the trees surrounding the adjacent fields and smelled pungent wood smoke on the air—hearth fires were being lit in nearby farmhouses. The short day was swiftly fading; evening was moving in. Stowing the ley lamp safely in her pocket once more, Wilhelmina hurried back to the mule and wagon and returned to the city, her mind filled with questions and half-formed possibilities. Indeed, it would take her some time to fully appreciate, let alone comprehend, the capabilities of the new instrument and what it all meant.

That could come later. There was something she had to do first. Right away. Before she did another thing.

Mina drove the mule and cart straight back to the city. The torches and smudge pots were being lit for the night as she passed through the gates; with a wave to the gatemen she rambled up the long street that led into the Old Town Square. She left the wagon outside the Kaffeehaus and went inside. The air was warm and full of the yeasty scent of dough on the rise. Mina drew a breath deep into her lungs. A few patrons idled over their coffee and strudel in an atmosphere of peace and calm. The warm scent of fresh coffee and rising dough mingled in the air. *I love this place*, she thought. *Is there anywhere better than this?*

She called a breezy greeting to her patrons and staff as she swept through the dining room and headed straight for the kitchen, where Etzel was instructing two of his young helpers about the next day's preparations.

"We will make braided raisin bread tomorrow," he was saying. "See that the baking trays are clean and ready before you leave tonight." He half turned as Wilhelmina entered the room. *"Ach, mein Schatz,"* he said, breaking into a smile when he saw her. "There you are. Hilda was looking for you."

"I will see her later." She gave him a quick peck on the cheek, then turned to one of the assistants. "Hans, the wagon is outside. Take it to the stable, please, and see the mule's water bucket is full. Give him an extra handful of grain."

"Jawohl, Fräulein Mina," replied the young baker smartly.

"Barthelm," she said to the other helper. "Go with him. I wish to speak to Herr Stiffelbeam alone."

The two kitchen aides left the room. "Come, Etzel," she said as soon as they were gone. She took his hand in hers and led him to the worktable. "I want you to sit down."

"Mina, what is it? Is something wrong?"

"Nothing is wrong," she assured him. "But I have to tell you something."

She drew a stool from beneath the table and perched him on it, then paused, thinking how to begin. Concern and curiosity wheeled across his good-natured face. Wilhelmina smiled.

"Dear Etzel," she sighed. "What will I do without you?"

"I hope you will not have to do without me, *Herzerl,*" he said.

"But that is what I have to say." She took his hand again and, clasping it in both of hers, raised it to her lips. "I think I may have to go away for a while, and I want you to know the reason so you won't worry about me."

"Go away?" His expression grew puzzled. "Why? Where will you go?"

"I have a confession to make," she said. "This will not be the first time I have gone away."

"I know you go out into the country," he said. "To talk to the farmers and the beekeepers."

"That is true," she allowed, "but there is more. I have been travelling to other places too. Many other places."

He stared at her in baffled silence.

"Etzel," she said softly, "it is time you knew the whole truth. Some of the places where I go are not of this world."

He continued to gaze at her until at last the light of understanding shone in his eyes. Nodding slowly, he replied, "*Ach, mein Schatz*, we are none of us belonging to this world."

CHAPTER 5

In Which Lord Burleigh
Takes a Stroll

Archibald Burley walked, as he walked everywhere these days, with a sprightly spring in his step. Life, in all its unique and unqualified splendour, stretched before him in glittering vistas of happiness, success, and unstinting prosperity. As the-man-also-known-as Lord Archelaeus Burleigh, Earl of Sutherland, his acumen in finding and securing the best artefacts and passing them on to London's elite collectors had established him on the upper rungs of London's social ladder. His eye for authenticity was extraordinary and his judgement second to none. As the premiere purveyor of the finest antiquities and *objets de désir* for the aristos and would-be upper-crusties, Burleigh's prices were as breathtaking as the artefacts were exquisite and beautiful and, with the current craze for all things classical, the young earl was squirreling away the dosh by the cartload.

If business was good, his personal life was even better. In fact, he could not recall a time when he had ever felt such joy: confident, optimistic, and so brimming over with good cheer he all but sloshed as he walked. Following the untimely demise of his guardian, mentor, and benefactor, Lord Gower, Archie had been at liberty to be, do, and go as he pleased, and he luxuriated in the freedom. He did not squander either his wealth or opportunity like so many of his ilk—the poor barrow boys, ragamuffins, and street urchins who, by one means or another, occasionally manage to rise above their station and gain a toehold on a higher rung of society's ladder.

His rising fortunes notwithstanding, topping Archibald's list of Reasons to Be Cheerful was the gladsome fact that he was in love. The object of his affection was the estimable beauty Phillipa Harvey-Jones, daughter of the notorious empire builder Reginald Harvey-Jones, whose roster of industrial conquests was precisely as long as his inventory of enemies. Truth be told, the Earl of Sutherland was not the man Harvey-Jones would have chosen for his beloved Pippa. Ever the shrewdly calculating businessman, Reg considered young Burleigh a jumped-up Northern bounder with a dubious title. Yet, for reasons he could not fathom, Phillipa loved the dark-haired lord, so there was nothing to be done about it but pour the champagne and announce the nuptials.

That this had not yet happened was not for lack of trying on Pippa's part. She nudged and coaxed her paramour as sweetly as any maid ever coaxed a beau, but there always seemed to be some excuse why this or that close date could not be countenanced. The latest obstacle was an urgent business trip to Italy to collect certain promised objects for an influential client.

"We will be married as soon as I return," Burleigh declared; he stroked her hand in the hope of making his words more palatable.

"You said that last time," she pointed out, her lower lip protruding in a pout.

"The situation is quite different this time," he insisted, not ungently. "If I win my way with Lord and Lady Coleridge, our future in society is secured. Clients will beat a path to my door. You'll want for nothing."

"All I want," she replied petulantly, "is you."

"And you shall have me, my sweet." He raised her hand and brushed it with his lips. "One more trip and you shall have me all to yourself forever after."

"How long will you be away?"

"Only as long as it takes the ship to sail there and back."

"Must you really go yourself? Can you not send someone to collect these trinkets for you?"

"If only I could," sighed the young lord. "But no, the thing must be done by me in person. There is less risk of anything going wrong, and I dare not hazard the loss of this sale." He patted her hand. "When I return we shall be married with unseemly haste, I promise."

"We had better," she replied, accepting his assurances at last. "I shall content myself with picking out my trousseau in your absence."

"And all the rest—china, linens, crystal, silverware, everything. Choose whatever you like, my love, for if you like it, then I am sure to like it too."

They talked about where they would like to honeymoon and other pleasantries, and this carried them up to the day of Burleigh's embarkation. He called on her a few hours before sailing time and made his final farewell. They shared a kiss or two, and then he departed. No one but the coach driver saw him walk onto the dock to board the waiting ship. And that was the last that anyone in London saw of him for a very long time.

As for Burleigh, the trip began as routine and uneventful as any traveller could wish. The ship—a fair-sized packet steamer christened *Gipsy*—called on ports along the French, Spanish, and Italian coasts; she was tight and seaworthy, the captain a capable and conscientious seaman who had served in the Royal Navy. The steamer made its appointed rounds, collecting and delivering mail and freight and passengers to their destinations, and picking up the same for return to England. When asked later, the captain did remember dining with the young earl during the voyage. The purser even recalled seeing Burleigh drive off in a hired coach at Livorno—this he remembered because the earl had made a point of booking the same cabin for his return journey when the ship was to call back in ten days' time.

In any event, the young lord failed to appear, and *Gipsy* returned to England without him.

After disembarking, Burleigh wended his way to Florence, where he acquired a small painting of the Duke of Montefeltro, two cameos from the time of Emperor Trajan, and a marble bust of Cicero. From there he went on to the capital to conduct his principal business. Somewhere between Florence and Rome, so far as anyone was able to figure out, disaster struck. The coach had put up for the night in Viterbo, and Burleigh checked into the inn. He had a fine supper of fresh river perch and a mushroom rissole, and went to bed early. The next morning the coach continued the journey, but a mile or so outside town, one of the horses threw a shoe and pulled up lame. This necessitated a wait while a blacksmith was fetched.

Burleigh and the only other passenger—a talkative Italian lawyer by the name of Lorenzo de Ponte—decided to stretch their legs. They began walking. The day was pleasant and the rural countryside a veritable medieval painting come to life.

"Have you ever seen one of the old Etruscan roads?"

"I cannot say that I have," replied Burleigh.

"I am not surprised," said the lawyer. "They are not well known beyond the region. Would you like to see one?"

The young lord regarded the rough-cobbled road on which they stood. "Am I to take it that this is one of them?" He indicated the bumpy, stone-flagged path stretching before them across the countryside.

Lorenzo chuckled. "By no means, my friend. This is a Roman road. Etruscan roads are far older. Also, they cannot be seen." At Burleigh's dubious expression, he laughed again and explained, "They are below ground, you see."

Burleigh's Italian was not as good as his French or German, so he asked, "Below ground? Underground, do you mean? Subterranean?"

"No, not like a tunnel." The affable lawyer pointed off across the landscape and said, "This way. I will show you."

As they walked the fellow explained, "I grew up in Tarquinia—not far from here. It is in what was once known as Etruria, which is called Tuscany now. The Etruscans were very clever people, yes? They invented many useful things. But they were also very mysterious. They invented many mysteries too, I think."

Lorenzo led them off the road, across a shallow ditch, and over a stubble field towards what appeared to be a cleft or fold in the landscape. "They built houses of stone with red clay tiles and running water. They built wonderful temples and palaces and tombs—many, many tombs. You never saw people who built so many tombs. They also built roads—two kinds. Ordinary roads they made for travel, and secret roads for their secret ceremonies."

"How very odd," replied Burleigh, his sense of interest quickening.

The mention of tombs and palaces brought the possibility of antiquities instantly to mind. Etruscan art was an area he knew little about—which meant it was an arena ripe for exploration and plunder. "Tell me more."

"These Etruscans carved their secret roads deep into the tufa stone—the soft volcanic rock, yes? And they carved for miles and miles." He waved his hands at the low hills around them. "Sometimes these roads connect the ancient towns and villages, but most times they simply connect one strange place with another. And"—he raised a finger for emphasis—"they are always, always lined with tombs also carved in the tufa stone."

"Extraordinary," said Burleigh. "These tombs—are they ever explored?"

"Always."

"And are there objects? Artefacts?"

"But of course. Wonderful things. They were very good craftsmen, and they made fine ceramics—and tiny little figures in iron. We find these things all the time."

"Fascinating. I would be most interested to see some of them."

"That could easily be arranged," Lorenzo assured him. "I have a friend in Firenze who can oblige." He stopped walking. "But now . . . Behold!"

Burleigh looked around, but saw nothing. They had come to the edge of the cleft, and so he took another step closer and looked down into a deep trench that, as the lawyer had said, was carved into the underlying tufa. The trench was perhaps twenty feet deep and no more than eight or ten feet wide, and it ran along the natural fold of the hill.

"The local people call them Spirit Roads—or Ghost Roads." He shook his head gently as he peered into the shadowed trench. "They were considered sacred, but how they were used no one knows. It is one of the Etruscan mysteries."

"Can we go down there?"

Lorenzo hesitated. "Getting down is no difficulty." He smiled. "Getting out again—that is the problem." He looked down the length of the Sacred Road. "You might have to walk many miles before you find a place to climb out again. I would not advise it." He stepped back from the edge. "Perhaps another time."

"I did not hear that!" came the shouted reply. "You'll have to speak up!"

When de Ponte turned back, Burleigh was nowhere to be seen. He stepped to the edge of the trench and saw the young earl's face smiling up at him.

"Sorry," he said. "Couldn't resist." He looked around. "This is extraordinary. Might as well explore a little as long as I'm down here."

"I would not take too long," the lawyer suggested. "We do not wish to delay the coach."

"You're right. I hadn't thought of that," Burleigh confessed casually. "I'll just walk along here a little way and see if I can find a place to climb out."

"Yes, that would be best." Lorenzo cast a hasty glance in the direction of the road, still empty. "Perhaps I should go back and wait for the coach. I don't see it yet, but it could be along any minute."

"Right-o," Burleigh agreed. "We don't want to miss it."

"Unless you think you will need help climbing out."

"No, no, I should be able to manage that easily enough," Burleigh said. "I'm just going to walk along here a little way and find a good place. I think I see one a little way ahead. You go on and hold the coach."

"Very well, if you insist."

"I do insist," Burleigh told him. "You run along now. I will join you in a moment."

Lorenzo hurried off and returned to the roadside, where he spent an idle twenty minutes watching the highway for the horses and carriage and searching the countryside for the earl. As he feared, the coach, with its newly shod lead horse, appeared first. The driver slowed the carriage as the Italian gentleman hurried to meet it.

"Signor de Ponte," called the driver as he brought the horses to a halt. "Where is our other passenger?"

"He will be coming along shortly," answered the lawyer, and went on to explain about the earl wishing to explore the sunken Etruscan road. "Please wait here, and I will go and bring him now."

"By all means," said the driver. "But hurry, please, or we shall be late arriving in Florence."

"Don't worry. He is just over there. I will fetch him at once."

Lorenzo began walking rapidly along the side of the trench, calling out for Burleigh as he went. When he failed to receive a reply one way, he turned around and walked a fair distance the other, calling for Burleigh every few yards or so. There was never any answer to his repeated cries.

"I fear something ill has befallen our friend," de Ponte announced upon his return to the coach. "I called as loudly as I could, but there was no answer. He might have fallen and struck his head. I think we must go down and search for him."

This is what they did. The driver and his assistant climbed down into the deep-cut road and proceeded to search for the lost passenger—one going north, the other south along the ancient pathway. They ended up searching the entire two-mile length of the sunken causeway, but failed to turn up so much as a muddy footprint.

So, after leaving word of the young man's disappearance with local farmers, Lorenzo reluctantly agreed that there was little more to be done, and allowed the coach to continue on to Florence, where he immediately informed the authorities of his companion's strange disappearance. To be sure, a formal investigation was begun at once. The next morning a search party was organised, the ancient Etruscan road scoured end to end, and flyers distributed throughout the area in case anyone should stumble upon a lost or injured foreigner. None of these efforts met with any success. And although the case remained officially open, without any new evidence there was nothing more to be done—save inform the British Embassy. This they duly did, allowing for the more relaxed attitude of the Mediterranean temperament. Then the *polizia* and *carabinieri*, and Lorenzo de Ponte, settled back to await further developments.

Sadly, no news was ever forthcoming. No one involved in the whole curious affair ever learned what had happened to the Earl of Sutherland.

CHAPTER 6

In Which a New Thing Comes to Pass

*K*it followed the little band of hunters along the frozen river as it wound in great, curving arcs towards the south and west. There were eight in all, seven clansmen and Kit, led by Dardok, forging a path through the snow lining the riverbank. They walked by day beneath low, heavy-laden skies, sometimes with a little wind at their backs, which seemed to urge them on their way. Ice narrowed the river margins, and chunks of snow and slush floated downstream.

They walked in a constant fog produced by their own breath crystallising in the frigid air, pausing every now and then to scan the rock walls of the gorge for any sign of predators. All the while, the snow fell lightly but steadily—small, hard flakes that dropped like frozen grit and squeaked underfoot. The air was cold, stinging all exposed flesh, but the exertion of the trek warmed him well enough, and after days lounging around the fire, the exertion felt good. Kit was reminded yet again of the clansmen's natural hardiness—their strength, stamina, and endurance far exceeded anything he had ever encountered in his own species, and as the day lengthened he hoped he would be able to keep up.

Eventually they came to a place where they were forced to scramble up a steep incline to a higher plateau. At the top Dardok paused, and Kit, puffing from the climb, joined the hunters as they stood gazing down into the gorge now far below. Kit thought they were looking at the river, but upon joining them, saw that Dardok had spotted a herd of the shaggy, long-horned bison that usually roamed the reaches of the higher forests. The beasts were moving slowly and laboriously along the river, forging through the snow. Kit experienced a visceral thrill at the sight and caught something of the band's instinctive urge to go after good meat on the hoof.

They watched for a moment as the dozen or so brown, hump-backed creatures ambled along; then Dardok, turning his head this way and that and sniffing deeply, gave out a little grunt. Kit followed his example and caught the merest whiff of a sharp sour scent on the air; the others murmured softly, having also recognised the smell. Kit looked to the Big Hunter for an explanation, and Dardok extended his finger and pointed to a stony outcrop across the gorge a little above the riverbed. Squinting his eyes against the white, Kit made out the pale grey muscular form of an animal he recognised as canine—a beast easily two times the size of a normal wolf: a dire wolf.

The creature was watching the bison herd traversing the valley and, no doubt, licking its chops. Dardok pointed again, and Kit saw another, slightly smaller wolf watching from a stone ledge below them. Clearly, the predators were tracking the bison, stalking the herd and awaiting a chance to make a kill.

Silently as shadows, the hunters edged away from the overlook and moved on. The river valley, which had been bending ever farther westward, now began swinging away to the south. The ground continued to rise, and the woodland closed around them, becoming a tangle of brush and close-grown trees with no clear path through. Progress slowed to a laborious crawl. The party strung out single file, and Kit, falling farther and farther behind, had begun to fear he would lose sight of his companions when Dardok suddenly came to a halt. The hunters quickly gathered around him, and Kit hurried forward to see what had happened. He found them all squatting in the snow, transfixed by something they saw there.

Peering over the head of the nearest hunter, Kit saw the tracks of a large and heavy animal in the snow. "Bear?" he asked, then remembered to use their word for the animal. "Gan-gor?" He held the image of a large black bear in his mind.

Dardok gave a forceful snort, which Kit had learned to interpret as a negative. The Big Hunter spread his fingers and placed them in one of the imprints. Then he raised his hand and made a clawed paw. "Kar-ka," he said aloud.

Kit had never heard the word before. "Karka," he repeated.

Dardok uttered a grunt of satisfaction and pointed to the line of tracks—first one, then the next. Then, with the tip of his spear, the Big Hunter indicated a long slash between two of the tracks and made a flourish with the flat of his hand. The action was so expressive Kit could not fail to understand: a beast walking, its tail sweeping the snow now and then.

Again Dardok pointed to the tracks. "Kar-ka."

Into Kit's mind came the image of a great shaggy animal the size of a small cow, but with a huge head supported by a huge neck and muscular shoulders. It had a short mane that wreathed its jaws and ran down its sloping back in the form of a ridge of spiky dark fur. Kit knew instantly what it was; he had seen one before: in another time, in another place, at the end of a chain. It was a cave cat, older brother to the beast the Burley Men called "Baby."

"Karka," breathed Kit.

With his broad hand Dardok swept the print away, then rose and resumed the trek. They soon came to a place where the river gorge made a wide, arcing curve, bending around to the north. The valley below widened and flattened out, and the cliff top on which they walked began to descend to meet it, falling to within thirty metres or so of the riverbank. A little farther on, Dardok found a trail and led the party down to the valley floor; he halted there to take a good sniff of the wind and, satisfied there were no predators lurking about, led them around the arc of the river to a massive wall of pale limestone. He stopped again and gazed around, scanning the rocks and cliffs above as well as the riverbanks, then moved cautiously towards the wall.

It was only as they neared this curtain of stone rising sheer from the valley floor that Kit saw the hole—an empty oval a few metres in radius and not more than three metres off the valley floor: the entrance to a cave. A tumble of rocks lined the base of the wall, and Dardok moved towards them, slowing as he came to stand below the hole in the wall. Kit felt a shiver of awareness, and the party instantly contracted into a tight knot. Scanning the area, he saw what had drawn the others' attention. On the rocks below the hole were more tracks, identical to those they had seen on the bluffs above. Kit stared at the tracks in the snow and then smelled the sharp animal pong. An image came into his mind: a great slab-sided dark beast with massive forequarters, powerful haunches, and a shaggy, brindled coat: karka.

The wooden vessel containing the embers was pressed into Kit's hands, and Dardok turned to the others. In his head Kit heard the brief flutter of thoughts as they passed among the hunters and, though he could not understand what he heard, he glanced up to where they were looking and saw the big cat standing in the entrance to the hole; it was watching them, its huge yellow eyes narrowed, its ears flattened to its enormous head.

Instinctively Kit stepped backwards.

Then everything seemed to happen all at once. The great cat sprang from the mouth of the cave, forelegs outstretched, scimitar claws extended. The hunters scattered, darting away in every direction.

Kit turned to flee, slipped in the snow, and went down, losing his grip on the ember-bearing vessel. The cave lion landed on the rocks below the cave mouth, its head whipping first one way and then the other as it determined which of the many victims provided the nearest, easiest kill. It saw Kit floundering in the snow and crouched, gathering itself to pounce. The huge head lowered as the immense body contracted, muscles bulging—a coil tightening before release—and Kit swam backwards through the snow, kicking his legs, his arms windmilling.

The cave lion leapt. A slight lift of its chest, and the creature was in the air. In the same moment Dardok darted to Kit's side. With a grace born of endless practise, Big Hunter's massive arm drew back. The spear point came up and, with only the merest pause, flashed forward. Dardok's shoulders and torso followed as he delivered the full weight of his body behind the throw. The rude weapon sliced the air in a tight arc and struck home.

With the sound of an open-fisted slap, the shaft buried its

razor-sharp flinthead between the ribs of the enormous cat just behind the front legs. Ears flat, baleful eyes glaring, its great mouth open in a snarl of pain and rage, karka spun to confront the attack. A second missile was already in the air—a blur of motion that ended as the spear sprouted from the beast's thick neck.

The lion swiped at the missile and succeeded in dislodging the shaft. It gathered itself to pounce, but Dardok gave out a cry, and hunters advanced on the run, darting in behind their spears to stab and jab before darting away again—first one side and then the other, keeping the angry animal off balance and confused.

Dardok turned and swooped on Kit, picking him up and setting him on his feet in one swift motion. Pressing a big hand to Kit's chest, he pushed him back, then with a mighty shout ran to join the fray. The lion, bleeding now from several wounds, roared to shake the stones from the earth. With great slashes of its claws, the cat tried to catch its tormenters as one at a time they darted nearer. Big Hunter dared the claws and, in an act of courage that took Kit's breath away, snatched his spear from the beast's side.

Growling, spitting, the great cat spun and raked the air with its claws. Dardok dodged just out of reach and then plunged the spear point into the creature's side. The cat loosed a scream of pure hatred and rage and turned—not toward Dardok this time, but away—just as another of the band leapt in to retrieve his weapon. Karka's huge paw met the oncoming clansman and ripped through his side, opening a four-fold wound across his belly.

The hapless hunter staggered from the blow and looked down, his fur clothing in shreds. And then the muscle cords severed, and a gout of blood and bowels gushed from the wound. The man crumpled as if made of paper.

Dardok gave a cry of rage and drove in again, stabbing down into the cave lion's huge muscled neck. He buried the stone blade deep and leapt away again. The other hunters continued their feinting attack, careful to remain just out of reach of those killing claws. Every thrust, nick, and stab drew blood, staining the snow in a wide circle as the beast thrashed and gyrated, trying to capture another of its tormentors.

Meanwhile, Dardok ran to the injured hunter and seized him by the arm. Kit ran to help him, and together they dragged him out of the way. Blood welled from his injury; the man's face was white and his lips were blue and trembling; his body shook. Kit bent over him, gripping his hand. The hunter, his eyes wide, gave out a sighing groan as a spasm seized him, then abruptly relaxed, leaving Kit holding the hand of a dead man.

Behind them the cave cat gave out a bone-rattling yowl. The creature reared up on its hind legs, towering over its attackers. It made another ineffectual swipe with a mighty paw, then turned to retreat.

The hunters were ready. As the big cat spun around to scramble back up the rocks and into the shelter of the cave behind it, the nearest hunter lunged, driving the stone point of his spear deep into the lion's side just behind the forelegs. The cat screamed and turned, half rising up on its haunches. The clansman held firm to the shaft of the spear, forcing it deeper. The lion raked at the hateful weapon, and a second hunter dashed in from the other side. He was followed by a third, and the three held the writhing beast pinioned as a fourth hunter took careful aim and plunged his spear into the lion's massive chest.

The last wound was fatal. The lion gave a final roar, and its legs collapsed beneath it. The great body rolled onto its side, and the creature subsided with a long, gurgling sigh. Even dead, the animal presented an aspect of tremendous power and fearsome grace. Dardok pulled his spear from the carcass and wiped the stone point on its bloody pelt. He then knelt and placed his hand on the big cat's head. One by one, the other hunters followed his example. They remained in this attitude for a long moment, and then rose and, taking up their spears once more, walked away without a backward glance. Kit hesitated. What about their dead comrade, he wondered. They had shown a moment's respect for the dead lion, why not their clansman?

"Wait!" Kit called after them. His shout was not understood, but it produced the desired effect of halting them. Stepping to the poor, mangled corpse of the hunter, Kit fought down a queasy sickness at the horrendous gaping wound; he knelt and began pulling together the bloody bits of fur, straightening the man's limbs, and wiping the blood from his face.

As he worked, Kit became aware that the others had gathered close and were watching him. When he finished arranging the body, he rose and, searching along the base of the limestone wall, gathered stones and placed them around the body. Once the corpse was outlined, he proceeded to cover it. Dardok was first to catch hold of the idea. Imitating Kit's example, he joined in building the burial mound. The others were quick to follow Big Hunter's lead; soon all were busy adding stone to stone until the body of the hunter was completely subsumed beneath a neat oblong heap of stone.

Kit stood and, feeling that he should say or do something to mark the occasion, stretched his hand over the grave, and after a moment's contemplation said, "Creator of all that is and will be, we give you back one of your creations. His life in this world was taken from him, but we ask that you receive him into the life of the world that has no end."

This impromptu prayer shocked Kit fully as much as it surprised his companions. What they made of it, he could not guess. The sentiment and words to express it had simply materialised on his tongue as he spoke. Still, now that they were said he felt there was a rightness about them; both words and sentiment seemed good and proper. He raised his head and gave a grunt of satisfaction the hunters could not mistake. Then, picking up the dead hunter's spear, he stepped away from the mound. He had gone but a few steps when he felt Dardok's hand on his shoulder; the gesture stopped him in his tracks and held him there for a few moments before releasing him again. No other communication took place, but Kit understood. A profound connection had been made, a link forged in the minds of all who had witnessed Kit's improvised burial rite. A new thing had come to pass, and it was now acknowledged. Nothing else was needed.

CHAPTER 7

In Which Subversion Is Plotted

L ady Haven Fayth was accustomed to skating on thin ice where her relationship with the vile Lord Burleigh was concerned. But cracks of doubt were beginning to show beneath her blades, and she was having to skate faster and faster to stay ahead of his racing suspicions. She could sense that a parting of the ways loomed. She would like to have learned more from him about ley leaping—at least sounded the depths of his knowledge to find out how extensive it was. But time was against her now, and the best she could hope for was to make sure that the inevitable separation happened on her terms, not his.

The Black Earl's present distraction might be, she reasoned, the perfect opportunity to make good her own escape. Her captor and erstwhile co-conspirator was at the present moment wholly consumed by the Kit Livingstone affair—and not without good reason. Secure in the knowledge that Kit—along with Cosimo, Sir Henry, and Giles— had met his ultimate end and been entombed in the sepulchre of High Priest Anen, Burleigh had come to Prague to collect the latest version of his ley-hunting device hot off the workbench of the emperor's chief alchemist, Bazalgette. The cunning little instrument was made of brass and was about the size and shape of a cobblestone, but that was about all she knew of it; Haven had only glimpsed it fleetingly and furtively, because his lordship kept it, like much else, entirely to himself. Haven suppressed a laugh, recalling the look of disbelief on Burleigh's face when he was informed that the presumed-to-be-deceased Kit Livingstone was . . . surprise! . . . alive and well and loose in the streets of Prague.

The resulting chase succeeded only in wounding the coachman, Giles; Kit had escaped and the Burley Men were held to blame for the debacle. For the last four days the Black Earl and his louts had been combing the countryside for Kit. At first they merely searched the physical geography of the area—the hedgerows, villages, barns, and even the river—and when that failed to raise any material evidence the search was expanded to include any ley lines within reach of the fleeing man. They had found a likely ley in the vicinity of their initial chase, but a thoroughgoing search of the destination on the other side failed to raise a trail.

As day gave way to day and reports from the Burley Men brought them no closer to finding the fugitive, his lordship's temper darkened the more. He was angry at everyone and everything: angry at being lied to—though the Burley Men denied this vehemently—angry at the lack of results, angry that his plans were being stymied by a mere know-nothing nobody, angry at his own failure to get his hands on the one piece of the Skin Map he knew where to find. None of this was Haven's fault, a fact she was not hesitant to point out. She most strenuously distanced herself from the current disaster, hoping to remain aloof from the steadily mounting storm of his lordship's wrath.

"There is some deception here that I have yet to penetrate," Burleigh declared on his return to the inn. It was the evening of the fifth night of the futile search, and his mood was toxic. "Livingstone has been aided and abetted in his escape. That is the only explanation—at least, it is the only explanation that makes sense."

The weather had turned cold and wet with a foretaste of the winter to come; Lady Fayth was sewing new buttons onto a coat she had bought in the market, replacing the wooden ones with silver. Lord Burleigh sank into a chair by the fireplace and summoned one of the inn's serving boys to come and remove his muddy boots.

"Clean them and bring them back when you are finished," he commanded, his German lumpy but understandable. "Have the landlord fetch me something to drink—a jar of mulled ale will suffice for now. Get on with you. And be quick about it!"

The lad scurried off. He had learned to obey swiftly and without question when the earl spoke.

"You say Kit is a know-nothing," Haven ventured, "and by all indications it would seem that you are correct in your assessment. If that be so, then what can it possibly matter that he has escaped?"

"Because he is a thorn in the flesh," snarled Burleigh. "He is an increasingly troublesome obstruction to the ongoing search for the map. He is a rival and a threat."

Haven did not raise her eyes from her work. "Hardly that, I think."

"Do you doubt it?"

"I doubt it very much indeed, sir," she replied. "He is as you have painted him—a nothing, a nobody. His only attachment to this enterprise was through his great-grandfather, Cosimo. That tether has been severed, and Kit has no idea what to do or where to go next.

In the brief time I was with him he showed no volition and demonstrated no extraordinary understanding of the enterprise in which he was involved."

"My impression too," affirmed Burleigh. "Entirely."

"Why not simply put him out of your mind? Kit Livingstone is of no consequence. Whatever his understanding may be, it can have no bearing on your designs."

"How is his presence in Prague to be explained?"

"Just coincidence, surely," she suggested, passing the needle through the button and into the cloth in a single smooth stroke. "Everyone must be somewhere, after all."

"But why here?" Burleigh growled, watching her. "I think he was here for a reason, and I want to know what it was. That woman at the coffeehouse is mixed up in this—I know it."

"Who?" Haven raised an eyebrow. "One of the serving girls?"

"No—not a servant, blind you. The other one."

Haven stared at him blankly. "I cannot for the life of me think who you must mean."

"The tall one," he snarled. "The English manageress or owner or whatever—I'm telling you she knows more than she lets on."

"You are chary by nature," Lady Fayth suggested, returning to her work. "It does you no good. Here we are, flailing about uselessly when we could be getting on with the hunt. That is surely more important than running down Kit Livingstone."

"She was poking around the palace, trying to ingratiate herself at court. That's where I met her, you know—the first time I came here. A right Miss Busybody."

Haven drew the needle up through the button. "Are we talking about the woman from the coffeehouse again?"

"She implied she knew about my travels, or something of the sort," Burleigh continued. "I warned the wench in no uncertain terms to keep her nose out of my affairs."

"Then I am certain she has taken your good advice to heart," concluded Haven sweetly. "Anyway, she can have no idea about any of this. Living here in Prague and running a coffeehouse—one is hardly liable to stumble across anything of value to our cause."

"Perhaps we should go talk to her," he said. "Find out what she knows."

Haven lowered her work into her lap and gave the exhausted earl a look of sharp appraisal. "The woman is hardly going to cooperate after your heavy-handed intimidation. If she does know anything, you would be the last person in whom she would confide."

Burleigh frowned, then brightened as a new thought came to him. "*You* could go."

"Me?" Lady Fayth feigned disapproval. "I cannot see what good that would do. I can think of nothing worthwhile to say to her."

"You could come alongside her—woman-to-woman, be her friend, gain her confidence."

"Do you honestly imagine that will achieve some positive result?" Haven asked, still shaking her head.

"She would talk to you," insisted Burleigh. "Get her to confide in you."

"A manageress?" Haven made a wry face. "What could she possibly know that would be of the most remote interest to us, or to the success of our venture?"

"*That*," declared Burleigh decisively, "is what you must discover." He thought for a moment. "No . . . no," he said slowly. "Better still, gain her confidence and invite her to dinner tomorrow. Lure her here, and I will take care of the rest. Once we get her upstairs, alone, we'll find out what she knows soon enough."

Lady Fayth, having given an entirely believable performance of the Reluctant Accomplice, agreed to take on the chore and took herself to the Grand Imperial the next afternoon. She was there, waiting, when Wilhelmina returned from another unsuccessful attempt to locate Kit. The two exchanged a knowing glance and Wilhelmina, after greeting Etzel, filled a pot with fresh coffee and sat down with her ally to share information on the state of the game so far.

"I cannot understand the Black Earl's interest in Kit," Lady Fayth mused. "On the one hand he insists that Kit knows nothing useful to the quest. On the other hand he refuses to simply let him go. We have already stayed in Prague far longer than originally intended, and there are no plans at present to leave."

"Burleigh is not being entirely truthful," observed Mina. "No doubt the shock of seeing Kit here in Prague, when he thought him dead and buried in Egypt, revived his interest—at least insofar as he assumes Kit must have had help to escape the tomb." She thought for a moment. "Has he said anything about this?"

"He has vouchsafed nothing specific or germane to the issue at hand. His lordship's hirelings have borne the brunt of his anger on that account, and they have paid dearly for their lapse." Her lips curled in a conspiratorial smile. "Nevertheless, they have helped our cause—unwittingly, it must be said—by maintaining the fiction that the prisoners were in the tomb when the wadi was abandoned. To admit anything more would merely bring even greater approbation down upon their sorry heads."

"Poor things," Wilhelmina said without the least shred of pity.

"As it stands, Kit is the object of the earl's present obsession. The quest, I suspect, will not go forward until Kit is found. As to that, our nemesis intends on casting the net wider. He intends to find out what you know about this affair." Lady Fayth sipped her coffee and watched Wilhelmina for a response.

Mina took this information in stride. "He *is* grasping at straws." She thought for a moment. "What form would this interrogation take?"

"You might well ask. He has prevailed upon *me* to be the agent of his inquiry." She offered a cheerful smile. "I am to gain your trust and induce you to confide in me. Under the guise of a dinner invitation, he would lure you to the inn, take you prisoner, and menace you into revealing your secrets."

Wilhelmina's brow creased with concern.

"Of course," Haven continued quickly, "it goes without saying that we must decide between ourselves what we want him to know."

"Then we must think very carefully what to tell him," agreed Wilhelmina. She reached for the little pewter pot. "More coffee, Lady Fayth?"

The young lady made no move to hold out her cup. "I suspect he knows you are a ley traveller, and I have no doubt he intends you harm."

Wilhelmina returned her gaze steadily. "He will have to catch me first."

"It would be unwise to make light of the threat. Lord Burleigh is fully capable of carrying out his nefarious designs, as we both know only too well." Lady Fayth gave her a solemn nod. "In regards to the dinner tomorrow night—you dare not for a moment even contemplate actually going."

"But if I refuse," countered Mina, "won't that make him even more determined and suspicious?"

"Perhaps." Haven pursed her perfect lips in thought; she glanced out the window at a man carrying a wicker basket. "Why not go away for a few days? Leave the city, go somewhere—anywhere. Stay out of his way completely."

"Run away, you mean."

"Why not? Only for a few days, mind. His lordship will soon grow tired of waiting and leave Prague. We would have departed long since if not for Kit."

Wilhelmina thought for a moment. "I could go away," she agreed. "I have been wanting to go back to—"

"Do not tell me," warned Haven. "It will be better for both of us if I do not know. Only make some excuse and depart as soon as possible. Leave at once."

Wilhelmina regarded her co-conspirator for a moment in silence, unable to tell if she was keeping something back.

"Please," urged Lady Fayth. Reaching across the table, she clutched Wilhelmina's hand and squeezed it for emphasis. "Please go."

"Very well." Mina rose and pushed back her chair. "If you will excuse me, I think I have some packing to do."

PART TWO

The Jagged Mountain

CHAPTER 8

In Which a New God Is Extolled

Chaos is loosed upon the Black Land, my brother," declared Anen, Second Prophet of Amun, with a solemn shake of his head. "Pharaoh pursues a dangerous course. He takes counsel only from his Habiru advisors and listens not to the voice of his own people. He taxes the land heavily to pay for the building of his new city in the desert." He paused and added, "There is even talk of closing Amun's many temples."

Arthur Flinders-Petrie shook his head in sympathy. "I am sorry to hear it."

"It is believed by many that unless he is stopped, Akhenaten will bring all the country to ruin."

Benedict, reclining at table next to his father, cleared his throat. He leaned close and whispered, "What is he saying?"

"Excuse me a moment, Anen." Arthur put his head near his son, and replied, "He is telling me that there is trouble in Egypt just now—the new pharaoh is pursuing a reckless course."

"The new pharaoh—Amenhotep, you mean."

Arthur nodded. "He has taken the name Akhenaten and is building a new city in the desert to honour his god. The people are unhappy."

"Perhaps we should leave," suggested Benedict. "If there's going to be trouble . . ."

"You may be right." Arthur turned once more to his friend. "It was my hope that my son could abide here awhile to study your language with the priests in the temple school—as I did all those years ago. But it seems that the Flinders-Petrie visit has come at an awkward time. Perhaps it would be best if we made other plans. You will not want us underfoot."

"Never think that," said Anen, taking a handful of dates onto his gold plate. "As always, your visit gladdens my heart. To see you and your son once more is a potent medicine to this old man. The troubles of which I speak are but wisps of smoke on the winds of time." He made a sweeping gesture with his hand. "But true friendship is carved in stone. It endures forever."

"It does indeed, my friend," agreed Arthur. He dipped a scrap of bread into the olive oil and then into the salt, put it into his mouth, and chewed thoughtfully. "I treasure our friendship."

Anen raised a finger, and a temple slave stepped silently to the table with the wine jug. Benedict swallowed the dregs and held up his cup for more. While the two older men talked, he contented himself with taking in the wealth of exotic sights around him. They had been in Egypt less than two days, and already he felt himself forgetting any other life but the one he saw around him—a life that seemed to flow as easily and effortlessly as the great green river Nile on which the High Priest's palace was built.

Benedict fingered the blue lapis scarab he had been given as a token of Anen's esteem and gazed around the intimate banquet hall—the smaller of the palace's festive chambers—marvelling at the richly painted walls, the elegant statues and carvings, the stately columns and regal sphinxes, the tall, dark-skinned servants in their embroidered white robes, the exotic scent of sandalwood on the air, the sumptuous banquet spread on the low table before him. All of it—from the endless marble corridors to the gold chains round the priest's neck—seemed fantastical, and far beyond what he had imagined from his father's stories. Yet here he was, reclining at table in the presence of Egyptian nobility. The way Benedict understood it, Anen as Second Prophet ranked a step below High Priest but was nonetheless accorded all the benefits of royalty because of his blood ties to the royal family.

As a child of six, Benedict had visited Egypt; his father had brought him to meet Anen. But other than being very ill the day of the journey and very hot the rest of the time, he could remember almost nothing about it. This time, however, he was determined to soak up as much of the experience as he possibly could—all the more since the current troubles meant their visit might be curtailed.

He listened to the sibilant susurration of his elders' speech and wondered how he would ever learn it. That was why they had come: to allow Benedict to further his education by learning the language— much as they had done a couple years ago when he spent time in China with his mother's sister and her family. Then again, if the troubles his father and Anen were just then discussing were to deepen or spread, he would not have to worry about it, since they would not be staying.

". . . the Habiru are hard workers and keep to themselves. Pharaoh has given them land in the Gesen, and they live there most peaceably. We have no difficulty with them. No"—he shook his smooth shaved head—"no, the difficulty is that Akhenaten has taken up their curious doctrine that their god, a formless spirit called El, is the only god worthy of honour and worship by anyone.

"Why? Why should this be?" Anen demanded. "It makes no sense. We do not say that only Amun must be worshipped, or only Horus, or only Anubis. There is room for all. You may venerate Sekmet or Ra if you like, while I am free to revere Ptah or Hathor or Isis as it suits me. There is room in Egypt for everyone, and each is free to follow the decrees of his own heart."

The priest smiled sadly. "But it is not so with the Habiru. Their god El makes many demands, and one of these is that there must be no other gods worshipped by those who call on his name. This, I think, is because the Habiru do not recognise that all the gods are but expressions of the One, the Absolute God."

"I have heard this said," remarked Arthur. Like the English gentleman he was, Arthur did not argue with his various hosts about religion; whatever world or epoch he visited, he kept his own views to himself. It was one of the rules he lived by as a ley traveller.

"But these Habiru must make even simple things—like sacrifice and offering—very difficult," Anen continued. "I do not understand it. Unfortunately, Pharaoh has become infatuated with the precepts of the Habiru and has turned his back on the gods of his own people. He shuns certain foods and will not cut his hair—all to appease this new god that he has named Aten." The priest's lips twisted with disapproval. "But this is merely El under a different name. This is where the difficulty lies."

"I see the problem," Arthur offered. "But what will you do about it?"

"In two days the Temple of Amun is sending a delegation to Aten City to discuss matters with Pharaoh—to see how this present difficulty may be resolved. You are welcome to come along."

Anen glanced at Benedict, who was now nodding on his cushion. "It seems as if we have exhausted our young traveller with our talk." He raised a hand, and one of the servants stepped up and knelt beside him. The priest spoke a few words, and the servant moved to the side of the sleeping youth and gave him a gentle nudge.

Benedict came awake with a start. "Oh!" He flushed. "Sorry, Father."

"No matter," said Arthur. "You are tired." He nodded and spoke a command to the servant. "Itara here will take you to our lodgings. I will follow shortly."

Benedict rose, and with a respectful bow to his host said, "Thank you for the wonderful dinner. I enjoyed it very much." He then wished his two elders good night and followed the servant from the room.

"You must be very proud of him," Anen observed when Arthur had translated his son's thank-you. "He has grown into a fine young man since I last saw him."

"Indeed he has," Arthur said. "I am very fortunate."

"It is good for a man to have a son to carry his name into the world and continue the work he has begun."

"That, my friend, is my fervent hope—that my son should succeed me one day."

"We must hope that day is long in coming." Anen rose, and instantly a servant stepped forward. The priest waved him away. To Arthur, he said, "Come, let us walk around the pool a little before we go to our beds."

Anen led his guest out into a private garden. The balmy air was sweet with the fragrance of jasmine and hibiscus. They strolled the garden lit by the lambent glow of candle-lit lanterns set along the paths around the sacred pool, which seemed radiant with the reflected light of a ripening moon and a bright spray of stars.

The garden, with its scented air and glowing pool, the blue, star-filled sky, and even the presence of Anen himself put Arthur in mind of that fate-filled night years before when, ravaged by fever, his dear, lovely wife, Xian-Li, succumbed to disease and died. The presence of his visitor must have brought the event to mind for Anen too, because after the two had walked awhile in silence, he asked, "Do you ever think about what happened?"

Arthur smiled. "Every time I look at Xian-Li." They walked a little farther, and he added, "I think I mentioned Benedict's troubled birth?"

"I seem to recall something about it, yes," replied Anen. "You took him to Etruria to be born—because the physicians in your country had not the skill to effect his birth." He thought for a moment and added, "In this Etruria, the High Priest is also king. Not so?"

"That is so," confirmed Arthur. "One day you will be High Priest. Think where you would be if you lived in Etruria."

Anen laughed gently. "I would not want to be king—too many wars, too much fighting all the time. It is not good for the soul."

"I agree. Yet somehow Turms has been able to thrive, and his people with him."

"Have you ever returned to the Spirit Well?"

"The Well of Souls?" Arthur nodded. "Two or three times. There is a mystery there I have yet to penetrate."

"The secret of its life-giving spring?" wondered the priest. "Do not be forgetting—you have promised to show me this marvel one day."

"I have not forgotten," Arthur assured him. "One day I will solve the mystery—but until then, I think it best it remain a secret known to a trusted few—as few as possible."

"I understand."

Two days later the delegation of priests departed for the Holy City of Aten, some distance north of the High Temple at Niwet-Amun. They travelled by barge—five of them: two for the priests and three smaller boats for the servants and attendants. While those around him tended to their business—the priests to their discussions and the servants to their chores—Benedict sat perched on the wide, low rail with his legs dangling over the side of the barge. For hours he watched the panoply of life unfold along the greatest river in the world. The slow progression of the boats was mesmerising; the river world seemed to glide effortlessly by, revealing wonders around every bend: tiny islands filled with snow-white birds; basking crocodiles the colour of jade; buffalos being washed by brown-skinned boys; lazy, grey hippos waggling their ears and yawning; towering palms with golden branches laden with shiny black dates . . . and on and on without end.

Owing to the sluggish summer current, it took three days for the wide, flat boats to reach the pharaoh's new city. The servants and minions disembarked first to prepare the landing place; they were followed by the priests in order of rank. The High Priest, a wizened old man named Ptahmose, who to Benedict's eyes appeared as wrinkled and dried up as a walking mummy, came last, assisted by Anen, his second-in-command.

Dressed in simple kilts of starched white linen and the broad, multi-leaved collars of gold that were a symbol of their office, they walked up the avenue lined by their servants, some of whom held banners while others carried trumpets; still others bore cloth-covered baskets on their heads. As the delegation approached the low, white-washed walls of the city, the trumpeters began to sound loud, rousing blasts on their instruments, heralding the arrival of their masters.

Arthur and Benedict, as guests of Anen, walked directly behind. Workers in the fields outside the city walls paused to watch the procession as it passed. At the gates they halted and waited while the guards hurried to push open the huge cedar trunks that formed the entrance; bound in iron and painted red, each of the two enormous doors took five men, straining at the rings, to open.

Once the way was clear, the parade resumed its stately progress. The stone-paved streets of the new city were wide and straight, the buildings low. The inhabitants on the streets paused to watch the spectacle; others came out of their dwellings to see what was happening. The streets were soon lined with curious onlookers.

As the priests made their way deeper into the new city, it became obvious that construction was still at an early stage: most of the structures, while roughed out in mud brick and plaster, had yet to be finished in stone. Only the temples—of which there were several of varying sizes—were complete; even the royal family's residence waited to receive its gleaming white façade.

Nevertheless, work seemed to be hastening on. Builders swarmed the various construction sites—hundreds of them, organised in gangs, each with an overseer. The squat, swarthy labourers were all stripped to the waist, oozing sweat as they chiselled or plastered or carried bricks to and fro, with a cloth headdress the only concession to the pitiless sun. The appearance of the workers was so unlike that of the taller, more graceful Egyptians, Benedict guessed that these must be the Habiru that Anen had mentioned.

That they were skilled masons and artisans was clearly seen in the reliefs and statues and paintings that appeared at regular intervals along the streets of the royal city. Everywhere Benedict looked, there was an image of Pharaoh: Akhenaten with his wife, the beautiful Nefertiri; Akhenaten with his children; Akhenaten receiving the life-giving rays of the sun; Akhenaten mediating his god's justice to the people of Egypt. Some of the statues appeared grotesque and misshapen—Akhenaten with big, blubbery lips, a round pot belly, and spindly bowed legs—absurd caricatures of the strictly codified official portraits.

"Look there," he said, nudging his father with a discreet elbow. "The pharaoh's face looks like a camel. Did they do that on purpose?"

"Apparently," Arthur whispered back. "I've never seen anything like that before."

"Is he sick?"

"Perhaps, but I think we'll soon find out." He nodded past the priests leading the parade as into the street ahead swept a chariot with a phalanx of spear-carrying soldiers trotting easily behind. Drawn by two white horses with ostrich-plume headdresses, the chariot gleamed golden in the bright sunlight.

The procession halted as the speeding vehicle came hurtling headlong towards them, its iron-rimmed wheels clattering on the pavement. The driver lashed the horses to greater speed and drove on, his long black hair streaming in the wind.

As the vehicle closed on them, the leading line of priests broke ranks and moved aside. At the point of collision, the servants threw down their banners and ran. Suddenly the decorous procession was a mad scramble as priests fought to get out of the way. Arthur and Benedict, some little distance apart, beat a quick retreat to one side and watched the mayhem. With a clatter of hooves and a whirl of dust, the chariot skidded to a stop. The priests, outraged at their treatment, began shouting and calling down curses upon the belligerent driver—who merely put back his head and laughed, his teeth a flash of white behind the rich black of his braided beard.

The soldiers came pounding in, their heavy sandals slapping the stones. The commander, an imposing fellow in a plumed helmet of gleaming bronze and a chest plate made of overlapping leaves of bronze scales, called an order, and the soldiers formed up, coming to attention with a smart crack of their spears on the pavement.

"This is an outrage!" shouted one of the senior priests, shoving forward, his robe in disarray and smudged with dust. "A curse on your house!"

The chariot driver merely gazed down, grinning through his beard. Benedict edged closer for a better look. He saw a compact, well-made man in the prime of life, clean-limbed and clear-eyed, his skin bronzed a robust hue from the sun—the symbol of the god he served. He had a high forehead, strong jaw, and fine white teeth that fairly gleamed through the dark forest of his beard.

This only served to enrage the priest all the more. Spitting with anger, he shook his fists in the air, threatening, "Your reckless behaviour and thoughtless treatment will not go unpunished! Pharaoh will hear about this!"

The charioteer laughed again, then passed the reins to his commander and climbed down from the vehicle. As he came around to face the angry priests, he raised his hand to reveal that he held a rod of gold and lapis. The mere sight of this implement brought gasps from the assembled priests, who instantly bowed from the waist, the palms of their hands extended at the knee.

"Pharaoh, I think, has already heard your complaint," said the cheerful charioteer.

"O Mighty King, forgive your servant's intemperance." The priest bent low and remained in an attitude of extreme supplication. "Forgive me, my king. I did not know you."

"You did not know your king?" wondered Pharaoh mildly. "How is that? Is not my image engraved upon your heart?"

"Great of Renown, it has been so long . . ." The priest, flustered now, began backing away, mumbling as he went. "You have changed, my king. I did not . . ."

Benedict's eyes grew round. "That is Akhenaten?" he gasped under his breath.

"So it would seem," whispered Arthur.

"What are they saying?"

"Shh! I can't hear. Be still."

Now the High Priest, on the arm of Anen, moved forward. The priests around him moved aside to open a way for the old man. He came to stand before the supreme king and, after the merest pause, bowed and then rose.

"Mighty Ruler of Two Houses, Supreme Son of Horus, Heavenly Warrior, Life-giver of Nations—the First Prophet of Amun greets you," he intoned in a thin, reedy voice.

At this Akhenaten's smile dissolved, and his features took on a stony cast. "I know who you are, old man." He cast a glance at Anen. "Who is this?"

"Great of Glory," said Anen, bowing nicely, "I am Anen, Second Prophet of Amun."

"*Two* prophets," observed the king with a snide curl of his lip. "It seems I am doubly blessed today." Gesturing to the assembled priests who had quickly gathered around, he said, "And are these all prophets of your god as well?"

"O Wonder of the Visible World, may you live in health forever—" began the High Priest.

Pharaoh cut him off with a flick of the rod in his hand. "Why are you here?" he demanded.

"Mighty King," said Anen, "we have come with gifts for you." He signalled to the servants carrying the baskets. They came forward to offer their gifts, but the king raised his hand and halted them.

"Do you think Pharaoh desires anything you have to give?" he demanded. "Am I one of your gods that you can placate with trinkets and sweetmeats?"

"By no means, Wisdom of Osiris," replied Anen smoothly. "We give you but your own from the largess your enlightened rule has ordained and made manifest."

"Humph!" sneered Akhenaten, turning away. He walked back to his chariot and climbed in. "Priests of false idols, hear me!" the king called, his voice loud in the silence. "This place is holy to the god Aten, the Only Wise Supreme Creator and Ruler of the Heavenly Realms. If you have come to forswear your worship of lesser gods, you may stay. If you have come for any other purpose, you are no longer welcome here."

"If our presence offends you, Great One, allow us but a word, and we will depart in peace."

"Be gone!" roared the king, gathering the reins in his hands. He levelled a cold gaze at the High Priest, who stood openmouthed in disbelief at his insolent dismissal. "Remove these people from my sight."

Upon Pharaoh's command the commander of the soldiers raised his spear and shouted an order to his troops. The soldiers levelled their weapons and, spear tips glinting bright in the sun, they all moved forward as one.

The priests and their attendants fell back. With much grumbling and muttering, they turned and began making their way to the city gate.

"Come, Benedict," said Arthur; he tugged on his son's arm, pulling him away. "Stay close to me and keep your wits about you. If anything should happen, run for the barge."

Fuming with frustration and humiliation, the priests retreated, pursued by the soldiers who, not content with compliance, began calling taunts and threats to provoke a response. The jeers were taken up by the citizens lining the streets, growing more angry and aggressive with every step. Though Benedict could not understand the insults, he knew trouble when he saw it—and this was trouble pure and deep. Looking neither right nor left, he kept his head down and walked quickly behind his father.

As they came into sight of the city gates, they saw that the way was blocked by a gang of Habiru workers. The procession slowed and then juddered to a stop. The priests demanded to be allowed to pass. The labourers refused to move and make way for the priests. Some waved their fists and some, holding hammers and mallets, began pounding on the ground.

The first stone sailed up from the ranks of onlookers, striking a priest in the front of the procession. He let out a startled cry, clutched his shoulder, and whirled around to see who had thrown the missile. Those next to him began demanding that the perpetrator be punished.

Arthur moved to Benedict's side and took his hand. "Hold on," he told him. "Whatever happens, hold on to me."

Even as he spoke, another rock struck a nearby priest, who crumpled to the ground. This missile was followed by a brick from one of the building sites. It hit the pavement hard and shattered, scattering chips and fragments. The crowd cried its approval, and more stones and bricks swiftly followed.

Anen pushed his way to the fore rank; with his arms raised above his head, he called on the Habiru to cease their assault and let them pass. When this failed to elicit a response, he turned to appeal to the commander of the soldiers to halt the stone throwing and allow them to depart in peace. His pleas went unheeded. More stones followed, coming faster now as the crowd took encouragement from the lack of intervention by soldiers, who merely stood by and watched.

"We're going to have to run for it," Arthur advised his son. "Don't let go of my hand."

Anen was struck next, receiving a grazing blow to the side of his head. Blood oozed from the wound, drawing a cheer from the crowd. Priests, frightened and confused, charged the labourers blocking the way. Some of the workmen stood aside—only to strike at the holy men as they passed. Others challenged them outright, shoving them or swinging hammers and fists.

The retreat became a rout. Everyone ran for the gate and the barges waiting at the wharf.

"Now!" shouted Arthur, pulling Benedict with him. "Run!"

Dodging and weaving through the angry throng, they scrambled.

The mob closed in behind them, pelting the fleeing priests with stones and bricks. They gained the gates and, pushing past the last of the workers, were free. Once beyond the city walls, they paused to wait for Anen and the High Priest.

When they failed to emerge, Arthur pulled Benedict close. "Go! Get on board," he ordered. "I'll join you in a moment."

"I won't go without you."

"Obey me, son. Go!"

Arthur released his son and pushed him towards the barge. He had only just turned and started back into the crush at the gates when a brick sailed out and with uncanny accuracy struck him on the left temple. The blow spun him sideways and he fell, unconscious when he struck the ground.

"Father!" shouted Benedict. He ran to his father's side and knelt, taking the wounded head onto his knees. There was little blood. The brick had barely broken the skin, but already an ugly red-blue welt was rising.

"Father, wake up!" urged the youth, cradling the wounded head. "Can you hear me? Father? Can you hear me? Wake up."

Priests were running past them. Benedict called out, "Help!"

One of those running past stopped.

"My father is hurt!" shouted Benedict. "Help me!"

The priest realised instantly what had happened; he snagged one of his fellow priests and, with Benedict's help, lifted the unconscious Arthur and dragged him to the barge, where they laid him carefully on the deck.

The next events would always be something of a distant confusion to Benedict. He remembered other priests joining them on the deck, and Anen himself taking command and directing the wounded man to be carried to the roofed pavilion in the centre of the barge and laid upon the cushioned platform there. When Benedict looked around again, the barge was already under sail and the royal city receding into the distance.

CHAPTER 9

In Which Wilhelmina Pursues a Mountaintop Experience

With Lady Fayth's timely warning to crystallise her thoughts, Wilhelmina decided her best course of action. She had been itching to put the new model ley lamp through its paces and discover its full potential; leaving Prague for a few days was the perfect excuse she needed and, having made a clean breast of it with Etzel, she was now free to travel whenever she pleased: much as before, of course, but now without the nagging guilty conscience for misleading her partner, her champion.

For indeed, dear Engelbert could not have been any more gallant a defender if he had worn a suit of shining armour and carried her colours into the joust on the back of a galloping steed. Never had she known anyone who so selflessly and consistently took her part and put her welfare and interests first.

Etzel did all that and more, and Mina had no doubt that when the quest for the Skin Map was finished, she would happily settle down to life in the Grand Imperial with him. Indeed, the more she thought about it, the more certain she was that she wanted nothing else.

Just now, however, she had other duties and entanglements that he could not share. First on the list was to elude Burleigh. Then she could devote herself entirely to discovering what had happened to Kit. The first task was simple and easily accomplished, thanks to Haven's timely warning. For the second chore, she would need help. Having come to the end of her own expertise, she determined it was time to go back to the one who had helped her find Kit the first time: Brother Lazarus.

With any luck at all, she might still be able to stay a step or two ahead of Burleigh and his brute squad. The chief problem, among many, was the risk of exposure. Knowing how Burleigh's new device worked, she now realised just how vulnerable she would be when ley travelling. If the treacherous earl ever took an interest in her specifically, the result could well be catastrophic.

Once the decision was made, Wilhelmina wasted no time in putting her plan into action. She bade Etzel farewell, promising to hurry back as soon as humanly possible, and then set off. The ley she needed was half a day's journey from Prague, and from previous experience Mina knew it to be particularly time-sensitive—that is, offering only a very narrow window of activity twice each day, a few minutes either side of sunrise and sunset. Miss either opportunity, and the ley traveller would have to wait until next time. This was not unusual; many ley lines and portals operated in a similar fashion, she had found. Some were more lenient and forgiving, some less so. Why? Wilhelmina had no clue.

With the hostler near the city gates she arranged for a carriage and driver to take her to her destination: an empty stretch of countryside a kilometre or so north of the tiny farming village of Podbrdy. Her plan was to disembark outside the settlement and walk to the ley unobserved, if possible. Two further jumps would put her in the southern Pyrenees within a stone's throw of her destination. Once there she would assume the guise of a nun on pilgrimage and seek out her mentor. In accordance with his wishes and her most solemn and sacred vow—he had made her swear on a hand-copied Bible not to reveal either his identity or whereabouts to another living soul—she had never breathed a word of Brother Lazarus' existence to anyone. The cautious monk was, in effect, her very secret weapon. A quaint arrangement, but it suited them both.

Wilhelmina dozed through much of the coach ride to the village so that she would be well rested for the next leaps in her journey. In the end, she need not have bothered because she arrived too late and the ley was dormant; she had to wait until sunrise. She begged a bed for the night in the barn of a nearby farmer and spent a pleasant, if odorous, evening with two cows, four ducks, and a black-spotted pig.

Just before sunrise she returned to the ley and made the leap; the next two were accomplished without incident and, pausing before the last jump, she took refreshment at a small café on the Via Bassomondo, the dusty road winding down the gently sloping hillside to the abbey of Sant'Antimo. She was, she thought, somewhere in the last century—1929, perhaps? Wilhelmina couldn't tell. Her Italian was strictly confined to *Buongiorno, Signor Rinaldi! Un cappuccino e una brioche, per favore.*

She drank her coffee and ate her pastry, making comparisons with her own brew and baking, paid the bill from her little stash of coins obtained on her various travels, and then walked on to the next ley, which ran through the valley outside the abbey. This part of the journey was always her favourite, and Mina often lingered a little while to enjoy the sublime view of the broad olive-groved and cypress-lined valley. Tradition had it that Emperor Charlemagne had been a major benefactor of the monastery in earlier days, and often used it as a convenient stopping-off place on his various journeys from Rome to his palace at Aachen.

Sometimes, when she had time to spare, she paused to take in the abbey church itself, a handsome Romanesque structure in rough white limestone with beautiful carvings inside and out. The location had been chosen because, like so many sites that now hosted churches of various kinds, it had been a holy place long before the monastery had been contemplated. That it remained a pilgrimage destination worked to Wilhelmina's favour in that the monks were used to strangers in their midst and welcomed them as best they could. Thus Wilhelmina blended in with the general comings and goings of the place, and her odd appearances and disappearances went unnoticed and unremarked. More importantly, however, it was at Sant'Antimo that she had first learned of the man to whom she owed much of her acumen and skill in ley travel.

This is the story of how she first came to meet Brother Lazarus and travel to his world:

Wilhelmina's experiments with Burleigh's first device had provided her with a ready means of recognising active ley lines as well as guiding her to them. She had made a number of test jumps—cautious to the point of timidity at first, but with growing confidence as she gained experience—beginning with a series of single jumps, then a few doubles, before progressing to what were, for her, the very daring triple jumps. In each of these experiments she noted the place and time of the ley activity and memorised the destinations. On one of those early triple jumps she had landed in the pleasant Italian valley near Montalcino, on a narrow dirt road that passed a grand old church and monastery. The date—local time—was 27 May, 1972.

Surrounded by ancient cypress trees, well-tended fields, and a little pasture for sheep, the place seemed to speak to her; she felt drawn to it and decided to indulge herself with a little sightseeing. Passing through the handsomely carved archway, she entered the quiet sanctuary; the cool air was heavy with the scent of frankincense. From somewhere near the altar at the front of the high-ceilinged chancel, a small bell chimed. There were a few other visitors walking the aisles, quietly, thoughtfully, and in spite of her old-fashioned clothes, Wilhelmina blended right in. As she made her first circuit of the church, she came upon a large hand-painted sign with a diagram of the floor plan. Seeing the explanation was in English as well as French and Italian, she paused to read it and discovered that, according to a series of measurements carried out some years earlier, no fewer than seven separate lines of electromagnetic force met at a point directly beneath the church's altar. These force fields were not leys; at least, not like any Wilhelmina had previously encountered. They were not straight, and culminated at a single point—unlike normal ley lines; nor was that term used in the fragmented English translation provided on the sign by the mapmaker. Were these lines of force something similar? Or something else entirely?

Mina, determined to find out all she could of these mysterious lines of telluric energy flowing beneath the church, immediately hailed one of the monks going about his business. *"Scusi, padre. Parla Inglese"*

"Sì, signora, a leetle."

Pointing to the sign showing the map of the curious lines, she said, "This priest"—she tapped the neatly lettered name at the bottom of the sign—"Fra Giambattista Becarria?"

"Fra Giambattista, *si*," agreed the monk.

"Is he here? May I speak to him? It may be important."

"No, *signora*, is not possible. Fra Giambattista, he no longer with us."

Mina frowned. "He is dead, you mean?"

"*Si*. Many years now."

"May I see his grave?"

"Alas, *signora*. Is at *Abbazia di Montserrat*, I think"

"Montserrat? Is that far?"

"*Si, signora*. Is in *Spagna*."

Wilhelmina thanked the priest for the information and continued her exploration of Sant'Antimo. By the time she reached the altar rail she was in the grip of a conviction as potent as it was absurd: the unanswerable certainty that the knowledge she so desperately needed would be found at a place that thirty seconds ago she had never even heard of. Moreover, this conviction entailed an insistence of such urgency that she plopped down in the front pew and stared at the light streaming in through the high, narrow windows behind the stunningly lifelike crucifix, her mind reeling with the single thought that she must drop everything and get herself to the abbey at Montserrat by the fastest means possible.

At the time, her ley mapping skills did not yet extend to the Spanish peninsula, and she wanted to make no mistakes, so she decided to travel by train. In a typically canny move, Wilhelmina decided that if she was to visit a Spanish abbey, she would present herself as a German nun. In Montalcino, she purchased a plain skirt and blouse, and with the addition of a gift-shop cross of olive wood and a well-arranged dove-grey headscarf, she was a passable sister—if of the modern variety.

Upon arrival in Barcelona, she found a convent and arranged to join a group of visiting French nuns on pilgrimage to the *Abadia de*

Santa Maria, which was located high in the jagged mountain range northeast of the city. It was a three-day trek on foot, but Wilhelmina enjoyed the fresh air and easy company of the nuns, who sang as they went and stopped in every village chapel and shrine along the way to pray and prepare for their sojourn at the abbey.

The little party finally arrived late in the afternoon of the third day. They entered the narrow gorge into which the abbey and its various buildings had been painstakingly shoehorned. The soaring peaks of the surrounding mountains rose sheer on every side save one, which gave onto a shimmering vista stretching from the sloping foothills all the way to the coast. As the covey of nuns stood marvelling at the magnificence of the abbey and its situation, the bell for vespers rang, so they followed the general flow of monks and visitors up the steep incline to the church.

At the top of the esplanade rose ranks of steps that terminated in a courtyard, the end of which opened to a gateway. Beyond the gates was a handsome atrium lined with statues of apostles and saints and paved with inlaid marble of many colours that marked out a geometric swirl of intersecting lines, at the centre of which was a circular mosaic representing the four rivers flowing out of Eden. The courtyard thronged with visitors behaving in a most peculiar way. They stood in a long line snaking back into the courtyard and, one at a time, each waiting patiently for the other, they took it in turn to step forward and stand in the central disc of the mosaic. Then they prayed—some in the classic attitude with hands folded and heads bowed, but many in apparent wild abandon with arms outstretched and faces turned to the clear blue sky above.

The faithful would stand like this for a time before moving off to join the general population making their way into the sanctuary.

This curious activity was not lost on Wilhelmina. *How very odd*, she thought. Clearly, there was something going on here, and she took it as a sign that vindicated her own decision to come.

She followed the others as they moved slowly towards the entrance and, upon approaching the centre of the mosaic circle, experienced the subtle but unmistakable frisson of pent energy that she always felt in the presence of an active ley. It was there, marked out in stone in the middle of the atrium where, apparently, pilgrims in their hundreds and thousands also perceived the latent energy in some way.

Once in the chapel, she sat through the service, listening to the ethereal voices of the choir and wondering how to make sense of it all. The end of the service found her in a pensive mood of rapt contemplation; for overarching all other considerations was a feeling of peace and, if not contentment, then at least a sense of rightness—she felt that all was as it should be.

She took a light supper in the convent refectory with sisters from a dozen different nations and was given a cot in the dormitory. Wilhelmina slept well and awoke at the sunrise bell to attend prayers with them. As soon as the service was finished, she set off to find the grave of Fra Giambattista and to learn more about him if she could. She waited until most of the congregation had left, then approached one of the monks who acted as usher and guide. *"Por favor, habla inglés?"*

"Lo siento, hermana, no," he said, shaking his head. He turned, then pointed across the spacious expanse of the sanctuary to a black-robed monk stacking blue service books.

"Excuse me, brother," she said, upon approaching him. "I am told you speak English."

The monk straightened, turned, and smiled when he saw her. "I have a little. How can I help you?"

"I am looking for the grave of a former priest by the name of Giambattista Beccaria," Wilhelmina replied, and went on to explain how she had been directed to the abbey to find it. She watched a thoughtful frown form and deepen on the priest's smooth-shaven face.

"I am sorry, sister," he replied at length. "I have never heard that name. Are you certain he is buried here?"

"That is what I have been given to understand. He was a former astronomer here—at least, that is what I was told."

"Ah! Then you must go to Brother Lazarus. He is astronomer now. If anyone knows about this, he will."

Wilhelmina thanked him for his help and asked where she might find this brother. The monk, who had resumed stacking books, shrugged. "At the observatory, where else?"

She hurried off and, after asking directions, found a signboard painted with a map of the extensive abbey grounds. The observatory was clearly marked. According to the sign it was at the top of one of the peaks soaring above the abbey; all she had to do was climb the winding path leading to the summit. This she did and discovered a small tower with a bulbous top perched on a pinnacle of stone. An iron rail enclosed a circular walkway around the base of the building, and a simple handrail of knotted rope assisted the ascent up a steep flight of narrow stairs leading to the door.

There appeared to be no one around, but as she started up the stairs she heard the sound of someone humming—low and rhythmically, if not exactly melodically. Mina could not see who was making this sound, but as she mounted to the top step and started around the base of the tower she found a monk in the black robes of the Benedictines down on his knees, surrounded by gardening tools—a small hand trowel, a rake, a pruning knife, an assortment of clay pots, and a sheaf of cuttings. The gardener was clutching a double handful of dirt and humming tunelessly while he worked. As she watched, he placed the dirt in a clay pot and pressed it firmly around a geranium cutting. A canvas bag of soil stood open beside him.

Wilhelmina cleared her throat. "Excuse me, please," she said, announcing her presence. "Hello?"

The priest gave such a start that Wilhelmina was ashamed of startling him. "Oh, I am sorry," she apologised. "I did not mean to frighten you."

The gardener's hand described a strange gesture around his head, and he whipped something out of sight in a fold of his robe. Then, steadying himself, he rose and turned to meet his visitor. *"Que?"* he said, rubbing dirt from his hands. *"Buenos días, hermana."*

"Sorry, *no habla español,*" she replied. Then, out of force of habit, she said, *"Sprechen Sie Deutsch?"*

"Ja, tu ich." His smile widened. A small man, with short snow-white hair and quick, dark eyes. His face was nicely browned by the sun, his hands made strong by the long hours he spent gardening. In all, he reminded Wilhelmina of one of the Seven Dwarfs. *"Guten Morgen, Schwester,"* he said in a rich, almost operatic baritone—the voice of a much larger man.

"Good morning, brother," she answered in the sturdy German of Old Prague, then offered him a little bow she had seen the other nuns make when addressing a priest of the order. "I am looking for the one they call Brother Lazarus."

"Then God smiles upon you, sister." He bent to brush dirt from the knees of his robe. He straightened again, the top of his head coming only to Mina's shoulder. "You have found him."

"*You* are Brother Lazarus?" she asked, unable to keep the note of incredulity out of her voice. "The astronomer?"

He laughed, and Wilhelmina's face went red with embarrassment. "Why?" he asked. "Is that difficult to believe?"

"Oh, I *am* sorry," Mina said quickly. "I took you for a gardener," she explained, indicating the assembled tools and pots.

He looked where she was pointing. "Yes, well"—he gave a little shrug—"such is a good grounding for stargazing." He reached out a thickly muscled hand and placed it gently on her sleeve. "An astronomer can only practise his craft at night. What is he to do with the rest of his time?"

"Forgive me, brother. I meant no disrespect."

He swatted away the apology with an impatient flick of his hand. "Now that you have found Brother Lazarus, what do you want with him?"

"I am searching for the burial place of one of your colleagues, a monk of this order. I have been told that he was once the astronomer here and that his grave is nearby. Can you tell me where it is?"

"Perhaps, yes," he replied, turning to resume his work. "If you will tell me his name, I can tell you if he is buried at the abbey."

"His name is Fra Giambattista."

At the name, the monk stopped, straightened, and went very still. "Fra Giambattista Beccaria?" he asked without turning around.

"Yes, that's the one."

"I am sorry, sister," he said, stooping once more to his tools. "Your search has come to nothing. His grave, if it exists, is not here—not at this abbey." He made a show of beginning to work again. "Good day to you. And Godspeed."

Wilhelmina pursed her lips, alarmed at the swift change in the man's demeanour. The mere mention of the name had brought about an abrupt and disagreeable transformation—the same as if he had slammed a door in her face.

"Good day," she said quietly. "I am sorry to have bothered you." She took a step backward, but as she prepared to take her leave, a force of will rose up inside her—a determination to hold her ground, come what may. At the very least, she owed it to herself: she had come this far and it would be a rotten shame to go away empty-handed.

In a moment, the monk, still on his knees, peered back over his shoulder at her. "You're still here."

"I am."

"Why?"

"I think," she began, feeling her way into it, "that I am waiting for a better explanation than the one I have just heard."

"Then you must resign yourself to waiting a very long time," he declared. "There is no other explanation."

"I beg to disagree. I think there is," she said, and even as she spoke the answer came to her.

"Oh, you do," he snapped, his voice taking on a brusque and officious tone. "Since you know, you have no need to ask *me*." When she hesitated, he added, "Nothing else to say? Then I will ask you kindly to remove yourself."

"There is no grave," Wilhelmina ventured, "because . . ." She drew herself up and, casting all caution to the wind, said, "Because *you* are Giambattista Beccaria."

CHAPTER 10

In Which False Identities Are Exposed

"Y"ou *are* him, aren't you," Wilhelmina maintained, growing more certain by the moment. "You are Fra Giambattista."

"Do not be absurd, young lady," he scoffed. "What a ridiculous notion!" He gave a choked little half laugh. "Utter nonsense."

Wilhelmina said nothing. His protest sounded contrived, and that fine, mellifluous voice had become pinched and tight.

"The very idea is preposterous," he blustered, shaking his head. "Absurd."

"Why?" asked Wilhelmina. "Why is it absurd?"

"Brother Beccaria lived in Italy, long ago. If he were alive today he would be"—he paused to do a rough calculation—"well, it is impossible." The monk made a dismissive wave and offered what was supposed to be mirthful chuckle. "Preposterous. Young people are so credulous."

"Yet I do not hear a denial," she observed. "Why is that?"

"I insist you go away before we both say something we will have need of confessing."

"My conscience is clear," Wilhelmina told him. "Is there something *you* would like to confess?"

The priest became very still, then slowly rose to his feet once more, stood, and turned to face her. He studied the woman before him closely, his eyes moving over her face and form. "Who are you?" he said at last.

"My name is Wilhelmina Klug," she said.

"*Fräulein* Klug, I think. Despite present appearances, I suspect you are not a nun, nor ever have been," he remarked. "Am I right?"

"I believe we are both somewhat other than we appear."

"Please, do me the courtesy of a truthful answer. Are you a sister of the order?"

"No," Mina told him. "I am . . . a traveller."

"A traveller." He made a face, dismissing her claim. "You are disingenuous," he replied. "Traveller . . . ha!" He raised a hand to her, and Wilhelmina thought he meant to send her away once more but thought better of it. Instead he asked, "How did you learn about Fra Giambattista?"

"I was visiting the abbey at Sant'Antimo in Tuscany," she replied. "I saw the name on a placard. One of the brothers told me he had been appointed astronomer here, and that he was buried here." She cast an appraising glance over the man before her. "But that is not true. There is no grave because he never died. In fact, he is standing here before me."

Astonishment, horror, but also relief played across the priest's round, good-natured face. "But how could that possibly be?" he said, his voice growing small.

"How could it be that you are that old?" she wondered. "Or how could it be that I know this?"

"Either," he mumbled, rocking back on his feet. "Both."

"It is possible," she replied, taking a step closer, "because you are a traveller too—like me. And like me, your travels are not entirely confined to this world."

"*Madre di Dio!*" he said, making the sign of the cross over his chest and kissing his clasped hands. Without another word he darted to the door of the observatory tower, put his hand on the brass knob, and pushed open the door. Wilhelmina expected that, fleeing her presence, he would shut her out. But as he disappeared inside, he motioned for her to follow.

She mounted the steps and entered a tiny vestibule; a narrow corridor led straight ahead to a pair of doors, and a staircase led to upper levels. Brother Lazarus went to the door on the left-hand side of the corridor and passed through. Wilhelmina followed him into a tidy little kitchen with a simple woodburning stove, a square wooden table, and four chairs. A curtained window opened to a view of the surrounding peaks and the lowlands beyond. The room was tidy and well kept; there were flowers in a chipped pottery mug on the table, and the rag rug on the floor was clean.

The flustered monk went directly to the little cupboard and removed a short glass beaker, a cup, and a jug of wine, which he carried to the table. He gestured to one of the chairs. "Sit."

Wilhelmina obeyed and was presented with a tot of wine. The priest sat down across the table and, taking his cup in both hands, guzzled down a healthy slug. He looked at Wilhelmina, who raised her beaker to him, then sipped, and he took another great gulp. "So! I am discovered at last." He shook his head slowly. "What is to happen now?"

"I really don't know," replied Mina gently. "I certainly did not come here to frighten you, or harm you in any way."

"Why did you come here?"

She did not know where to begin to answer that—there was just too much. She wanted to know how to manipulate the leys, how they worked, what caused them, where they led; there was the nagging matter of Kit and getting in touch with him again so that she could tell him to stop worrying about her; and then there was the whole business of the Skin Map and the Burley Men, and so on. Wilhelmina decided to skip all that for now and settled for a much simpler, "I came here seeking knowledge."

"Knowledge," repeated the monk. "What do you want to know?"

Wilhelmina gazed at the wine in her glass. "There is so much—I hardly know where to begin. I have so very many questions."

"Pick one," replied Fra Giambattista. Perhaps it was Wilhelmina's soft-spoken assurance, or the soothing influence of the wine, but the priest's fractured attitude seemed to be on the mend. "It does not matter where one starts; it is where one finishes that makes all the difference."

She seized on one of the many questions wheeling around in her head like a flock of noisy seagulls. "For an Italian living in Spain, why do you speak such good German?"

He laughed, some of his former good humour returning. "That is what you have come here to ask? I thought it would be about the Holy Grail."

"King Arthur's Holy Grail?"

"Is there another?"

Charmed by the idea, she gave a small laugh. "Why should I ask about that?"

"That is what everyone wants to know!" he cried. "We have no end of seekers looking for the Grail of King Arthur—and the brothers always send them to me. Legend has it that the fabled cup is buried here on Montserrat."

"Is it?"

"I have no idea!" Fra Giambattista laughed again and was his former self. "Why ask about my German?"

"As you say, we must begin somewhere." Mina took a drink of wine. "Who knows where we shall end up? Well?"

"It is obvious. All the best physics is German," he declared. "I learned it in order to read and converse with my fellows in Bonn and Berlin, Hamburg, Vienna . . ." He shrugged. "It helps to know a little of the language of science."

"I can well appreciate that," agreed Wilhelmina. "How did you discover ley travel?"

"*Ley* travel?" he wondered. "Is that what you call it?"

"It is how it was described to me," she answered. "I suppose you could say I fell into it by accident."

"Dear lady," offered the priest with a smile, "there are no accidents." He took another sip of wine and refilled their cups. "But I know what you mean. I suppose I came to it in the same way. In the course of my various experiments, I had become aware of the lines of force operating beneath Sant'Antimo. In the course of mapping them for further study, I was caught in a storm, and in trying to run to shelter inexplicably found myself . . ." His voice trailed off, remembering.

"Where?" asked Mina after a moment.

"Here!" he said. "At Montserrat."

"The two places are connected, you mean."

"Indeed they are. Of course, I thought I was going mad," he chuckled. "It took me years to work out what had happened and still more to learn how to manipulate it for my purposes—as much as anyone can ever impose one's own purposes on such an elemental power." He shook his head again. "That was a very long time ago, yet I remember it all as if it were yesterday."

They talked then, sharing their observations of, and experiences with, the unconventional properties of ley travel. And the more they talked, the more Wilhelmina was convinced that she had found someone who could do more than simply provide her with information. In Fra Giambattista she had found a mentor, someone whose knowledge was extensive and who could capably guide her search.

"Why did you change your name?" Wilhelmina asked. They had moved their conversation to the cloister garden, where they could be seen by those who cared to notice—this was to avoid any discussion about a nun visiting a monk in his quarters.

"Well, dear lady," he had replied with a laugh. "It was because I was living so long! You see, travelling between worlds affects the aging process. I was outliving all my contemporaries, and it was beginning to be noticed."

"I can see that would be a problem."

He nodded. "One day—after the funeral of our dear old sacristan, and in the company of everyone—the abbot of Sant' Antimo was heard to remark, 'Brother Giambattista, you must have more lives than Lazarus!' Everyone laughed, but I got the hint. Something had to be done." The priest spread his hands. He gazed up at the clear, cloud-speckled sky for a moment, then shrugged. "What could I do?"

"What *did* you do?" asked Wilhelmina, chin on hand, fascinated.

"Well, it was obvious, no? Brother Beccaria could not go on. One spring, I received permission from my abbot to go on a pilgrimage to Montserrat, and on arrival to stay and use the observatory. Of course, I had been here before, but none of the brothers at Sant' Antimo knew that. Once here, I contrived to become ill, and reported this to my brothers. Eventually, I sent back a message that poor Fra Giambattista had succumbed to his maladies and gone to his heavenly reward."

"Fra Giambattista died," Mina concluded, "and Brother Lazarus was born."

"A deception, I admit. But all this has been confessed and God will forgive, for my heart is pure and the work I do, I do in the service of the Almighty." He nodded, satisfied with this arrangement. "After that I travelled many years in Germany, learning the language and reading physics, talking to my colleagues and studying, studying, all the while studying." He brushed a bit of fluff from the lap of his fine black robe. "When I had learned enough, I came back here."

"As astronomer?"

"Oh no. All my contemporaries here had passed away by then— that was part of the plan, you see. Fra Giambattista was remembered, of course. But no one then at the abbey knew "Brother Lazarus." I worked in the gardens at first and helped at the observatory. In time, I became assistant to the chief astronomer and climbed my way up the ladder once more." He put a rough gardener's palm on Wilhelmina's hand and confided, "Patience was ever a virtue."

Wilhelmina's first visit extended to more than two weeks. Every other day or so, she met Brother Lazarus in the cloister garden to discuss some particular aspect of ley travel, its uses and attendant problems and implications. The astronomer monk proved himself a thoughtful and erudite instructor; his study of astronomy and physics embraced cosmology, philosophy, and, being a priest, theology as well. As a patient and capable teacher he was second to none, and Wilhelmina, the eager and willing student, was soon firmly under his spell. His enthusiasm, she suspected, derived from the fact that he had previously had no one with whom he might share his greatest discoveries and insights. In Wilhelmina he had at last found someone who not only understood but could partake in the wonder of the enterprise at the deepest level. And inasmuch as her experience of ley travel, although undisciplined, was no less extensive in its way than his own, Wilhelmina was someone who could help further his inquiries. Nor did it hurt that he genuinely liked her and enjoyed her company.

That first fortnight passed in a blink. Wilhelmina could have stayed much longer, but to do so would draw unwanted suspicion. Instead the two conspirators agreed that she should leave soon, but return in the spring when they could continue Mina's education to the point where she could eventually collaborate on Brother Lazarus' work of mapping the intersecting dimensions of the cosmos.

"Many people make annual pilgrimage to the abbey," he said. "Your presence need not draw suspicion—and if anyone should ask, you can always say it is in fulfilment of a vow for answered prayer."

"That is nothing more than the truth, after all," Wilhelmina decided.

The day of departure came and she took her leave—but not before learning the whereabouts of the nearest ley and how it connected with Sant'Antimo. "What about the circle in the sanctuary atrium?" she remembered asking. "Is that a ley threshold?"

"There is a force there, very powerful. I have measured it, but never attempted to use it. I believe it to be unstable, unpredictable. It must be studied further. Besides, it is too public," the monk told her. "Nevertheless, these mountains are seamed through and through with lines of power—these leys, as you call them. The one nearest the observatory—the one I showed you?—that one joins Sant'Antimo."

"That is how *you* got here the first time."

"Exactly." He raised a finger in warning. "Use it, but use it carefully. We never know who may be watching."

Wilhelmina thanked him for his care and departed, returning the next spring and then again the following autumn—a pattern that was to repeat until she became a familiar sight around the monastery grounds. Her friends there were happy to see her, and she slowly became attached to the place.

"Do you know Thomas Young?" Brother Lazarus asked Mina on that first visit. "A physician in London? Have you ever crossed paths with him at all?"

"I feel certain I would know if I had," she replied. "But no. Is he a fellow traveller?"

"I have never heard that he was, but it would not surprise me. His experiments in 1807 established the foundation on which the edifice of quantum physics is constructed." Brother Lazarus went on to explain, in almost reverential tones, about the man who had discovered the dual nature of light as both particles and waves. "If that was not enough, he also helped establish archaeology as a science and in 1814 succeeded in cracking the code of Egyptian hieroglyphic writing."

"He sounds fascinating," she concluded. "He lives in London, you say?"

"He did." The monk nodded. "A most fascinating man is Thomas Young."

That was the first time Wilhelmina heard of Dr. Young. It would not be the last.

CHAPTER 11

In Which Tracks Are Made and Covered

I agree it is something of a coincidence," allowed Lady Fayth judiciously. "Then again, why should this bakery woman not go wherever she likes?"

"I find it highly suspicious," declared Burleigh. "On the eve of receiving our dinner invitation, she picks up and flees the city. Coincidence? I think not."

"She can hardly be said to have *fled* the city," Haven countered smoothly. "The baker said she had business in Vienna. There is nothing odd about a woman of commerce travelling on business. Some would say that such an eventuality was an inevitable consequence of trade."

Burleigh's expression hardened. "Why are you always taking her part?" His tone was dark and insinuating.

"The way you talk." Haven sighed lightly and rolled her lovely brown eyes. "I take no one's part, my leery lord. I merely point out the folly of your insistence on viewing even the most perfectly innocent event as part of some vast conspiracy to overthrow your plans."

"Watch your mouth, girl," growled Burleigh. He glared at her. "I grow sick of bickering with you over every step I take."

Haven knew she had pressed the matter far enough. It was time to make amends. "Oh dear, I have angered you," she said, suddenly contrite. "I am sorry." She lowered her head in a submissive gesture. "Offending you was the last thing I intended."

"Get out!" he shouted. "I cannot think with you simpering on like that. Go to your room until I call for you. I will decide what to do."

Without another word she turned and moved to the door, glad to escape the Black Earl's foul mood.

"Do not imagine that I will forget your insolence," he called after her.

"No, my lord," she answered, shutting the door behind her. To herself she added, "I imagine you will soon have cause to long remember it."

She stalked off down the corridor, seething with rage: against Burleigh, against wicked circumstance that forced her to behave like a debauched wanton, against the guilt she felt for abandoning her uncle and the others to die in the tomb—rage against the powerlessness and humiliation she felt every moment of her waking day. It was bad enough that she had been made into a plotter of plots and a schemer of schemes—it was the price paid for joining the quest, so be it—but that she must travel with the brute, be seen by one and all as his confidante, nay, his paramour. The sound of his voice, his supercilious manner, his handsome features—which might have been admired in a better man—turned her stomach.

The pretence of obedience was wearing on her. She detested the odious man and his bestial morality, and it was now almost impossible to hold her tongue in his presence. Burleigh himself sensed that all was not as it seemed with her; soon, if not already, he would decide to sever their partnership, and she would become another victim sacrificed to his insatiable ambition.

Aside from simple survival, she had hoped to learn from him—at the very least learn his methods, plans, his ultimate aims. But beyond Burleigh's obsession with the Skin Map, she had learned very little. What he wanted, why he drove himself, what he hoped to gain from his ruthless exploitation of everyone who crossed his path she still did not know. But she sensed she had learned all he was willing to teach her. Now, as she stood in the darkened corridor staring at the door to her room of this fetid, bug-infested inn, she knew she had reached the end of her endurance.

The inn, the grandest Prague had to offer, was insufferable; the stink, the noise, the squalid surroundings did not befit a lady of her station. She refused to spend one more night listening to cats rummaging through garbage in the street beneath her window, listening to the drunk and snoring sleepers in the rooms on either side of hers, smelling the slops as they were sluiced into the gutters.

The moment she closed the door behind her, she changed into her travelling clothes and, taking only her coat, crept from her room. Once in the corridor, she slipped like a sprite down the stairs and tiptoed across the inn's hall, risking a glance into the common room to see that Burleigh was still sitting where she had left him, brooding, a drink at his elbow. She moved to the entrance and, with a last look around to see that she was unobserved, departed.

She moved through the streets of Prague, descending the palace hill towards the old town and the city walls rising beyond the square.

The sun was already down, but the sky held a glimmer of light. She hoped there would be no difficulty in departing the city; she did not care to leave behind any witnesses who might be interrogated later. This, as much as the fact that her German was nowhere good enough to concoct a plausible story for inquisitive guards, determined another, slightly less desirable course of action. Quite simply, she would linger in the shadow of the gates until a departing wagon or coach rumbled through. Using the vehicle to shield her from view, she would slip through and then disappear into the countryside.

Upon approaching the gatehouse, she slowed her pace, keeping to the far side of the street, watching the activity and trying to determine the whereabouts of the guards. She found a narrow alleyway within sight of the gate, crept in, and, perching herself on an upturned crate beside a rain barrel, settled back to wait for her chance. A short time later she heard the clip-clop of horses' hooves on the cobbles. She eased herself off her perch and moved to the mouth of the alley. The torches had been lit on either side of the big timber doors, and one of them was open. A wagon loaded with barrels was just then negotiating with the guards to open the other half to let the wagon through. Plucking up her courage, Haven darted from her hiding place, moving alongside the boxy vehicle just as the driver flicked the reins and called to the horses to walk on.

Both Haven and the wagon passed through the portal out onto the road at the same time. To the best of her knowledge, the gatekeepers had not seen her, nor had anyone else. Casting one last glance over her shoulder, she satisfied herself that she was indeed free, then turned and hurried to the jumping-off place—the site Burleigh used to reach Prague. She had memorised the location and had no difficulty finding it again.

A brisk walk through the chilly grey countryside brought her to a secluded spot in the hills north of the city. There, amidst farms of beets and turnips, was a preternaturally straight crease—a shallow ditch marking the boundary between two fields. These were ancient features, she knew; her uncle called them Hollow Ways, and they were older than the farms and fields they marked; as old as the hills themselves, Sir Henry said.

At the fleeting thought of her beloved uncle, Haven felt another stab of guilt for having failed him. "I am so sorry, Uncle," she murmured, then shoved the feeling aside. Revenge, she decided, would drive her from now on. She would avenge her uncle's death and punish the Black Earl for his needless cruelty and for the humiliation he had inflicted on her.

The stars were alight in the eastern sky when Haven reached the ley. Without a moment to spare she hurried across the high-furrowed field to the Hollow Way, stepped down into the ditch, and aligned herself with one of the stones that served for field corners. Then, putting her feet in the centre of the path, she started down the narrow trail. Within four determined paces, she felt the familiar tingle on her skin. A breeze gusted over the crest of the bank and swirled around her long skirt. Three more steps carried her to the next stone marker. The banks of the Hollow Way grew hazy. The twilight dimmed, and she felt the path fall away beneath her feet. For an instant her ears were filled with the howling screech of the void, and misty rain spattered her face and neck. By now a more experienced ley-leaper, she was ready for the awkward lurch as the trail came up beneath her once more, the ground level slightly higher this time. Taking the jolt in her knees, she managed to remain upright, took two more steps, and stopped to look around.

The world around her had changed. The gentle hills and ploughed fields of Bohemia were gone, and in their place was a chilly, mist-covered wilderness of wide valleys and treeless heights—somewhat like Yorkshire, she thought. But it was not Yorkshire—as least not the one she knew. Burleigh maintained that it was, like so many other worlds, only a connecting place, a waypoint between one dimension of the multidimensional universe and another. Two more leaps would bring her back to England.

Haven had no doubt she could reach London, but there was some uncertainty in judging the leap just right in order to achieve the desired time. Without the benefit of the Black Earl's little device to aid her, she would have to rely on her native wits. Nevertheless, she was happy to have successfully made her escape and to be on her own at last.

The next ley line was some distance away—a peaty upland nearly half a day distant on foot, and, as this was a remote and deserted landscape, there was nothing for it but to walk. She started off at once, making what time she could. Likely she would have to wait for sundown once she got there, but she would rather wait than miss it and have to spend the night out on the desolate moor.

As she walked along she rehearsed in her mind what she would do when she got to London, and how she might proceed to further the quest. Clearly she could not conduct the search for the Skin Map alone. No doubt she should have made plans to meet Wilhelmina in London. Thinking of it now, that would have been the perfect solution—they could have evaded Burleigh and furthered their alliance. But in the urgency to get out of Prague, neither of them had thought of that.

It was late in the day by the time she reached the ley—a nameless trackway high on the crest of a broad headland where two valleys met above a grey river. She found a stone beside the trail and sat down to watch the low-riding sun sink farther below the line of barren hills to the west, shivering in the chilly, damp air as night came on. She comforted herself with the thought that she would soon be home again, dry and warm.

Then, as the evening shadows darkened the valleys, and wraith-like vapours snaked along the river below, she stood and, carefully pacing off the distance from the beginning of the ley, once again composed herself for the jump. This one, like the first, was accomplished without undue discomfort—which Haven took as a sign that she was perfecting her abilities. The thought pleased her and filled her with confidence as the battering rain shower announced her arrival in England on a lonely hilltop somewhere on the southern downs.

When her vision cleared she made out the line of the London Road—flanked by barley fields in neat rows, the thatched houses of farmers, the mail coach rumbling up the long chalk hills. Haven took in the sight, and her heart leapt. She had done it! She had successfully navigated the journey home all by herself.

It was early in the day yet; the sun was high in a cloud-flecked sky, the air soft and balmy. Haven paused to catch her breath and let the incipient nausea pass. She drew the sweet, fresh country air into her lungs and gazed down the smooth green slope of the hill; she could see wagons and some foot traffic on the road below. As soon as she felt stable once more, she hiked up her skirts and hurried down the hillside, secure in the knowledge that she would soon beg a ride with a passing merchant or farmer or, better still, a carriage heading for the city.

In any event she had to make do with a hay wain, an ox cart, and a brewer's wagon pulled by a team of heavy horses—each slower than the last. As a result it was already nightfall by the time she reached

London and made her way to Clarimond House, Sir Henry Fayth's London home. Through streets intermittently lit by torchlight she flitted like a ghost, keeping to the shadows. A young woman alone on the streets of the city after dark was asking for trouble—Haven Fayth had not come this far only to end up at the end of a footpad's knife.

Darting along the houses fronting the wide, cobbled boulevard— sometimes so close she brushed the doors with her elbow—she heaved a sigh as she came in sight of the stately redbrick mansion. A few last running steps carried her through the iron gates, and she was safe within the grounds. Hurrying up the drive, she bounded up the front steps and rapped sharply on the door. At her second knock the door opened slowly. A servant dressed in black barely deigned to glance at her, a frown of disapproval on his face.

"His lordship is not receiving visitors," he informed her in tones that left her in no doubt that she was not welcome. He made to close the door.

"Do you not know me, Villiers?" she said, putting her hand to the door.

"My lady?" The door opened again, more widely, and the servant produced a candle. "Lady Fayth," he gasped, holding the candle high to see her. "You should have sent word of your arrival."

"Am I to spend the night on the doorstep?"

"I am dreadfully sorry, my lady." He stepped aside, bowed, and ushered her quickly into the vestibule, closing the door firmly behind her. "Pray forgive me. We were not expecting anyone. If I had known you were coming, I would have sent a carriage for you."

"There was no time," she told him. "I am starving. Is there dinner?"

"Cook is preparing it now," Villiers replied. "I will have a place set in the dining room." He gazed at her intently. "I can see your travel has fatigued you. I will have hot water and towels sent up to your room. If you care to freshen yourself, I will inform the household that you are in residence."

"Thank you, Villiers. I leave it in your hands. But first I have to see Giles. Is he here?"

"Indeed, my lady. Mr. Standfast is convalescing. He has suffered a gunshot."

"Yes, I know. Terrible accident. It should never have happened." She turned to the staircase. "I must see him straightaway."

"I believe the doctor has ordered bedrest and quiet."

"I shan't disturb him overmuch," she replied, ascending quickly. "Which room is he in?"

"The Plum Room, my lady. Allow me to announce you."

"No need. I would prefer that you see to dinner. I will announce myself." Abandoning propriety, she took the candle and ascended the stairs quickly, reached the gallery, and hurried to the landing off the staircase used by Sir Henry's staff and retainers. She paused at the third door along, composed herself, then knocked.

"Enter," came a familiar voice from the other side.

She turned the brass handle and pushed open the door.

Giles lay in bed, the entire upper left side of his torso bound in white bandages. A lighted lamp glowed on the bedside table and, beside it, a jar and cup. On the floor was a chamber pot. At the first glimpse of his visitor standing in the corridor, the wounded man started upright.

"Miss Wilhelmina? Have you fo—" he began.

Haven stepped across the threshold and into the room, coming into the light. "Hello, Giles," she said.

He slumped back against the pillows. "Lady Fayth. I never thought—" Then, realising the implications of her presence, he bolted upright once more, threw aside the blanket, and made to climb out of bed. "Is Burleigh here?" he asked. The effort made him wince with pain as he struggled to rise. "Is he—"

"Calm yourself, Giles," Haven said gently. "All is well. I am alone. Like you, I have escaped him."

With the slow, measured movement of an aching man, he lay back once more. "Then why are you here?" he said, his tone sullen and unwelcoming. "You must know that I have nothing to say to you."

"Perhaps not," she allowed. She picked up the edge of the blanket and pulled it back into place over him. "But you might care to listen, for I have something to say to you."

He glared at her, his expression full of hurt and distrust at what he considered her former betrayal. "Go on, then," he said at last, curiosity overcoming his suspicion.

"First," she said, "I have to know—are you well enough to travel?"

CHAPTER 12

In Which Kit Learns the Uses of a Marmot Skull

The interior of the cave seemed warm to Kit, and drier than he would have imagined. He followed the hunters, carefully working his way over the jumble of rocks that littered the cavern floor. The air was still and smelled of dry leaves laced with the sour scent of cat. The deeper they probed into the side of the gorge, the warmer it became. Sweating from the fight with the cave lion, Kit felt like shedding his shirt—and maybe would have if he had not effectively sewn himself into it. Of greater concern at the moment, however, was not to lose sight of the tiny light bobbing along a few steps ahead of him.

Following the battle with the beast outside, the hunters had climbed up into the hole in the wall of the gorge, where Dardok scrabbled around in a dark recess of the cave and extracted from a cleft in the rock three small marmot skulls. The skulls had been broken down, leaving just the brainpan that formed a shallow bowl. These were quickly revealed to be primitive lamps—left there, apparently, the last time the clansmen had visited the cave. Using live coals from the wooden vessel, retrieved from the snow bank where Kit had dropped it, Dardok set about lighting the lamps. With braided hair for wicks and animal fat for fuel, the skull lamps stank and gave off a grudging oily light, but in the absolute darkness of the deep underground passages they were surprisingly effective.

The lamps were handed out and the clansmen set off, pushing deeper into the cave; owing to narrow walls and cramped spaces they were forced to go single file and were soon strung out. Kit lost sight of the first two lamps, and was desperate to keep the last in sight as the troop followed the passage ever deeper into the earth. Occasionally there would be level stretches where the channel became wider; other times it was all Kit could do to wriggle through the gap. The rocks were damp, and some were wet where water seeped from a seam or leaked from somewhere above. Where there was a continuous trickle and plink of dripping water, stalactites hung from the cavern ceiling, and these had to be avoided—likewise the stalagmites erupting from the floor like giant teeth in a stony jaw.

Kit followed the group, trying to stay out of the standing water pooled on the floor. At one point he slid over a boulder and suddenly found himself at the entrance to a large gallery; both roof and walls opened out beyond reach of the crude lamplight. Up ahead he saw the reflection of Dardok's lamp in a pool of water on the cavern floor. The light had stopped moving, and Kit guessed Big Hunter was waiting for the group to gather once more before pushing on. Indeed, when all were assembled, Dardok moved off; they came to the end of the gallery and entered a tunnel. They followed this a few hundred paces until it branched. Taking the right-hand branch, the band moved along a corridor that, though he could not see the ceiling, was nevertheless narrow enough for Kit to touch either side with arms outstretched. Here they stopped.

Taking his skull lamp, Dardok held it close to the wall, and Kit saw in the dull glow cast by the greasy light the unmistakeable bulk of a large, long-horned aurochs painted on the stone wall. The beast was rendered in ochre, red, and brown with black ears and eyes; its mouth was open and its forelegs bent as if it was running. As Kit watched, Big Hunter moved the little lamp back and forth below the image, and to Kit's amazement the carefully drawn creature seemed to take on breath and life right before his eyes. The flickering light rippled along the uneven surface of the stone, lending the illusion of movement.

The trick of light was delightful, and Kit chuckled aloud, which brought curious looks from his companions. Dardok gave a gruff snort and shifted the skull lamp to another position, revealing an elk with huge splayed antlers. The hunter with the second lamp stepped across to the other wall and held up his lamp. Kit saw a phalanx of earth-coloured horses—six chubby, short-maned, thick-necked beasts—all in profile, each head in a slightly different attitude, all running together, their forelegs churning in unison.

There were more—scores of them, an entire panoply stretching down the gently arching wall of the cave: a brown bison with its young one, a pair of leaping antelope, a cave lion roaring with its mouth open to show its fangs, a bear on its hind legs, an ox, a bear, a fat-bellied cow with a skinny calf nuzzling up to suck, and even the head and shoulders of a woolly mammoth with its high-domed head and red shaggy pelt. All the paintings were drawn with exquisite skill, but in something of a naïve style—as if executed by highly skilled schoolchildren. The way the artists had captured the demeanour of individual creatures with just a few lines—a stroke here for a mouth, a bit of shading there for a bulge of muscle—was remarkable and revealed a long familiarity with the animal life depicted. At the same time, there was a distinctly fanciful element in the portrayal—as if the artist were at play with his subjects or engaged in a light-hearted dance.

Drawn deeper into the gallery, Kit saw that, apart from the creatures on display, there were sections consisting of symbols—spirals and wavy lines, dots and circles of various sizes, shapes that looked like eggs, and many handprints. The handprints were made the way a kindergartner makes a hand by outlining his own digits with a crayon; on the cave wall, however, instead of drawing around the hand and fingers, the pigment had been sprayed somehow over the hand, leaving a shadow print on the surrounding rock, a void where the artist's hand used to be. Were these the painter's signatures? Or were they simply a way of announcing a presence—like the "Bill woz' ere" graffiti one saw scrawled in London subways?

And then Kit saw something that made his heart beat a little quicker. There on the wall opposite him was a spray of smaller figures. Kit moved in for a closer look at the pattern of swirls and spirals, squiggles and dots—the strange characters of a deranged alphabet. Despite the crude tools used to make them, each was precisely rendered, and each unique. Bending near, he peered at them in the dimly flickering light and knew he had seen these queer pictograms before: on the Skin Map.

Mind reeling with amazement, Kit gaped at the devious signs. How could this be? How was it possible? He drew a deep breath and forced himself to rein in his racing thoughts. *Okay, think! What does it mean?* The first thing that came to mind was that either Arthur Flinders-Petrie had been here, or someone who had access to his map—because, on closer inspection, Kit noticed that the technique of the artist was very different from that displayed in the surrounding paintings. Each pictogram was precise and cleanly drawn, with no false starts or smudged lines. Obviously, the person who painted the symbols on the wall knew exactly what he was doing.

Standing there in the quivering darkness of the cave, Kit heard again the words of Sir Henry Fayth: *No coincidence under heaven.*

"No such thing as coincidence," whispered Kit, brushing the stone with a trembling fingertip. It was true.

The light shifted abruptly, and Kit glanced around to see that the clansmen were moving on. "Wait!" he called instinctively, his voice ringing hollow along the gallery walls. The last clansman looked back but did not stop, and Kit was soon enveloped in darkness. With a groan of frustration, Kit abandoned the Skin Map symbols and hurried after the light, determined to return as soon as possible to study the symbols some more and try to commit them to memory.

Dardok led them by winding turns deeper and ever deeper into the cavern until at last they came to a stretch of wall where there were few paintings. Placing his skull lamp on a flat rock, Big Hunter busied himself with something in the shadows; Kit edged closer and saw that Dardok was kindling several more lamps, lighting them from the single flame of his own. As soon as they were lit, he handed them out, giving one to Kit as well.

Besides the lanterns, there was a supply of shells from river clams, twigs, and clumps of earth. Taking up smooth river rocks obtained from a little heap beside the place where Dardok was lighting lamps, the clansmen began pounding the dirt clods. At first this activity appeared meaningless to Kit; but as he watched, the men took up some of the clamshells, also obtained from the river, heaped some of the pounded earth into the shells, and then added water from a dripping stalactite to make a thin mud.

It's a workshop, Kit realised. *They're making paint.*

This mud was mixed on the half shell with a grubby forefinger, each artist making his own. When the paint was ready, Dardok produced hazel twigs. These were handed around and promptly popped into their mouths. The clansmen chomped away for a while, gnawing on the sticks, fraying the ends to form rudimentary paintbrushes. Every now and then they removed them for examination before chewing again. When all was ready, there followed a lengthy consultation that Kit could follow only in part. He sensed the buzz of thoughts flitting among the group—he could always tell when they were discussing something—but the impressions did not settle and crystallise as when En-Ul addressed him directly. Moments later the huddle broke and the clansmen took up places along the wall, singly or in pairs, and began to work.

Kit found a comfortable perch on a low rock and settled back to watch as the hunters-turned-artists sketched their designs. Each artist, following contours of the rock only he could see, roughed out a basic body shape—an ox, a deer, or a bear—and began filling in the body, dabbing the paint with their crude brushes. They worked quickly, adding shade and colour to the shapes they created. Kit gradually became aware of an odd sound—a low droning hum almost below the threshold of hearing. Rising and falling like waves washing on a distant shore, the sound waxed and waned: the clansmen were humming while they worked—not vocalising exactly, something more like purring. The sound seemed to come not from their throats, but from their chests; and once it started, it went on and on and on.

Kit watched the progress of the painting, and it occurred to him that if he made some paint he might imitate Arthur Flinders-Petrie and copy the glyphs onto himself; he could become his own Skin Map, and thereby carry them out of the cave for further study. Taking one of the clamshells, he filled it with some of the pounded earth, mixed in some water, and then started back to the main channel of the cave. Passing Dardok, he paused and whispered, "I need a drink." He held the image of a man cupping water to his mouth. Dardok glanced around at him and gave a grunt of assent before resuming his work.

Message delivered and received, Kit took his lamp and walked back along the tunnel leading to the main passage and the gallery of animals where he had seen the Skin Map pictograms. He followed the twisting, turning corridor of stone and came to a divide and paused. He had not remembered that junction, but then coming from the other side he would not have seen it; he took the larger path and continued on. After a few steps, his decision was rewarded by the sound of water dripping into a pool—a solid, almost metallic clink echoing along the stone corridor from somewhere just ahead.

Kit resumed his slow progress along the passage. The plinking sound, however, seemed to move with him, remaining just a little ahead of him. Sometimes it seemed to be closer, and other times farther away, but curiously, the sound seemed to remain just a little way ahead. Against all reason, he picked up his pace—as if he might overtake the sound somehow. He felt a breath of air on his face—the merest touch of flowing air, nothing more than a sigh against his cheek. But it halted him once more. The tiny breeze ceased. *Must have imagined it,* thought Kit, moving on. He had taken four or five steps when he felt it again—a feathery light touch of warm on his skin.

He pushed on. The single-flame lamp gave off little light, but drawing closer to the metallic clinking sound Kit imagined he saw a movement in the darkness just out of reach of his puny lamp—a low, sinuous motion close to the floor. It was there—just a flicker of shadow in the deeper gloom—then it was gone again. Yet the metallic clinking sound continued, a little louder than it was before.

Now air flowed over and around him—fresh and clean, not the stale, still stuff that filled the cave. At this, Kit felt the first flutter of worry: had he taken a wrong turn somewhere? Kit stood for a moment, frozen by indecision. Should he go back and try to find where he had gone wrong, or continue on? He felt the air on his face and decided to go forward. If nothing else, he reasoned, following the fresh air would eventually lead him out of the cave. He lurched ahead. He heard the plinking sound again and sensed a rush of movement just ahead of him. He glanced up to see a dark shape moving against the deeper darkness. In the same instant, his foot snagged something loose on the floor. He felt a jerk, lost his balance, and went down. The clamshell fell from his hand and clattered against the stone floor. The skull lamp's fragile flame snuffed out.

Absolute darkness—intense, complete, and impenetrable—descended on Kit. It felt as if the weight of the earth had collapsed upon him. The darkness was so oppressive that for a moment he felt as if he might suffocate.

Relax, he told himself. *Take a breath. Your light's gone out, that's all. It is only darkness—you won't smother.*

With these and other thoughts he comforted himself as he lay on his side trying to decide if he was injured or merely unnerved. Other than utter blindness, he seemed to be intact. His best, if not his only, option was simply to keep following the fresh air until he came out of the cave and then wait at the entrance for Dardok and the others, who would eventually emerge to discover him. Rolling over onto all fours, he climbed unsteadily to his feet and heard the clinking sound echoing off the rocks some distance away. Turning his head towards the sound, he glimpsed a faint glow of pale light ahead—a ghostly gleam so weak it might have been imagined. Kit closed his eyes and counted to ten, then opened them again. The light remained. He looked away. Looked back. The pale cast of radiance persisted— along with that maddening rattling clink.

Kit pushed himself along with one hand on the wall beside him, stumbling towards the distant glint of light. After a few dozen steps the light seemed to grow brighter, showing grey-white from an unknown distance ahead. The sound was moving that way too, it seemed. Then again, perhaps the source of the *plink-clink* emanated from there. Given the reverberating nature of the cave, there was no way to tell. He shuffled forward, holding the glow in the centre of his vision. The shimmering radiance grew accordingly larger and brighter until Kit realised he was looking at sunlight reflected off the stone sidewall of the passage ahead.

A few more steps carried him to the place where the tunnel twisted sharply to the right. Kit rounded the corner, and the light grew brighter. He worked his way along the uneven floor, scrambling over rocks and loose rubble. Up ahead, the passage turned again. The *plink-clink* sound stopped.

As he rounded the corner, he saw the cave mouth. Brilliant white streamed in through the irregular opening. To Kit's light-deprived eyes it was like looking into a blazing furnace or a miniature sun. He squeezed his eyes shut; then, putting his hands over his face, he allowed the light in a little at a time until his pupils had time to adjust. He looked again. The opening was still there, still ablaze with radiance, and sitting in that warm sunlight was the unmistakeable, larger-than-life form of another cave lion; looking more than anything like a grossly oversized housecat, it sat on its haunches, licking a forepaw the size of a soup bowl.

Kit was already in midstep and could not stop himself in time. His foot came down on a loose bit of rock, which tipped and skidded under his weight. The resulting clatter startled the beast, and it turned its head towards him. Seen entirely in silhouette, the animal appeared smaller than the one the hunters had killed earlier in the day—a young one, perhaps—but still big enough to fatally maul Kit with a single swipe of its rapier claws. Kit could not see the creature's eyes, but it was looking right at him. He held himself perfectly still in the hope of being downwind, of being invisible in the darkness. The cave cat simply watched him for a moment, then rose.

Slowly, slowly, Kit bent down and felt on the floor for a rock. Sweat beaded on his forehead and ran down his neck. His sweaty hand closed on a ragged stone, and he gripped it tightly. At least he would not go down without a fight.

He straightened again.

The cave lion took a step towards him, and Kit drew a breath and shouted. He ran forward, screaming like a crazy man. The big cat halted, turned tail, and fled. As it leapt from the cave opening, Kit glimpsed something in its flash of movement that almost made his heart stop: the cave cat was wearing an iron chain. As the beast bounded away, the chain swung out. Standing in the cave mouth, Kit saw the trailing links clearly in the light. The end of the chain struck the rocks—*clink-plink, clink-plink.*

Time telescoped. How long had he been with River City Clan? How long since he had seen a fully evolved human being, conversed in a modern language, worn real clothes? His mind reeled as he tried to place himself in an altered perspective, for Kit knew this cat; he knew it from another time and another place, another reality. This cave cat was the property of the thugs known as the Burley Men. *This* cat had a name: Baby. And the last time he had seen Baby, that chain had been in the hands of a Burley Man named Mal.

Stunned, Kit hurried to the cave entrance and looked out. The gorge was gone, the snow vanished, and winter with it. Instead, he gazed out on a scrubby green hillside. The slope fell away steeply, and at the bottom far below, he saw the cave cat streaking for the wide silver arc of a river and, just beyond the river, a two-lane blacktop highway.

CHAPTER 13

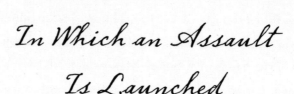

In Which an Assault Is Launched

Sunrise was Cassandra's favourite time of day in Sedona. The air was fresh and cool from the previous night and the sky pale pink, the rising sun still hidden from view behind the rim of towering red rock stacks that formed the horizon in every direction. Cassandra put the key into the ignition of one of the small white utility vans, started the engine, and eased out of the parking lot of the King's Arms motel. There were few cars on the road, and she made the familiar drive out to the dig site in good time. She pulled into the site staging area and parked behind the mound of rubble bags so the van would be less visible from the highway.

Taking her hat, sunglasses, and camera, she tucked the keys under the vehicle's rubber floor mat, cracked the windows, and left the van in the little shade provided by a small canvas awning attached to the sorting shed. She shouldered her day pack and wove her way through the excavation potholes and trenches, moving towards the escarpment shielding the deep arroyo known as Secret Canyon. She breathed in the morning air, heavy with the scent of sagebrush, and fell into an easy rhythmic stride, enjoying the crunch of scree beneath her thick-soled boots. Cass had come dressed for action, wearing her good, well-worn hiking boots and thick socks, her long-sleeved chambray shirt, her lightweight cargo trousers, and the oversized cotton scarf she used as a sun shield. In her day pack she carried two litres of water; a margarine tub full of raisins, peanuts, M&M'S, and dried cranberries; a tube of factor 100+ sunscreen; a folding knife; her emergency first-aid kit with snakebite accessories; and lightweight travel binoculars—everything she needed for a desert assault. If what happened today was at all similar to what had happened the evening before, she would be ready. In any event, she wanted to take some pictures and write some notes, to begin documenting the phenomenon. When her father arrived later in the day, they could sit down together and design a more thoroughgoing investigation. First, however, she intended to test her theory that the phenomenon that Friday called the Coyote Bridge was actually a space-time anomaly connected to or embedded in the physical landscape of the earth.

After speaking to her father, Cass had gone to bed, but was way too keyed up to sleep, so she spent the night online researching such things as shamanistic flight, soul travel, and astral projection. Most of what she read as she sat in bed hunched over her laptop was incoherent blather—a mixture of New Age tripe and bizzaro fantasy—but she found enough level-headed material to convince her that what she had experienced the day before was not a dream, vision, or mental aberration such as a hallucination or some kind of hysteria. The violent storm, sudden and short-lived; the weird vertigo; the abrupt arrival in a foreign place—these were, apparently, more or less common features of the phenomenon, attested to in many cultures and times. Some writers ascribed mystical significance to the experience and others were quite workaday in their appraisal.

Moreover, while many outlandish claims and explanations were offered, and there was very little agreement among people with startlingly divergent orientations to life—some exhibiting an extremely loose grip on reality—Cass was able to tease out a few common threads: a belief that travel to other dimensions or parallel realities was shared by many different cultures in many different ages, and that such travel was not only possible, it was a practise that could be taught, learned, and mastered. The author of one intriguing article—a woman with waist-length white hair who went by the name of Star Eagle—offered the observation that not only were specific locations on the landscape important for Shamanic Flight, but the specified locations were time sensitive; that is, the would-be flyer would be most likely to achieve success if he or she embarked at sunrise or sunset. Dawn and twilight were the best times to fly, she said.

Hardheaded scientist that she was, Cass would have written off all this as so much malarkey and mumbo jumbo. If not for her own firsthand experience the day before, she would have consigned astral travel to the loony bin along with rainbow worship, crop circles, and almond-eyed aliens. Yet something had happened and, whatever it was, she could not ignore it. Like a good open-minded researcher, she had come prepared to test and document her discovery, however unsettling; plus, she wanted to have something tangible—a few photographs, at least—to show her father.

She walked easily through the desert, enjoying the stroll among the cacti and creosote bushes with the almost giddy sensation of a little girl on Christmas Eve, that flutter in the stomach and a feverish anticipation. When she reached the arroyo she paused for a moment to take a few snaps of the Secret Canyon entrance, still deep in shadow. She could feel the night-cooled air issuing from the mouth of the gorge, wafting over her and dissipating. The darkened opening yawned like a cave and seemed somehow forbidding. Cass hesitated, taking a few more pictures. Finally, as the rising sun cleared the ragged hill line to the east, spilling light across the valley, she drew a breath and whispered a simple prayer: "God, don't let me break my neck." She put her arm through the dangling strap of her pack and stepped into the canyon, adding, "Also, please, oh please, don't let me get lost."

The walls closed around her. She walked slowly, placing her footsteps with exaggerated care as if measuring distance, alert to whatever sensations she might feel. Aside from the sound of her own footsteps pinging off the high sandstone walls, there was nothing. She had reached the straight track and was a fair way into the gorge when it occurred to her that when she had been here the first time she had been chasing Friday, trying to catch him. So she picked up her pace. A cool breeze gusted down from the stony heights of the undulating walls. She stepped up her pace still more.

From somewhere high on the canyon rim above her, Cass heard a sound like that of a hawk—a keening, whine-like whistle—and felt a spatter of rain strike the back of her hand. She glanced up and got another raindrop smack on her brow. A low mist cloud hung over the gap between the narrow rock walls. She kept moving, noting the sudden change in the weather as gusting wind whipped around her legs, blowing loose sand and dry yucca leaves down the path ahead of her. The mist descended, enveloping her, slicking her face with moisture.

In the same moment, a queasy sensation squirmed through her, and her step faltered—as if the surface beneath her feet had dropped half a step lower. She saw light ahead where the sun was burning through the all-enveloping fog and moved towards it, emerging to find herself on a vast plain stretching away in every direction to a horizon of black hills far away.

She had arrived in the Ghost World.

The travel sickness hit her all at once, slamming into her even as she stood looking at the emptiness opening around her. She doubled over and retched into the dust at her feet; hands on knees, she stood for a moment, breathing through her nose until the dizziness passed. She dabbed her lips and rinsed her mouth with a swig from her water bottle, thankful that this time there was no headache. She swallowed some more water and then, raising her camera, began photographing the bleak, monochrome landscape in a wide panoramic sweep to take in the open, empty, bone-dry, flat-as-an-iron volcanic pan around her. The sun stood low in the western sky, almost touching the tops of the far distant hills, illuminating the lines that covered the cinder plain stretched away arrow-straight across a totally featureless waste-land—no cacti, no boulders, no rocks larger than any other, nothing in any direction as far as the eye could see . . . except the mysteri-ous lines. Some of the lines were arrow straight; others curved into immense spirals splayed across acres of empty landscape.

Lowering her camera, Cass squatted down to take a few pictures of the path on which she stood, then put down a hand to feel the gritty texture of the pumice and discovered that the layer beneath was lighter than that which was above.

"Oxidation," she breathed to herself. "So that's how they're made."

It was simplicity itself: by moving the surface layer off to either side to expose the lighter material beneath, a stripe of light-coloured stone was created. She remembered pictures of chalk drawings presented in prehistoric anthropology lectures at university where, to create a drawing on a hillside, primitive people simply removed the turf to expose the white chalk just below the surface—a technique requiring few tools, but lots of manpower. The principle here was the same.

Cass stepped off the line and took a photo of the trail from another angle. The light dimmed somewhat; the sun was beginning its descent behind the hills. Cass decided that, having done what she intended, she should go back while the Coyote Bridge between the worlds was still open. She stepped onto the track once more and started back the way she had come, walking with quick purpose.

Almost at once, the wind sprang up. It howled around her in whirling dust devils, raising clouds of fine volcanic dust. Cass shut her eyes tight against the blowing grit, and in a moment felt the sheen of moisture on her face. She continued a few more paces, and the wind died away with a last trailing shriek; she was back in the canyon, in the shadowed cool of early morning, the tall stone walls rising sheer on either hand.

She managed a few more steps before the incipient motion sickness caught up with her. It was dry heaves this time, and she put a hand to the nearest wall to steady herself, drawing deep breaths through her nose until the queasiness passed—to be replaced by a surge of joy at having successfully navigated the Coyote Bridge between worlds without a guide, and without a hitch. *Wait until Dad hears about this!* she thought. *He'll be so amazed.* Wiping her mouth on her sleeve, she moved on.

Her moment of blissful triumph ended abruptly as she stepped from the mouth of the canyon and was met by the sight of a wide green valley with a broad river flowing through it in graceful arcs beneath a sky dappled with small, white powder-puff clouds. A line of stately poplar trees rose above the rich brown earth of newly ploughed fields on the hills either side of the river. The gentle rural scene met her astonished gaze, and her heart clenched in her chest.

Wherever she was, it was definitely *not* Arizona. Her brain thrummed with a single thought: *Now what? Now what? Now what?*

Cass's first inclination was to promptly sit down, hug her knees to her chest, close her eyes against the sight, and wish it all away—as one would with an ordinary nightmare. Her second thought was to calmly, carefully enumerate and categorise her options. She did neither of those things. Instead, she gave in to a far more instinctual urge and simply turned and fled the way she had come, darting back into the canyon once more. She raced along the sandstone walls, her heart in her mouth, hoping against hope that the Coyote Bridge was still accessible.

Before she had taken a dozen flying steps, her vision grew misty and a blast of hot wind swept down upon her, driving her forward. The ground gave way beneath her and she lurched a falling half step, stumbled, and pitched forward. Her camera banged into her forehead, causing her eyes to water; all knees and elbows, she landed in a heap, raising a cloud of dust.

As before, the light filtering down from on high was dim, the air cool on her skin, and she sighed with relief at the sight of the Secret Canyon's familiar sandstone walls. But as her eyes adjusted to the faint light and she looked around, the walls turned out to be whitewashed plaster and the path was a cobbled stone alley. Just ahead, a low and narrow archway opened onto a brighter, sunlit way beyond.

"Oh great," she muttered between gritted teeth. "*Now* where am I?"

Determined this time not to give in to panic, but to approach this admitted setback in a calm, rational, scientific way, Cass dragged herself to her feet, swatted the dust from her clothes, and moved towards the archway. With a calming breath, she stepped through. A white sun blazed in a cloudless sky of intense blue, beating down upon a street lined with ruined columns and bounded by tiny shops sporting colourful striped awnings and, directly before her, a cobbled thoroughfare straight as a plumb line and squeezed to near impassibility by a formidable gauntlet of street merchants selling from carts and stalls and barrows.

She stood at the entrance to the alleyway and gazed down along the avenue. Clutches of people moved among the vendors, examining the merchandise, bargaining, buying, and bearing away their purchases. All were dressed in billowy garments: long head-to-heel robes of black, brown, or blue-and-white-stripes for the women; and for the men, baggy striped trousers—ballooned around the legs and tight at the ankles—with floppy white shirts and truncated waistcoats in yellow, green, or blue. Every head was covered: the women wore scarves or veils of netted lace; the men wore hats in brick tones or blood red.

Cass took one look at the fez-topped heads and came to the conclusion that she had arrived in Turkey—Istanbul, maybe? In any case it was a city she had never visited before and had no wish to be in right now. Glancing quickly right and left to make sure no one was watching, she ducked into the alley from which she had just emerged and strode back the way she had come. Passages opened on either hand, but she continued straight on until reaching a blank wall. The old track had once passed through the wall; she could see the outline of an arch framed in stone, but the opening had been bricked up some time in the past.

She spun on her heel and headed back the opposite way, moving with the same swift, purposeful steps that had brought her this far; this time, however, they did not produce the desired result. The air remained still, the alleyway did not grow misty, there was no sudden gust of wind or rain or mist, no momentary lurch into another world. She paused, drew a deep breath, and repeated the attempt . . . with no better result.

Cold sweat beaded between her shoulder blades. "No," she whispered under her breath. "Fear will get you nowhere. Turn around, and let's try this again."

After one more effort, Cass concluded that she was stuck—at least until sunset or, failing that, early the next morning. In the meantime, she would find somewhere to hide and lie low until nightfall. That would keep her out of sight and out of trouble. Looking around, she decided to hunker down in one of the little passageways branching off the alley; it was shady and cool, and though other doors opened onto it, there was no one around. Slipping off her backpack, she sat down on the ground and settled in to wait.

An hour or so passed, during which she grew bored, and she was rethinking her strategy when a pack of dogs came wandering down the alley. They saw her and began barking. Cass did not like dogs all that much, and disliked being barked at even more. She tried to hush them and made shooing motions with her hands to drive them away. While she was doing this, one of the alley doors opened and a man put his head out to see what had stirred up the pack. He saw her and started towards her, calling out in a language Cass could not identify, and Cass, to avoid an explanation or a confrontation, shouldered her pack, gave him a cheery wave, and hurried away, leading her doggy escort.

Back on the street once more, she decided that she might as well make the best of it and at least explore the place while she was here. She had taken but a few steps from the alley entrance when she heard a shout and spun around in time to avoid a man on a motor scooter bearing down on her. Balanced on the handlebars was a tray of pomegranates. Cass scrambled out of the way as the scooter spurted past, the man still shouting and weaving wildly, narrowly missing a donkey cart carrying crates of live chickens stacked in a high, unsteady tower. The dogs followed the cart, yapping at the donkey, and Cass proceeded on her way down the street, looking for any hints that might tell her where in the world she was.

The signs she saw on the shops and in windows, or hanging over the streets on wires, were all in some form of Arabic—which did not entirely square with her scant knowledge of Turkey. The snatches of language she caught as she passed—from those nearby and the street sellers who called out to her—sounded to her like Arabic too. So, not Turkey then, but somewhere in the Middle East. This impression was immediately strengthened when a group of women emerged from a side street, each wearing a black veil and carrying a parcel on her head—bags bulging with fruit or neatly folded sheets of flat bread.

One of the women saw Cass, nudged her neighbour, and pointed. The group stopped, turned towards her, and stared.

My clothes! Cass suddenly felt very conspicuous and vulnerable. Her first thought was to buy something from one of the street merchants, but realised she had only a handful of loose change in a foreign currency. Ducking behind one of the marble pillars lining the street, she hastily readjusted her wardrobe; buttoning her floppy shirt to the top and pulling out the shirttails, she put her belt around the outside to make it look like some sort of short tunic. She could not do much about the trousers, but unfolded the cuffs and pulled them down over her boots. Then, taking her scarf, she arranged it to cover her hair, roughly in the manner of the other women. In all, this thin disguise was not the best way to pass unnoticed by the locals, but it would have to do.

When she ventured into public view once more, she kept to the shadows and tried to remain inconspicuous. Carrying her backpack like a parcel under her arm rather than wearing it, she slowly made her way along, pausing now and again to take surreptitious photos of the place—for future reference, if nothing else. For some reason, she was especially drawn to doors and doorways—these, and even some of the walls of surrounding buildings, were of a distinctive black-and-white stone in wide alternating bands. Basalt for the black, Cass decided, and pale limestone or marble for the white.

On closer inspection, there were traces of other periods of architecture mixed in here and there, a melange of styles, each distinctive of an empire past—Greek and Roman from the classical period, Byzantine, Arabic, and, though Cass was no expert, what looked to her like Ottoman. She passed beneath a ruined Roman arch, still standing, with distinctive Acacia-topped columns on either side, and a few yards or so farther on another arch in the characteristic Arab onion shape framing a Byzantine bronze door.

She walked on, eventually coming to the city wall set with a huge triple gate—two smaller doors flanking a large central portal; all three doors were open wide, and through them she could see a wide boulevard of palm trees with traffic passing to and fro outside the wall. Oddly, for a busy city there were few vehicles plying this thoroughfare—Cass would have expected more—and all of them appeared as if they belonged in a museum for vintage motors. With low-slung chassis and small windows, and fat, white-walled tires below wide, rounded fenders that swooped into running boards, these automobiles and small trucks were definitely from another era. Cassandra had the sensation of having wandered onto a movie set of a film about the 1930s.

So, as well as moving through space, she had also travelled in time. The scientist in her rose up in a cry of *Impossible!* Even as this thought entered her head, another voice asked, *More impossible than travelling from one place to another in a pretty good imitation of "Beam-me-up-Scotty"?*

The possibility of chronological migration had simply never occurred to her, and it took her a moment to adjust to yet another radical new paradigm shift. Clearly, everything she knew was wrong. A new theory would have to be created to account for this new reality. Cass turned and gazed back down the street. Nothing she saw contradicted the time-travel premise; neither did anything readily confirm it. The architecture certainly was archaic—but that was true of most places throughout the region. The people were dressed in simple garb that might belong to any decade in the last two hundred years or more—again, that was inconclusive. The vehicles alone gave her a clue; one or two might be explained away, but every single one of them belonging to the same era? No. So, taken together, these clues led to the conclusion that, in addition to moving through space, she had somehow slipped backward in time.

Reluctant to wander any farther from the one street she knew, Cass turned around and started back the way she had come, walking along, taking in the simple brick-and-timber style construction mingled with more substantial stone structures. She passed a church behind a gate of iron filigree and, across the street from it, a mosque with a green dome topped with a crescent moon in brass. She walked beneath the Roman arch once more and noticed, immediately on the other side, a generous gated doorway contained within an arch of alternating black-and-white stone. The huge wooden doors were open, revealing the entrance to a covered marketplace. Veiled and shrouded women were congregating around the entrance chatting to one another; they darted glances at her but did not stare, and for that Cass was grateful. Beyond them she could see merchants selling vegetables and cloth from stalls either side of a long aisle that disappeared into the dark interior of the bazaar. She moved towards the entrance, keeping to the edge of the milling throng. As she neared the archway wall, her eye fell upon a sign—a single sheet of orange paper printed in neat black letters—written in English and pasted to the plaster of the wall. She stopped automatically and read:

Lost? Lonely?
Looking for Something to Believe In?
We Can Help

For Information Ring
Damascus 88-66-44
Or Come to 22 Hanania Street nr.
Beit Hanania

The Zetetic Society

She read the words again with the uncanny feeling that in some inexplicable and wholly improbable way the message on the sign was meant for her. She stood, transfixed by the simple orange sign as by the dancing flame of a fire, while the conviction hardened within her that she must go to this place at once, and that if she could only find the Zetetic Society, all her questions would all be answered.

Already one question had been answered: she now knew that she was not in Turkey but in Syria. What else could this mysterious society tell her?

PART THREE

The Street Called Straight

CHAPTER 14

In Which Some Things Are Not to Be

The Nile flowed on without so much as a ripple beneath the barges carrying the priests of Amun back to Niwet-Amun and the temple. Though the sun blazed high in the clear Egyptian sky and life along the river continued serene and quiet as always, Benedict's small world was shaken to the very core. He looked upon the lush green banks sliding silently by, and all he saw was desolation. In his mind, moment by moment, he relived the riot in Akhenaten's Holy City; he heard the angry cries and saw the stones striking the priests, striking his father.

Refusing to leave his injured father's bedside, he sat in misery, rarely stirring, filled with dread and fear, while a succession of ministering priests came and went.

"I will not swear falsely," Anen told him. "Your father's injury is very grave."

Benedict turned anxious, uncomprehending eyes upon the priest.

"But know you," Anen continued, "our skills are great, and every possible remedy will be availed for him. Take courage in this knowledge." He placed a comforting hand on the young man's shoulder. "On this, I have made my vow. In the name of Amun, it shall be."

Unable to understand the language of those around him, Benedict derived little comfort from this assurance. Still, he heard the sound of hope in the priest's voice and felt his encouragement in the gentle touch. He did take courage, and he prayed as he had never prayed before, using the only prayer he knew well, and saying it over and over until it became only *Our Father who art in heaven, hallowed be Thy name, Thy kingdom come, Thy will be done . . . Amen.*

It took two days for the barge to sail upriver to Amun's Holy City; by the time they reached the temple, Arthur had rallied somewhat. He was able to sit up and take a little water and, though the priests were reluctant to give him too much food, they allowed him a little of the flat bread sprinkled with salt. Benedict was relieved and took this as a good sign.

Upon arrival at Niwet-Amun, a cadre of servants carried Arthur's pallet from the dock to the House of Wholeness and Healing, a large square structure occupying the eastern quarter of the temple compound. There the injured man was placed on a low bed in a cool, dark room to be watched night and day. The temple physicians busied themselves with a thorough examination of the livid wound, which had swollen the entire left side of Arthur's head. Arthur endured their gentle probing, groaning and grinding his teeth.

"You're going to be all right," Benedict assured him.

When the physicians finished, Arthur sank back into a deep sleep and did not awaken again until sunset. "Water," he said, his voice a croaking whisper.

The priests in attendance did not know what he said, so Benedict repeated it and mimed drinking from a cup. One of the younger physicians poured a shallow bowl of water infused with honey and herbs.

"Here, drink this," Benedict said, bending near. "How do you feel?"

"Hurts," whispered Arthur. "Inside . . . it hurts." He made to turn his head, but the effort defeated him. "Where are we?"

"We are back in the temple. There are doctors here. They are taking care of you," Benedict told him. "They are going to make you well. You're going to be all right."

"Good." Arthur offered the bare hint of a nod. "Well done, son."

The young physician offered the cup once more, and Arthur was given a little more to drink. After taking a few sips, he tried to sit up. The movement brought him pain, and he lay back, panting with the effort.

"Just rest now," Benedict told him. "They will take care of you."

Arthur slept then and awoke in the night complaining about the noise in his ears. Benedict tried to convey to the priest in attendance what his father was saying; he pulled on his ears and made a sound like the buzzing of angry bees. The doctor nodded and hurried away, returning with two senior physicians. He pointed to Benedict and gestured for him to perform the pantomime again, which he did. The elder doctors nodded, and one of them stepped close to the patient; holding his hand before Arthur's face, he clicked his fingers. When this failed to elicit a response, he clapped his hands—first in front of his face, and then next to his ear.

Arthur's eyelids fluttered, and he opened his eyes.

"Did you hear that?" asked Benedict. When his father did not reply, he asked again, more loudly.

"Ah . . . yes . . . I heard." He opened his mouth and swallowed. ". . . Mouth is dry."

Benedict took up the cup of honey water and, gently raising his father's injured head, gave him another drink. Arthur seemed to relax somewhat; he closed his eyes and went back to sleep. The next time he awoke, he called out for Benedict who, asleep beside him, rose and bent near. "I am here, Father," he said. "What do you need?"

Arthur raised a trembling hand and pawed the air. "I can't see you," he gasped. "I can't see."

Benedict took his hand and held it. "I am here."

"My eyes . . . I can't see."

The young physician, hearing the exchange, appeared, and Benedict explained as best he could what his father had said. The night doctor ran to fetch the two senior physicians, and they examined Arthur, carefully lifting his head and feeling the massive discoloured lump and gazing long into the injured man's left eye using a candle and disk of polished bronze.

They exchanged a few words over their patient, then sent the younger one away. He returned a short time later with Anen, and the three held close consultation for a moment. Then Anen nodded and turned to Benedict.

"What is wrong?" said the young man. "What does it mean?"

"I am sorry," Anen said, placing a hand on the young man's shoulder. "There is bleeding inside his head. It is making a swelling and a pressure in the brain."

Benedict did not understand a word of what he was being told, but he understood the priest's grave tone. "He's going to be well, isn't he? He's going to get better."

"We must open his skull to let out some of the blood and relieve the pressure."

"What are you saying?" demanded Benedict, frustrated at not being able to comprehend the priest. "I don't understand."

Anen gestured to the young physician, who came forward and offered his own head for examination. Anen proceeded to demonstrate what he was talking about by way of indicating on the young man's head what he intended. He drew a small circle on his subject's scalp, then lifted it away and proceeded to tap and pick at the centre of the imaginary circle.

"You are going to open my father's skull?" wondered Benedict, aghast at the very idea.

Anen caught the disbelief in the youth's tone and shocked expression. He sought to reassure him. "It is dangerous, truly. All such procedures carry great risk. Yet this treatment is well established among us, and our physicians are skilled in its application." He gazed intently at Benedict. "We must begin at once."

Benedict could only nod helplessly. He gazed at his father's inert form. "Do what you must."

Anen led the youth to his father's bedside and with a gentle touch roused the suffering man. "We will treat you, my friend, using a special procedure. I have every confidence in its success, but if you have anything to say to your son, you should speak now."

Arthur understood what Benedict did not. He stretched out his hand to his son and gripped it hard. "I am not afraid," he whispered.

"They are going to make you better," insisted Benedict, clasping his father's hand tight in both his own. "Do you hear? They are going to make you well again."

"I love you, son," replied Arthur. "Take care of your mother. Tell her I . . . I am sorry."

Anen, stepping near, took Benedict by the arm and drew him away. "We must begin at once if we are to save him."

The senior priest clapped his hands, and four physicians appeared. They wore white linen robes and small white caps, and each carried a tray of instruments, jars, and vials. Temple servants scurried behind them with stands on which to place the trays; other servants brought torches on high stands, which they placed around the bed. Still others appeared bearing basins of water and piles of folded cloths.

They went straight to work. While one of the priest physicians shaved the left side of Arthur's head, one administered a tincture of herbs mixed with opium, and a third undressed him. His shirt had to be cut off; the priest applied the scissors, pulling the cloth away in strips to reveal a torso decorated with bright blue tattoos—all in the same neat hand, all of them utterly incomprehensible symbols. When the last shreds of his shirt had been removed, the priest spread cloths under Arthur's head and shoulders and washed his neck, shoulders, and chest; while all this was going on, the fourth priest prepared the instruments, rinsing them in a special mixture of distilled vinegar.

When everything was ready and in order, Anen gestured to one of the attendant servants, who turned to Benedict, bowed low, and, taking him by the hand, led him to a far corner of the room where the youth could watch but would not interfere. Then, at a nod from Anen, the operation began.

The foremost of the priest physicians knelt down beside the bed and took up a small knife with an obsidian blade; he clicked his fingers before Arthur's eyes, then tapped him lightly on the cheek— raising no response. Then with quick, decisive strokes he applied the blade and cut into the scalp around the discoloured lump above the left eye—once, twice, and again. Blood flowed freely from the deep cut. Instantly, wet cloths were applied that had been soaked in some astringent solution, because the gush of blood ceased almost at once.

The physician made another quick incision and then pulled back the flap of scalp to reveal a black clot of blood and tissue with white bone beneath. A cloying, sweet smell wafted into the room.

While the first physician held back the flap with a little bronze prong, a second moved swiftly forward with a pair of long, golden tweezers and began picking out bits of clot and dead flesh. When the area was clean, he turned his attention to tweezing out fragments of crushed bone and dropping them into a small silver bowl.

Anen stood by, arms folded across his chest, supervising the procedure. When the priest finished removing the splinters of bone, Anen motioned to the third priest—a short, stocky man with a shaved head and round, cherubic face—who stepped to the bedside and took up a bronze instrument that to Benedict resembled a carpenter's auger. As the first priest carefully held back the flap of scalp he had freed, the auger was applied to the freshly scoured bone.

The fourth priest moved in to steady the patient's head, and Benedict heard a sound like that of a millstone grinding corn. Unable to watch, he turned his face and looked away. The grisly sound seemed to go on and on, and when it finished, Benedict glanced around to see that a neat round hole had been bored in his father's skull. In the centre of the hole was a ghastly clot of blood glistening red-black and virulent. Anen turned and offered Benedict a knowing smile to tell him that all was going well.

The stocky priest stepped back from his work, and another moved into his place. Taking up a tiny golden knife, the physician began gently scraping at the clot, cutting it away, pausing now and then to dab away the blood oozing from the fresh wound and to remove the scrapings and rinse his blade in a bowl of vinegar solution. It was soon finished, and the golden tweezers applied once more to remove every last fragment, sliver, and fleck of broken bone. Greyish pink flesh glistened through the hole.

Anen stepped forward then; the other priests stood back to allow him to examine their work. He bent close, and with the most delicate touch probed the neat incision and felt the smooth edges of bone. He inspected the wound and spoke to his fellow priests. They held close consultation for a moment, whereupon Anen crossed the room to join Benedict.

"There has been much bleeding beneath the bone," the priest said, willing the youth to understand. "The bleeding is stopped and pressure is relieved. Now we can but watch and wait."

Benedict heard in the priest's tone a note of reassurance and clung to it. "Thank you."

Anen squeezed the young man's shoulder, then returned to supervise the binding of the wound. A small disk of gold was washed in the vinegar solution and then applied to the naked skull. Working with deft efficiency, the priests closed the wound, replacing the scalp and sewing the edges back together; they then wrapped strips of clean linen around and around the patient's head. When they finished, Arthur's head was swathed in a turban. All four doctors stepped back, bowed to the patient and to Anen, then took up their trays and instruments and departed, leaving one behind to watch the patient. Anen released Benedict to approach his father once more.

Despite the ordeal just endured, his father seemed to rest peacefully. His breathing, though shallow, was regular and even. Benedict took this as a good sign. He settled onto his bedside stool to resume his vigil.

Sometime before morning there arose a commotion out in the temple courtyard. Benedict, dozing on his chair, awoke to the sound of raised voices and running feet. Glancing around, he saw that the priest keeping vigil was gone. He went to the door of the Healing House and looked out. Priests with torches were running here and there; they seemed to be barring the gates. No sooner was this accomplished then they raced away, and the courtyard grew quiet once more.

Benedict returned to his father's room. Taking up a lamp, he moved to the bed and examined his father. Although it was difficult to tell, he sensed a change: his father seemed to rest more peacefully, the lines of tension in his face relaxed, his features composed. Benedict turned to replace the lamp on the stand and heard a faint clicking sound. Looking back, he saw his father's mouth move, but no sound emerged.

He leaned close once more. "I am here, Father. What is it?"

Again the dry lips moved, and Benedict heard the merest ghost of a breath utter a word.

"I did not hear you, Father. Say it again."

The voice, rising to a hoarse whisper, repeated the words. "The Spirit . . . Well . . ." Arthur sighed and seemed to sink deeper into the bed.

"What? Father, tell me again." Benedict stared at his father, fear twisting his gut into a knot. "What did you say?"

Receiving no response, Benedict leaned closer. "Father, I can't hear you." He put a tentative hand on his father's shoulder and jostled him in an attempt to keep him awake just a little longer. "Please, tell me—what did you say?"

"The . . . Spirit Well . . ." The words came out as a moan. With the last of his strength, Arthur moved his hand to his chest. Benedict observed where the hand came to rest. "I have . . . marked it," he gasped, his voice trailing into silence.

Benedict gazed at the tattooed symbols on his father's chest—the familiar spray of curious emblems he was only just beginning to learn how to navigate. He shook his father's shoulder again.

There was no response.

"Father!" Benedict, growing frantic, shouted. "Please! I don't understand what you mean."

Turning from the bed, he ran to the door and called for help. The priest assigned to bedside duty reappeared almost at once. Hurrying across the yard, he bowed to Benedict, then pushed past him and moved quickly to kneel beside the bed, placing a hand on Arthur's chest. He put his ear close to his patient's nose and mouth, and paused as if listening.

"He was just—" began Benedict.

The physician raised a palm for silence and then placed his fingertips against Arthur's neck. Rising, he retrieved a small rectangle of polished bronze from his tray of instruments and held it beneath the stricken man's nose.

Benedict, his heart in his throat, knew what this meant. Dreading what he would see, yet unable to look away, he stared with growing apprehension as the physician turned the little square of bronze towards him. There was not the slightest smudge of fog or moisture on the polished surface. His father was no longer breathing.

The physician shook his head, then stood and, raising his palms shoulder high, bent at the waist and began chanting in a low, droning voice.

Benedict slumped back against the wall, his eyes on his father's body. "No. It cannot be," he murmured, pounding his fist against the wall. "He was just talking to me. He cannot be de—" The boy refused to say the word.

Rushing to the bed, Benedict threw himself down upon his father's body. There was no movement, no resistance. He clasped his father's face in his hands and was surprised to feel the warmth there. "Don't leave me." His voice cracked. "Please . . . don't leave me."

Strong hands gripped the young man's arms and pulled him away. Upon release, Arthur's head rolled to one side. Benedict shook off the priest's hands and struggled forward once more. "I think he's unconscious," he insisted. "We should try to wake him."

The priest said something to him and shook his head, then went back to his chanting.

An almighty walloping *thump* sounded in the courtyard—something had crashed into the temple gates. Benedict turned towards the sound, and a servant burst into the room; the servant took one look at the praying priest and disappeared again. Benedict, sinking under the weight of grief rising within him, clasped his hands and began to pray as well. He squeezed his eyes shut and prayed as he had never prayed in his life.

The next thing he knew Anen was standing before him, his expression grim, sadness filling his dark eyes. The priest gestured to the body of his friend and said something Benedict could not understand. The young man shook his head, whereupon Anen took him by the hand and led him to the bed. Placing the young man's hand against his father's body, he held it there. The flesh was cooler now.

Anen spoke again, his voice gentle with sorrow. "We tried to heal him, but it was not to be. His soul has entered the House of the Dead and has begun the journey into the afterlife." He pointed to the body in the bed and seemed to expect a response.

Benedict gazed upon that inert form. The transformation had begun; the animated presence he had known all his life was no longer there. All that was left was a shell, a rather sad and damaged husk. The man he knew and loved was gone.

CHAPTER 15

In Which Old Haunts Are Revisited

Wilhelmina enjoyed her visits to the abbey at Montserrat and looked forward to them with an anticipation that far exceeded any expectation she held for the journey or destination itself. In some ways it was reminiscent of the feeling she had had as a schoolgirl the night before the annual field trip to the British Museum, a place she loved; or maybe it was the way a pilgrim felt when, after weeks or months of preparation, the day came to set foot on the peregrine path leading to a sacred destination. Perhaps, by a little stretch, that was what she was—a pilgrim.

Just thinking about working with Brother Lazarus at his kitchen table in the observatory high on the mountaintop, sipping his sour wine and talking astronomy, cosmology, and physics in an attempt to unravel the mysteries of ley travel, made Wilhelmina's heart beat that little bit faster. She had found him—or had been guided to him, as he insisted—to further her education for the work ordained for her to do. She was stretched and challenged, always, but also comfortable in his presence; he was the wise uncle she had never had.

And so it was that on one of those early visits it was decided that as a test of Brother Lazarus' theory of time calibration between alternate dimensions, Wilhelmina should return to London to find Kit and, as she put it, settle her affairs. Aside from explaining what had happened to her during that first ill-considered jump, she wanted to tell him not to worry about her, that she had found her bliss running a coffee shop in Prague and was making a better life for herself in the seventeenth century than she had ever known in the twenty-first and, incidentally, that whatever romantic attachment they might once have shared was now irrevocably severed. Time had passed, events had transpired, and as a consequence they were no longer what they had once been. Selflessly, magnanimously, with every blessing for his future happiness, she graciously freed him from any entanglements, real or imagined, he might feel. For this last part she rehearsed various scenarios, all of them ending with a tearful, regret-filled Kit bidding her farewell as she strode—shoulders back, head held high—out of his life forever.

The inevitable breakup was not owing to any vindictiveness or hard feelings towards Kit; she bore him no ill will whatsoever—just the opposite, in fact. She was extremely grateful to him for introducing her to the wonders of ley travel, if accidentally, and any resentment or bitterness she initially felt—and there was plenty of that in those first traumatic days—had long since evaporated in the sunny prospect of a far brighter future than she could have imagined, much less engineered, on her own. That it was a future taking place in a post-medieval version of Prague gave her no end of pleasure;

the paradox was delicious. *I guess I'm just an old-fashioned girl at heart*, she mused happily.

Now that she was familiar with ley travel in its broadest, most general sense, and growing in confidence by leaps and bounds, as it were, Wilhelmina was keen to master the finer points and intricacies and so had become a willing guinea pig for Brother Lazarus' experiments.

"Getting the time period right," he said during one of their sessions. "That is most crucial if we're ever to effect a reunion between you and your friend."

"Or any other useful purpose, for that matter," suggested Mina.

"To be sure." He tapped his fingers on the table. "Are you certain you wish to try?"

"Why not?" She shrugged. "What have we got to lose? I know how to get back here. If anything goes wrong, I can always return. And who knows? Whatever happens might prove useful."

"There is rarely advance without experiment," he observed, then leaned forward, elbows on the table in the posture of a lecturer instructing a pupil. "If this experiment is successful, we will add a great deal to our store of knowledge. See here, now. Listen carefully. Thomas Young was active in London between 1799 and 1829. He was a president and member of the Royal Society, so you should be able to make contact with him through the society secretary—providing you can get back to London in the first place. The ley that took you to Prague should lead you back to London—although this is far from certain."

Mina agreed that it was worth a try. "I just wish there was a way to calibrate the time frame more precisely."

"That, my dear, is what the experiment is designed to explore," he said with a smile. "If my theory is correct, each physical point along any particular line corresponds to a specific time reference. That being so . . ." He smiled and shook his head. "Well, you'll just have to try making a jump and see where that gets you. A leap or two along the same ley should give you the means of comparison. Again, this is assuming you end up in London."

"I have my ley lamp to help me," she pointed out.

"An extraordinary instrument," Brother Lazarus enthused. "I would give my right arm to know how it works." He regarded her across the table. "Are you certain you wish to try this? Going home again could be distressing."

"I was born and raised in London. I'll be all right."

"When will you go?"

"I'm ready now," Mina told him. "There's no time like the present."

As the sun began to sink beyond the crags to the west, Brother Lazarus walked with her to the high mountain ley to see her away. *"Vaya con Dios!"* he called as Wilhelmina embarked on her long-delayed return to London.

Her attempt employed the line she now called the Bohemian Ley; the landscape was as she remembered it from that first traumatic leap, and visiting the place again brought a curiously nostalgic feeling. The little blue lights on the lamp confirmed the presence of an active ley, and her first jump proved marginally successful in that she reached the outskirts of a sizeable town set in a place that in most ways resembled the English countryside. At first glance the landscape looked familiar; but as she stood on a bluff overlooking a wide, generous valley with a small village of thatched-roof cottages, the absence of paved roads and motorways gave her to know that if it *was* anywhere near London, the day of the combustion engine had yet to dawn. Immediately turning around, she doubled back before the ley closed—and tried again.

In all, it took her two days and no fewer than seven leaps before she happened to strike the winning formula: roughly a metre every four hundred years, or thereabouts. She worked out that if one paced off the stride and matched stride to leap, so to speak, one could home in on England's capital city in a particular epoch. Her seventh attempt brought her to a suitably modern period.

The sound of the gusting wind receded, blending into the whine of an ambulance siren echoing down the brick canyon of Stane Way. The alleyway looked familiar, and she was mightily encouraged. It remained to be seen precisely *when* she had arrived, but that mystery was cleared up the moment she emerged onto Grafton Street. A bus bearing an advertisement for Virgin Mobile phones was the first vehicle to pass, and it was quickly followed by a British Telecom van advertising their speedy 30 MB service for £16 a month.

"I made it!" trilled Wilhelmina. "I actually made it!" She shivered with equal parts excitement and dread at the prospect of a return to her old haunts, then started down Grafton Street. Her progress soon had her reeling with the brute force assault on her senses. The ordinary sights of the city were garish and gaudy, the sounds strident and confusing—everything blared and screamed and contested for her attention. After the relative peace of a less-mechanised time, the modern pace of the world seemed an ordeal—too loud, too fast, too rough. She had the feeling of running an obstacle course full of unnecessary shock and alarms.

Everywhere she looked, the view appeared designed to deliver a blow. A low-slung black car with black-tinted windows cruised by, booming out a bass beat designed to disturb; a motorbike zipped past in the opposite direction buzzing like an oversized hornet; the pavement teemed with French language students lugging matching orange backpacks and drifting along in amorphous crowds like multi-headed amoebas; a tower block undergoing renovation was a gutted noise box echoing with the clatter of jackhammers and diesel generators filling the air above with a noxious pollution of high-decibel clashing and blue fumes; the signs in shop windows screamed in fluorescent letters *Sale!* and *Ultra Discount! Everything Must Go!*

Yet . . . and yet—these streets heaving with traffic, bristling with advertising, and thronged with oblivious pedestrians bowling along in pursuit of their own private agendas were exactly the same as she remembered. The bleak skyline of grey apartment blocks, the dreary sky crisscrossed with vapour trails of roaring jetliners, the litter and garbage discarded in the gutter, the thrum and thrust of a busy metropolitan street—all of it was precisely the same as it had always been. Funny, she had never noticed the casual brutality of it before. Well, she noticed now, and she did not like it.

The assault on her senses staggered her; she felt the city closing in on her, and her stomach grew queasy. At the first opportunity she ducked into a side street and slumped onto the bottom step of a townhouse to gather her wits and regroup. *You don't live here anymore, Mina,* she told herself. *Just let it wash over you.* After a few minutes she was able to regain her composure enough to continue on to her old neighbourhood.

Since leaving, Wilhelmina had had plenty of time to consider what she would do if she managed to return to London again. Her first inclination was to avoid Giovanni's Bakery—too many memories, too much explaining to do—but now, as she entered more familiar streets, she changed her mind. Part of settling her affairs involved making a clean break with her old life so that there would be fewer questions left unanswered, fewer loose ends left dangling. If nothing else, she reckoned she had back pay coming, and she could use some ready cash for getting around the city.

First, however, she had to find out the present day, month, and year so she would know how much time had elapsed since that first fateful journey. She passed a W. H. Smiths and stepped inside, moving directly to the wall of magazines and newspapers. A quick examination of *The Times* caused her to do a double take; a glance at the dateline on the nearby *Guardian* confirmed it. The newspapers were dated the month and year she had left, and the day . . . . what day had she departed? A Sunday—yes, Sunday—she and Kit had planned to go shopping on her day off. It was Monday's edition of *The Times* that she held in her hands.

Flabbergasted, she stumbled back onto the street, her mind spinning with the implications. By the time she reached her old work-place, Wilhelmina was slightly dazed and not at all certain what her reception would be. She paused across the street from the little shop and watched for a moment. Nothing seemed to have changed: the green-and-white striped awning was the same, the sign on the window proclaiming *Artisan Breads Our Specialty* was exactly as she had last seen it. Fixing a smile to her face, she crossed the street and pushed through the door. The bell over the door tinkled, announcing her arrival, and the girl behind the counter looked up.

"Mina!" screeched Tatyana, the cashier. "You're here!"

"I, uh—"

"What are you wearing?"

Wilhelmina glanced down at her travelling attire. "Clothing crisis," she explained. "Don't ask."

"You didn't come in this morning," Tatyana pointed out. "What happened?" Before Mina could answer, she continued, "We tried to call you. We were worried. It's been crazy here all morning."

"Sorry," said Wilhelmina.

Just then John, the bakery owner, bustled into view carrying a tray of sticky buns. "Who's sorry?" he asked, then glanced around. "Mina! What happened? You didn't open this morning."

The sight of her employer, the shop, the warm yeasty smell of baked goods in the display cases brought a surge of emotion Mina had not anticipated; she had not spared a single thought for the place in all the time she had been gone. "I think I ate a bad shrimp," she muttered. "Sorry. I couldn't get my phone to work."

"No kiddin'. I tried to call you." He set down the tray and regarded her closely. "You look different. You okay?"

"Actually, I need a sick day," she replied gamely. "If that's okay."

"Sure," agreed John. "Take a couple days if you need to. I'll cover for you tomorrow."

"Thanks. I appreciate it." She hesitated, then said, "I don't suppose I have any pay coming?"

"Isn't it direct deposited?"

"Right," said Mina. "I wasn't thinking." Her salary would have been deposited electronically into her account; to get any money would require a visit to the bank and production of her bank card—which she no longer possessed.

"Well, I'd love to chat," John was saying, "but I've got another tray of buns coming out. See ya later." He turned and retreated to the kitchen. "Go up and see Rachel—maybe she hasn't done the end-of-month stuff yet."

Wilhelmina called her good-bye as he disappeared around the

corner. Two women customers entered the shop, followed by a mum with a pram. The place was suddenly filling up.

"Hope you feel better, Mina," said Tatyana, turning to serve the newcomers. "Hi, can I help you?"

Wilhelmina backed toward the door. Somehow, now that she had seen them, she could not make herself say good-bye for good. A cheery, "See you later," was all she could manage.

A quick visit to John's wife in the office upstairs confirmed that her paycheck had been, as always, deposited directly into her account.

"Is anything wrong, Mina?" asked Rachel.

"Um, no—not really. It just that I seem to have lost my card. It's a huge bother." She sighed. "Oh well."

"I can give you last week's," suggested Rachel, "if that's any use. That hasn't gone in yet."

"You can? That would be a *big* help." She waited while the middle-aged woman took out a key and opened the bottom desk drawer and withdrew a metal cash box.

"I'll need you to sign for it," said Rachel. She withdrew a handful of bills and began counting them out onto her blotter. "You sure everything's okay?"

"Never better," said Mina. "Why?"

"I don't know—you look different is all." She handed a tidy stack of bills to Wilhelmina. "Six hundred. Here you go."

"Thanks." She stuffed the money into her pocket and scribbled her signature on the slip Rachel offered. "Thanks a lot. I'll see ya."

A minute later she was back on the street. Next stop, Kit's flat. The walk to his front door gave her time to think about what she might say to him—how she might explain not being able to see him for a while, if ever. There was no easy way to do that, so she decided a clean break was best. Taking a deep breath, she gave the door a few solid raps and waited, then knocked again. She tried two more times before giving up. Kit was out. *Typical,* she thought, and considered leaving him a note, but she had nothing to write with or on, so she let it go. She could break up with him some other time.

Back on the street again and buoyed by the thought that it had only been a day since she was last in London, she resumed her walk and her feet directed themselves to her old flat. *Why not?* she wondered. She could at least check on the place and see if there was anything worth taking away with her; and while she was there, she could let the landlord know she might be gone for a while.

Ten minutes later Mina turned onto the street, and a few minutes after that was bounding up the steps of the building. She paused briefly to collect her spare key from the old lady who lived in the apartment below.

"Did you lock yourself out, dear?" asked Mrs. Parker as she handed over the key.

"Silly me," replied Wilhelmina. "I'll put this back through your letter box when I'm finished."

"You do that."

"Cheerio, Mrs. Parker." Mina moved away and climbed the stairs to her flat. She slid the key into the lock and stepped inside. One look at her cosy little nest and she was overcome by a surge of melancholy that weakened her at the knees. There was mail on the doormat, which she collected and tossed on the hall table. She stepped into the lounge and took in the sight of her couch and pillows, and the fleece blanket she used to curl up in, the book she had been reading—it was almost too much to bear. She went into the kitchen, and one glance at the flowers still fresh in the vase on the windowsill and she lost it. Tears welled up in her eyes, and she stood in the centre of the room and bawled.

If anyone had asked her why she was crying, she would not have been able to provide a reasonable answer. In fact, even as the tears flowed she told herself she was being a big baby and that she was far happier with her life now than she had ever been and that she would not trade her new life for anything. Still, the tears flowed.

When she was finally able to drag her ragged emotions together, she went into her bedroom, emptied the stale water from the glass beside her bed, and straightened the duvet, then proceeded to look around for anything that might be useful to her in her new life. From her wardrobe she selected a lightweight black wool jumper and a pair of smart lace-up ankle boots she had worn only once; the rest she could live without. Closing the door to the wardrobe, her eye fell on the jar of pennies and obsolete coins—shillings and ha'pennies and the like—she kept on the bureau. She carried the jar to the kitchen and upended it into a plastic carrier bag, then went to check out the bathroom.

One look at the gleaming white tile, and she knew she had to have a shower. She turned on the taps, stripped quickly, and stepped into the free-flowing hot water and lathered up. Oh, such luxury! It had been so long since she had had a proper shower, she had all but forgotten just how truly delicious it could be. She washed her hair and then just stood and let the water run over her until the room filled with steam. With a sigh of regret, she turned off the water and dried herself on a fluffy towel. She brushed her teeth, keeping the toothpaste and brush to take with her. She used the toilet, flushed, and turned out the light. Okay, it wasn't all bad, she thought as she padded back into her bedroom to dress; there was a lot to be said for the convenience of modern plumbing.

Then, having wallowed enough, she decided it was time to be about her business. She bundled the items she was taking with her into the carrier bag of coins and had a last look around. As she locked the door, she drew some comfort from the idea that she did not really have to abandon anything just now; she could keep the flat just the way it was. Now that she knew how to reach London again and arrive within a day or so of her initial leaving, her home in this particular world would always be there waiting for her. She could come back anytime she chose. What is more, it would be a bolt-hole for her, should she ever need a safe house.

Pleased with herself for having generated this consoling thought, she proceeded in a much better mood and treated herself to a wild shopping spree—which, to her practical mind, meant a visit to the big Marks & Spencer flagship store on Oxford Street. She took her time browsing the ladies' section and eventually settled on a long flowered skirt, three good-quality cotton T-shirts, two of them long-sleeved, a thin leather belt, an assortment of utilitarian foundation garments, a smart white overblouse, a short wool jacket in navy blue, two pair of thick tights, and a tri-pack of cotton socks. She dressed in the changing room and then continued to Selfridges a few doors down, where she indulged in the splurge purchase of a fine cashmere pashmina in radiant sky blue.

At a smart boutique called Sweaty Betty she found a lightweight, multi-pocketed suede bag with strap handles that could be worn as a day sack, into which she bundled her purchases and the plastic carrier bag. Satisfied with her new gear, she popped into the nearest Pret A Manger and bought a chicken-Caesar-and-bacon baguette, a three-bean and couscous salad pot, grapes, a packet of sweet potato crisps, and a bottle of Pure Pret Pomegranate drink. As the day was still fair, she crossed the street to Hanover Square Park and found a shady bench on which to enjoy a leisurely lunch and watch the world go by while waiting for the Stane Way ley to become active.

This simple lunch was followed by a long, lingering coffee at Café Nero with a slice of millionaire shortbread for desert. She dawdled over the coffee—partly to kill time, but also out of professional interest—observing the operation of the coffee shop closely, critiquing the service and savouring the hot, black brew—analysing the entire experience in a way that never would have occurred to her before. On the street once more, she passed a Waterstones Bookshop and, on a whim, worked her way up to the fourth floor, where in a little-visited side room she pulled science books off the shelf, spread them on the floor, and chose three for Brother Lazarus: *The New Physics: A Guide to Life, the Universe, and Everything*; *Quantum Physics for Dummies*; and *Advanced Cosmology—Comprehending the Cosmos*.

She resumed her promenade along Oxford Street, window-shopping. When at last the sun began to lower in the west, Wilhelmina bade farewell to the city and turned her steps towards Stane Way in preparation for phase two of her plan: a rendezvous with Dr. Thomas Young. While she did not entertain any notions that it would be easy to locate a man who had, in the present world, been deceased for almost two hundred years, she could not have predicted just how crooked that particular path would prove.

CHAPTER 16

In Which a Long-Promised Tea Is Taken

The blue light on the new-model ley lamp indicated the presence of an active line. It was time to go. Wilhelmina tightened the laces on her new boots and, tucking the lamp into a pocket of her new blue jacket, started down the narrow service alley. The wind kicked up suddenly, and a few errant raindrops spattered around her. The world grew dim—as if she had passed into deep shadow. A few steps more and she emerged from the darkness and into a passage in every way similar to the old Stane Way . . . yet different. This alleyway was bounded by wooden walls, not brick, and the path was paved not with tarmac but with uneven cobbles.

She moved quickly towards the end she could see ahead and emerged into the light of a sun-bright seaside village. A tall-masted schooner stood docked at the wharf a short distance away, and in the harbour another lay at anchor. A few smaller fishing boats plied the waters farther out, rocking in the gentle swell, and sea gulls filled the soft, salt-scented air with their high-pitched chatter.

Her immediate thought was that the jump had gone wrong. She had expected to connect with the Bohemian Ley, and this place was definitely not Bohemia. Pulling the ley lamp from her pocket, she detected only the faintest glint of light, a sign that the ley activity had indeed waned. The sun was high overhead, so there would be a few hours to kill before she could resume her journey; in the meantime she might at least find out when and where she had arrived, and make a note of it for future reference. Stepping out onto the street, she moved along the waterfront trying to appear inconspicuous in her new clothes, and alert to any clues that might help determine the time and place.

Along the wharf, the warehouses and stores were open and either receiving or dispatching cargo in the form of barrels, crates, and bundles bound in burlap and hemp—all of it toted one way or another by stevedores in short trousers and long, floppy shirts. Everyone she saw wore a hat. The men wore either shapeless knit caps, straw hats, or felt constructions with round crowns and wide brims. The few women she saw wore bonnets; they also had shawls or scarves tied around either their shoulders or hips, and all wore long skirts and blouses with scooped necklines and short sleeves. Wilhelmina pulled her blue pashmina from her bag. *If only M&S carried bonnets in its new line, I'd be set,* she mused and, draping the scarf over her head and shoulders, continued with her amble along the harbour and soon found herself enjoying the fresh air and the relaxed and peaceful atmosphere of the little fishing village—a welcome relief after modern London.

As she strolled along she became aware of the feeling that she knew this place. Although she was certain she had never seen or set foot in the town before, there was something vaguely familiar about it—something that eluded her ability to pin down, yet persisted in her awareness. What was it?

"Come from the Indies?"

The voice startled her out of her reverie. She spun around to see a dirty-faced girl of perhaps ten or so watching her with a keen and vaguely disapproving expression.

"Excuse me?"

"Yer from the Indies, ent ya?"

"You speak English," said Wilhelmina.

"Aye," agreed the girl. "Here'bouts, we does. And are ye speakin' the King's English in the Indies?"

"How do you know I'm from the Indies?" asked Wilhelmina.

"It's yer rags." The girl raised a filthy hand and extended a slender finger at Wilhelmina's shawl and blouse. Her own clothes were bedraggled and dirty; her long brown hair was lank and clearly had not been brushed for some time. "We don't wear aught like here'bouts."

"No," agreed Wilhelmina, "I suppose not." Directing her attention to the wharf and docklands, she made a sweep of her hand and asked, "Where am I? What is this place?"

"This be Sefton," the youngster replied.

That's it! she thought. *Sefton!* That was the name of the place Kit had told her about—the place he had been taking her to see when they had become separated on that first climactic leap. She gazed up and down the seafront, taking in the harbour and village with new eyes. So this was the little seaside town Kit had wanted to show her. It was much as he had described it—at least the little she could recall of his description. On that fateful day, Kit had promised to take her to tea at the seaside, to demonstrate the truth of his nutty claim about ley lines and alternate dimensions. "Sefton-on-Sea?"

"Aye," confirmed the girl. "I be Maggie."

"My name is Mina. I am pleased to meet you, Maggie." Wilhelmina extended her hand to the girl, who, after a moment's hesitation, took it and gave it a halfhearted shake. "Can you tell me what year it is?"

"Ye don't ken the year?"

"No," answered Wilhelmina. "I've been travelling a long time."

The girl's round face scrunched up in thought. The answer forced its way to her lips, and she proclaimed, "This be the year of Our Lord and King William 18 and 18!"

Wilhelmina smiled. No doubt the youngster was simply parroting back something she had heard, but it was enough. Wilhelmina thanked her and asked if she was hungry. The girl hesitated. "I was thinking of having some tea and a bun, maybe. Would you like to take tea with me?" Mina invited.

Maggie frowned. "I never, my lady," she said, growing suddenly shy and polite. "I ent allowed."

"Something else? A glass of milk, maybe?" Mina offered. "I have money, and no one to talk to. Maybe there is someplace you could show me where we might get something to eat and drink?"

The girl thought for a moment. "There's the Old Ship," she said. Extending a grubby finger, she pointed to a storefront a little farther along the street.

Wilhelmina glanced around and saw a low building painted white with a black door. A sign overhead bore the image of a ship under full sail on a stormy sea, the waves crashing against its prow. "Well," said Mina, "I'm going to go there. I hope you'll come too."

She turned and started towards the public house. Maggie watched her for a moment, then followed a few steps behind. The door of the pub pushed open easily, and Wilhelmina entered a dim, low-ceilinged room. The air, redolent of stale beer and coal smoke, was thick and muggy, but not unpleasant, and unlike anything of Wilhelmina's experience.

A plump young woman stood behind the heavy oak bar drying thick glass jars with a rag. "G'day, m'lady," she called cheerfully. "What can I get ye?"

"Good day," replied Mina. "I would like a cup of tea. Is that possible?"

"To be sure, m'lady," replied the barmaid. Her eyes flicked to the youngster who had entered behind Wilhelmina. "You! Haven't I told you 'bout comin' in here? Now, get on wi' ye."

"Sorry," said Wilhelmina quickly. "She's with me. I asked her to join me."

"That's as may be, m'lady. But young'uns ent allowed in t'pub. An' she knows better, that one."

"Oh yes, of course. You're right. I wasn't thinking."

"You ent from around here, are you, m'lady," said the young woman behind the bar.

"No, I—no, I'm not."

"Just off t'ship, then?"

"Travelling, yes." Wilhelmina, keen to change the subject, glanced around the pub. "Do you think I could have my tea outside? And maybe some cake if you have it?"

"We have some nice oat cakes just come out t'oven. I can give ye o' that wi' some good jam."

"Would you?" said Mina. "That would be perfect. Bring me a pot, please—and a glass of milk. I'll be waiting outside."

Wilhelmina stepped back onto the seafront and, with Maggie in tow, found a pleasant spot on a wharfside bench to wait. The sun was warm on her back, and she gazed out on the peaceful little harbour, the sea glinting blue and silver beneath a cloudless sky. Presently the tea came—served in a brown crockery pot with two chunky cups—one filled with milk—a plate of small round oat cakes, and a tiny bowl of red jam.

"Will there be anything else, m'lady?" asked the serving girl.

"This is lovely," said Mina. "Thank you, no. That will be all just now."

"Just bring the tray back when you're done." She cast a last dubious glance at Maggie, then returned to the pub.

After a moment Wilhelmina poured her tea. "Sefton seems a pleasant place," she observed, passing the cup of milk to her young companion. "Have you lived here long?"

"All me life long," replied Maggie. "An' have ye always lived in the Indies?"

"No," replied Mina. "I used to live in London."

"London," mused the girl. The way she said it made it sound as exotic and far away as China. But then, Wilhelmina reasoned, being a deep-water port, little Sefton probably saw more folk from foreign climes than from the capital.

The two chatted amiably, and then a bell in a church tower somewhere in the town tolled the hour: three o'clock. Maggie jumped up and, curtsying awkwardly, took her leave, saying, "My da' will be comin' home wi' the catch."

"Then you'd better run along," Wilhelmina agreed. "I wouldn't want you to get into trouble. Good-bye," she called as the girl scurried away. "Maybe I'll see you again sometime."

Wilhelmina sat for a while longer enjoying the day, and thinking what a strange life she now led. Her experience in London, far from arousing any lingering feelings for her life there, merely confirmed what she had known, or at least suspected, all along—that she did not miss the place and no longer cared to live there.

When the clock in the unseen church tower tolled four, Mina gathered up the tray and took it back inside the Old Ship Inn; she paid for the tea and cakes, holding out an assortment of coins from her penny jar from which the barmaid selected a few coppers. She then returned to the alley to see if the ley was active yet. With a quick glance around to see that she was unobserved, she drew the ley lamp from her pocket and ascertained from the absence of blue lights that the ley was still dormant. Stuffing the device back into her pocket, she stepped back from the mouth of the passage and, as she did so, her eye fell upon a word scrawled low down on the wooden siding of one of the walls. The mere glimpse rooted her to the spot.

She blinked her eyes to make sure she was indeed seeing what she thought she saw. There, written in black grease pencil, was a name: *Wilhelmina.*

There was more—a brief message that read simply, *Collect letter from Molly at the Old Ship Inn—Cosimo.*

"What on earth . . ." She stared at the unexpected communication. Cosimo! That was the name of the man Kit had met in the alley, his great-grandfather—the one Kit had tried to tell her about the day they made that fuddled jump.

Wilhelmina made quick strides to the pub. The round-faced girl was still there, still behind the bar. "Was there something else?" she asked.

"Yes. Are you Molly?"

"Aye, I am."

"My name is Wilhelmina. I forgot to ask earlier, but did someone leave a letter for me—someone by the name of Cosimo?"

Molly the barmaid disappeared into the room behind the bar and returned a moment later with a thick yellow envelope. "Ye be a friend o' Cosimo's?"

"Yes, I think I am."

"What's yer full name, then?"

"Wilhelmina Klug," replied Mina, then spelled out her last name so there would be no misunderstanding.

Molly peered at the writing on the envelope, then passed it to Mina, who thanked her and went outside. She resumed her place on the bench and carefully tore open the envelope. Inside was a single, tightly folded page written in smudgy pencil. She opened it to find a handful of shillings, two guineas, and a large silver five-pound coin. She scooped up the money and quickly scanned the note.

It read:

My Dear Wilhelmina, I can well imagine how confused and frightened you must be. But take heart in the knowledge that we are looking for you. I urge you to stay here. Take a room at the Old Ship on my account, and remain in Sefton until we come for you. Kit is with me, and sends his greetings.

Your servant,

Cosimo Livingstone

Pocketing the money, she read the message again, then turned the page over. On the back, scratched hastily in one corner of the page, was a little list of sorts—as if someone had been quickly jotting down ideas. There were six items, and three of those had lines drawn through them. The six were: *Mansell Gamage, Sefton-on-Sea, Wern Derries, Much Markle Crosses, Black Mixen Tump,* and *Capel-y-Fin.* They were place names—employing odd, old-timey words—and certainly none that Wilhelmina had ever heard before. The first three on the list had been crossed out—apparently considered and then discarded for whatever reasons the list maker had deemed appropriate. But why? Even as she considered the question, it occurred to her that if Kit and his great-grandfather were searching for her and, obviously, leaving messages for her in likely places, this might be a list of such places. The inclusion of Sefton clinched it in her opinion. The three crossed out were places already visited and, presumably, where messages had been left. The last three, then, were next on the list.

The thought that they were worried about her and looking for her made her smile. *Bless 'em,* she thought. But they were not to know what she had been up to since she and Kit had parted company. The situation had changed, and she certainly did not need rescuing.

Mina returned to the letter and list once more and noticed something else: beside three of the place names was a tiny equal sign, a simple = as found in mathematical equations—written in lighter pencil as one might make when thinking on paper. Taking these additions into account, the list read *Mansell Gamage = China . . . Wern Derries = Ireland . . . Black Mixen Tump = Egypt . . .*

"How very interesting," she said to herself, tucking the note away. Rising from the bench, she went back to the Old Ship and inquired of Molly whether there might be a carriage or coach she could hire to take her to London. "Anything at all, really," she added. "I don't mind."

"Mail coach comes through at six," the barmaid replied. "Going up t'London from Plymouth. It stops here for the driver to wet his whistle. Be in London by morning."

"Splendid," said Wilhelmina. "I'll just wait outside."

"Suit ye'self, m'lady," said Molly, resuming her work of lining up clean jars for the evening's custom.

Mina returned to her bench in the sun to await her transport and determine how to make best use of her new information. By the time the mail coach arrived in a clatter of hooves, trailing plumes of dust, Wilhelmina had a new plan firmly in mind.

Sorry, Cosimo, she said as the carriage came rattling down the street, *but I've got a better idea.*

CHAPTER 17

In Which an Unwanted Partnership Is Forged

Burleigh's fortuitous return to London after his disappearance in Italy meant different things to different people. To the winsome young socialite, Phillipa Harvey-Jones, his long-suffering fiancée, it meant heartbreak when the young lord eventually called off the wedding; to his clients, it meant a veritable treasure trove of rare and precious objets d'art, each more wondrous than the last; to his bank manager, it meant joy unbounded as the earl's fortunes increased, swelling his coffers by leaps and bounds. For now that he had discovered ley travel, Burleigh was secretly employing his remarkable ability to amass a fortune through the acquisition of rare and precious artefacts. What better place to acquire invaluable antiques than directly from antiquity? His lordship's early experiments with ley travel swiftly gave way to an all-consuming obsession; thus, he no longer had time for Phillipa. Who could blame him? If his newfound ability to leap into parallel worlds could result in something so mundane as obtaining expensive knickknacks to sell to a hungry clientele in late-nineteenth-century London, what else could it do? Lord Archelaeus Burleigh, Earl of Sutherland, was on a quest to find out.

"Lord Burleigh," intoned His Lordship's valet, "forgive the intrusion."

"What is it, Swain?"

"A letter has arrived from Sotheby's." The gentleman's gentleman extended a small silver tray with a cream-coloured envelope addressed to the Earl of Sutherland. There was no stamp; it had been hand delivered. "I thought you would rather be apprised sooner than later, sir."

"To be sure." Burleigh took the envelope and, while the servant waited, he opened it and scanned the few lines. Then, placing the letter and envelope on the table beside him, he rose. "Inform Dawkin to ready the carriage. I am going out."

"Very good, sir."

Within the hour Burleigh was sitting in the office of Mr. Gerald Catchmole, the principal broker at Sotheby's auction house. He had been offered whiskey and a cigar, but declined owing to the hour of the day, accepting tea instead. While waiting for the tea, they chatted about the dismal lack of quality among the items currently coming out of the Levant. "We are obliged to auction them, of course," sniffed Catchmole, "but it does go somewhat against the grain."

"Not that your average punter knows the difference," replied Burleigh. "You make your commission all the same, I daresay."

"But *you* do know the difference, my lord," asserted Catchmole in an ingratiating tone. "Which is why I contacted you as soon as this came in." There was a knock on the door, and a middle-aged woman entered with a tray of tea things. "You may pour, Mrs. Rudd," instructed the broker. "And leave the tray, if you please. We'll help ourselves."

She poured, handed out the cups, then withdrew without a word. When she had gone, Catchmole took a sip from his cup, then set it aside. "I thought you should be the first to see this," he said, rising. He crossed to his desk, retrieved a wooden cigar box, and passed it to Burleigh. "Have a look."

Lord Burleigh took the box and opened the lid. Inside, nestled in tissue paper, were three small objects: an Egyptian scarab, a small statue of a woman in a long, multitiered skirt holding two writhing snakes, and a carved cameo of a man with a laurel wreath. They were, in fact, exactly the kind of objects currently in fashion, imitations of which were flooding the antiques market throughout Europe just then.

Burleigh glanced up at the broker. "Yes?"

"Take a closer look," invited Catchmole with a smile.

Balancing the box on his knee, the earl picked up the statue. It was about six inches high and painted with painstaking skill; the woman's eyes were large and open wide, her dark hair piled in an elaborate braided style, and the snakes she held in either hand curled up around her arms, their mouths open. The tiny statue had been painted green, and her long, high-waisted skirt was blue and green striped. The figurine had been glazed to a fine standard.

"I see what you mean," said Burleigh softly. "Sixteenth century BC—the Minoan snake goddess votive figure. Extraordinary preservation. It looks as if it could have been made yesterday. Was it?"

Raising his eyebrows, he glanced up at the broker, who merely indicated the next piece.

Burleigh picked up the scarab. It was crafted from a single flawless piece of lapis lazuli of deepest blue, and the carving was exquisite, the hieroglyphs fresh and clean; a cartouche contained the name *Nebmaatra*. On the underside, a tiny carved eye surmounting a rod and flail identified the maker. His lordship's brow wrinkled in thought.

"Neb-Ma'at-Ra," he mused, sounding the name aloud as he tried to place it. "Upon my word," he gasped, glancing up at Catchmole, who was watching with interest. "This is from the royal workshop of Amenhotep—the pharaoh's own craftsmen."

"I knew you would be impressed," chortled Catchmole, nodding and smiling. "If anyone can tell gold from glister it is yourself, Lord Burleigh."

"Where did you get these?" Burleigh demanded. He flipped down the lid of the box. It was an ordinary wooden container for a middling brand of cigars—a crude carrier for such treasure.

"May I direct his lordship's attention to the remaining piece?"

Burleigh flipped open the lid and lifted out the tiny stone cameo. Like the scarab, it was an elegant and finely worked piece of deep red carnelian. The profile was of a man wearing the laurel leaf crown of a Roman emperor. There was no doubt but that it had once been owned by an ancient citizen of great wealth and, no doubt, taste. There was an inscription on the backside: *G.J.C.A.*

Burleigh stared at it. "Extraordinary," he breathed. "Caesar Augustus?"

"None other—or so I am told by Searle-Wilson. Our resident classicist assures me there cannot be more than a dozen of these in existence."

"I suppose not." The earl held the cameo to the light. It would make a splendid ring, or a broach set in gold. "Where did you get these?" he asked again.

"I can take it that your interest has been sufficiently piqued?" said Catchmole smugly.

"They are genuine artefacts of the highest quality—of course I'm interested. But I must know how you came by them."

"As to that, I am not presently at liberty to say," replied the broker, taking possession of the box once more. "I can say that I am authorised to offer them for auction." He paused, his eyes shifting involuntarily towards the door as if he feared being overheard. Lowering his voice, he said, "I wondered if we might come to a more private arrangement?"

"I'll have them," said Burleigh, rising from his chair. "Yes, of course, I'll have them. I'll have the lot—but under the condition that you tell me where you got them."

Catchmole hesitated. "I gave my word the transaction would remain in strictest confidence."

"And so it shall," countered Burleigh. "The transaction necessarily involves three people—the seller, the broker, and the buyer—and only those three people need ever know about it."

The auctioneer regarded the box longingly. "One does not like to disappoint a client . . ."

"There is no need for anyone to be disappointed. Tell me where you got these items, and I will authorise a draught on my account at once."

"I can tell you that they came from a young man up at Oxford," Catchmole replied, placing his fingertips atop the box. "A university student. I do not know how he came by them. One doesn't ask such questions."

"Be that as it may, if we are to agree on a price I must ascertain the provenance of these artefacts," declared Burleigh. "They could be stolen from a private collection, after all."

"Upon my word, sir!" the broker protested. "If it was known that I was party to—"

"It has been known to happen," suggested the earl, removing his leather wallet from the inside pocket of his frock coat. "I am afraid I must insist on having the fellow's name." He withdrew two five-pound notes and laid them on the desk.

"Charles," sighed the broker, giving in. "Charles Flinders-Petrie."

"Where can I find him?" asked Burleigh, adding two more notes to the stack.

"He is a student at Christ Church, I believe." The broker pushed the cigar box across the polished top of his desk towards the earl and collected the bank notes. "I was told they are heirlooms from a family collection."

"I'm certain that they are." Burleigh scooped up the cigar box and tucked it securely under his arm, then turned on his heel to go. "You will do well out of this, Catchmole. I will see to that."

"I am only too glad to be of service, my lord."

"Good day to you." Burleigh opened the door and stepped from the office. "As always, it has been a singular pleasure."

"I assure you the pleasure is mine," replied the broker, folding the bank notes and slipping them into his pocket.

Outside Sotheby's, Burleigh climbed into the waiting coach. By the time he reached his Belgravia townhouse, the earl had determined his next course of action. "Do not put the carriage away, Dawkin. I will be leaving again within the hour." He dashed up the steps and burst through the front door, shouting, "Swain, come here at once! I need you."

The servant appeared momentarily, the only alteration in his customary nonchalance the lift of one eyebrow. "Was there something, sir?"

"I'm off to Oxford on the next train. Ready a valise this instant— a change of clothes and necessities for one night. Go!" As the senior servant padded off, Burleigh amended the order, "Wait! Better make provision for two or three days in case I run into difficulty."

"Of course, sir."

Before the clock in the foyer had struck the hour, his lordship's travelling case was packed and the earl was on his way to Paddington Station to catch the next train to Oxford. A pleasant journey through the rolling countryside brought him to the university city late in the afternoon. He sent his valise along to the Randolph Hotel with instructions for booking a room, then walked from the railway station to the centre of town, taking in the warm glow of the rich Cotswold stone that made up the greater buildings of the town's architecture. He arrived at Christ Church and, finding the gate open, stopped to inquire at the porter's lodge.

"Good day, porter," he said, "I have come to see my nephew."

"Yes, sir," replied the porter, stepping up to his window. "And who might that be?"

"Flinders-Petrie," replied Burleigh. "Charles Flinders-Petrie."

The man scanned a ledger book. "I don't see that anyone is expected."

"Surprise visit." He removed a calling card from his wallet and passed it to the porter, who, upon seeing the title and name engraved upon the card, instantly became obsequious. "Do you think you could tell me where to find him?"

"Of course, my lord." The porter put on his black bowler and stepped from the lodge. "I shall take you there myself. Right this way, sir, if you will. Right this way."

He led the earl across the wide expanse of the quad, through a warren of corridors, gardens, and hallways, and to a narrow stone staircase. "This way, sir," said the porter. "Right up these stairs." The college official started for the door.

"A moment, my good man," said Burleigh. He fished out a handful of coins from his pocket and stacked them in his palm. "I have a question or two first."

"Of course, sir," replied the porter, trying not to look directly at the silver in his lordship's hand. "If I can help in any way . . ."

"I promised Charles' father I would render a report upon my return. It is late, and I don't particularly care to go to the trouble of hunting down tutors and whatnot." He fingered the stack of coins. "I was hoping you could enlighten me."

"Well, sir, I can tell you that he is a good lad. Cheerful. Always a smile or a joke for the porters and bulls."

"I will accept that for what it is worth," observed Burleigh dryly. "What about his studies?"

"I wouldn't know about those, sir. You would have to ask his tutors about any of that."

"And how is Charles regarded about town?" At the porter's hesitation, he pressed quickly, "The truth, now. I won't land you in the soup, don't worry."

"I don't like to speak ill of anyone—"

"Noted," said Burleigh. "But?"

"But . . . well, sir, there have been occasions when I have had call to fetch the young man from some . . . shall we say . . . less than salubrious places." He laid a finger beside his nose. "If you know what I mean."

"I think I can guess. Anything else?"

"Lately, there have been men calling round to collect debts."

"What sort of debts? Food, drink, clothing—the usual things?"

"Gambling, sir."

"I say!" Burleigh feigned surprise. "Are you certain of this?"

"I fear so, sir. There are several gaming clubs around town. It is difficult to keep the young gentlemen out of them."

"And are they very great, these debts?"

"I'm sure I don't know, sir. We don't let them past the gate, you see, and they decline to leave a message."

"Well," harrumphed Burleigh. "We shall certainly have a serious talk about that."

"Oh, I wouldn't be too hard on him, sir," said the porter apologetically. "A young gentleman must sow a few wild oats. That seems to be the way of the world."

"No doubt. Is there anything else?" Burleigh became officious. "Come, if I am to have any influence in the matter, I must know all. What else?"

"There is just the matter of the battles, sir."

"You've lost me."

"The battles—accounts, sir," repeated the porter. "The bursar can give you the pertinent details, but there is a debt owing for drink and such within the college."

"I see."

"Would you like me to take you up now?"

"Thank you, but no. I can find my own way." Burleigh smiled and dropped the stack of silver coins into the servant's hand. "Let us keep this a surprise, eh?"

"Very good, sir." The porter pocketed the coins. "It's the first room on the right at the top. Please, feel free to make your way up in your own good time."

"Good evening," replied Burleigh.

The servant lingered. "I will just mention, sir, he may be in hall at dinner just now—that is, if he's chosen to eat early. Most of the young men do. If you like, I can send for the gentleman."

"I don't mind waiting," said Burleigh, waving the servant away. "If Charles is out, I will simply make myself at home until he returns." He started up the staircase. "Again, my thanks, porter. You've been most helpful."

When the man had gone, Burleigh made his way up the stairs. At the top of the staircase, he found two doors. On one, a calling card in a neat brass holder indicated that the occupant was indeed one Charles Flinders-Petrie. Burleigh knocked quietly; when there was no answer, he tried the door, found that it was unlocked, and let himself in to a large square room with a window overlooking Christ Church meadow and, beyond it, a willow-lined stretch of the Isis River. There were cows in the meadow and a herder with staff and dog moving them towards a barn for the night.

Burleigh stood for a moment, studying the interior. Two large overstuffed leather chairs sat on either side of a generous fireplace and, between them, a small round table bearing a silver tray with a crystal port decanter and four glasses. There was a painting on the wall of a country scene, and clothes spilled from an untidy wardrobe. A coat rack beside the wardrobe held a black student gown, a satin waistcoat, a long overcoat, two hats—one black beaver skin, one grey felt—and the distinctive striped scarves of several colleges, none of them Christ Church. One wall was taken up with a floor-to-ceiling bookcase, half full of books; the lower shelves held items of clothing, a pair of shoes, a battered straw hat, a cricket bat, ball, and gloves. He moved closer to scan the shelves; judging by the titles, the subjects were mostly to do with history. The tops of the books were dusty.

Across the room, the bed had been made, but was rumpled; a small pile of clothing—trousers, a shirt, a waistcoat, a black tie—lay on the floor beside it. A reading table at the window held a dirty plate with a rind of cheese and crumbs of bread, an empty mug with tea stains, a half-eaten apple. A bottle of wine, empty, stood on the floor beneath the table. Hanging from a strap on a peg by the door was a leather satchel.

In all, it was the room of a fellow who spent little time in it, and less time studying—a more or less typical student, Burleigh decided as, taking in his surroundings one last time, he lowered himself into one of the worn leather chairs at the fireplace.

Little by little the light grew dimmer as evening settled. A chill crept into the room, and Burleigh was considering whether to light a fire in the grate when he heard voices on the staircase. Presently there was a click at the doorknob, the door opened, and in stepped a sandy-haired youth with his dinner jacket slung carelessly over one shoulder. He was tall, but not gangly; slender, but not gaunt; his features were regular and well-formed and would have been fairly unremarkable if not for his eyes, which were subtly oval-shaped and ever so slightly aslant, giving them an almost Oriental appearance.

The youth threw his jacket on the bed and began unbuttoning his shirt.

"Hello, Charles," said Burleigh.

The young man jumped and spun around. "Good lord! Who the devil are you?"

"Forgive me for startling you," said his visitor, rising slowly to his full, imposing height. "My name is Burleigh—Earl of Sutherland. I think we share a common interest."

"Oh?" said Charles warily. He made no move to come nearer. "And what might that be?"

"Antiquities."

"Oh, that!" sniffed Charles dismissively.

"Yes, that," affirmed his dark visitor. "Why, what did you think I was going to say?"

"I don't know—bear baiting, dog fighting, I suppose. Gambling, what have you."

"Nothing quite so exciting." Burleigh turned and poured out two glasses of port from the crystal decanter on the table. "Come," said Burleigh, and held out one to the young man. "Sit with me a little. Let us talk about artefacts. Ancient artefacts."

"I think you have the wrong fellow," protested Charles. He moved to accept the proffered glass. "I know nothing whatsoever of antiques." He flopped into the chair. "Not my line at all, don't you see."

"But it *is* mine," said Burleigh, seating himself once more. "I am a dealer in such things."

"Bully." Charles raised his glass. *"Yum sen!"*

Burleigh drank and then set aside his glass. "I will not impose on you any more than necessary, but as a courtesy I will insist that you attend me in a matter of some importance." With this, Burleigh reached into his coat pocket and retrieved a black velvet wallet, which he unrolled to reveal the lapis scarab, the Sumerian votive figure, and the carnelian cameo of Augustus. He lined them up on the table beside him.

Charles glanced at the objects and feigned indifference. "Charming," he said. "But I feel it only fair to warn you that if you mean to *sell* me these baubles, it is a rum go from the start." He took another sip. "Don't have any dosh, you see. Fresh out. Skint as a lizard."

Burleigh regarded the young man with intent: his manner was not what he had expected; clearly, the fellow was playing at something. "You are disingenuous," observed the earl. "Could it be that you still cling to the mistaken belief that I have not guessed the provenance of these items?"

The erstwhile scholar put back his head and offered a tepid laugh. "Provenance, sir? Why, how you talk. I've never seen the trinkets in my life."

"We both know that is a lie," Burleigh countered, keeping his voice level, his temper cool.

"How dare you!" Charles began, but the objection lacked force. "I will have you know—"

"Spare me, please," interrupted the earl. "I have been dealing with antiquities of this sort longer than you have been alive, and I know whereof I speak." Burleigh picked up the votive figure of the snake goddess and held it to the light. "These are genuine. What is more, they are in almost perfect condition—untouched by the ravages of time or the grave. In short, they were not dug out of the deserts of Egypt or Babylon, nor recovered from any tomb." He fixed the young man with a stern gaze. "I will ask you in plain language—how did you come by them?"

Charles threw back his drink, then poured himself another. He slouched further into his chair and with a forced nonchalance said, "That is none of your business."

"I have just told you that it is very *much* my business." Burleigh's voice, though calm, took on a steely note. "Why do you persist in this feeble attempt at dissembling? It is a waste of time."

The young man glared at his visitor, but remained silent.

"Let us begin again." Burleigh replaced the figurine and picked up the scarab. "I am happy to pay a fair price for this piece—and for the others as well. More than you would have made at auction."

At this Charles perked up. "How much more?"

Burleigh gave him a sour smile. "Enough to give me the right to come here tonight with an offer—and a very handsome offer, I might add."

"Well then?"

"I am prepared to buy all the pieces in your collection, singly or in a job lot—subject to examination, of course—at fair market value plus fifteen percent. No, let us make it twenty percent. An auction house would take at least that much in commission. You might as well have the benefit instead."

"Twenty percent above market value?" repeated Charles. "And who, might I ask, determines market value? You, I suppose?"

"Anyone you like," Burleigh answered. "But if you want my opinion, Catchmole at Sotheby's will not steer you far wrong. I trust him."

The profligate young man frowned as he mulled over the offer.

"There are conditions," Burleigh continued after a moment. "You will tell me how you came by these objects—and any others I acquire through our arrangement. Further, you will agree never to sell any such artefacts to anyone else."

"Impudent rascal, see here—!"

"From now on, I am your sole partner in the antiquities trade." Burleigh gave him a cold smile. "Fair price plus twenty percent and a ready sale. You will never have to chance the whims of a fickle public."

"Don't want much, do you?" sneered Charles. "Anything else?"

"Only that you will not breathe a word of our partnership to another living soul."

Charles dashed down the rest of his drink. Then, arranging his features in an expression of defiance, he said, "I won't do it. I refuse."

With the grace of a pouncing cat, Burleigh leapt from his chair. He snatched the young scholar by the throat and yanked him to his feet. "Listen to me, you prodigal prig. I know very well what you have been up to. I know about the gambling, the drinking, the whoring. I know the places you've been and the company you've been keeping."

"Unhand me, rogue," began the frightened Charles in a somewhat strained voice.

Burleigh tightened his grip and cut off any further protest. "You owe money all over town, and men have been sniffing around to collect your debts. It is only a matter of time before they catch you and you end up dead in a ditch with a broken head or a knife in the back."

Charles scrabbled at his attacker's hand, but Burleigh held firm. "Listen very carefully. You will agree to the terms I have outlined, and you will keep your mouth shut. Nod your head if you understand."

Charles, his face growing red, gave a feeble nod.

Burleigh released him then and threw him back into the leather chair. The young man bent forward, clutching his neck and gasping for air. In a moment his colour and breathing returned to normal.

"No need to glare at me like that. You aren't hurt," Burleigh said, standing over him. "Tell me how you got these pieces."

"Private collection," muttered Charles, still rubbing his neck. "Been in the family for donkey's years."

"Who collected them?"

"My grandfather—there's a whole chest full of the stuff."

"Where did he get them?"

"Haven't the foggiest," Charles began, then, seeing Burleigh flex his hands, quickly amended his reply. "He travelled a lot—spent most his time on ships to foreign parts. Had an eye for the odd trinket. He collected them." He thrust out his chin. "Satisfied? Or are you going to choke me again?"

"His name. This grandfather of yours—what was his name?"

"Arthur," answered the young reprobate. "Arthur Flinders-Petrie."

"Where can I find him?"

"You can't." Charles shook his head. "Died before I was born. Caught an ague or something on one of his travels. That's all I know."

"And your father? What is his name? What does he say about you selling off the family heirlooms?"

"My father passed away last year. But I doubt he would approve. He didn't approve of much, my father—at least where I was concerned. His name was Benedict. Anything else?"

"Arthur and Benedict Flinders-Petrie," said Burleigh, making a mental note. "That's all for now." He stepped away. "I will contact you if I require anything more."

"What about the money?"

"You will get your money. It has already been arranged through Catchmole at Sotheby's. All we need do is agree on a price; I will tell him and he will do the rest. He is being paid for his silence and discretion. How much do you owe in gambling debts?"

Charles frowned. "Fifty pounds, give or take."

"And your battles?"

"Another twenty, perhaps."

"We'll make it an even hundred, then," decided Burleigh. "And don't look so disappointed. It is more than any decent labourer earns in a year, and more than you would have made at auction. There, you see? I've saved you no end of trouble."

The young man frowned. "That's it, then?"

"Do cheer up. Think of it this way—you now have a new and supremely influential partner in business, and your pecuniary worries are over." He moved towards the door. "Still, I wouldn't go running up any more whacking great debts about town—I may not feel so generous next time."

"What if I don't want a partner?"

Burleigh put back his head and laughed. "Farewell, Charles." He opened the door and stepped out onto the landing. "Until we meet again."

"How do I contact you?" asked Charles, following him onto the staircase.

"You don't. If I should need to see you, I will contact you."

"When I want to sell something," suggested Charles, "how do I reach you?"

"Whenever you wish to sell"—Burleigh started down the steps—"you will send to Catchmole. He will do the rest."

"Why are you doing this?" Charles called after his visitor's disappearing form.

"I already told you," answered Burleigh, receding down the steps. "It is my business."

"Just business? Nothing more?"

Burleigh gave a laugh as he disappeared into the shadows. "You have no idea how far my business interests take me."

CHAPTER 18

In Which Kit Takes a Detour

Cupping his hands to his eyes, Kit blinked at the black stretch of highway as it shimmered gently in the full sun of a blistering summer day. The shock of seeing that road rocked him backwards a step. An image so drearily commonplace in his home world . . . in this world the sight jolted through him like lightning. It was a moment before he could properly frame his thoughts, and then the best he could manage was a feeble and ineffectual *How . . . ?*

The narrow passage in the cave contained a ley line—that was the only explanation. He had unwittingly crossed over and was now . . . where? Judging solely by the highway, it was somewhere reasonably modern. In other words, a world about as far away from the Stone Age as Marylebone from Mars. Kit gazed at the asphalt artery as it curved through the valley, hugging the sinuous curve of the river, and the sight filled him with dread bordering on despair. *Why?* he wondered. *Why now?*

There was a time when his first instinct would have been to run to that dusty band of tarmac, fall on his knees, and kiss it for everything it signified. But he was past that. Now he wanted nothing more than to dive back into the cave and take the leap back to rejoin his clansmen in the cave. *His* clansmen! Being part of River City Clan, learning their ways, discovering all the little mysteries of their existence, of another form of human life . . . this was his life, and he was not done with it yet, and he was in no way prepared to leave them without so much as a "So long, see ya later."

"No," he muttered with a determined shake of his head. "Not now. Not like this."

He glimpsed a burst of motion far down on the slope below as the cave lion disappeared into the thick brush of the riverbank. "Bye-bye, Baby," he murmured. "You go your way, and I'll go mine." With that, he turned right around and scrambled back into the cave.

Kit fumbled his way along the interior of the cavern, leaving the world of air and light behind. It was a slow and nerve-wracking process, but stubborn resolve kept his feet moving. When it grew too dark to see anymore, he steadied himself with one hand on the near left wall and worked his way along until he felt the passage straighten out and reckoned that might be the end of the ley.

Bracing himself for a blind leap, he started off. Trying to walk normally and with purpose in total darkness—one hand on the rough rock wall beside him and the other waving out in front—was more difficult than he expected. After a bit of practise he was able to achieve a respectable gait, but to no discernible effect.

He stumbled over the uneven floor, willing the transition to happen. When he reached the end of the straight section, he turned around and hobbled back to start again. After two failed attempts to make the leap, he remembered Wilhelmina's ley lamp in the inner pouch sewn into this shirt. He fished it out and waved it around. The little blue lights flashed, gave off a dying flicker, and winked out. Turning this way and that in the passage, he held the lamp before him, but could not raise another signal and was forced to conclude that any ley activity present in the cave was now dormant.

With a grumble and grinding of his teeth, Kit turned on his heel and headed back to the cave entrance to wait until the ley grew active once more. The day outside was hot and bright; it took him awhile to get used to sunlight again, and heat. He was soon sweating in his furs and wishing he had something else to wear. He shed the long, heavy tunic shirt, rolling it up and stashing it carefully under a rock just inside the mouth of the cave; he would need it later.

Returning to the hillside, he took the opportunity to more properly spy out the land. It was fairly arid hill country with a ridge of jagged grey mountains rising to the northwest, a river winding through a green valley below, and what appeared to be olive trees dotting the hillsides within view. The mountains looked vaguely familiar, but he could not place them. Aside from the olive trees, he might be almost anywhere—not that it mattered, because he did not plan on hanging around long enough to find out more. It irked him that he had been transferred to this place. Just his luck, he moaned; when he wanted to leave, the ley line he knew refused to open. Now that he had a reason to stay a little longer, he had been ejected by a ley he had not known was there.

Consoling himself with the thought that knowing a way back to his clan was the main thing and he could return later, Kit sat down in the shadow of an overhanging rock to wait for the sun to go down. Even sitting in the shade, the heat began to wear on him— the abrupt change from winter to high summer was a shock to the system. He closed his eyes and was soon dozing. Sometime later, a distant sound roused him from a deep sleep. He opened his eyes and looked around; everything was as before, but now he was aware of a burning thirst.

Looking down towards the river, he saw the gleam of shining water and decided that nothing would be gained by allowing himself to get dehydrated, so he rose and started down the hillside. He reached the riverbank and, keeping an eye out for the young cave lion, began searching for a place where he might be able to access the water, scrambling through the brush growing thick on the bank. He came to a flat stretch of pebbled shingle on the bank and, kneeling, scooped up handfuls of fresh water, still cool from the mountain springs.

He drank his fill and was just about to rise when he heard a tremendous commotion in the brush behind him. Fearing that Baby had found him, Kit grabbed a good-sized stone from the strand and crouched, ready to fight. Out from the brush bounded two big hounds—lean, long-legged beasts; one grey, one brown—and both of them extremely surprised to see him.

They halted in midchase and froze, heads low, ears flattened, hackles raised.

"Easy, fellas," said Kit, raising his free hand to show it empty. "Good boys. Stay." At the sound of his voice, the brown dog raised his snout and gave a single long yowl. The other remained fixed on him, snarling gently.

As if in answer to the first hound's yelp, Kit heard a thrashing in the wood, and into the clearing stepped a man in a red shirt and leather hunting vest. He was wearing a black beret and carrying a double-barrelled shotgun. He took one look at Kit and breathed, *"Madre de Dios!"*

Kit, still clutching the stone, said, "Okay, let's not get excited. Let's stay cool."

At this, the man in the black beret raised the shotgun and pointed it at Kit's chest. *"Qué?"*

"English?" countered Kit. *"Anglais?"*

Neither word had any effect. The man, still goggle-eyed at the apparition before him, remained unmoved, the gun unwaveringly aimed at Kit's chest. This standoff seemed to last an age, and then the man gestured with the gun barrel for Kit to throw down the rock. Kit complied without hesitation.

"Don't shoot, okay?" he said, raising his hands slowly. "I'm just a traveller. You can put the gun down. I won't cause any trouble. See?"

The man gestured for Kit to move away from the riverbank, which he did, and Kit was then led at gunpoint out of the brush and into the field beyond. Once in the open, the man gave out a long, rising whistle. It was answered by another in kind. A moment later, a second man appeared from out of the bushy scrub along the river. Like the first, he was dressed in a red shirt and black beret; he also had leather leggings on his trousers and wore a pouch for birds or rabbits or other small game slung over one shoulder.

The second hunter took one look at Kit and said, *"Santa María!"*

The first hunter nodded.

The second hunter approached Kit cautiously. *"Dónde consiguió usted eso?"*

"English?" said Kit. He thought for a moment how to frame the next question, but found that his own facility with English had all but dried up. After so long a time with River City Clan, he could barely make his mouth say the words. "Speak English?" was all he could manage.

The two men looked at each other and then at Kit. The second hunter shrugged and said, *"Padre Tadeo."*

"Si," agreed the other. *"Padre Tadeo lo sabrá."*

The first hunter motioned with the shotgun once more, and Kit was marched away with the two men behind him and a dog on either side. They followed the curve of the river around a wide bend and came to a bridge joining a dirt road to the highway. Parked at the side of the road was a tiny three-wheeled vehicle of muddy green; it had a cab for the driver and an open bed for haulage. One of the men got into the driver's seat and the other motioned Kit into the back. Then the man and hounds climbed in with him, the engine fired up, and they juntered off.

They drove a few miles to a village just off the highway. The place was the centre for a small farming community, boasting a single main street lined with a few simple shops, a watering tank for live-stock, a greengrocer, and a post office. The signs Kit saw on the sides of buildings and in the store windows were all in Spanish. The main street ended at a town square with a large stone church on one side and, facing it across the square, a rambling stucco edifice with white pillars and black doors. The town square had a large marble fountain, but the fountain was dry.

The three-wheeled truck pulled up outside the church, and the driver beeped the horn and went on beeping it until a priest in a long black cassock emerged and stood on the steps. The driver got out and ran to the priest; the two exchanged a few words, and the clergyman approached the little pickup where Kit sat under guard in the back.

A short man with heavy dark eyebrows above deep-set black eyes, the priest took one look at Kit and crossed himself.

"Hello," said Kit, having decided his best option was to remain calm and quiet and try not to alarm folk unnecessarily. "Do you speak English?"

The priest's eyebrows shot up. He glanced at the two holding the shotguns, who nodded knowingly, then said, "I speak English, yes."

"Good," said Kit. He made to get out of the vehicle, then glanced again at the two men who still held their shotguns at the ready and decided to stay put for the moment.

The priest hesitated, but the hunter who had discovered Kit nodded his encouragement. "This is El Bruc, *señor*," replied the priest. "Who are you?"

"My name is Christopher." He considered asking where he was and the year, but decided those questions could wait until he knew his captors better. "You can call me Kit." He smiled in what he hoped was a reassuring manner. "Who are you?"

"I am Father Tadeo." Waving an expressive hand at the patchwork of furs Kit wore, the little priest said, "*De dónde*—ah, where came you from?"

"Where did I come from?" echoed Kit. He paused, considering how to answer. "I am from England. I have been, um . . . I have been exploring."

"*Explorar?*" echoed the cleric. Turning to the others, "*Es un explorador,*" he explained.

The gun-toting hunters nodded. "*Explorador,*" they murmured. The second one loosed a volley of rapid-fire Spanish at the priest, who then turned to Kit and said, "Ricardo wishes to know why you dress like this."

Kit glanced down at his shaggy, handmade trousers. The fur was matted and ratty-looking, his stitched-together shoes caked with mud. He stank, and his hair was a mass of wild tangles, his beard a bushy thicket around his face. He suddenly felt very silly wearing this ludicrous outfit. "I lost my clothes."

The priest relayed this to the hunters; one of them answered, and all three men laughed, whereupon Father Tadeo replied, "We think you have lost more than your clothes, Senõr Christopher."

"Yes," agreed Kit, running a hand through his beard. "You might be right about that."

This small convocation outside the church did not go unnoticed for long. A portly man in a brown suit and white shirt appeared from the large pillared building and hurried across the square to join them. "What is this?" he demanded in Spanish. Father Tadeo explained briefly, and the man turned and commanded one of the hunters, "Go and bring Diego. Tell him we have a problem."

The hunter hurried off, and Father Tadeo said to Kit, "This is Senõr Benito. He is *Alcalde*—the mayor of this town."

"Tell him I am pleased to meet him," replied Kit. His tongue seemed to be working better now as it loosened with use.

The man in the brown suit gave a curt, officious nod and spoke again, watching Kit narrowly. Father Tadeo translated for Kit. "Alcalde Benito wishes to know if you are *loco*—crazy?"

"Please tell him that, so far as I know, I am in my right mind."

The priest and mayor conferred over this. The mayor shook his head and frowned. He crossed his arms over his paunch of a stomach and watched Kit. A moment later the hunter returned with a policeman in a blue uniform with *Guardia* on a shoulder patch. He wore a white bandolier to which was attached a holster with a large revolver. He greeted the mayor and priest, and the three briefly conferred in Spanish as Kit sat looking on.

"Ramón and Ricardo have found this man at the river below the cave," said Father Tadeo.

"It is true," said Ramón. "We were hunting rabbits, and I found him."

"We think he is crazy," added the mayor.

"Has he been making trouble?" asked the policeman.

"No trouble yet," said Ramón. "But," he added, "he speaks only English."

The policeman nodded, then directed a question at Kit, which Father Tadeo translated. "Señor Diego wishes to know why you are living in the cave."

"Ah," replied Kit, trying to maintain his placid demeanour despite the stakes, which seemed to be rising by the minute. "Please tell Señor Diego that I was not *living* in the cave. I was exploring it." He shrugged and raised his palms. "I lost my way."

This explanation was duly repeated and was discussed by the five townsmen gathered around the three-wheeler where Kit sat like a dishevelled dignitary conducting an al fresco audience.

"Do you have papers?" asked the priest at one point, to which Kit shook his head.

The men conferred again, with much gesturing and head scratching. "What shall we do with him?" asked Father Tadeo.

"He has broken no laws that I know of," suggested Diego. "I do not think I can arrest him for getting lost in a cave."

"Arrest him? I don't want him arrested," said the mayor. "I want him gone. Look at him. He is a barbarian."

"He is an Englishman," said Ricardo.

"He was exploring and got lost," added Ramón. To the priest, he said, "You should give him a bath and a meal."

"Me! I should do this? *Madre de Dios!* This is none of my affair." Father Tadeo put up his hands. "It is none of my concern what you do with him."

"But you are the priest of this town," asserted Mayor Benito.

"What has that got to do with it?" countered Father Tadeo.

"The duties of hospitality fall to you," said the mayor.

"No such thing," replied Tadeo. "You are mayor—hospitality is yours to provide."

"We must do something," insisted Ramón. "He cannot live in my truck. I have to go home and feed the cattle."

"He has no papers," said the mayor.

"Does he need papers?" wondered the policeman.

"All respectable people have papers," suggested the mayor. "Another reason he cannot stay here."

"Where can he go?" asked Ricardo. "He is lost."

"I know!" said Father Tadeo. "Take him to the abbey. They are always having so many visitors—pilgrims from everywhere. They will know what to do with him."

"He is not a pilgrim," said Ramón. "He is an explorer."

"No matter—it is the same thing," replied the mayor, making an executive decision. "Padre, you will take him to the abbey, and they will deal with him."

"Me?" Father Tadeo put up his hands. "I have no automobile, as you know. I cannot possibly take him. I have my homily to compose."

All eyes turned to the policeman. "Diego, my friend," said the mayor, putting his hand to the policeman's shoulder, "this is official business. You must take him in your vehicle." He glanced at Kit, then added, "Use the siren."

So it was that Kit was transferred from the back of the three-wheeled truck to the official police cruiser—a dented blue-and-white tin can that spewed acrid smoke as it rattled along. The policeman kept a wary eye on his unusual passenger. For his part, Kit smiled a lot and tried not to make himself appear any more of a problem than he was already.

They passed through another village and another before the highway turned and headed up into the mountains. The road snaked higher and higher, following a series of rising switchbacks into the sharp-angled peaks. The police car chugged ever more slowly, straining at the steep incline, eventually rolling to a halt before a high iron gate overarched by a sign in wrought-iron letters painted white that read *Abadia de Montserrat.*

CHAPTER 19

In Which a Sisterhood Is Joined

With the warmth of a dazzling Damascus sun on her back, Cassandra stood outside a shiny black-lacquered door bearing a small brass plate engraved with the words *Zetetic Society* in a fine, flowing script. The doorknob was also brass, and both were polished bright. The close little street was quiet and shaded by high whitewashed walls and the grey stone flanks of Beit Hanania, the house of the man known to the western world as Saint Ananias—who first healed and then befriended the murderous zealot Saul of Tarsus and helped ease him into his role as the apostle Paul. A sign on the wall outside the shrine had informed her in three languages, as if she had not already guessed, that she was in the city's ancient Christian quarter.

The doorway before her, like many Damascene portals, was constructed in the distinctive black-and-white-banded stonework. A small and extremely dusty window, enclosed by thick iron bars, opened onto what appeared to be a pokey little bookshop.

Cass saw unkempt shelves and a table stacked high with books and pamphlets, and her heart sank. A *bookshop*? Was that all there was to it—some kind of weird cult pushing their odious literature and trying to convert unsuspecting suckers to their occult beliefs? Disappointment turned down the corners of her mouth. How *dare* they, she thought—pasting up signs promising help as a way to lure in gullible travellers; they ought to be ashamed of themselves. These and other thoughts were riffling through her mind as, thoroughly disgusted—with them for lying, and with herself for letting her hopes get so high on the basis of such flimsy evidence as a handwritten poster—she turned to go.

No doubt all this bouncing around between worlds or dimensions or whatever—finding herself in new places every other minute—had momentarily thrown off her judgement. That could not be allowed to continue. She had to apply the rigour of her scientific mind to the situation at hand, and she would begin this very moment.

With a last disdainful glance at the shop, she stepped away and started down the street when there was a click behind her, and the glossy black door opened. A stout older woman with straight white hair cut in a short bob stuck out her head. "Oh!" she said, "I have company. I thought I heard someone on the step." Dressed in a long-sleeved blouse with a large jade brooch at the throat, a green tartan skirt, and sensible brown shoes, she peered at her visitor through small, wire-rimmed glasses, offering the thin smile of a strict elder aunt or a Scottish school mistress á la Miss Jean Brodie who, in her prime, tolerated no nonsense in her classroom. The woman opened the door a little wider. "You must come in, dear."

"You speak English," Cassandra observed with some relief. "I mean—that is, I was looking for the Zetetic Society."

"And you have found us." The lady stepped to one side. "Please, this way."

"No, I—I was just leaving. I think I made a mistake."

"If you have come all this way," the woman said, her enunciation precise and slightly clipped, "it is certainly no mistake."

She said it with such simple conviction that Cass was persuaded to agree. "Well, just for a moment, perhaps," she allowed.

Cassandra crossed the threshold and entered the bookshop. The interior was muted—the only light came from the window, and that was filmed with age and dust. But the shop itself was reasonably clean, and the soft furnishings of sofa and overstuffed chairs gave it the feel of an old-fashioned reading room or private library. The woman shut the door and regarded Cass over the top of her glasses. Cass caught a whiff of lavender water.

"What brings you here, if I may be so bold?"

"To Damascus?"

"To the *society*," corrected the woman, stressing the word for emphasis. Before Cass could answer, a shrill whistle sounded from another room. "There's the kettle. Would you like a cup of tea?"

"Um," Cass hesitated.

"I was just going to have one myself. Please, make yourself comfortable. I shan't be a moment."

She hurried away, leaving Cassandra to gaze around the little shop. In addition to the bookshelves lining the walls, there was a round brass table of the kind much favoured in the Middle East, consisting of a tray balanced on a carved olive-wood stand. Two large easy chairs sat on either side of the table and, between them, a floor lamp with a purple silk shade. There was no counter or cash register, which Cass thought odd for a bookshop, nor any other accoutrements of commercial enterprise.

Cass moved to the nearest shelf and took in some of the titles.

The History of the Assyrian Empire . . . A Walk in Old Babylon . . . Life in the Ancient Near East . . . The Lost Treasury of Nebuchadnezzar . . . and other tomes of history, their leather spines creased and cracking with age. She moved along to a section of religious writing: *The Habiru of Palestine . . . The Collected Writings of Josephus . . . The Desert Fathers . . . A Sojourn in the Carpathians . . . Sumerian Culture . . . Who Were the Hittites? . . . The Tombs of Catal Huyuk . . .* and so on.

Presently the woman returned carrying a wooden tray laden with a brass teapot, glass beakers half filled with fresh green leaves, and a plate of tiny almond cookies. She placed the tray on the table and invited Cass to join her. "I hope you like it with mint," she said, and began pouring the hot tea over the leaves. "It is a local custom of which I've grown quite fond." She passed a glass to her guest, settled back in her chair, took a sip, and sighed, "There, that's better."

"Mm," Cass remarked after an exploratory sip. "Delicious."

"There is sugar, if you like." The woman nudged a tiny china bowl. "Where are my manners?" she said, replacing her cup. "I am Mrs. Peelstick."

"My name is Cassandra," replied Cass.

"What a pretty name. I'm very glad to meet you, Cassandra. I don't believe I heard your answer when I asked what brought you here today." She blew on her tea while waiting for a response.

"Well, I guess I was just curious."

The woman nodded and said, "'Curiosity does, no less than devotion, pilgrims make.'"

"Pardon?"

"A scrap of old poem." She stirred sugar into her tea, swirling the green leaves around and around. "After all, we are pilgrims—are we not? Help yourself to biscuits."

Cass reached for one of the small round cookies. It was a relief just to sit and do something normal for a moment—if one considered taking mint tea with an English ex-pat in Damascus in any way normal. "Thank you."

The two sipped their drinks for a moment in silence. From somewhere in the next room a clock chimed the hour. "I hope I'm not keeping you from anything," said Cass. "I was only curious about the society." The old woman made no reply, so Cass, to fill the silence, continued, "Zetetic is an odd word. I don't believe I have ever heard it. What does it mean?"

"It comes from the Greek *zetetikos*—to seek. The Zetetic Society is a society of seekers."

"What do you seek?"

"Ah, *that* is the question." The old woman smiled and sipped her tea. At first Cassandra did not think she would answer, but the woman put down her glass and said, "I suppose one could say something pompous and embroidered. If Brendan were here he would no doubt offer up a phrase such as . . . 'We seek not the treasures of knowledge, but the treasury itself!'" She paused to frame a more considered answer. "Perhaps the simplest way to put it is that we of the society seek answers to life's biggest questions."

"Which questions are those?"

"The usual questions. Why are we here? Where are we going?" The woman paused, leaned a little forward, and regarding Cass meaningfully, added, "What is the true nature of reality?"

"I wish I knew," sighed Cass under her breath. The woman's continued gaze made her uncomfortable. She seemed to be expecting Cass to say something, so she asked, "These books—are they for sale, then?"

"Oh, dearie me, no," the woman replied, retrieving her tea. "They are resource materials."

"I see." Cass nodded, sipping thoughtfully. "But you do have some literature?"

"No, I'm very much afraid that we do not."

"Nothing about the society—its aims, beliefs, membership requirements?"

"You make us sound very grand—very grand, indeed. No, I'm afraid we're just a small congregation of oddballs and eccentrics dedicated to the quest. There are no formal requirements." She hesitated, again regarding Cass with that direct, appraising look. "No formal requirements other than finding your way to our door."

"That's it? That's all? A potential member only has to find his way to this shop?"

"What made you think this was a shop?" she asked, picking up the brass teapot. "More, dear?"

Cass offered her glass. "Thank you."

"As I was saying, there are no membership requirements because, you see, we find that only those who wish to become members of the society would bother inquiring at all."

"Your membership is self-selecting," mused Cass. "Then I suppose it must be a very large society."

"Why would you think that?" wondered the woman. "True seekers are very rare. Those willing to pay the price to join the quest are rarer still." She shook her head. "No, we are a small, rather exclusive group. But the exclusion is not on our side, I assure you. People either choose to join us or not. Mostly, we find, they do not."

"That's a shame," quipped Cass. "At very least they'd get a nice cup of mint tea."

"They would indeed, dear."

Cassandra finished her cup and placed it on the tray. She stood. "Thank you for the chat, and for the tea. You're very kind, but I really must be going. I didn't intend to take up your morning."

"Didn't you?" wondered the woman. "Then why did you come?"

"The poster," explained Cass. "I saw the poster—the orange one?—at the entrance to the bazaar. I thought it sounded interesting, so I came."

The old woman placed her glass on the tray and faced her visitor, her gaze pointed and uncomfortably direct. After a moment she said, "Would it surprise you very much if I told you that not everyone can see that poster?"

"Because it's written in English, you mean?"

"I did not say they could not read it," replied the woman, adopting a pedantic tone. "I said they cannot *see* it. Our little advertisement is effectively invisible to all who are not ready and willing to see it. You, my dear, *are* ready—otherwise you would not be here."

Cass felt a queasy apprehension squirm over her. "I'm not sure I understand what you mean."

"I mean exactly what I said. No more. No less." Her smile became tight and sharp. "Do you think I cannot tell who and what you are?"

Anxious now to terminate the interview and leave, Cass said, "Well, I really must be going." She rose and stepped backward, edging towards the door. "It was nice meeting you."

"And you as well." The old woman rose and followed her. "But I have a suspicion that we shall be meeting one another again very soon."

Cassandra nodded. Moving quickly to the door, she fumbled with the doorknob, twisted it, pulled open the door, and stepped outside.

The woman followed her as far as the threshold. "There is a

convent not more than a hundred paces farther on. It is run by the Sisters of Saint Tekla, and they offer beds and simple fare to pilgrims of all faiths or none." She gestured vaguely farther along. "If you have no place to stay, I recommend them without reservation."

"Thank you," said Cass. "Good-bye."

"God be with you."

Cass stepped away quickly and started off down the narrow, meandering street, aware that the woman was watching her until she was out of sight. A few dozen paces later she saw a small red-and-white sign hanging into the street from its place over a wrought iron gate. The sign read *Le couvent des soeurs de Sainte Tekla*, and had a cross in the shape of a capital T with crossed palm fronds beneath it. In small letters at the bottom were the words *Troisième section*. Another sign in Arabic featured the same crossed palms and capital T. Slowing her pace as she neared the gate, Cass heard children laughing, the sound drifting up over the convent walls. Although she had no intention of asking for a bed in a convent, Cass paused to look through the gate.

She saw a plain, paved stone courtyard surrounding a neat, white church with small stained-glass windows and wide, brown, nail-studded doors. In one corner of the courtyard a handful of young girls were playing some sort of game with an older woman dressed in a voluminous blue gown topped with a long white headscarf—one of the sisters, Cass decided. Two other nuns were sweeping the already clean-swept courtyard with branches of natural green broom bound together around short handles. The scene looked so homely and happy that Cass lingered longer than she intended.

"*Puis-je vous aider?*"

The voice and face suddenly appearing at the gate startled Cass. She took a step back. "Sorry! No—I was just passing."

The face was that of a young woman about her own age with large dark eyes and dark hair beneath a tight-fitting white scarf; she was dressed in the habit of the nuns. *"Parlez-vous l'anglais?"* she asked, her voice rising gently.

"Oui," confirmed Cass. *"Mon français . . .* is . . . um—*est très petit."*

The nun offered a blithe smile. "Then we speak English together," she declared in a workmanlike, if heavily French-tinted accent. "Would you like to come in, *mon amie?"*

The invitation was so kindly and innocently offered that, as the iron gate swung open, Cass found herself stepping into the courtyard. To one side of the church grew a palm tree; a fig tree with broad green leaves shaded a simple wooden bench upon which another nun sat shelling peas into a big brass bowl.

"Welcome to Saint Tekla's," said the nun, closing the gate once more. "I am Sister Theoduline."

"I am glad to meet you, Sister," replied Cassandra. "Please, call me Cass." She glanced around the neat yard. "What kind of church is this—if you don't mind my asking?"

"Non," replied the sister. "We are not only a church. As you see, we are also a *couvent*—an order of nuns and some lay sisters. We belong to a Syriac order. Very old. One of the oldest. Would you care to take some refreshment with me?"

"Thank you, no," declined Cass. "I had some tea at the Zetetic Society." Then, feeling the need to explain, she added, "Actually, I am just passing through. I won't be staying."

"No?" wondered the nun. "That is a pity. Damascus has many wonderful places to visit—including Saint Tekla's. Come, I will show you."

Cass spent a pleasant half hour examining the church with its garish icons and, in the buildings behind it, the orderly little school and dormitory.

"We operate an orphanage for girls," Sister Theoduline explained. "So many children lost their parents in the revolt, and to disease. We have twenty-seven girls with us, and thirty-three more at Ma'aloula, our parent *couvent*."

"I see," replied Cass. "They seem happy here. I am sure you are doing a very good work."

"Pray God this is so," agreed the nun. "But caring for orphans is a secondary service, you might say. We were originally charged with aiding and providing hospitality to pilgrims on their way to and from the holy sites here in Damascus and beyond." She sighed. "We get so few pilgrims these days—times being what they are. If you have nowhere else to go, you are most welcome to stay here with us during your sojourn in Damascus." She offered a hopeful smile. "It would support our mission simply to have you here."

Cass thanked her, but said, "I don't expect to be in Syria very long."

"Oh, I thought you said you had been visiting the Zetetic Society, *n'est-ce pas?*"

"I did, yes, but—" She paused, then changed tack. "Excuse me, why do you ask?"

"We have, from time to time, extended hospitality to the society members. They are very fascinating people. If you are with them, you must be fascinating too, I think."

"I don't know about that," replied Cass diffidently. "I'm not really with them—that is, I'm not a member of the society."

"Oh," remarked Theoduline. "Forgive my presumption." Her smile returned instantly. "But you are still very welcome to stay with us if you wish—however long your visit."

"Thank you," said Cass. Considering that she had nowhere else to go and no money anyway, she surprised herself by saying, "I think I would like that."

This pleased the young nun, who offered to show her to a room at once—a small, clean, cell-like apartment with a bed and table, a chair, and a bright Persian rug on the floor beside the bed. On one wall was a plain wooden cross, and on the other a painting of a young woman in a flowing robe, a halo around her head. Cass took one look at the painting and felt her stomach tighten. The young woman in the painting was making her way between two towering walls of stone— unmistakably a canyon.

It was such a vivid depiction of what Cass herself had experi- enced that she felt an instant connection to the woman; she stepped closer to inspect it in more detail.

Sister Theoduline, who had been instructing her about soap and clean towels, noticed her interest and moved to her side. "That is Saint Tekla," she explained. "Do you know the story?"

Cass confessed that she did not.

"It is quite interesting," the sister said, and went on to tell the leg- end of the Syrian saint who, as a young woman, became a Christian and was baptised by Saint Paul. One day she was being pursued— perhaps by a ruthless suitor because of her exceptional beauty, or perhaps owing to her refusal to abandon her faith and bow to the emperor—the reason was not entirely clear. But having fled into the wild hills, she found her way blocked by a steep impasse of stone. "Tekla offered up a prayer, and miraculously a way opened through the stone—a *sentier*. You know this word?"

Cass shook her head.

"It is like a path—a small road—a *crevasse*."

"I see," murmured Cass, transfixed by the picture. "A path through the rocks."

"*Oui,*" agreed the nun. "Tekla fled into the rocks and disappeared. Her pursuers were never able to find her. Later she returned to establish one of the first churches in Syria. And it is still there," concluded Theoduline. "It is at Ma'aloula."

"The same place as the orphanage?"

"The same, yes. It is our mother church."

"A fine story," replied Cass, her mind racing freely along trajectories of extreme improbability. Later, after a nap and a ramble through the city, then a simple supper of soup, bread, olives, and hummus, followed by a sung evensong by the nuns and their young charges, Cass retired to her room and ended her eventful day sitting on the edge of her bed and meditating on the painting of the beautiful young Christian fleeing through the canyon of stone. She went to sleep thinking she knew very well the makings of Tekla's miracle. The neophyte saint had stumbled upon her own Secret Canyon and, like Cass herself, had travelled a Sacred Road to become a World Walker.

CHAPTER 20

In Which a Good Doctor Is Hard to Find

L ondon in the year 1818 took some getting used to but, thankfully, the layout of the main thoroughfares had not been altered since the Romans first laid them down over the footpaths made by the Celts along the wide rolling river known to the locals at the time as *Afon Tamesas*, but now known as the Thames River. Wilhelmina did not know the original name of the river, but not many did. As the coach rumbled over the engineering marvel that was the London Bridge, Mina shook her head at the multitude of water conveyances on show below. Boats of every size and description filled the grey water: ferry boats, both oar-driven and coal-powered; steamboats pulling barges loaded with cargo; sailboats, from ocean-going schooners with crews of a hundred to single-manned ketches; ironclad warships bristling with guns; sleek pleasure boats with striped canopies; tug boats, tenders, and taxis plying the waters looking for employment . . . so many boats that Mina imagined she could have hopscotched across the water from the Embankment to South Bank one boat deck at a time.

Nor were the city streets less crowded. As with the water, every manner of land vehicle ever invented seemed to want to cross the bridge at the same time. Horse-drawn coaches and carriages accounted for most of the traffic, but there were also carts aplenty; Wilhelmina counted no fewer than forty-nine handcarts, seventeen donkey carts, nine mule carts, eight goat carts, five horse carts, and a dozen or so pulled by dogs. Foot traffic filled in every available gap, and Mina thought it a wonder pedestrians were not continually falling beneath moving wheels of one sort or another.

When the coach finally reached its destination, Wilhelmina disembarked and was pleased to find that she recognised some of the more familiar city landmarks such as Blackfriar's Bridge and the Tower of London; navigating her way around would not pose undue difficulty—providing she knew where to find Thomas Young. The only scrap of information she possessed was that he was a member of the Royal Society. Find the society, she reckoned, and with any luck that would lead to the good doctor.

Thanks to her judicious purchases at M&S, she blended in well enough with the other pedestrians as she walked along the road she knew as Victoria Street, heading towards Whitehall. As she came in sight of the Palace of Westminster, she saw a line of street vendors selling everything from tortoise shell combs to sugared almonds; they were standing by their handcarts pestering passersby with their sales pitches. The nearest one was selling ribbons; he, like many of the others, had bushy sideburns and a droopy moustache and was plying his wares with gusto.

"Good day to you, sir," Wilhelmina said nicely. "A bit of the red, please." She pointed to a glistening spool of crimson satin.

"Right away, miss." He fetched the spool and produced a pair of scissors from his apron pocket. "How much would 'ee like?"

"Oh, about—so much." She held out her hands a few inches apart. "How much would that be?"

"Well, this red is very dear, it is. Comes all the way from China, don't you know." He held the shears, ready to snip.

"How much?"

"Thruppence, miss. A'right?"

Mina nodded. She fished around in her sack of coins for three pennies—grateful once more for Cosimo's thoughtfulness in providing some ready cash. The ribbon man snipped and rolled the ribbon carefully. "That'un won't run in the rain, miss."

"Thank you." She paid the man and pocketed the ribbon. "I was wondering if perhaps you could tell me how to find the Royal Society?"

"Eh? Royal Society, is it?"

"Please." She batted her eyelashes. "If you could point me in the right direction, I would be much obliged."

"Much obliged, is it?" Removing his cap, he looked her up and down. "Well, if I was wantin' to find the Royal Society, I would just trot along the way you're going like, and when I got a little way past Whitehall Palace, I'd start asking folk around there the way to Somerset House. It ent far."

"Somerset House," echoed Wilhelmina.

"That's where they keep it, my darlin'."

"My thanks, sir. You have been a gentleman."

The compliment made the fellow smile; he raised his hat to her, which brought a hoot from his near neighbour. "Hoo! Lookit Sweet William there!"

Wilhelmina blew the fellow a kiss and resumed her walk and, following the ribbon seller's advice, was soon standing outside the pale stone façade of the sprawling edifice of Somerset House—an impressive, imposing pile built right on the Thames so that visitors could arrive and depart by boat. The size of the place and the overpowering grandeur took her aback somewhat, and she spent a moment planning her assault. Then, with a plan firmly in mind, she made her way to the nearest of several doors off the street, pushed through, and found herself in a large garden. An arched entrance stood across the courtyard, which she crossed before entering the main building. She was immediately met by a man in the black livery of a servant, who demanded to know her business.

"I am looking for Dr. Thomas Young," she replied simply.

The doorman regarded her sceptically. "Women are not permitted entry," he intoned dryly.

"I do not wish to *join* the society," Mina said crisply. "I merely wish to speak to Dr. Young. I have it on good authority that he is a member of the society."

"Indeed, madam," confirmed the servant. "Dr. Young is the current president of the Royal Society." He tilted his head so that he looked down his nose. "It is my opinion that he would not wish to be disturbed."

"I thank you most kindly for your opinion, to be sure," countered Mina sweetly. "But I believe that the good doctor himself will be the best judge of whether he wishes to see someone who brings him valuable scientific information." She had made up that last bit, but thought she could back up the claim in any case. "Now, if you will be so kind as to tell me where I might find him, we will put your ill-considered theory to the test." She gave the man a superior smile. "Shall we?"

Perhaps unaccustomed to dealing with such stroppy, head-strong females as the one standing before him, the doorman quickly acquiesced, saying, "I regret to inform you that Dr. Young is not in residence, madam. But if I were of a mind to locate him, I would inquire at his medical practise, the offices of which are to be found in Harley Street."

"There, now," said Wilhelmina. "That wasn't so difficult, was it?" She thanked the fellow for his help and was soon making her way to Harley Street, the traditional home of London's medical establishment. She located Dr. Young's offices by reading the large brass nameplates outside the doors and went inside, where she was politely informed that Dr. Young was away on one of his scientific expeditions.

"He is in Egypt this time of year," the woman explained. "We do not expect him to return before the autumn."

That was that. Wilhelmina was back on the street within two minutes and heading for the nearest café or restaurant where she could collect her thoughts. She found a tidy little eatery on a nearby cross street where she sat with a warm pork pie and pot of tea, contemplating her next move: a visit to Black Mixen Tump. That was the next place listed on the back of the note Cosimo had left for her at the pub in Sefton-on-Sea. She reasoned that if she went there she might find another note, or another clue of some kind. Though where Black Mixen Tump might be—or even *what*—she had no idea, but reckoned a visit to the British Library would give her access to whatever maps or geographical guides were to be found.

Nor was she disappointed. The Ordnance Survey, recently published, contained an exhaustive index that did indeed list the place. It gave precise coordinates to said feature in Oxfordshire, which Wilhelmina copied down, drawing a neat little map of the area for future reference. The day was advancing as she left the library, and the sun, having long since crossed the midday meridian, was now beginning to fade in the west as clouds drew in. To save time and shoe leather she hailed a hansom cab and told the driver to take her to the nearest overland coaching office.

As the cab jostled its way across cobbled streets, Wilhelmina marvelled again at the amount and variety of street life. Pre-Victorian London was veritably awash with a restless tide of surging humanity and a multitude of wheeled conveyances. In her time in Prague, she had grown used to a more mannered, less frenetic pace, and she much preferred it. Still, the sights, sounds, and smells—garbage and horse manure chief among them—occupied her until she reached her destination.

The office was in the stable yard of the George Street Inn across the river in Southwark, where a clerk in a short green jacket and long brown apron advised her that she could go to Oxford and take another coach from there to Banbury and then prevail upon the locals there to help her find the place. "There's only a day coach to Oxford," the clerk told her. "It leaves at crack o'dawn. You're welcome to wait for it here, but if you've got a penny or two, you'll find more comfortable accommodation at yonder inn."

Mina purchased her ticket and, taking the clerk's advice, crossed the stable yard and took a room at the inn. She endured a rather loud supper in noisy company and a rather sleepless night in a flea-infested bed, but was waiting, washed, and breakfasted when the coachman called for passengers to board. There were five, of which Wilhelmina was the only woman; she slept some and made polite conversation with her fellow passengers. The coach reached High Wycombe late in the afternoon, which necessitated another night at an inn, before undertaking the final push to Oxford early the next morning.

After a third night at a coaching inn—this one a cut above the others, in the centre of Oxford—she hired a private carriage to take her to Banbury, where, at the Fox and Geese public house, she was given directions to the tump and a bit of friendly advice from the landlord. "I wouldn't go up there after dark if I was you, miss. It ain't safe—leastwise not for respectable folk."

"Whyever not?" wondered Wilhelmina.

"Strange happenings up there." He frowned and, laying a finger beside his nose, added, "Say no more."

Mina thanked him for his advice and took a light dinner and an early night. The next morning she attempted to hire a coach to take her to the tump, but when that failed, she set off on foot. Armed with her sketched map and a packed lunch provided by the innkeeper, and aided by a well-marked track and a fresh, bright day, she had no difficulty finding her way.

Seeing it for the first time as a shadowy, hulking mass against the yellow sky gave the place a weird, menacing cast that brought her up short. She stood in the farmers' track and stared at the dread Black Mixen as at an apparition. Something about the shape—so unnaturally perfect with its smooth tapering sides and perfectly flat, level top surmounted by three aged oaks twisted and gnarled by time—suggested sinister rites and unspeakable practises. Despite the fine afternoon sunlight all around, the tump itself seemed steeped in perpetual shadow, brooding and ominous.

Mina retrieved her ley lamp from a pocket and held it up, as if it were a flashlight and Black Mixen a darkness to be illuminated. There was no sign of activity from the device, so she stowed it away again and found a dry place under a tree to sit down and relieve her feet. There was no telling what she might find on the other side; it was best to rest while she could. She opened the cloth square containing her lunch and started in on the brown bread and thick slab of pale cheese the innkeeper had prepared for her. After that, she peeled the boiled egg and had a bit of the pork pie; she also had a bottle of small beer and an apple. She ate slowly, and the afternoon dwindled around her; then, much refreshed by the meal, she resumed her assault on Black Mixen Tump.

Upon reaching the base of the hill, she saw a narrow footpath spiralling up the side of the mound and followed it to the top. The way was steep, but she soon reached the summit and paused a moment to catch her breath. The high plateau gave unobstructed views of the countryside all around, and Wilhelmina walked all the way around the perimeter but saw no one about. *So much the better*, she thought. If she was going to experiment with ley travel on the tump, she did not want an audience.

She took out the ley lamp once more—still no activity, so she conducted a closer examination of her surroundings. This was quickly accomplished. Apart from the three old oaks, fascinating as they were, there was not much to see—except for a single stone she found embedded in the turf near the centre of the hill. Broad and flat as a paving stone from someone's garden, there was nothing at all remarkable about it. As twilight was a little way off yet, she decided to sit down and wait to see if anything might happen.

She sat, her legs drawn up, her chin resting on her knees, and closed her eyes. Tired from her long walk, she was soon asleep. Fragments of dreams, disjointed and disturbing, flitted through her subconscious. She awoke with a start to the sound of raucous laughter. Looking around, she saw that the sun had gone down and the sky above was filled with circling rooks—their cackling call the disembodied laughter of her dream. Having grown stiff sitting on the stone, she unfolded herself and stood, and instantly became aware of a warmth emanating from her pocket. She took out the ley lamp; it was not only warm to the touch, but the little blue lights were all aglow within the filigreed metallic carapace.

On her initial survey of the tump top, Wilhelmina had detected no indication of a ley line anywhere. Not only that, but there did not seem to be room enough for a line of any length. But the blue lights were aglow, and they did not lie. So, holding the lamp in front of her, she began walking slowly, first one direction, then another, watching the lights. She quickly noticed that the little blue indicators glowed more brightly as she neared the centre of the mound and dimmed as she moved away. The strongest reading came when she stood directly on the flat stone marker.

"This is it," she murmured. "Now what?" How did one traverse a ley that was not a line, but a point?

As she was considering this, she caught a movement out of the corner of her eye and glanced around to see two dark shapes racing towards her across the level plain of the tump. Shielded by the trees until they were almost upon her, she had but a glimpse, but it was enough to know that they were after her.

Whipping the ley lamp out of sight, she turned to meet her pursuers.

"Oi!" shouted the nearest one. "Stand right there! Don't you move a muscle, me darlin'!"

Wilhelmina felt a sudden surge of energy flash up around her. The hair on her arms and the back of her neck stood erect. She could feel the tingle on her skin and a faint crackling of static snapping around her ankles. The very air tingled.

The men rushed closer. Dressed in long, dark cloaks and wide-brimmed hats, their faces grim and determined, they closed on her with swift strides. One of them produced a pistol. "Put your hands up, girly," he ordered.

His companion threw out a hand, caught his arm, and spun him around. "Don't tell her that!" he cried. "That sets it off!"

But it was already too late. At the sight of the gun, Wilhelmina had instinctively raised her hands. Her fingers tingled with the pent power flowing around her. She raised her arms higher, the air grew misty, and she saw the disbelief register on the men's faces. One of them let out a shout, but his words were lost in the scream of the wind suddenly swirling around her.

The world grew hazy and her vision quavered and she was enveloped by the shimmery, glowing halo of high-energy photons—an earthbound aurora borealis. At the same time she became aware that pressure was building around her, crushing down, squeezing the air from her lungs. Instinctively she resisted, holding herself upright. Burleigh's two thugs made a rush towards her. She gave a little hop, and the world winked out in a fizzing pop like that of a firecracker tossed into the air.

Mina blinked, and when she opened her eyes again she was standing in the dazzling white light of a blistering sun on a wide, stone-paved path lined on either side with statues, hundreds of them, stretching for a thousand metres or more, each one with the head of a man and the body of a lion—an avenue of sphinxes. One look at the impassive granite face gazing at her from the nearest statue and Wilhelmina Klug knew beyond any doubt that she had arrived in Egypt.

PART FOUR

The Omega Point

CHAPTER 21

In Which Time Is Measured in Empires Crumbled to Dust

Somewhere between shutting her eyes and opening them again on the new day, Cass had changed her mind and decided that instead of trying to find her way home by herself, she would to return to the Zetetic Society. They were offering help, after all, and help was what she needed right now. If they could describe for her what was happening and how it worked—well, that was well worth hanging around an extra day to find out. While she still had no intention of joining them, or getting mixed up in their mysterious machinations, whatever they were, simply getting a few answers to some questions— like: what was the best and quickest way home—would be no bad thing.

That decided, Cassandra shared a noisy breakfast with the nuns and orphans of Saint Tekla's and helped with clearing and washing the dishes. Then, free to follow her bliss for the day, she started off for her visit to the society. At the convent gate, one of the sisters approached with a thin cotton robe of drab green. *"Pour vous, mon amie,"* she said, holding out the garment.

"For me?" wondered Cass. "But—"

"S'il vous plaît," insisted the nun. *"C'est mieux, ma soeur."* She pointed to Cass's clothes and held out the gown for her to put on. It came to Cass that it was the same kind of drab robe she had seen on women going into the bazaar—less than a burka, but more than a house-dress—that would, in her case, be useful for keeping her modern dress covered. She understood then that the sisters, having noticed her odd garb, were trying to protect her from difficulty.

"Merci," said Cass, accepting the robe. She allowed the nun to help her into it. *"Cella-là est bonne, ma soeur. Merci."*

Smiling, the nun also arranged Cass's cotton scarf into a more convincing head covering, then opened the gate for her. *"Bonne journée."*

Cass wished her a good day and, stepping through the gate and into the street beyond the walls, made her way back to the society's black lacquered door. She knocked once, waited, then knocked again. When there was no answer, she knocked a third time and waited some more. *Still too early*, she thought, and deciding to try again later, she spun on her heel and started off to explore a little more of Damascus. Deep in thought, she reached the end of the lane and rounded the corner onto the busy main street—where she collided heavily with a tall, thin man in a three-piece suit of pale cream linen topped off with a natty white panama hat.

Cass was thrown backward into the road. The man hooked her elbow to keep her from falling.

"Steady there." He helped her to right herself, then moved back a step and regarded her with the disinterested concern of a stranger. "Are you quite all right, miss?"

"Yes—fine," she said, embarrassed. "Very sorry. I wasn't watching where I was going."

He glanced beyond her in the direction from which she had come. "You've been to the society."

"I have. Yes," she said as if this explained everything. She made to edge past him and move on.

"Rosemary said there was someone yesterday. Was that, by chance, you?" He spoke matter-of-factly, and Cass placed a soft Irish accent.

"I suppose it was," she allowed. "Are you one of *them*?"

He chuckled. "We're not as bad as all that, I hope." Before Cass could draw breath to apologise, the thin man smiled and offered his hand. "Brendan Hanno at your service," he said, his light Irish burr going down like butter. She took the offered hand and clasped it diffidently. "And you are?" he asked.

"My name is Cassandra."

"Yes," he replied pleasantly. "I expect it would be. I was on my way to the society just now. Would you like to accompany me? We can have a cup of tea and see if we can find answers to all your questions." He gestured towards the lane. "Shall we?"

Cass fell into step beside him. "How do you know I have questions?"

"Everyone who comes to us has questions," he observed mildly. "I have a few myself—such as, how do you find Damascus?"

"It's nice," replied Cass lamely. "I've never seen any place like it. Then again, I've only been here a day, and I haven't seen very much."

"Well, we must do something about that," he said. "To know Syria is to love Syria."

They reached the society entrance, and Brendan fumbled a key out of his pocket and into the lock, opened the door, and beckoned her in, snapping on electric lights as he went. From somewhere they could hear a warbly humming. "That will be Mrs. Peelstick making tea. We live on tea, it seems. Take a seat, and I will tell her we're here."

Cass sat down in one of the damask-covered overstuffed chairs and took in the room once more—the shelves of books, the old-fashioned sitting room furniture, the dusty windows barred to the street.

A moment later Brendan poked his head back into the room to announce that they would take their refreshment in the courtyard. "This way, please. It is far more pleasant outside."

He led her along a high-ceilinged corridor to a door that opened onto a commodious enclosed courtyard of the distinctive black-and-white-banded stone. The square, paved yard was open to the sky, but half shaded by a striped canvas awning. The air was cool and fresh and alive with the gentle tinkling splash of a small octagonal fountain standing in the centre of the courtyard; the bowl of the fountain was covered in a blanket of red rose petals floating on the surface of the water. A tall potted palm stood in a large terracotta pot in one corner, and in another stood a round teak table beneath a square blue umbrella.

"It is so very pleasant this time of day," Brendan observed, waving Cass to a seat. Presently the woman from the day before appeared with a tray full of tea things. "I think you have met Mrs. Peelstick," announced Brendan.

"Yes, good morning, Mrs. Peelstick," replied Cass.

"Please, call me Rosemary."

"Rosemary, then. I am sorry if yesterday I seemed somewhat . . . brittle. I am still a bit uncertain about all this."

"Understandable, dear," replied the woman. "Think nothing of it."

"Rosemary has been with the society since its inception," explained Brendan with a teasing smile.

"Nonsense!" scoffed the woman lightly. "Not by a long chalk." She bent to the teapot and began the ritual of pouring black tea into glasses containing fresh mint leaves. Passing a glass to Cass, she said, "I want you to know that you are among friends. From now on we will treat one another like the friends we hope to become."

"In short," continued Brendan, completing the thought, "we will speak frankly."

"Please," replied Cass, taking a sip of hot minty tea. "I welcome it."

The sun was warm, and the palm fronds rustled gently in the light breeze. Small white butterflies flitted here and there among the jasmine strands growing up the courtyard wall. Cass felt the anxiety and trepidation that had marked her first visit melting away. Inexplicably, everything seemed right and in order; all was as it should be—although nothing much, really, had changed at all.

They drank their tea, and Cass listened to the Irishman talk about the courtyard and the building the society maintained and how they had come to own it. He described what it was like to live in Damascus—a place that, as he said, "In the immortal words of Mark Twain, measured time not in hours or days or even years, but in empires that arose and flourished and crumbled to dust."

Finally they came back around to the reason for Cassandra's visit. "We know you are a traveller," Mrs. Peelstick said, "a traveller for whom time and space are little impediment. Otherwise, you would not be here. That is a fact. It is also a fact that there are only two ways to become such a traveller: either you are initiated by another traveller, or you are simply born with the ability—passed on, perhaps, genetically. The former is the usual way; the latter is more rarely the case."

Brendan, nodding slowly, added, "One means confers no great benefit over the other, although those born with the ability to leap from one dimensional reality to another may be physically more sensitive to the active mechanisms involved." He fixed her with a quizzical expression. "Which sort of traveller are you, Cassandra?"

"So far as I know," she answered thoughtfully, "no one in my family has ever experienced anything like this. I think I would have heard about it if they had. I guess I was initiated."

"By whom, may I ask, were you initiated?"

"A man—a Native American. We call him Friday."

"You knew this fellow well, did you?"

"Not well, no. We worked together sometimes, is all. He was a member of an archaeological dig that I was—that I *am*—involved with in Arizona." She thought a moment. "But I don't think you could call it an initiation at all," she said. "I followed him into a canyon near the site one day and . . . it just happened."

Brendan sipped his tea. "That must have been something of a shock for you."

"It was," Cass agreed. "It still is. I don't even know how I ended up here."

"You have a gift—or have been given one," said Rosemary. "Either way, it amounts to the same thing in the end. You are now an astral traveller."

"I like the term *inter-dimensional explorer*," put in Brendan, "because it carries no unfortunate occult overtones. You simply cannot imagine the amount of blather and nonsense that has crept into the subject over the years."

"And always, it seems, by people who do not know the first thing about it," Mrs. Peelstick said, extending a plate of tiny, round sesame-seed-and pistachio biscuits. "Try one; they are delicious."

246

"Much of that nonsense is useful, of course," observed Brendan, his Irish lilt dancing, "for it obfuscates the subject sufficiently to protect our work."

"Protect it?" wondered Cass. "Why does your work need protecting?"

"This would merely be a somewhat arcane, not to mention fool-hardy, pursuit if it did not serve a far greater purpose," Brendan told her. "It is not too much to say that the future of humankind may depend on the work of the society. We are engaged in a project of such importance to humankind that its success will usher in the final consummation of the universe."

"Gosh!" remarked Cass; to her embarrassment it sounded like sarcasm, which she had not intended.

Brendan paused, gauging her receptiveness to hear what came next. "I suppose it does sound a little overblown," he admitted, "but it is true nonetheless. In short, the Zetetic Society was formed to offer aid and support to our members who are engaged in a very particular project. Our aim is nothing less than achieving God's own purpose for His creation."

"And what *purpose* would that be?" Again, Cass hoped her response was not an offense to these kind and hospitable—and probably delusional—people.

Mrs. Peelstick fielded the question. "Why, the objective mani-festation of the supreme values of goodness, beauty, and truth, grounded in the infinite love and goodness of the Creator," she con-cluded, her tone suggesting that this should be obvious.

"Human beings are not a trivial by-product of the universe," Brendan continued. "Rather, we—you, me, everyone else—all human-kind is the reason the cosmos was created in the first place."

"I am familiar with the anthropic principle," Cass replied. It was a favourite hobbyhorse of her father. "The theory that the universe was designed to bring about human life—that the universe exists not only *for* us, but *because* of us."

"Succinctly put," commended Brendan. "You do know your cosmology."

"My dad is an astrophysicist." Cass lifted a shoulder diffidently. "I might have picked up a few things."

"We go further," said Mrs. Peelstick. "We extend the principle to say that the universe was conceived and created as a place to grow and perfect independent conscious agents and fit them for eternity."

"Independent conscious agents," echoed Cass softly. "Human beings, you mean."

"Yes, dear—human beings."

"Why, one might ask?" said Brendan. "What is the aim, the purpose for such an elaborate scheme?"

"That," Cass suggested, "is where all the controversy begins."

"Truly," agreed Brendan. "Our view is that the aim of the process of creating all these independent conscious agents is to promote the formation of harmonious communities of self-aware individuals capable of knowing and enjoying the Creator, and joining in the ongoing creation of the cosmos." He paused, then added with a shrug, "In a nutshell."

Cass bit her lip. This sort of talk always made her uneasy: the grand claims of visionaries, charlatans, and madmen sounded very much alike to her. She had had a bellyful of that in Sedona, and before that from various cranks with whom her father had, at one time or another in his career, chosen to entertain. She was fed up with their quasi-scientific and irrational beliefs.

"I see we're confusing you," Brendan observed. "Perhaps we should start again." He bent his head in thought, pressing his fingertips together beneath his chin. Then, brightening suddenly, he asked, "Have you ever heard of the Omega Point?"

"Not as such," Cass replied. She searched her memory, then shook her head. "No."

"The Omega Point is conceived as the end of time and the beginning of eternity, the point at which the purpose of the universe is finally and fully realised. When the universe reaches the point where more people desire the union, harmony, and fulfilment intended by the Creator, then the balance will have been tipped, so to speak, and the cosmos will proceed to the Omega Point—that is, its final consummation. The universe will be transformed into an incorruptible, everlasting reality of supreme goodness."

"Heaven, in other words," Cass concluded.

"Yes, but not another realm or world," corrected Mrs. Peelstick. "*This* world, *this* universe, transfigured—the New Heaven and the New Earth. It will be a place of eternal celebration of God's love and goodness where we will live and work to achieve the full potential for which humanity was created."

"Which is?" wondered Cass, acutely aware that she had managed to sound sarcastic again.

Mrs. Peelstick returned her wondering glance as if to say, *Don't you know?*

"I'm not trying to be difficult," blurted Cass. "I'd really like to hear your theory."

"Human destiny," replied Mrs. Peelstick, "lies in the mastery of the cosmos for the purpose of creating new experiences of goodness, beauty, and truth for all living things."

"And," added Brendan quickly, "extending those values into the rest of the universe at large. You see, the universe as it exists now is but Phase One, you might say—it is where living human souls are generated and learn the conditions of consciousness and independence. The ultimate fulfilment of the lives so generated, however, will only be found in the next phase of creation—a transformation we can hardly imagine."

Cass shook her head. Clearly, she had paddled into deep water—but what did any of it have to do with inter-dimensional travel or, come to that, with her?

"The quest for the Skin Map is merely the beginning," said Mrs. Peelstick. "But there is so much more."

"The Skin Map?" wondered Cass.

"Has no one mentioned that?" asked Brendan.

Cass shook her head. "Not in so many words."

"Well then, I will tell you a story, shall I? Many years ago a man named Arthur Flinders-Petrie—"

Mrs. Peelstick put up a hand. "Please, spare the poor girl."

"Mrs. P. has heard all this a time or two before," Brendan confided.

"Yes, and I don't need to hear it again now." She gave them both a sunny smile. "If you two will excuse me, I am going to pick up some things at the grocer's—and if you will take my advice, you will get out and enjoy this beautiful day. Cass has never seen Damascus. Why not show her around the Old Quarter, Brendan?"

"That is a splendid idea, Rosemary. I'll do just that."

"Good." Rosemary started away. "Don't wear her out with your ramblings, Brendan—you know how you are—and try not to be too late. I'll have a nice supper ready when you return."

CHAPTER 22

In Which Despair Gives Birth to Audacity

The journey to Black Mixen Tump always filled Charles Flinders-Petrie with dread. Although the gentle hills of the Cotswold countryside appeared benign enough, it was the destination that cast a pall over all that went before. He felt it now—and he could not even see the great mound from the window of his carriage. But it was there, hidden from view, waiting for him. The thought made his heart skip a beat.

Almost fifty years had passed since his father, Benedict, had introduced him to the infamous mound—and still the thing occupied a baleful place in his psyche. An earthwork of incalculable age, the tump had been raised by the hands of primitive labourers using nothing more than deer-antler picks and reed baskets. Why this primitive society thought it necessary to build yet another hill in a landscape of nothing *but* hills remained a mystery. "The Age of the Monument

Builders," murmured Charles to himself. An age, so far as he could tell, that was rife with mysteries of every kind.

The carriage lurched and took the turning in the road, leaving behind the village of Banbury, and Charles regretted his decision to come to this godforsaken place. Even more, he regretted that the decision was necessary. But something had to be done. His last exchange with Douglas had made that abundantly clear.

The boy had always been headstrong; as a child he had been willful, wayward, intractable. Charles, bereft after the death of his dear wife in childbirth, despaired of the boy's rebellious and destructive nature and packed him off to boarding school in the hope that a stern institution would instil the discipline he himself was unable to generate. Stoneycroft School had made the lad more mannered and well behaved, to be sure; but it had also made him far more devious. That, combined with a self-confidence bordering on reckless audacity, cast Douglas as a most formidable adversary to anyone or anything that crossed him. In short, from a selfish, unbearable youth, Douglas was fast becoming a cunning, implacable, and dangerous young man.

"I do *not* see what difference a piece of paper makes anyway," Douglas had complained during their last in a long series of confrontations. "Nothing they teach is any use on the quest. Anyway, it is my birthright." He glared at his father. "Or will you deny me that—as you have denied me everything else?"

Charles exploded. "Ingrate! How can you say that? In all good conscience, how can you possibly even think it? I have denied you nothing." Rising from his chair, he began pacing about the parlour. "All I ask is that you gain a little more learning, apply yourself to your studies, show me you can achieve something through your own efforts." He looked at Douglas' sullen face and saw he was not getting through to his unruly son. He tried another tack. "You are not stupid, Douglas. In fact, in many ways you are amongst the most intelligent persons I know. If you were to apply even the smallest portion of your native wit and mind to your studies, you would achieve wonderful things.

"Listen, I've secured your place at Christ Church, and all is arranged," Charles continued. "Three years is nothing—you'll be busy, make new friends, and establish associations that will serve you through the rest of your life. If you apply yourself, time will pass just like that." Charles clicked his fingers. "On the day you finish your exams, I will personally place the map in your hands."

"Why should I believe you?" grumbled Douglas. "How do I know you'll keep your word?"

"Now, son—that's not fair."

"You should know—you're the one who sold grandfather's collection and gambled away the money. Was that fair?"

"That was wrong. It was a sad and terrible mistake, and I've been paying for it all my life." He thrust out pleading hands. "Douglas, please, try to understand. I know I have kept it from you—I admit as much—but the last thing I wanted was to see you make the same mistakes I made when I was your age."

"So just because *you* failed, now I have to make up for it. Isn't that what you mean?"

"All I want is for you to be prepared. I want you to be better at the quest than I was." He paused. "And yes, I failed. But you have it in you to succeed. To do that you must be thoroughly grounded in language and history. Oxford can give you that."

"And if I refuse to go? What then?"

"It is not as if I am asking the impossible," Charles pointed out. "It is for your own good, after all."

"Since when have you ever known what was *good* for me, Father?" The question was a slap in the face.

"Douglas, there is no cause for—"

"I see it now, Father," he sneered. "*You* get sent down in disgrace, so now I have to go and restore the family name. You tried the quest and failed, so now you want to keep everyone else from even trying."

"This discussion is over," declared Charles, collapsing behind his desk. "I have told you what I expect and what you must do to inherit. You either take up your studies or suffer the consequences."

Douglas rose from his chair, his fists balled at his sides. "You don't frighten me with your threats, old man." He turned and stormed from the room, slamming the door so hard it rattled the lamps on the mantle.

"Douglas!" called Charles after his son. "Come back!"

Another door slammed in the hall, and the house was quiet once more.

Why does it always have to be like this? wondered Charles, shaking his head sadly.

That was a two-year-old argument, and still it rankled. Douglas had taken up his place at Christ Church, but from all Charles was able to learn, his son rarely attended lectures and was never seen in any of the university's libraries. Douglas might as well have been a ghost as far as his tutors were concerned. Then, when the demands for money from the town's merchants and publicans began arriving, Charles read the writing on the wall. He sent pleading letters, one after another . . . letters that went unanswered, never a reply.

Then came the straw that broke the longsuffering camel's back: an urgent message from the college chaplain stating that, along with two other students, Douglas had been arrested for being drunk and disorderly and starting a public affray. The Rev. Philpott indicated that the young miscreant could be released on bail of fifty pounds; otherwise he would be forced to spend time in gaol until the case was called to court.

Filled with despair, Charles had made up his mind before he had even read the signature on the letter. Douglas would remain in gaol and take his chances with the magistrate. He could not count on his father to save his worthless hide this time; it might even do the boy some good to suffer the consequences of his actions. But gaol was at best merely a stopgap, not a solution—and a solution was desperately needed. If Charles was ever to have any peace, he would have to be bold and ruthless—more audacious than he had ever been in his life to now.

He spent three days and nights in intense cogitation, thinking up and then discarding one desperate plan after another until he hit upon an idea that offered the perfect solution. Thus, as the sun rose early in the morning on a clear May day, Charles made the decision that would solve his immediate problem. Unfortunately, this decision, born of despair, would also confound the quest for generations to come.

The carriage jolted back and forth over the rutted road, moving deeper into the countryside. When Charles stirred and looked out the window once more he saw the dark, unnaturally conical shape of the mound looming in the near distance and felt the skin on the back of his neck tingle with apprehension. Black Mixen Tump was only a portal, he told himself. He had used it before; there was nothing to fear.

Charles drew a deep breath and glanced at the flat wooden box beside him on the seat. He pulled the box closer and rested his hand on the polished lid. If ever he needed assurance that he was doing the right thing, he needed it now. "God help me," he whispered. "Give me a sign."

He turned his gaze to the imposing dark mass of the tump and saw the Three Trolls—the ancient oaks growing from the flattened top of the mound. As he watched, three crows rose from the uppermost branches—one from each tree. Was it the sign he had requested?

Charles shrugged. It would have to do.

CHAPTER 23

In Which Kit Plays the Waiting Game

They have *all* gone, you say?" wondered Abbot Cisneros. He raised his eyes from the work on his desk and pushed his glasses up his nose.

"Yes, Your Eminence—all are gone," replied Brother Antolín, the abbot's secretary.

"Where have they gone?" The abbot put down his pen and blew on the ink, still wet on the page before him.

"To the ecumenical conference, Eminence," replied the brother. "The one convened by Cardinal Bernetti."

"The Lucerne Conference, yes, I remember." The abbot picked up his pen once more and waved it in the air. "Is there no one else?"

"It would seem not, Holiness."

The abbot replaced his pen on the desk once more. "Am I to believe that no one else speaks English in this entire abbey? One of our many international visitors, perhaps?"

"We considered that, of course," replied Brother Antolín. "But it was thought unwise to involve outsiders in what may turn out to be a sensitive matter."

"Ah." The abbot picked up his pen yet again. "You are right. Best keep this to ourselves until we know what the outcome might be." He paused, thought for a moment, then wondered, "Have you asked at chapter?"

"I did, Eminence—before bringing it to you. But it seems those possessing a fluency with English are all in attendance at the conference."

"How extraordinary." The abbot resumed writing.

The secretary folded his hands before him and awaited the result of his superior's deliberation.

Presently the Abbot of Montserrat finished the sentence he was writing and asked, "Have you seen this fellow?"

"Yes, Eminence. He appears ordinary enough—though he *is* dressed very oddly."

"Some would say the same of us," observed Abbot Cisneros.

"Indeed, Eminence."

"You say the local police merely dropped him off at the gate with the porter, is that right?"

Brother Antolín nodded. "That is what I understand."

"And no one can be found to speak to him?"

"It is thought that Brother Lazarus knows someone—an occasional assistant, a German nun, I believe—who speaks English."

"Aha!" The abbot raised his pen triumphantly. "Summon the sister and proceed accordingly." He returned to his writing. "Oh—and, brother, I think Prior Donato should deal with this from now on. See that he is informed of all pertinent details."

"Tomas is in Lucerne at the conference, Eminence."

"Of course he is." The abbot waved him away. "Bring word when the matter has been successfully concluded."

"It will be done." Brother Antolín backed from the office, closing the doors as he went, and returned to his own desk in the outer vestibule where a young novitiate was waiting. Addressing the monk, he said, "Abbot Cisneros has decided to leave the matter in my hands for the time being. Take word to Brother Lazarus that I wish him to meet me at the porter's lodge. He is to bring his assistant—the German nun. She will serve as our translator."

After being dropped at the gate by the policeman, Kit had been left in the care of the porter, a squat Spaniard with pudgy hands and the face of a cherub. Kit spent the next few hours idling in the gate-keeper's lodge as a sort of quasi-captive—he was not locked up, nor was he free to go, for every time he got up and tried to leave, the porter came running after him, scolding in Spanish, and he was pushed back into the lodge. Kit was given to know that he was being made to wait until adequate provision could be made for him. In the meantime he was given cool lemon water to drink and some small, dry biscuits. Occasionally church bells sounded, and once a priest came to look at him, exchanged a brief word with the porter, and disappeared again. Kit, none the wiser, was left to himself once more.

There was no point in getting stroppy with the fellow, Kit decided, and in any case getting stroppy in Spanish was quite beyond his abilities. His best option was simply to remain pleasant and compliant, and wait for whatever Providence would toss his way. The waiting continued, and the day drew on towards evening. Then, shortly after the bells in the abbey tower sounded for the third time, Kit heard voices in the gravel yard outside. The door opened, and the gate-keeper motioned for Kit to come out. He was met by three priests: two very large hulks in dusty, worn habits—manual workers, Kit decided—and the priest who had looked in on him earlier.

"Gracias," he said, marshalling the little Spanish he possessed. The priest smiled, patted him on the bare shoulder, and motioned him to follow. Happy to oblige if it meant he could at last leave the confines of the gatehouse, Kit stepped out into a day fading towards evening. The jagged grey peaks, blushing pink in the light of the setting sun, soared high above the abbey precinct, casting all in shadow. The air was already starting to cool with the approach of night.

The little delegation climbed a long, winding boulevard to an enclosed courtyard. One side of the courtyard fronted the great abbey church, which seemed to be carved into the very stone of the mountain; on another side was a grand stone edifice with a baroque façade. Kit was conducted into the building, where a tiled vestibule gave way to a long panelled corridor that smelled of beeswax and wood polish. He was marched to a waiting room that contained nothing but wooden chairs lined up around the perimeter.

"Siéntense, por favor," said the priest.

Kit entered the room, and the door was closed behind him. "What a palaver," he muttered.

Having spent most of the day sitting, he decided to pace instead, and occupied himself with the same questions he had been asking since his arrival. What were they doing? Why couldn't they just let him go? What were the chances of getting a proper shirt and trousers? His animal-skin clothing, in this setting, made him look and feel ridiculous.

He was on his fourth or fifth circuit of the room when he heard voices in the corridor outside. He turned to the door just as it opened to admit an elderly, white-haired priest in a black cassock and a young woman in a crisp grey nun's habit.

"*Mio Dio!*" cried the priest, upon confronting the wild man standing in the doorway. He gave a little jump, colliding with the woman entering behind him. She steadied the priest with a hand and moved around him into the room. Taking in the hairy apparition before her, the nun's mouth fell open and her eyes went wide.

"Wilhelmina!" gasped Kit.

She leaned forward, studying his face. "Kit—is that really you under all that hair?"

"It's me, Mina." He started forward, his arms outstretched to embrace her. "I can't tell you how glad I am to see you."

Her hands flashed up; she reeled back. Kit hesitated. "What are you wearing?" she said. Her face wrinkled. "What *is* that smell?"

"It's a long story," replied Kit. "What are you doing here? Where are we, anyway?"

"Don't you know?"

He shook his head. "Nobody tells me anything."

The white-haired priest, having overcome his shock, stepped forward. "Wilhelmina," he said in German, "do you know this . . . this man?"

Mina turned, grinning with joyful disbelief. "Let me introduce you to my dear friend, Kit Livingstone."

The priest let out a little gasp of amazement. He gaped at Kit, letting his astonished gaze sweep from head to toe and back again. "*Unglaublich!*" he breathed, shaking his head in wonder.

"I know," Wilhelmina agreed, watching Kit as if he might

suddenly vapourise before her eyes. "It is unbelievable—but here he is! All this time we were trying to find him, and—voilà! He finds us. Incredible."

Then, turning suddenly, she grabbed Kit in a fierce hug. "Where *have* you been, my dear, filthy, wild-haired man?"

Kit kissed her cheek and then buried his face in the hollow of her neck. "Oh, Mina," he sighed, surrendering to an overwhelming relief. "It is so good to see you. You don't know—"

"Come on," she said, pushing him away and taking his hand. "Let's get out of here." She cast a glance over her shoulder and spoke German to the priest, who answered, offering his hand, which Kit shook. "This is Brother Lazarus," she said, making a quick introduction. "He is the astronomer here. We'll go up to his quarters—we can talk and we won't be disturbed up there."

She said something else in German, and the priest replied with a nod. To Kit she said, "Brother Lazarus will take care of the details. He will fix things with his superiors and make the necessary arrangements. You are to be his guest."

"Okay," agreed Kit, "but could we eat something first? I haven't eaten since . . . I don't know when."

"Sure—I'll fix you a nice meal," she told him. "But first we're going to get you a bath—and a haircut if possible. I'll have to find some clothes." She regarded Kit's furry trousers and laughed. "How do you feel about a monk's robe?"

They moved into the corridor, where a few curious brothers had gathered outside to catch a glimpse of their unusual visitor. Brother Lazarus called to the onlookers and conducted a brief conference while Wilhelmina steered Kit away.

"Don't worry," she whispered. "He'll take care of everything. He has a fair bit of seniority around here. They all love him and trust him completely. You'll like him too."

Kit nodded. They reached the vestibule and stepped out into a balmy evening where the stars were just beginning to kindle for the night. The ethereal sound of singing reached them on the soft night air—the monks were chanting evensong. Once out of sight of the others, Wilhelmina looped her arm through Kit's and pulled him close.

"Are you really a nun?"

Wilhelmina laughed, her voice full of delight. The sound was delicious in the evening twilight. "Don't be silly. It's a role I play when I come here. The habit just makes everything so much easier." She gave his arm an affectionate squeeze. "A lot less explaining to do."

"It suits you."

Indeed, she was more attractive than ever—and it showed in her figure as well as her face. She had filled out a little and now had curves where before there had been only angles. Her dark eyes fairly gleamed with health and well-being. "You look wonderful."

"You think so?" She smiled, enjoying the compliment. "There's a lot to be said for the convent life. What about you—what's the explanation for what you're wearing?"

"What do you mean? This is the height of fashion where I've come from."

She laughed again. "Look at you! I hardly recognise you under all that hair. You look like a big old bushy bear. What—they didn't have clippers or razors where you were?"

"Actually, no," Kit said, running his fingers through the tangles of his beard.

"And those muscles!" she hooted, giving his biceps a squeeze.

"No more puppy fat. You're positively brawny—a lean, mean fighting machine," she said approvingly. "Whatever they were feeding you, it didn't do you any harm."

"Thanks, I guess." He looked down at his torso. Beneath the layer of smudgy dirt he could see the ripples of a six-pack, and his arms were corded muscle. Now that she mentioned it, he supposed he had trimmed down and bulked out a bit.

"Oh, Kit, it is so good to see you and have you back safe and sound. I've been worried about you. Where have you been, anyway?"

"You won't believe the half of it," Kit replied. "I'm not entirely sure I believe all of it myself." He fell silent, thinking about where to start, or even how to begin to frame an explanation.

"Well?" she said after a moment. "Are you going to keep a girl in suspense?"

"No—no, I don't mean to, it's just . . . I don't even know where to start."

"Well," she said, "the last time I saw you, Burleigh was hot on your tail. He chased you and Giles out of the city, and you made for the river." She went on to describe the chain of events as she knew them. "Giles is okay, by the way. The bullet did no irreparable harm, and as soon as he could move, I took him home. He should be good as new very soon, if not already."

"Good. I'm glad he's okay," mused Kit, and explained how he had come under gunfire but found the ley and made the jump, landing in the place Mina had told him about. "But the time was all off, and I ended up in what I guess you could call the Stone Age."

"That would explain the fur trousers."

"I was found and, well, more or less adopted by a tribe of people— River City Clan, I call them. They live in this enormous gorge—"

"The one I've visited," surmised Mina.

"The same one, but in a different time—far different. Anyway, they are the most amazing people. They don't speak much—they have a very limited vocabulary. They communicate mainly by a sort of telepathy—kind of like a mental radio."

Wilhelmina gave him a sideways glance.

"It's true," he insisted. "I could hardly believe it the first time it happened. But one of them, this incredibly old chieftain called En-Ul—he's a master at it, and he taught me how to—"

He stopped walking—so abruptly that Wilhelmina took two more steps without him. She turned, and he blurted, "Mina, I've been to the Well of Souls."

"You *what?*"

"The Spirit Well," Kit said, his voice ringing in the empty plaza. "I've been there, Mina—I know how to find it."

CHAPTER 24

In Which Communication
Breaks Down

The death of Arthur Flinders-Petrie could not have come at a worse moment. The land was in upheaval, and it was all Pharaoh's fault. If the crisis did not pass soon, the kingdom would descend into civil war.

"You had the misfortune to die at a very bad time, my friend," Anen sighed, then smiled ruefully at the foolishness of his own thought. For the young and healthy, death always arrived at a bad time, did it not?

As senior priest of the Temple of Amun he had scores of minions at his command, yet Anen took charge of the funeral preparations himself out of respect and honour for a friendship that had spanned decades. In his mind, there was no question but that Arthur's body would be embalmed and a suitable tomb made ready. The embalming procedure—from the ritual washing of the corpse with water from

the Nile to its nitre bath and the final anointing with oils and swath-
ing in linen—would require seventy days. Under the circumstances,
it would not be possible to build a tomb in such a short time; therefore, an extension of Anen's personal tomb would be carved out and
painted, and a wooden sarcophagus constructed to hold the earthly
remains of the late Arthur Flinders-Petrie.

This would also give time enough for young Benedict to return to
his home world and break the sad news of his father's decease to his
mother. The two of them could then return to attend the grand funeral
ceremony and oversee the entombment. As head of the Flinders-
Petrie family, Benedict would host the funeral feast. This is how it was
done. This is how it had always been done since time out of mind.
Observing the rituals of life and death in proper order—including the
time-honoured rites of embalming and entombment—brought order
to the affairs of men, which in turn led to order in the universe.

Satisfied that he had thought of everything, he summoned the boy
and, through the use of signs, communicated to Benedict all that must
be done in the days ahead. Benedict appeared to understand, whereupon
Anen ordered a mild sleep-inducing herbal infusion to be prepared and
commanded his personal servants to see the grief-stricken lad to his rest.
He then turned his attention to readying Arthur's corpse for transfer to
Per-Nefer, the House of Embalming, to begin the process of readying it for
life in eternity. As the shroud was being wrapped to secure the body for
transport, however, commotion erupted in the courtyard—accompanied
this time by angry voices from beyond the wall.

Anen stepped from the House of Wholeness and Healing; the
moon was high and bright, spilling light into the sacred enclosure. In
the moonlight he saw priests and temple soldiers milling about the
gates. He hailed one of the servants just then hurrying past. "What is

the reason for this uproar?" he demanded. "I was given to understand that the mob had gone away."

"They dispersed, my master," answered the servant. "The temple guards drove them back to the river."

"Well?" demanded Anen, as if this should have been the end of the matter.

The servant lifted his palms. "They have returned."

With a flick of his hand Anen sent the impertinent fellow on his way and proceeded to the gate, where a group of priests and servants had gathered. "Where is Tutmose?" he demanded, scanning the crowd quickly for the commander of the temple guard. "He should be dealing with this breach of the peace."

"Commander Tutmose is out there," explained the nearest priest. He turned and saw that it was Anen who addressed him. He bowed low. "My master, I did not know—"

"Outside the gates?" he said, cutting off his subordinate's instinctive apology.

"He went out to talk to them," said the priest. "To find out why they are doing this and demand that they leave us in peace."

Anen cocked his head to one side, listening to the hubbub of voices from over the wall. "Tell the commander I wish to see him as soon as he returns. I will await him in my chamber."

The priest bowed low, and Anen took his leave, returning to his rooms in the palatial Prophet's House. He bathed and dressed in a clean robe, then lay down on his bed. He had just closed his eyes when he heard swift footsteps in the corridor outside his sleeping chamber. His housemaster came padding into the room an instant later, saying, "Loath as I am to disturb you, my master, Commander Tutmose has returned with word of the uprising."

"Bid him enter." Anen rose and stood ready to receive the chief of the guards.

"The wisdom of Amun Ascendant be yours, master," said Tutmose, entering on the heels of the servant. He bowed and waited to be addressed.

"What news?" said Anen impatiently. "Come, man. Speak."

"We are besieged by a rabble of common labourers from Akhenaten's city," said Tutmose. "They are demanding that the temple be closed."

Anen stared at his commander. "Impossible! Are they insane?"

"It is likely," affirmed Tutmose. "But they say they possess an edict from Pharaoh himself."

Anen gaped in astonishment. "Such a thing has never been known."

"I do not say it is true," Tutmose added, "only tell you what they themselves have told me."

Anen gazed at his chief of guards and saw that he was bleeding from a cut on the side of his face; blood also trickled down his leg from a gash in his thigh. "You are injured, commander," he observed. "They did this to you?"

"They refused to show this decree to anyone but you, master. They demand an audience at once."

"Do they!" sneered Anen. He drew himself up. "I will speak to them. But by the power of Horus, I will not have them run riot on holy ground. Tell them, 'Thus says Anen, Second Prophet of Amun, you are to choose four from among your number to represent you. These four representatives and these alone will be admitted to the temple court-yard after morning prayers. We shall sit down with the High Priest and discuss this matter like civilised men.' This is what I have decided."

"So shall it be done, master." Tutmose bowed and hurried away to deliver Anen's message.

Before Anen could return to his rest, the commander was back with word that the workers refused to enter the temple precinct because they considered it an unclean place. "They insist that you come out to them," Tutmose reported.

The demand was so audacious, Anen could only stare in disbelief at his commander. That this should come to pass so swiftly after their confrontation with the workers at Akhetaten could not be a coincidence. It was a deliberate act of aggression. But why send mere labourers? It made no sense. Pharaoh commanded armies; he had only to whisper a word, and his royal bodyguard would march into the sea at his behest. Either the mob was lying about the edict—which seemed only too likely—or there was some darker purpose at work that he did not yet perceive.

"My master?" asked Tutmose, stirring him from his thoughts. "What is your will?"

"This rebellion must end. I will go out and speak to them."

Tutmose inclined his head. "The temple guard stands ready to attend you."

"No," countered Anen. "I go out alone. They should not feel threatened by a solitary priest. Return to your troops and see they are armed and stand ready behind the gates. If anything should happen to me, you are to march on them." He began removing his robe and collar. "Go."

A few moments later Anen emerged, dressed in the simple *shendyt* and belt of an ordinary priest. At his approach those gathered at the gate bowed. "Open the door," he commanded.

The gatemen pulled, and the gates swung slowly open. Anen stepped forward and was instantly confronted by a crowd of swarthy men who, at sight of him, began shaking fists and tools and shouting abuse. He held up his hands to quiet them and waited to be heard. After a moment a grudging silence came upon the throng, and he said, "Who speaks for you? Who among you is leader?"

A long-haired fellow moved out from the rabble; bearded in the Habiru fashion, dark from long hours in the sun, muscled arms crossed over his massive chest, he carried a hammer in his thick hands. "I speak for my people and carry the demands of Pharaoh that this temple be closed and the priests dispersed. The stones of these walls and buildings are to be carried off to Akhetaten."

Anen regarded the fellow with a dubious expression. He paused to let his gaze travel around the close-packed ring of angry faces. "If that is so, how is it that I have heard nothing of this until now?"

"I bring an edict from Pharaoh," the labourer proclaimed loudly, glancing around at his men, some of whom shouted in support of this assertion.

"May I see this edict of yours?"

The man nodded to one of those behind him. A papyrus scroll was passed forward into the hands of the priest.

Anen calmly unrolled the papyrus and read the contents. What he saw there brought the blood to his head. It was much as the Habiru labourer had said—by decree of Akhenaten, the temple was to be dismantled and used for building stone at Akhetaten, Pharaoh's new city. Anen took a deep breath and forced himself to answer calmly, "If this is truly from Pharaoh's own hand, it will have to be studied and verified. I will take possession of it and begin an inquiry."

The belligerent fellow snatched back the scroll. "We have come to begin the work of tearing down this temple."

"That is over-hasty and premature," Anen told him, his voice flat. "No one will be permitted to begin anything until we have made petition for clarification and received confirmation from Pharaoh's own lips." He paused and added, "For all I know, that is a false document—a fraud and a forgery."

"By the Living God!" swore the labourer. His fellows muttered dangerously, "You dare accuse us so?"

"I make no accusations," Anen replied coolly. "I only state a simple fact. Since I was not present when Pharaoh made this proclamation, I cannot be certain it carries his true intent."

This argument might have continued some considerable time, but the mob, having heard enough, began shouting that the temple must be pulled down at once. Someone threw a stone, striking Anen high on the chest. The priest staggered back, bleeding from a gash below his collarbone. The angry crowd surged forward.

The commander of the guard, having seen enough, drew his sword and dashed to Anen's side. Raising his shield, he thrust his master behind him and backed away as the crowd began hurling paving stones ripped from the street with picks and pry bars. "Close the gates!" shouted Tutmose, and the gatemen leapt to obey as the stones smashed against the massive timbers.

"What will you have us do, my master?" asked Tutmose as soon as the doors were sealed and barred once more.

"If any of them should try to get inside the temple precinct," said Anen, "they are to be resisted—by force, if necessary." He hurried off to have his wound dressed. Halfway across the courtyard he paused, changed direction, and proceeded to the guest lodge instead.

Benedict was asleep, but lightly, and woke when the priest came bustling into his room. "Trouble has come to the temple," Anen announced, knowing the youth could not understand him. He gestured for Benedict to rise and follow him; once outside, he cupped a hand to his ear and said, "Listen."

The young man heard the sound of voices raised and paving cobbles rattling the gate beams.

"We must get you safely away from here," said the priest; he pointed to Benedict and mimed the action of a bird flying away.

Benedict caught the meaning on the second repetition and replied, "I understand. It would be best for me to leave." He mimed the bird-flying motion, nodded, and pointed to himself. "I am ready."

Anen turned and called for one of his senior priests to attend him. "You must take our guest from here by way of the hidden gate. Accompany him to the Sacred Road and see that he departs in safety."

"As you command, my master, so shall it be," replied the priest. He turned to the young man, bowed, and gestured for him to follow.

Benedict thanked Anen for his care. The priest put his hand on the young man's chest over his heart, and then pressed it to his own heart. Benedict returned the gesture. "Farewell, Anen," he said, and in that moment was a boy no longer, but a man with alliances and responsibilities. "Until we meet again."

The senior priest put a hand to Benedict's arm and started to lead him away. Benedict hesitated. The priest gave his arm a tug, urging him to follow, pointing at Tutmose, who was waiting to conduct them out of the temple by way of the hidden gate.

"Wait!" Benedict said, making a flattening motion with his hands. "There is something I must do." He turned back and called to Anen. "I am sorry, but I cannot leave without copying my father's map."

Anen regarded the youth quizzically.

"My father's *map*—see?" At this, Benedict opened his shirt and began drawing symbols on his chest with his finger in imitation of

Arthur's many tattoos. He then pantomimed drawing them. "You see? I must copy the map."

Understanding broke across Anen's broad features. "You want the skin," he said, placing his own hand against his chest and making little curlicues with his finger.

"The map, yes." Benedict nodded, confident that the priest had understood.

"This will take time." Anen pulled on his chin and frowned. "But we must get you away from here now before the fighting starts." He turned and spoke a rapid command to the priest he had placed in charge of Benedict's safety. "A new command—take him to the servant's precinct beside the river. Go to Hetap and tell him to watch over our guest until I send for him. He will be rewarded."

The senior priest bowed in acknowledgment of the command, and then beckoned Benedict away. The young man hesitated. "You will bring me the copy of the map?" he asked, retracing the symbols on his chest.

Anen smiled and pantomimed the symbols, then made a motion with his hands as if folding a cloth, which he then presented to Benedict.

"Thank you, Anen," Benedict repeated. "I am in your debt."

At the far end of the temple in a dusty little corner was a small door—large enough to accommodate a goat or dog, or a man on hands and knees—and after withdrawing the bolts and catches, Benedict was led out into the night-dark streets of Niwet-Amun. Once away from the temple, the city remained placid and quiet, the people asleep in their homes. They walked through a district of large houses—the homes of the wealthy nobility—and progressed by degrees through neighbourhoods of more modest means until they reached the humble mud-brick huts of the servant class that lined the river. Here there were people awake and already working: hoeing or watering their gardens, tending their chickens, sitting at looms, repairing tools, and other chores—labouring for themselves before going off to serve in the houses of their masters.

They stopped at a house with a neatly tended garden and approached a squat, fat old man sitting on a stool outside the front door. The senior priest bowed and spoke to the man, then indicated Benedict. The fellow rose, bowed, and made a lengthy reply to the priest, then bowed again. Turning to his charge, the priest indicated that Benedict was to remain with the man.

The priest departed then, and the old man addressed his guest. "Hetap," he said, placing his fingertips against his pudgy chest.

Benedict repeated the name, then said his own, whereupon the old temple servant took him by the hand and led him into the house to meet his wife, a plump, grey-haired woman with a ready, dimpled smile. Benedict was given the only chair in the house and, as the sun rose on a new day, he was fed figs, slices of sweet melon, and flat bread fried in palm oil and dipped in honey. Then he was shown where he could sleep.

All this was accomplished with simple sign language and an impressive dose of goodwill. At each transaction, Benedict thanked his hosts and hoped they would be richly rewarded for their kindness to him, a stranger who could not even speak their language.

He lay down a little while, but could not rest. Thoughts of his father's last moments crowded out all other considerations. It was still difficult for him to accept that his father was dead. He continually relived the awful moment, and wondered how he would break the news to his mother. What would she do when she learned her husband of so many years would never return to her? How would she bear it?

Bereft, lonely, grieving, unable to understand anyone or make himself understood save for blunt gestures that passed for sign language, Benedict spent the day in misery, watching the road for any sign of Anen bringing the copy of his father's map. But the priest did not come. Toward the end of the day he saw a barge approaching on the river; as it passed the village, he saw that it was filled with soldiers. This he took as a sign that the trouble at the temple had come to the notice of the authorities and the situation would then be resolved.

By the end of that first day, he went to his rest feeling certain that the map would arrive the next day and he would soon be on his way.

The second day dragged by, and though Benedict rarely took his eyes off the road, no one came from the temple. The third day passed similarly—the only change was that the commotion in the city seemed to be spreading. The villagers were becoming restive, and many seemed fearful; there were furtive discussions amongst neighbours and everyone was wary.

Almost beside himself with frustrated impatience, the young man determined that he would not wait another day but, come what may, would return to the temple to see for himself what was happening. Obviously, something had gone wrong. How long did it take to make a simple copy of the tattoos on his father's chest? Benedict berated himself for leaving without insisting on making the copy himself—much as he would have dreaded the task, at least it would have been done. He spent a last restless night and rose at first light the next morning to set out; Hetap and his wife attempted to prevent him, but he remained adamant. He thanked his guardians for taking care of him and departed.

He was halfway through the village when he saw a chariot speeding towards him. He waited, and as it drew near he recognised Tutmose.

The chief of the guards had clearly been in a battle; he wore bandages on his right arm and left leg just above the knee, and his eye was black and discoloured from a nasty blow.

Tutmose halted the horses and stepped from the chariot. From a bag on a strap over his shoulder he produced a parcel wrapped in papyrus and bound with a band of linen dyed red. The commander greeted Benedict and placed the parcel firmly in his hands.

"Thank you," said Benedict. The parcel, flat and decorated with a row of hieroglyphic symbols in black along one side, was so light as to weigh almost nothing.

As Benedict tugged at the red band to untie the bundle, the commander reached out and prevented him, saying, *"Rewi rok."*

"No?" asked Benedict.

Tutmose shook his head and indicated that he was to get into the chariot at once. Clutching the parcel, Benedict climbed into the vehicle, and with a jolt the horses clattered out of the village. Soon they were speeding past fields of beans and barley, heading up into the hills and out into the desert.

By the time he had mastered his balance in the swerving, jouncing vehicle, the long avenue of ram-headed sphinxes came into view. But a few moments later, the chariot was drawing up at the end of the avenue where the sacred way leading to the temple commenced. Tutmose gestured for Benedict to get out, then turned his team and, raising his hand in farewell, sped off once more, leaving Benedict to make his departure alone and unseen.

It was early yet. The sun was just rising above the line of hills to the east. Benedict knew which sphinx to mark in order to make the leap—his father had taught him well. But first he had to look at the map copied from his father's tattoos. Kneeling down where the stone pavement ended, he carefully untied the red linen band and unwrapped the papyrus.

What he saw caused him to jump to his feet and take two involuntary steps back. He stared at the parcel on the ground, amazement and revulsion churning through him in waves that made him gasp and fight for breath.

For on the ground before him was no mere copy of the map made by the temple scribes, but the map itself: his father's skin made into parchment. His inability to communicate had led to this monstrous misunderstanding. No mere copy, the embalmers had preserved the original. The horror of the deed overwhelmed him, and Benedict retched into the dust at his feet.

When the dry heaves subsided, he stood gazing at the ghastly artefact, wondering what to do. He could not bear to take it, neither could he leave it. Caught in a spiral of indecision, he stared at the grisly thing—a roughly rectangular piece of near translucent integument covered with the blue symbols applied during the life of its owner—knowing he must decide, and quickly. The sun climbed higher above the hills. Time was fast approaching when the ley would cease its activity and he would be forced to spend another day in this hateful place.

Benedict swiftly reached the conclusion that he had only one option. He knelt down and gathered up the ends of the papyrus, carefully folding them back into their original shape and retying the red band. Then, tucking the packet into his shirt, he turned and stepped to the centre of the Avenue of Sphinxes outside the half-finished temple. He walked to the fifth sphinx from the end, stopped, cast a last look around at the unforgiving desert, and, with the even, measured pace his father had taught him, began making his long way home.

CHAPTER 25

*In Which the Best
Theory Is Expounded*

*B*rendan proved himself an able and erudite guide to the attractions of Damascus. He led his willing charge on a leisurely tour of the Old City, visiting the Great Umayyad Mosque with its golden domes and shrine to John the Baptist; the Pasha's Palace with its serene palm-shaded fountains and room after room of ornate tile and scrollwork screens; the Chapel of Saint Paul on the very spot where he escaped the city in a basket from the city wall in the dead of night; Bab Faradis, or Gate of Paradise; the Great Souq al-Hamidiyya, with its miles of aisles and dizzying myriad of shops; Straight Street and its marble columns and Roman arches. And while they strolled and took in the sights, they talked, and Cass got a better grasp on the nature of ley travel, to be sure, as well as the work and philosophy of the society, which, she learned, had all started with a man named Arthur Flinders-Petrie.

"An extraordinary fellow—inquisitive, resourceful, fearless as the day is long—an explorer of the highest order." They were sitting at a tiny round table under a striped awning sipping sweet, fragrant hibiscus tea from glasses in silver holders as the day faded around them. "Ever come across that name at all?" asked Brendan.

"No, never," said Cass.

"Pity. But I'm not surprised. That he is not now remembered in the annals of human achievement is due to the fact that his work was largely clandestine and confined almost exclusively to exploration of the lines of telluric energy—ley lines, in other words. That alone, I suppose, would be reason enough to found a society in which to carry on his work. But there is more." Brendan paused and regarded her closely, as if gauging her readiness to hear.

Cass felt her pulse quicken. "I'm listening."

"Arthur discovered something," Brendan said, lowering his voice. "On one of his many journeys he discovered something of such unimaginable magnitude that it changed the course of his life. Though he continued his travels, he held his discovery a close-guarded secret, refusing to speak of it to anyone."

"What did he discover?"

Brendan leaned back, frowning. "The truth is, we do not know."

"That's it?" blurted Cass, exasperation pinching her voice. "Since we're speaking frankly, I don't mind saying that, frankly, I expected more."

"And I truly wish I could tell you more. Members of our society have been working over many lifetimes to answer the riddle of what it was that Arthur discovered and did not feel he could share with the rest of the world. We have sworn life and blood to this quest, and some have died in pursuit of it. We trust their lives have not been given in vain."

Cass leaned back in her chair and stared at the gentleman across the table, fighting down her frustration and disappointment. "But you must have *some* idea what you are searching for?"

"We have no end of ideas, theories, notions, suppositions, and so forth," Brendan replied with a rueful laugh. "Too many, in fact. But the very best theory—and this is not mine alone, others share it—is that Arthur Flinders-Petrie discovered nothing less than the means to alter reality."

"Excuse me?" said Cass, disbelief edging into her tone once more. Scientific training and her own native scepticism—honed by years in academia fighting from her corner against considerable odds—made her wary of anything that sounded even remotely oddball. "For a moment I thought you said *alter reality*—what does that even mean?"

Brendan nodded. "I don't blame you for being dubious. It took me years to accept it myself. Even now I'm not sure I fully grasp all the implications, but it would seem to be bound up in the ordinary mystery of time. Arthur may have found a way to manipulate time itself."

"That would be the greatest discovery in human history," Cass observed dryly. "Your man Flinders-Petrie must have been one heck of a discoverer."

"Oh, he was," agreed Brendan. "Of course, that is only a theory—but it is the best one we have so far. Consider," he said. "What if, just for example, you possessed the ability to change the past—"

"Then instead of a dirt-sucking PhD grunt, I would be fabulously wealthy and living on a tropical island paradise, and we would not be having this conversation—that is, if *I* could change the past."

"I'm afraid I've presented you with too much, and all at once," Brendan sympathised. He drew a deep breath and gazed at a sky fading from gold to violet as evening came on. "We should get back. Rosemary will wonder what has become of us."

He laid a few coins on the table, and they resumed their walk through the Old Quarter's rabbit warren of streets. After a moment he said, "Here in Syria, the grand panoply of the past is all around us—everything from pre-historic to Assyrian, Babylonian, Persian, Roman, Byzantine—you name it—every epoch of human existence has left its mark on the land. Here, it is easy to imagine travelling to the past because the past is never far away."

"You are talking to a palaeontologist," Cass said. "I spend a lot of time with my head in the past."

"Then you should have a good feel for the mystery that lies at the heart of time itself. We live and move in time, but none of us really knows much about it. For example, in normal experience time flows in only one direction—from past to present. We can visit the past, at least vicariously, through photographs, the written word, our memories, the fossils you find, and such like. The past is always with us; we carry it around with us in the form of memories, we live in a world shaped entirely by it, and it continually exerts a direct influence on the present, yes? The choices you made yesterday affect what happens to you today, and the choices you make today will affect what happens to you tomorrow. We all reach the future at the same rate, and we have to live with what we find when we get there."

"In large part because of the choices we've made," said Cass. "We shape our reality through the exercise of intention, through the application of our free will as conscious beings."

"Correct," agreed Brendan. "With ley travel, however, the experience of time and reality is somewhat more fluid."

"So I've noticed."

"Indeed, ley journeys normally involve visits to a particular version of the past—a past where many things will be the same as we remember them, but other things are different. People, events, and, in some cases, even places will differ from those we recognise from our personal experience." He paused and raised his eyes to take in her expression. "But what if the past was fully as malleable, as ripe with potential, as the future seems to be?"

"Then, by changing the past, we might make a better future than we might otherwise have had," Cass suggested.

"That is why you get to be fabulously wealthy and live on your island in tropical splendour—because of the changes you made to your past reality." Brendan regarded Cass with a knowing look. "In short, by changing the past one also creates a future that might not have existed if things had stayed the way they were."

"If only," remarked Cass. "The fly in the ointment, of course, is that you never know exactly what the outcome of any change might be. Since everything is intertwined with everything else, even a small change in one tiny area might result in terrible, or at least unwanted, consequences somewhere else—chaos theory in a nutshell."

"What if there was another way?" suggested Brendan. "One hypothesis of time holds that the future exists only as a cloud of possibility—no form or substance, just pure potentiality. Now then, what if you had the ability to reach into that cloud of possibility— that fog of all possible outcomes to any action—what if you could reach in and pluck out the particular outcome you desire?"

"Choose the future you want," mused Cass. "Which would alter the present reality and also, by logical necessity, change the past as well."

"*That*," declared Brendan, "is what I believe Arthur Flinders-Petrie discovered."

No more was said; Cass remained quietly thoughtful as they made their way back to the society headquarters, where Mrs. Peelstick welcomed them and said, "You two carry on. Supper's almost ready. I'll call you in a few minutes."

"Thank you, Rosemary. You're a peach," Brendan told her. Crossing to the stairway, he called to Cass, "Come, I want to show you something."

Cass followed her guide up two floors. Taking a key from his pocket, the Irishman unlocked a heavy door and stepped across the threshold. He twisted a switch on the wall, and lights in sconces flickered on to reveal an absolutely enormous room with a high, beamed ceiling and small diamond-shaped windows. The room occupied the entire second floor of the building, and appeared to be stuffed with books and scrolls and manuscripts and papers of all kinds. There were books in wooden crates and crammed into the floor-to-ceiling shelves lining the long wall on either hand; books piled on the floor in unsteady towers; books lying in untidy heaps in the corners, cascading from under canvas sheets, and spilling from disintegrating boxes. Three large library tables groaned under the weight of oversize volumes, and another table was piled high with rolled parchment scrolls and bundled manuscripts tied with ribbon and string. The air was musty with the scent of mouldering paper and dust.

"Come in, come in," he said, ushering her inside.

Cass took in the chaotic clutter. "This reminds me of the graduate reading room in the library of the university," she said.

"Oh, it's not a library," countered Brendan. "Nor a reading room. This is a *genizah*."

"Genizah," repeated Cass. She had never heard the word before.

"The ancient Jews considered it sinful to throw away a book, and it was anathema to destroy any book bearing the tetragrammaton—the four letters making up the name of God. So, when their holy texts or other materials became worn out, they were consigned to a genizah to await official burial on holy ground." He spread his hands to the room. "This is our genizah, but we do not bury the books anymore. They are far too valuable."

"Your treasure is books." Cass stepped to the nearest table. The volumes were old and well worn, it was true, and most were in languages other than English. "Where do they all come from?"

"They are gathered from here and there by society members on their various travels and donated to the cause. Those books we deem most worthy of preservation we keep. Who knows when something written in one of these pages—some little scrap of observation, an obscure record of an historical event, a word, a name, a report from a source now forgotten—some little gem of truth will prove valuable to furthering our investigations. Then the book will be resurrected, so to speak, to fulfill its destiny."

He walked to a smaller table at one end of the room. "Here, I want to show you one of the rarest of those gems." He reached for a large, rectangular, but very thin, book bound in red leather. The cover was stamped in gold with the words *Maps of the Faerie*. Brendan pulled the book to him and opened the cover. "This was compiled by a Scottish eccentric writing under the name Fortingall Schiehallion—not his real name."

"You think?" sniffed Cass.

"His real name was Robert Heredom, and somewhere around 1795 he published this treatise on the cartography of what he called the Faerie Realms." Brendan began leafing through the book, pausing now and again to show a page of elaborate drawings of strange landscapes with stranger names.

Displayed on the yellowed pages, Cass saw tracts of enchanted forests with twisted trees, magic fountains and rivers, islands of glass, and valleys ruled by immortal kings—all of it rendered with the precision and skill of a draughtsman.

"As you can see from the maps he has drawn, Heredom had an active imagination." Brendan turned to a page and directed Cassandra's attention to an odd map unlike any of the others she had seen so far. "But this map," he said, "this map is different."

He turned the book so she could see it clearly. It was a drawing done all in sepia tones as if to evoke a bit of parchment made from the skin of a goat or sheep. The piece was roughly oblong, with irregular edges and crease marks, a few tiny holes, a number of cracks or tears—the better to make it look as if the artist was actually copying an object from life. The surface of the parchment was decorated with a number of fanciful markings: spirals and whorls with dots, intersecting lines and overlapping circles, curious cryptic symbols that looked like primitive petroglyphs of the kind found on rocks in deserts, or letters from an imaginary alphabet, or stylised monograms from names in languages that never existed.

"How very strange," murmured Cass. "Maps to imaginary places."

"The map before you"—he brushed the page lightly with his fingertips—"*this* map is different. It is a record of what must be one of the most remarkable discoveries in the history of the human race."

Cassandra lowered her head and peered at the drawing more closely, concentrating her attention on the arcane hieroglyphics. She had seen such things before, scratched or painted on rock walls by long-extinct tribes the world over, and like all the rest the symbols meant nothing to her. "Parchment, is it?"

"It is that," confirmed the Irishman, "but of a very rare and special kind. What you are looking at is a drawing of the map Arthur Flinders-Petrie kept to record his more significant discoveries—discoveries that he inscribed on his own skin."

"They're tattoos," concluded Cass.

"That is exactly what they are. When Arthur died, his skin was removed and made into parchment in order to preserve the map, that the record of his discoveries should not be lost. We call it the Skin Map, and it is of central importance to the work of the society. Those symbols hide wonders. For example, somewhere on that map is the Well of Souls." Brendan glanced up. "I see you are not familiar with the legend?"

"Not as such," Cass confessed.

"It is a myth that finds expression in many cultures. One of the most common is an Arab belief associated with the Dome of the Rock in Jerusalem; the Spirit Well is known as a place of limbo where the souls of the dead await Judgement Day, or maybe the chance to be reborn. But the myth is far older than that—in fact, it seems to be as old as the human race itself. Almost every culture has a similar tale—the Fountain of Youth, the Elixir of Eternal Life, the Philosopher's Stone. All variations on a theme, you might say—the myth of the Spirit Well. Many other sources indicate that the well is located in the original paradise, Eden."

Cassandra's mind leapt ahead to the conclusion. "You believe that Arthur found this Spirit Well, and that this has something to do with manipulating time, selecting the future, changing the past, and all that—is that what you're telling me?"

"We cannot prove it," confessed Brendan. "But some of our members have reason to believe that Arthur discovered it and recorded its location on his map."

"And this," Cass said, indicating the open pages of the book before her, "you think this is a drawing of that map?"

"I do, yes." Brendan pursed his lips in a frown as he contemplated the image on the page. "Alas, it is not a reliable copy of the original map—merely an artist's conception, no doubt based on a verbal description of the map—perhaps someone who had seen it described it to Heredom, who made the drawing. Unfortunately, Heredom doesn't say. But inadequate as the drawing may be, it nonetheless serves to authenticate the original provenance of the map."

"Forgive me, Brendan," objected Cass lightly, "but who is to say this artist's rendition isn't itself simply based on pure fantasy—like all the other fairy-tale maps in this book? Is that not a more likely explanation?"

The thin Irishman smiled. "I shall very much enjoy working with you, Cassandra. Your scientific instincts serve you well."

Cass brushed aside the assertion that they would be working together. So far as she was concerned nothing was decided yet. "The simplest explanation is the most likely to be true. In this case, the simplest explanation is that Schiehallion, the fantasist, merely dreamed up the map—in the same way he dreamed up all the others."

"And you would be right, of course, if not for the fact that we have independent corroborating evidence that confirms the existence of the map. I can assure you that it is much as you see it here." He took a last look at the picture, then closed the book and returned it to its place. "I have seen it with my own eyes."

"You have the original Skin Map?"

"A piece of it, yes." He frowned. "Unfortunately, it has been stolen. We are working to get it back."

Missing evidence is no evidence at all, thought Cass, and once again felt the worm of suspicion squirm in her gut. Yet here she was in Damascus, about eighty years out of joint, and with no rational way to account for it. "I don't suppose you have anything else you could show me?"

"To *convince* you?" He laid particular stress on the word. "Isn't that what you mean?"

"Well, if you put it that way—what have you got to convince me?"

"One might be forgiven for thinking that your experiences up to now should have taken you a fair distance towards conviction." He turned and gestured towards the door. "After you."

Cass felt the mild reproach of his words as she moved towards the door. "Do you travel, Brendan?"

"Ley travel? Sadly, no. It is not for me." Brendan followed her out and locked the genizah again. "But like it or not, Cassandra, you have become a traveller. You have traversed the hidden dimensions of a universe far more vast and varied than present science imagines— although some enlightened thinkers—like Einstein or Neils Bohr, for instance—are beginning to theorise about it and describe it in ways that are strikingly close to our conception of the way things are."

Brendan allowed these words to sink in a moment, then said, "We are on the cusp of a monumental discovery. I can feel it." He paused on the landing and turned before starting down the stairs. "I have no doubt that we will do great things together."

"Assuming I agree to join you," Cass stated flatly. "I still have a choice, you know."

"Oh, of course you have a choice. You can join us or not as you wish. But ultimately, knowing what you know, I believe you will find it comes down to a choice between accepting your destiny or forever denying it. Either way you will choose, and either way you *will* move forward. Because, you see, there is no turning back."

CHAPTER 26

In Which Astral Dislocation Finds Explication

S nipe! Put down that toad," shouted Douglas Flinders-Petrie. "Did you hear me?"

The pale-skinned youth paused in his experiments; he glanced around at his master storming towards him across the stable yard and whipped the bloody knife out of sight.

"Stop torturing that creature, and come here. It is time to go."

With grudging reluctance Snipe dropped the wounded toad and stood. Still hiding the knife, he wiped the blade on his trousers.

"Come with me." Douglas started away.

Snipe waited until his master's back was turned, then stamped on the struggling animal and ground it beneath his heel.

"Now!" called Douglas. "We've got work to do."

Mouthing incoherent curses, the truculent servant fell into step behind his master, fists clenched at his sides.

"We've got to cut your hair, get you washed up and dressed," Douglas told him. "And we've got to get to the ley by sundown if we are to have any chance of meeting up with Brother Bacon tonight."

Having established himself in the guise of a visiting monastic scholar from Ireland, Douglas now felt free to come and go as he pleased on the streets of medieval Oxford. In the past six months he had consulted the learned professor twice on matters related to deciphering the mysterious text of a book he had stolen from the British Museum—an arcane little volume written in the form of an alphabet of intricate symbols, which the monkish professor euphemistically termed the Language of Angels.

Brother Bacon had yet to admit to composing the manuscript, but did allow that he had copied the text from another source. Douglas suspected the scholar was being overly modest, if not disingenuous— no doubt to protect himself from too-close scrutiny by nosy church authorities who tended to see heretics under every bush. The tome, handwritten on fine vellum, bore the intriguing title *Inconssensus Arcanus*, which roughly translated as *Forbidden Secrets*. A book like that would have spelt trouble for its author, and no wonder: its little pages were dense with close-crabbed, inscrutable text detailing all sorts of secrets—any one of which would have had the book's owner tied to a stake in the marketplace with pitch-soaked kindling bundled around his naked feet. If, that is, anyone had been able to read it.

Roger Bacon was no heretic, but science and magic were uncomfortably close bedfellows in the thirteenth century, Douglas knew, and so he did not press his prime source on the matter. In any event, he was more concerned with achieving practical results than arguing metaphysics with a church-bound mystic.

Six months of migraine-inducing labour and dogged persistence had paid off, and Douglas had finished his deciphering work. It had not been easy, and without the aid of Master Bacon's key—purloined by Snipe on their first visit to the scientist's sanctum—it would have been impossible. He was now ready to test the accuracy of his work. To that end, the journey he planned now was to confirm all that he had learned about reading the code and how it applied to the symbols on the Skin Map.

As to the latter, he was certain Bacon knew more about inter-dimensional travel than he let on. There were tantalising references scattered throughout the book, and Douglas, already well versed in the subject, was not slow to pick up the hints. Most of the text was devoted to a discussion of an abstruse philosophy of which Douglas could make neither head nor tail but somehow embraced what the writer referred to as *astralis dislocationem*. The treasure buried in pages of this obscure volume was a table delineating the symbology of the coded language itself, a key of sorts, showing how to interpret the symbols as they related to this so-called astral dislocation.

Douglas pulled on his monastic robe and cowl and passed a critical eye over Snipe, who was now dressed as a lay brother—as far, per-haps, from angelic as the founders of the Cistercian Order could have reasonably anticipated. But shorn of his pale, wiry hair, his oval face scrubbed pink, he could pass for a being somewhat less diabolical than was his natural bent.

"Tighten your cincture," Douglas instructed. "And tie up your sandals."

Muttering, Snipe obeyed. Douglas, satisfied that they were ready, locked the room and departed for the ley. As it was a damp night in late autumn, the streets would be dark and, he hoped, fairly deserted. The weather was cold, and a misty fog had seeped into town from the river, so it was hoped that they could make the leap without drawing unwanted attention. Monks suddenly appearing or disappearing in plain sight tended to have a disconcerting effect on the citizenry; the uninitiated were apt to make much of the event—even in a city as sophisticated as nineteenth-century Oxford. The less dramatic Douglas could make their clandestine comings and goings, the better.

They entered Queen Street from their rooms at The Mitre and walked with purpose into the gloaming. "Look for the mark," instructed Douglas. "It should be right about . . ." His gaze swept the pavement for the chalk mark he had placed earlier in the day. "There it is." He reached around behind him. "Your hand, Snipe."

The surly servant slipped his hand into his master's. "Ready? Step lively. On three." Douglas strode out. "One . . ." He took a step. "Two . . ." And another. "Three . . ."

He felt his feet leave the ground and then the always slightly unnerving sensation of weightlessness and falling—but only for a step—followed by the familiar jolt in his leg bones as the ground became solid beneath him once more. The mist cleared, and he saw directly ahead the same street as before, only this time it was paved with cobbles, and instead of traffic lights there were log-burning iron braziers set up at the crossroads.

The streets of medieval Oxford were patrolled by pike-wielding bailiffs who could be expected to challenge strangers, but Douglas did not see any around. He heard a retching sound behind him and glanced back to see Snipe bent over with his hands on his knees. "When you're ready," he sighed impatiently.

While he was waiting, he heard the clock in Saint Martin's ring. "It must be compline," Douglas mused aloud. "Come on, Snipe. Wipe your mouth and be quick."

He started towards the crossroads and turned south onto the Abbingdon Road leading to the river and the bridge upon which stood the old defensive tower—a half-ruined structure now known as Friar Bacon's Study, or, by those of a less charitable disposition, as Bacon's Folly. The two walked along the road, their sandals slapping the damp stones. Douglas wondered what day it was, or even what month; guesswork told him it could be any time between late November and mid-January.

The light from the crossroad beacons faded, and they walked in darkness until reaching the bridge, where another set of braziers was set up to illuminate the passage under the tower. Douglas walked around to the side and climbed the few steps leading to the stout wooden door, only to find that it was barred: rough boards were nailed across the door frame.

"What the bloody—" muttered Douglas. He had expected to find the scholar at work in his study, as he invariably was every night.

Snipe took one look at the boarded-up entrance and uttered a sharp bark, which was his attempt at laughter.

"Not funny," growled Douglas. "We'll have to go back into town and see if we can find out what's happened."

They trudged back up the street, and this time were challenged by the bailiff at the crossroads. *"Pax vobiscum,"* offered Douglas in greeting. He raised his hand in the sign of the cross, and the town official, seeing the gesture and monk's habit, raised his pike to let them through. *"Benedicimus te, filius meus,"* Douglas pronounced in his best clerical tone and passed.

"Salve, frater" replied the bailiff in rough Latin.

Douglas nodded and moved on. As the bells for compline had gone, he decided to call in at Saint Martin's and see if he might speak to one of the senior clerics. With a muttered warning to Snipe to be on his best behaviour, the two slipped into the church quietly to stand at the back of the simple sanctuary. A group of monks in white robes with black scapulas was standing below the altar at the front, chanting the last prayer of the day.

They soon finished and began shuffling out, some of them yawning, others talking in low voices. Douglas identified one he thought he recognised from a previous visit and, stepping out from the shadows, said, "My apologies for interrupting, brother." The Latin felt odd on his tongue, but he remembered to dip his head in a slight bow to acknowledge the other's seniority. "Brother Thomas, is it not? I was hoping to have a word."

The monk sent his brothers on ahead, stopped, and turned to Douglas. "Do I know you, brother?"

"I am Brother Douglas," he said, smiling, "a visitor from Tyndyrn."

"Ah, yes—I remember you. How can I be of service, brother?"

"Pardon my rude speech," Douglas said. The other gave him a nod of indulgence. "But as you may recall, I have been engaged in scholarly consultation with Friar Bacon—a question of language and interpretation."

"Yes?"

"I have just arrived in the city and was hoping to find him at work in his study at the bridge, but—"

Brother Thomas completed the thought. "You have discovered that Master Bacon's tower is boarded and barred."

"Verily, brother. I was hoping you might tell me the reason for this?"

The senior monk pursed his lips as he thought how best to frame his reply. "Brother Bacon has been placed under arrest and confined to his living quarters."

Douglas raised his eyebrows in surprise. "Can you tell me the reason for his arrest?"

"Pray, permit me a moment's consideration," replied Thomas. The monk steepled his fingers and placed them against his lips in thought. "I can tell you that our brother has been charged with attempting to corrupt the students under his care, and has been confined pending the outcome of an investigation into his teachings."

"This is a very serious charge, to be sure," allowed Douglas judiciously. Through his research, he knew Master Bacon had once been placed under house arrest on flimsy charges of heresy—brought, it was thought, by rivals jealous of his patronage by Pope Clement IV. He had, however, not been able to find out when this house arrest began; now he knew. "Is he allowed visitors?"

The elder monk shook his head slowly and offered a thin smile. "Alas, no. It is a condition of his arrest that until the charges are tried and proven one way or the other, Brother Bacon is not to see or speak to anyone—lest he spread the contagion of his noxious teachings."

"Of course," replied Douglas, sensing an underlying hostility in his informant. "No doubt that is as it should be."

"To be sure." The priest drew himself up. "Now, if there is nothing further, I will wish you a good night." He raised his hand in a parting blessing. "God speed you to your rest."

"And you, brother," said Douglas, stepping aside to allow the other to depart. The senior cleric joined his fellows, who were waiting for him at the church door. After the others had gone, Douglas drew Snipe aside. "We wait here until everyone has gone to bed," he said. "You sleep too. I will wake you when it is time."

PART FIVE

Five Smooth Stones

CHAPTER 27

In Which a New Recruit Is Canvassed

The soft evening deepened around them as Cassandra and her two guides sauntered along the quiet streets of Old Damascus, listening to the sound of distant church bells. Cass—a little dazed and dazzled by all she had heard that day—was in a quiet, thoughtful mood. From a minaret somewhere the droning sound of the muezzin arose, echoing through the near-empty streets, calling the faithful to prayer. The purple twilight and the sound of the bells and quavering chant suited her perfectly.

"I still don't know why you'd want me to join your society," she declared finally. "I have zero experience and know next to nothing of any of this. I really don't think I have a single thing to offer."

"My dear," said Mrs. Peelstick, "you have the one thing we need most—*youth*. All the rest can be learned."

"The plain truth is that the Zetetic Society has been active a very long time and, regrettably, our membership has aged," Brendan pointed out. "We may age more slowly than our fellows, but age we do. The simple truth is that most of us are simply too old to go adventuring anymore."

"It is a fact of life," agreed Mrs. Peelstick wistfully. "We do all get older."

"These days, our best and highest use is to recruit new members and provide support for the active questors," continued Brendan. "We're all of us searching for young blood, but it's not easy. For example, we have several members hoping to pass the baton just now, but hand-offs can be awkward. The travel itself can pose difficulties." Turning to Mrs. Peelstick, he added, "I'm thinking about Cosimo and Kit."

The older woman nodded knowingly, then sighed. "They are in my thoughts constantly."

"We mustn't give up, Rosemary. Until we know more, we simply cannot allow ourselves to assume the worst."

"You're right, of course, Brendan." She offered a sad, hopeful smile. "Still . . ." Her voice died away, leaving an uneasy silence.

Cass glanced at Brendan, but he seemed lost in thought. When she could restrain herself no longer, she asked, "Excuse me, I don't mean to pry—but who are Cosimo and Kit?"

"Ah," replied Brendan, coming to himself once more. "Cosimo Livingstone is one of our questors. He has been intent on bringing his great-grandson into the fold—a young man named Christopher— about your age, I should think. Cosimo had tried unsuccessfully to enlist his son and grandson, but in Kit he had found someone who could carry on his life's work."

"Handing such responsibility from one generation to another can be fraught with difficulty," observed Mrs. Peelstick.

"Cosimo had high hopes for Kit," Brendan continued, "and he was preparing the young man to take a full and active part in the society. They were to have attended our last convocation."

Again the shadow passed over the two elder members' faces. They shared an anxious glance.

"We were looking forward to meeting the young man," continued Mrs. Peelstick. "But we seem to have lost contact with Cosimo completely. It is feared they may have been taken."

"Missing in action," corrected Brendan. "Our last communication with Cosimo indicated that he and our dear friend Sir Henry Fayth were on a mission, and Kit is thought to have been with them. This is cause for concern, because they are pillars of the society. What has become of them is yet to be determined."

A queasy foreboding formed in the pit of Cass' stomach. "Taken?" she asked. Turning to Mrs. Peelstick, she said, "You used the word *taken* just now—what does that mean?"

"I was speaking out of turn."

Brendan stopped walking and looked around. The dusky sky had faded to inky blue, deepening the shadows on the street. They were standing outside the gate of a tiny church. A sign in English beside the gate read *Chaldean Christian Church*.

"Shall we go in? You deserve a full explanation, and it will be best absorbed sitting down." He opened the gate, and they crossed the courtyard to the door of the church and stepped in.

The interior was dark and quiet, the air fragrant with spent incense. The only light came from candles, which burned at stands set up beneath particular icons around the sanctuary. To Cass it felt like entering a cave, or perhaps a womb. An altar, with a simple golden cross flanked by two enormous beeswax candles, stood at the far end of the chancel. The short pews were empty; neither priests nor worshippers were to be seen.

"I come here sometimes to think," explained Brendan. "It is a safe place, and we won't be disturbed. Have a seat." He ushered Cass to a pew.

Mrs. Peelstick continued towards the front of the sanctuary; she paused, genuflected towards the altar, and then moved to a little stand set off to one side. Taking a candle from a bundle, she lit it from one of the candles already burning and placed it in the holder with the others. She bowed her head, then crossed herself and returned to where Cass and Brendan were sitting.

Cass remained silent, letting the peaceful atmosphere wash over her. After a moment, Mrs. Peelstick said, "Go on, Brendan."

"Where to start—that is the question." He frowned and gazed down at his clasped hands.

"Silly man!" sniffed Mrs. Peelstick. "You're frightening the poor girl with your theatrics. If you won't tell her outright, then I will." Brendan nodded. "It comes to this—there are forces that do not care to see our quest succeed. They are against us, and try to thwart us whenever and wherever they can. They pose an extremely potent threat and a very real danger to life and limb." She concluded with a grim smile. "There. That wasn't so bad, was it?"

Cass considered this. "You used the word *forces* just now. You mean people?"

"Human agents, yes," replied Brendan, rousing himself once more. "But spiritual agents as well, lest we forget. As our guide Saint Paul put it, 'For ours is not a conflict with mere flesh and blood, but with the despotisms, the empires, the forces that control and govern this dark world—the spiritual hosts of evil arrayed against us in the heavenly warfare.'"

"Now you *are* scaring her," chided Mrs. Peelstick. "Honestly!"

"Do we sugarcoat it, or tell it plain?" replied Brendan. Turning once more to Cass, he said, "On the human level, our principal adversary is a man who goes by the name of Archelaeus Burleigh. He has in his hire several low thugs of varying intelligence, none to match their leader in cunning and ability. He is a clever and resourceful enemy."

"And also, it must be said, completely ruthless," added Mrs. Peelstick. "I have little doubt he is behind the disappearance of Cosimo and Sir Henry—assuming they have come to harm."

"And the spiritual forces you mentioned?"

"The same as have always sought to wreak havoc on humanity and obstruct God's good purposes in the world," she replied in a soft voice, as if reluctant to speak aloud.

"Ancient enemies they may be, but we must never underestimate them on that account," Brendan pointed out. "They do not grow weak and toothless in old age. Rather, they are particularly active in our special sphere of interest." He saw Cass' uncertain expression. "Do you doubt this?"

"Not at all," she answered, with more conviction than she intended. "I was just wondering why these spiritual forces you mention might have any special interest in what you're doing?"

Brendan glanced around the church. "It is well we are talking about this here," he said, lowering his voice. "A church is the one place they cannot eavesdrop, so to speak, on our thoughts and prayers, our plans and intentions. Remember that; it could prove helpful to you one day."

"As to *why* they take a special interest," said Mrs. Peelstick, "we believe it must be that we are probing very close to a very great spiritual breakthrough, and they know that their time is running out."

"The transformation of the universe we talked about earlier—is that what you mean?"

"Indeed. Whatever form it takes, the fact is that opposition to our efforts has intensified out of all proportion to our somewhat meagre resources. The array of weapons against us is formidable. This leads us to believe that the quest so long and ardently pursued is nearing a critical stage."

"The Omega Point you talked about?" said Cass.

Brendan nodded.

"And if you fail?"

Brendan spread his hands. "The world will slide back into the chaos that you see rampant around us already—wars and rumours of wars, nation against nation, brother at the throat of brother, economic instability with the rich growing ever richer and the poor suffering on a scale heretofore unimagined. But it will intensify. The universe will continue on its long, slow decline."

"So," concluded Cass, "Almighty God is not strong enough alone to bring about His purpose for the universe. He needs you and your society to make it happen; otherwise it has all been for nothing. Is that what you're saying?"

Brendan only smiled. "Your cynicism is a well-honed tool."

"I'm not cynical," countered Cass. "Maybe a little sceptical, but believe it or not, I want to understand. I really do. I've experienced something that two days ago I would have said was impossible, and now here I am bouncing between Arizona and . . . *this*." She gave a sweep of her arm to take in not only the ancient building in which they sat but the Old Quarter and city beyond. "So cut me some slack, okay? I want to believe, but you're not making it easy."

Brendan regarded her quietly. Mrs. Peelstick leaned nearer and said, "It is true that as a society we may be small and insignificant, weak in the face of a monstrous and powerful opposition, dwarfed by the towering magnitude of the task before us. But you know, God has always worked through the small, the insignificant, the powerless—it seems to be sewn into the very fabric of the universe.

"If you consider it for a moment," suggested the elderly woman, "you will see that it has only ever been that way. Over and over again, we see that when anyone willingly gives whatever resources they have to Him—whether it is nothing more than five smooth stones gathered from a dry streambed or five little loaves of bread and two dried sprats—then God's greater purpose can proceed. Small and insignificant? Undoubtedly. But on the day of decision, everything depended on those five smooth stones—with them, David killed Goliath and saved a nation."

"Five loaves of bread became a banquet for five thousand hungry people," Cass said thoughtfully, remembering the Bible story.

Nodding towards the front of the sanctuary where a wooden cross stood on the altar, Mrs. Peelstick concluded, "And one poor, wandering country preacher—homeless, penniless, friendless, and despised by all but a handful of no-account fishermen and a few women—gave himself so fully to God that the combined might of the two most powerful forces in his world—the Roman empire and the religious authorities—could not stop him."

"They crushed him and killed him," murmured Cass, gazing at the empty cross on the altar. "And look what happened."

"Yes," agreed Mrs. Peelstick softly, "they killed him . . . and look what happened."

CHAPTER 28

In Which the Moment of Decision Arrives

Cass gazed at the simple wooden cross, pondering the depths of this sacred mystery. Five smooth stones gathered from a dry streambed changed the course of history; a nation was saved. And that other lad—given a lunch of five small loaves and a couple of dried fish and packed off to hear the wandering rabbi preach. Before the day was half through he would provide the substance for a miracle. He had been asked to give the little he had and, in the hands of the Master, it became a feast for thousands. Did that boy suspect that would happen? No—how could he? All he knew was that he had been asked to choose which side he would serve—just as Cass was being asked now.

"What do you say, Cassandra?" asked Brendan at last. "We have told you about our work and how you can help. It is time to make a decision. Will you join us?"

Despite all the outlandish claims and untethered assumptions, all the convoluted and eccentric propositions she had heard throughout the day, Cass did feel drawn to the quest. Somewhere, in the core of her being, she knew that what she had been told was true. Still, she hesitated. Joining them meant leaving behind everything she had ever known—her life, her work, her place in the world . . . not to mention her father. The thought of her father waiting for her back in Arizona—frantic over her disappearance—pulled her back to reality.

"I can't," she sighed at last. "I can't sign up to anything I don't fully understand. Besides that, I have commitments elsewhere. My father, for one—he must be beside himself with worry, wondering what happened to me."

"If I told you that you could return to the place you left within a day or so of the time you left," offered Brendan, "would that make a difference?" He saw Cass hesitate and pressed her further. "It is true. Travellers have been known to spend years away from home only to return within a few days—or even a few hours—of their departure."

"Well, I—"

"You could join us and still alleviate your father's worries. Perhaps, if we—"

"Don't badger the poor girl," interrupted Mrs. Peelstick. "She is intelligent, reasonable, and capable of making up her own mind." To Cass she said, "We will respect your decision, my dear, and consider that it was simply not to be. We will, of course, help you get home again."

"Thank you," murmured Cass. "You've been more than kind."

The old woman turned and, closing her eyes, drew in a deep breath of the frankincense-laden air. "It is nice here, isn't it? So peaceful. It is truly a shelter from the storms that rage across the world."

The three sat for a while soaking in the serenity of the ancient church, then Brendan stood and made his way out. Mrs. Peelstick followed; stepping into the aisle, she genuflected towards the cross and then paused to wait for Cass. They met Brendan outside, and the three walked slowly back to the convent. The gate was closed, but unlocked. Cass wished them good night and entered the silent courtyard. Halfway across to the dormitory building, she shivered with a sudden chill, paused, and glanced around the courtyard—still and empty as before. Crickets chirped in the far corner, and the scent of jasmine drifted on the night air. All seemed well.

Shaking off the chill, she hurried on, pulled open the door, and shut it firmly behind her. The corridor was dark save for a single candle burning in a red glass jar on the table outside her room. She moved to the door and slipped inside, taking the light with her.

She undressed quickly and climbed into bed, but had difficulty falling asleep; for a long time she thrashed about, unable to make herself comfortable. When sleep finally came, it was troubled with odd, incoherent, and unsettling dreams. Towards morning, Cass experienced a dream that was more lucid than usual; in it, she saw herself as a little girl standing on a ledge of red Sedona sandstone looking out across the desert wasteland. In her dream, she gazed far beyond Earth's atmosphere and into space, beyond the moon to the very edge of the solar system itself and an endless heaven filled with stars and a multitude of galaxies, all wheeling in harmony with the slow, elegant rhythm of creation. The magnificent extravagance of the display stole her breath away. She sensed that her father was there, and when she turned, she saw him dressed in a black suit with his eye pressed to the lens of an enormous telescope. "I want to see," she said. In her dream she heard her father reply, "It is not for you."

She turned away, and this time saw a wall of darkness at the distant edge of the cosmic horizon, far beyond the spiral arm of the Milky Way. Somehow she understood that this was not the darkness of deep space, but was instead an active and invasive darkness, expanding and growing beyond the galactic boundaries. Cass watched as this alien darkness began to seep into the cosmos and swallow the nearer stars and galaxies. Growing, expanding, gathering strength and speed, the darkness surged, and with its increase came an unmistakable feeling of malevolence—as if the darkness were driven not by a mindless force of nature but by a burning hatred as vast and limitless as its galactic reach. On and on it came, devouring everything in its path, growing, expanding with every speck and morsel of light it swallowed.

The childlike sense of wonder Cass had felt only moments before was obliterated by blind, icy panic as the manifold lights of heaven dimmed, faded, and died, annihilated by the insatiable darkness. And still it came, faster and faster, gaining strength and speed as it gathered mass from all the ingested star systems. Now darkness filled her vision, stretching from one end of the solar system to the other. Now the nearer stars blinked out. Now the sun grew cloudy, as if covered by a shroud, its light dimming and dimming until it was gone, leaving only the moon. Then that, too, faded, dimmed, and was gone.

All that was left was darkness made visible.

Cass looked into the gnawing void, and her heart shrank within her breast. She heard a howl—a disembodied shattering shriek of triumph—as the darkness swooped to consume the Earth and all living things. Death, extinction, the annihilation of the entire biosphere and everything in it followed with stunning swiftness. Cass felt an inexhaustible, fathomless cold as the last light of life disappeared into the merciless abyss.

She woke up shivering beneath her blankets and aching with a sadness akin to grief. Her heart, still racing, drummed in her ears. She glanced around the room, terrified, her breath coming in gasps. Never had she been so frightened.

Dragging together the tattered shreds of her courage, Cass rose, threw on her clothes, and dashed across the convent courtyard to the nuns' chapel. She let herself in and hurried down the aisle to the front of the sanctuary; she lit a candle at the little stand and then sat in the front pew, candle clasped tight in her hands, praying—for peace, protection, she knew not what—until it grew light enough outside to see. Then, leaving the church, she crept out of the convent gate. The empty street soon echoed to the sound of her running feet as she raced back to the Zetetic Society door.

Standing on the step, Cass pressed the doorbell, waited ten seconds, and pressed it again. The sky was showing a rosy hue as the sun lit up the heavens; the streets of the city were quiet yet. From somewhere a rooster crowed. She was on the point of pressing the bell again when she heard muffled footsteps in the vestibule beyond; there was a click, and the door opened to reveal Mrs. Peelstick in a lavender dressing gown. "You must be very keen to get home."

"I'm not going home," Cass blurted. "I'm staying."

The old woman observed her for a moment. "Something has happened to change your mind, hasn't it, dear?"

As Cass drew breath to answer, Mrs. Peelstick raised her hand. "No, don't tell me. We'll have some tea and toast first. And then when Brendan gets here we can all sit down together and talk about it." She ushered Cass inside, then closed and locked the door behind her. "It will save repeating. Is that all right? Do come along to the kitchen."

She padded off in her slippers, and Cass, exuding relief from every pore, hurried after her.

CHAPTER 29

In Which a Debt Is
Paid in Candles

Douglas awoke to the sound of the bells of Matins. Sore from his night in the cramped confines of the confessional cubical, he stretched and then peeked out from behind the drape. Seeing that no worshippers had yet entered the church, he quickly roused Snipe, and both crept away. Though the sky was light with the coming sunrise, the streets of Oxford were still steeped in shadow. At the crossroads the bailiff was dozing at his post; Douglas gave him a wide berth all the same. Once past the guards' station, the two furtive figures proceeded along Cornmarket Street to the market square—empty save for a bench in front of a butcher's stall that was occupied by a sleeping man wrapped in a cloak with his hat over his face. On the upper floor of a large house in one of the narrow side streets leading from the square, Roger Bacon, friar and professor, had his private chambers. Douglas had marked the place on previous visits and, assuming that was where the ecclesiastical authorities were hold-ing the professor, Douglas reckoned he might be able to reach him.

The entrance to the lodging house was not locked, so Douglas and Snipe slipped into the tiny vestibule and made their way up the wooden staircase that creaked with every step. A single door at the end of the hall gave access to the only room at the top of the house. Surprisingly, there was no lock on the door; neither was it chained. It, like the door to the master's tower study, was barred by simple board planks nailed crossways to the doorposts. The door itself could be opened to allow food and drink and other necessaries to be passed through. A determined captive could easily have escaped, but the renowned "Doctor Mirabilis" was a captive of conscience; no doubt honour held him more securely than iron.

Douglas put his hand to one of the boards and pulled; the resis-tance offered gave him to know that they would require tools if they were to gain entry—not an insurmountable problem, but likely to be more noisy than he would prefer. Waking up people at the crack of dawn would not advance the cause.

"Come, Snipe," he whispered, turning away. "I've seen all I need to see."

Outside they found a dry place to hunker down until a more convivial hour. Later, when the town began to stir, they crawled from hiding and joined the early-rising folk. Douglas bought two savoury pies from a baker and two jars of beer from a brew mistress with a cask in a barrow; they ate their pies and drank their ale, and watched the square slowly trundle to life.

As they sat eating, there arose a tremendous squawking and honk-ing. From the street to the east there appeared three figures—a man and two young girls—herding a flock of long-necked geese. The man held a slender staff, and the girls each wielded a bendy willow switch, expertly keeping the flock together. They moved into the square and began setting up a flimsy pen made of wicker hurdles pulled from a stack against a wall. While they were about this chore, another poulterer likewise set up his pen a little distance away.

The next arrivals were a farmer and his wife who carried a long pole between them on which a dozen or more live chickens were hung by the feet. The two placed the pole on a simple wooden frame that appeared to be set up for this purpose. The farmwife then produced a basket of eggs and settled herself on a stool to wait for customers. Other farmers appeared—some with chickens, others with ducks or pigeons—and several folk bearing great billowing sacks of feathers.

"The poultry market," Douglas mused, finishing the last of his beer. "Come, Snipe—let's go before I start sneezing."

Douglas rose and returned the wooden jars, then went back to the lodging house where Master Bacon was incarcerated. As before, no one was around, so Douglas simply knocked on the door; it was opened a few moments later, and the long, unshaven face of the great scientist peered blearily out.

Douglas was taken aback at the change in the master's appearance: stoop-shouldered in a filthy robe, his flesh slack and pasty, the eyes usually so keen with the bright light of an unquenchable intellect were now dull and watery; indeed, the scholar's whole demeanour seemed bowed with a grinding fatigue of care.

"Yes?" he said, his voice a creaking rasp. "Was there something?"

"Master Bacon," began Douglas, somewhat uncertainly.

"Do I know you?"

"Indeed, sir. It is Brother Douglas—from the abbey at Tyndyrn." There was no immediate response, so he added, "We have spoken in the past about your work with a particular manuscript in which we share an interest."

This last produced a result, as a glimmer of recognition lit the face briefly, then flickered out once more. "Ah, yes. I remember you," the master replied vaguely. "God be good to you, brother. I hope this day finds you well."

"And you, brother." Douglas hesitated, then asked, "Are you permitted to receive visitors?"

A faint smile touched the scholar's lips. "Strictly speaking, no. But"—he peered beyond his guest into the narrow corridor and landing—"as you see, visitors are not exactly clamouring for my attention. It will do no harm to allow an exception."

"I would not like to make trouble for you, master. Or make your present difficulties worse."

"The worst, I fear, has already happened." The most intelligent man in Oxford shook his head lightly. "A brief visit cannot further aggravate my present difficulties, I assure you. And a visitor is cheer itself to me just now. Pray, speak—and let me feast on the sound of a voice not my own."

"As you will, master," replied Douglas. Turning to Snipe, he gave a whispered command, and the feral boy turned and started away.

"A moment, if you will," called Friar Bacon after him. He moved aside, leaving the door ajar, only to reappear a moment later bearing a large crock with a wooden lid. "If you would do me this kindness," he said apologetically. "My night pot—it must be emptied, and I so loathe tossing it out the window into the street. I find the practise barbaric."

He offered the crock through the lattice of boards blocking his door. "I do most humbly beg your pardon, but—"

"Of course." Douglas took the crock and passed it to Snipe. "Empty this outside," he said, "and stay at the bottom of the stairs. Give me a whistle if anyone comes in."

Snipe uttered a low, throaty growl of displeasure, but took the crock and retreated into the shadows of the staircase. They heard the door slam, and all grew quiet once more.

"I am indebted to you," said Roger Bacon.

"On the contrary, master. It is I who am in debt to you, and I mean to repay you as best I can."

"You are too kind, brother, too kind." He offered his wan smile once more. "It is months since I had a visitor. I have almost forgotten how to behave. I could wish I had some refreshment to offer you, but I have only what they bring me one day to the next, and that is little enough. What was it that you wanted to see me about?"

"It is about a manuscript," replied Douglas. Putting his hand into his sleeve pouch, he withdrew a small scroll of parchment and passed it through the wooden bars.

Friar Bacon slipped off the binding ribbon and unrolled the scroll, holding it before his face. "My eyes have been giving me difficulty of late," he explained as he read. "These rooms are so dim, and I never can get enough candles." He scanned the scroll more closely. "Yes!" he said, his voice quickening. "I remember this. You are the scholar from Tyndyrn. Did you write this?" He shook the parchment in his hand. "I once made a simulacrum of this, I believe."

"Yes, master, that is so," confirmed Douglas.

"I cannot think what happened to it."

"We discussed the origin of the text, and you most generously provided a translation," Douglass offered, quickly skating over the fact that he had ordered Snipe to steal the professor's notes to aid his deciphering work. "I came to ask you to ascertain if I have rendered the text correctly."

"Ah!" Bacon returned to his scrutiny of the manuscript. He read, his lips moving slightly now and then, nodding to himself. "Well, well," he said, looking up at last. "I think we shall have to begin calling you professor."

"But is it accurate? What I have written—is it correct?"

"Oh, indeed. Correct in the main, and in most particulars."

"Most?"

"There are a few small errors," allowed the master, falling naturally into the role of a teacher. "But considering the difficulty you faced, it is a most worthy achievement. You are to be congratulated, brother."

"Thank you," replied Douglas. Relief, unexpected as it was pleasurable, swept through him. It was better news than he had hoped to hear. "But would you mind showing me where I have gone astray?"

"Not at all." He held the scroll up to the makeshift bars of his cell. "You see this symbol—how it curves to the left? What does a left-curling spiral indicate?"

"A retrograde interval," answered Douglas.

Bacon nodded. "And the four small points along its length?"

"Those represent physical way markers to be used for calibrating time."

"Just so," said Bacon. He raised a cautionary finger. "*When* such marks as these are above the line, or on the outer side of a curve, they represent way markers, as you say."

"Yes?"

"But the meaning changes when such marks are to be found below the line or on the inner side of the curve." The priest smiled. "What have we here?" He tapped the symbol in question with a long finger.

"Three dots on the inner curve," replied Douglas.

"And what does this configuration represent?"

Douglas stared at the tiny symbol and wracked his brain to remember. "Intersections?"

"Portals would be more precise, I believe—conjunctions of several pathways—a nexus, if you will."

"Portals," sighed Douglas in agreement. "Of course."

"As for the rest, the orientation and location alignments—these are all rendered correctly." He re-rolled the scroll and passed it back through the barrier. "Of course, I would need access to my papers in my tower study before I could offer a definitive judgement on your work. But for purposes of discussion, I think we can conclude that you have translated the cypher with admirable success. It is a most subtle and demanding art, but you have plumbed the depths of the mystery set before you. I salute you, brother. My congratulations."

"Your praise means more to me than I can say, master."

"I hope I do not have to remind you that the knowledge you have gained is to remain the province of your own keeping. It is not to be shared by a wider public." He regarded Douglas with solemn urgency. "As you can see"—he indicated his own predicament with a wave of his hand—"the authorities do not treat kindly truths that confound their own more limited understandings. The stake awaits anyone who ventures too far into realms deemed unacceptable for investigation." He paused, nodding for emphasis. "Do I make myself clear?"

"Completely," Douglas assured him. "I hasten to assure you that no one shall hear of our inquiry from me. I intend to guard the secret most jealously. Indeed, I have already destroyed all my notes and jottings regarding the phenomenon and its delineation in theory."

Roger Bacon offered a sad smile. "That is for the best—though one could well wish otherwise. One day, perhaps, the world will be a place where knowledge such as this can be lauded—not hidden."

There was a noise in the stairwell below, and a moment later Snipe's pale moon face rose in the shadows. He placed the chamber pot on the landing and made a hurry-up gesture before disappearing again.

"Someone is coming," said Douglas. He picked up the crock and passed it to the master. "I will leave you now."

"Yes, you should go," urged Bacon. "My keepers are bringing me bread and water. It would be best for both of us if they did not find you here."

"Unfortunately, I must return to the abbey tonight. But is there anything I can get you before I depart—anything at all?"

The master shook his head. "My needs are simple, and as such are supplied. Still," he added as the thought occurred to him, "one could wish for a little more parchment."

"Say no more," replied Douglas, moving away from the barred door. "I will see that it is in your hands before I leave."

"And a horn of ink?"

"You shall have it—and candles too."

"Thank you, dear friend. You are a very saint."

"Not at all," Douglas answered from the staircase. "It is I who should be thanking you. Farewell, Doctor Bacon—until we meet again."

"Go with God, my friend," called Bacon, closing the door once more.

On the landing below, Douglas met a robed church official ascending the stairs and, behind him, a squat fellow carrying a pail in one hand and a pike in the other. He could not avoid being seen, so he smiled, bowed, and wished them both a good day—all the while moving towards the door. He collected Snipe, who was hovering about the entrance like a sullen cloud, and hurried off across the market square. He lingered in town long enough to visit the chandlers and purchase a dozen large candles, then went on to procure some parchment and a flask of ink, some uncut quills, and a new pen knife. He arranged for all these things to be taken to Master Bacon's lodgings when the church bells tolled prime.

"Come, Snipe," he said. "We had best make ourselves scarce for a while." He struck off down the street in search of an inn where they could wait for the Oxford Ley to become active and the assault on the Skin Map to begin in earnest.

CHAPTER 30

In Which Priorities Are Realigned

*I*ncredible as Kit's unprecedented appearance seemed to everyone concerned, the tale he unfolded for them was more incredible still. Sitting in the tiny kitchen of the mountaintop observatory, Kit held his listeners rapt. Over big bowls of Brother Lazarus' spaghetti puttanesca, Wilhelmina's floury bread, and numerous glasses of the abbey's hefty red wine, he described life in the Stone Age as he knew it: River City Clan and its organisation; the order and rhythm of daily existence; the flora and fauna; the various individuals and their orientation to the clan and to their world; their unstinting care, support, and respect for one another; and their extraordinary means of communication.

Wilhelmina, leaning on her elbows with chin in hand, her dark eyes wide, kept up a steady, murmuring stream of translation for the priest, who shook his head in continual amazement. Shorn of his matted, shaggy locks and shaved clean, Kit no longer looked like the Wild Man in a circus sideshow. In his clean black cassock he might have passed for one of the abbey's resident monastics—except the things he was describing were things no monk had ever put into words. Story after story, each more astounding than the last, poured out in a flood of verbal astonishments. Every now and then Brother Lazarus would jot down a note for later reference, or a question. But neither he nor Mina wanted to interrupt for fear of missing something amazing.

They talked long into the night and the next morning. After broaching the subject of mounting a return expedition to explore the cave and retrieve the painted symbols from the walls, Brother Lazarus beetled off to consult his superiors. Meanwhile, Kit and Wilhelmina sat outside the observatory tower on a wooden bench, taking in the bright morning sun.

"I found that plaque in the church at Sant'Antimo in Italy and followed the trail," Mina explained, "and it led me here to Brother Lazarus. His real name is Giambattista Beccaria, and he is a traveller—like us." Her voice took on a no-nonsense tone. "That is a secret you will take to the grave—for his good as well as for ours, no one must know about any of us." She lightened again. "You can trust him, Kit. He is one of us. Actually, he's the one who's responsible for finding you the first time."

"I've always wondered how you managed to pull that off."

"It's complicated."

"I figured." Crossing his arms over his chest, he stretched his feet out in front of him, leaned his head against the back of the bench, closed his eyes, and tilted his face to the sun, enjoying the warmth. "Have a go."

"Okay," she agreed, turning her eyes to the valley, lost in a blue haze of morning mist. "I don't know about you, but my life has ceased to have linear chronology. I seem to be here, there, and everywhere. Time gets a little fuzzy."

"You got that right," affirmed Kit, his voice hoarse from talking more in the last twelve hours than he had in the previous twelve months combined. "Go on."

"I've been coming to Montserrat for a few years now. On one early visit I actually arrived and realised that I had returned *before* the last time I was here! From Brother Lazarus' point of view, we had not yet had the previous visit." She gave a little laugh. "That was a real mind bender. In the end, I had to go away again because it was all just too weird."

Kit gave a passable imitation of an En-Ul grunt of agreement.

"Anyway, it has taught me not to make any assumptions, to keep quiet and observe what's going on around me and try to blend in so I don't alarm anyone. I've also learned how to calibrate my jumps better. I can leave right now, go back to Prague for a month or two, and then come back here and you won't have arrived yet."

"Yeah," murmured Kit. "But you *would* know that I was going to arrive eventually, right?"

"Maybe. Sometimes." She clasped her hands and unclasped them. "I don't always *know* what I'm going to remember. You just said I found you in Egypt."

"Right. You *do* remember that, don't you?"

"Kit, I have no memory of that at all. For me—the Mina you are talking to right this moment—it hasn't happened yet."

He raised his head, opened his eyes, and stared at her. "Man, that *is* weird," he said after a moment. "Mina, you showed up in Egypt just in the nick of time to break Giles and me out of the tomb. You were wearing something like army fatigues, and your hair was tied up in a scarf—it was light blue. You got us out of that terrible crypt where Burleigh had locked us and left us to die. Are you telling me you don't remember *any* of that?"

"I have the scarf. But the rest of it?" She lifted a shoulder in a shrug. "Sorry. I don't have any memory of that."

"Well, what is the last thing you recall?"

"I remember going to Egypt to meet Thomas Young and to collect you and Giles and the map," she said slowly. "Then we all went back to Prague and ran into Burleigh. I sent you to the gorge, took Giles home, and came here. That's all."

"But before that—you don't remember coming to Egypt the first time and breaking us out of the tomb?"

"Sorry."

Kit sat up and put his head in his hands, rubbing his temples with his thumbs. Fearing she had caused an information overload, Mina put a comforting hand on his neck and massaged it gently.

"But it happened," he said, his voice falling softly.

"Not to me," she told him. "Not yet."

Kit nodded, trying to penetrate this new mystery.

"Listen, when we're together we occupy the same time frame, and the sequence of events is the same for both of us," Mina suggested. "But when we are separated we go to different times, right? So if we meet up again in a third place, like we are right now, why assume that we'll meet each other at the exact point where we left off? We might be catching one another before or after some arbitrary point in the sequence of events." She offered a reassuring pat. "Does that help at all?"

"A little," Kit allowed. "Maybe."

The silence stretched between them for long moments that seemed like hours.

"Cosimo said it wasn't time travel," observed Kit at last. "He was always at pains to point that out, and I never understood why. He'd say, 'Remember, Kit—this isn't time travel.' I remember thinking: when it so obviously *is* time travel, why make such a big deal of denying it?" He looked around at Wilhelmina and gave a half smile. "I think I'm finally beginning to understand why."

"Well, it is time travel, and it isn't. When we make a leap, we do travel in time, after all. But that isn't *all* we do."

"That's right. We leave one reality and enter another that is on a different time stream—like stepping from one merry-go-round onto another. Maybe one merry-go-round has not made as many revolutions as the other, but everything else is more or less the same." He considered this for a moment, then said, "I once asked Cosimo whether it was possible for you to meet yourself in another world. You know? Suppose you popped into London and went to your house, knocked on the door, and—Ta-da! There you are meeting yourself face-to-face. Could that ever happen?"

"What did he say?"

"He said he didn't know if it *could* happen, but that it somehow never did," Kit replied. "It must be that the same person cannot occupy the same reality in two different bodies—something like that."

"I went back to London and visited the bakery and my flat. I even went around to your place, but you weren't there. It was strange, but it didn't occur to me to wonder if I would meet myself there." She thought a moment. "So if I went to a place where there was another Wilhelmina, I would . . . what?" She looked at Kit.

"I don't know. But this idea that once we start jumping around in space and time our lives no longer maintain a linear chronology must be tied up with it somehow."

"Brother Lazarus is convinced that it all has to do with consciousness," Mina said. "If that is true, then it might be that you have only one consciousness, and it cannot be in two places at the same time."

"So you've been coming here and consulting with Lazarus a lot?"

"He's the best," Mina said. "A trained astronomer with a deep knowledge of cosmology and physics—a huge asset. All that, *plus* he understands ley travel."

"I wish *I* did," sighed Kit. He regarded Mina thoughtfully for a moment. "I wonder when we're going to catch up to one another. We have to get synchronised at some point, don't we?"

"I suppose we'll just have to wait and see." Her gaze was earnest and sympathetic. "You endured such hardship. I had no idea, or I wouldn't have sent you there."

"Really, it's okay."

"I looked for you every day—for weeks. Why didn't you just stay put like I told you?"

"But I did," Kit insisted. "If I'd waited any longer I would have taken root. I went back every day for as long as I could, but the line never became active again. I waved your little ley lamp around until I was blue in the face, but could never raise a signal."

"And here was I thinking you'd just got bored and wandered off somewhere." Mina regarded him with a sympathetic look. "I'm really sorry."

"Don't be."

"I feel responsible."

"You're not hearing me, Mina," he said, force coming once more to his ragged voice. "I count it a privilege to have had the opportunity to spend time with the clan, and to learn what I did. I'd go back there any day." He smiled knowingly. "Besides, if none of that had happened, I never would have discovered the Spirit Well."

"If it *is* the Spirit Well."

"What else could it be? There is no such thing as coincidence, remember?" He turned his gaze to the blue-misted valley stretching into the distance far below their mountain perch. "I used to think that was just something Sir Henry and Cosimo said—one of their little mottos."

"And now?"

"Now I know different." His eyes lost focus, as if gazing through a window into a wider, more intricate landscape beyond. "Everything happens for a reason. You don't have to convince me. I'm a believer."

Kit fell silent for a moment, lost in contemplation.

"Tell me again how you found the Spirit Well," Mina suggested at last.

Kit nodded, considering how best to explain. "I mentioned the Bone House, remember?" he began.

"I remember," she replied. "But I can't quite picture what it looks like or exactly what it's for."

"Think of an igloo made of the skeletons of prehistoric animals—a huge mound of intertwined bones—and that'll give you a rough idea. The clansmen carried bones from a kill zone to a clearing in the forest—it's the dead of winter, right? Then En-Ul—I told you about him, remember? Well, the Bone House was made for him—so that he could go and sleep in it. He called it Dreaming Time—"

"The Dreaming Time," repeated Wilhelmina softly.

"No," corrected Kit. "Not *the* Dreaming Time, just Dreaming Time."

Mina's face scrunched up in bewilderment. "What does that mean?"

"I'm not exactly sure. But it seemed that En-Ul went to sleep so that he could dream, and what he dreamed was *time*."

"Like looking into the future, something like that?"

"Maybe," Kit allowed with a shrug. "I got the sense that he somehow entered into the flow of time and was able to manipulate it, or create it. Maybe he saw the future and was able to shape it. I don't know. He was better at reading my thoughts than I was at reading his. Anyway, he took me down there to sit with him while he did it, and while I was there, a ley portal opened up. It registered on your ley lamp. I fell through it and ended up in the most breathtakingly beautiful place I've ever seen—definitely not of *this* world."

"The Bone House *created* the portal?"

"Either that, or the clansmen built the hut there because they sensed the portal was there."

"Just like the mound builders who made Black Mixen Tump," concluded Mina. "They knew it was there."

"Exactly," agreed Kit. "It seems that primitive humans were far more sensitive to earth energies and things like that than we are."

"Which is why they marked them," suggested Wilhelmina, thinking of the standing stones, wells, dolmens, mounds, crosses, cairns, and such scattered willy-nilly across the whole wide world. "Okay, so you fell through the floor of the Bone House and ended up in this amazing place—what happened then?"

"I walked around a little, taking it all in, and I came to a pool of light—I don't mean an area of sunlight in a shadowy place, I mean an actual pool filled with a sort of liquid light—think of honey made of light, or . . . or . . ." Words failed him, so he shrugged. "You'll just have to see it for yourself to understand. I was standing there looking at it when I heard a noise on the other side of the pool." Once again Kit's eyes lost focus as he revisited the memory of a miracle.

"Then what happened?" asked Mina softly.

"I look up, and this man appears, and he's carrying the body of a woman . . ." His voice took on the reverent quality of one reporting a marvellous dream. "She was wrapped in a long white robe and had long black hair; her skin was sickly pale, like grey clay. She was obviously dead in his arms. He comes up to the pool and without a second's hesitation he simply strides into the pool with the dead woman and sinks down into the liquid light. He keeps walking until they are completely submerged in this syrupy liquid." Kit shook his head in awe at the memory. "They seem to be under for a long time—but it must have been only a few seconds . . . you know how time stands still? But then when he surfaces again, the woman is alive."

Wilhelmina gave him a sceptical look. "Are you absolutely certain she was dead? You only saw her across the pond—how do you know she was dead?"

"Mina, she was dead—stone cold dead. You weren't there. You didn't see her. But trust me, Arthur was carrying a corpse."

"How do you know it was Flinders-Petrie?"

"Because," Kit explained, "when he came up out of the pool with her and put her down on the grassy bank, I saw his chest. It was covered with tattoos—the Man Who Is Map, just like in the tomb painting. He was wearing the Skin Map. Mina, he *was* the Skin Map."

"And that's how you guessed the pool was the Spirit Well?"

"That's the first thing that popped into my mind. I remember seeing those symbols and thinking, that's Arthur Flinders-Petrie at the Well of Souls." He paused. "It *is* the Spirit Well, I just know it."

Wilhelmina considered this. "I wonder . . ."

"You doubt me?" said Kit. "You think I'm making this up?"

"No, no," Mina countered quickly. "It's just that since we don't know exactly what the Well of Souls is supposed to be, we can't say for certain that is what you saw."

Kit stood. "Come on, let's go. I'll take you there and show you."

"Right now, this instant?"

"Why not? I can easily find my way back." He gazed down on her with an intensity Mina had never seen in him. "What are you waiting for? If I'm right, we're this close to solving the mystery of the Skin Map."

"Okay, okay," she said, "just pause a minute and let's think about this. If we have to travel back to the Stone Age, we should have some equipment. Knocking about in a cave in total darkness is not my idea of fun. We should have torches, at least—maybe ropes too, and . . . I don't know—a weapon of some sort in case things get sticky?"

"Sure. Whatever," agreed Kit. "Then you'll go with me?"

"Yes, and we'll take Brother Lazarus with us."

"Fine."

"Right. So, as soon as he gets back we'll start assembling the things we need. It will take a bit of time to get everything, and anyway, if this is as important as we think it is, then it is worth doing right."

Kit had to admit that she had a point, and in any case there was nothing to be gained by arguing about it, so he let it slide. "There's something I haven't told you," he said, taking his seat again. "I saw Baby—the cave lion?—I saw it in the cave. In fact, it sort of led me out."

"You followed it?" Mina regarded him askance. "Brave man."

"I didn't know I was following it at the time," conceded Kit.

"I lost my light and then heard the chink of the chain and moved towards the sound."

"You're sure it was Baby?"

"Positive. That chain."

"All the more reason to take a weapon with us," Mina concluded. She thought for a moment, then asked, "These cave paintings—are you sure you can find them again?"

"Pretty sure. Why?"

"Because we can copy the symbols in the cave and test them against those on our piece of the map."

"But we may not need the map anymore," Kit pointed out. "I can find the Spirit Well again without the Skin Map."

"Don't get me wrong," Mina said. "I'm all for it. But we don't know that the Spirit Well *is* the great treasure Cosimo and Sir Henry were looking for. It might be something else, something even bigger. In any case, it won't hurt to spend a few minutes copying the symbols."

"So we'll stop off on the way and make a copy. No problem."

Wilhelmina nodded. "Do you think Arthur Flinders-Petrie was really there?"

"He must have been. How else did those marks get on the wall of that cave?" said Kit. "Either our old buddy Arthur was there and drew them himself, or somebody copied them off his skin."

"We still don't know how to read them," Wilhelmina pointed out.

"True," agreed Kit. "But we may not need them anymore."

They talked a little longer, and then Wilhelmina went in to make some more coffee. She was just pouring the first cups when Brother Lazarus returned with the news that he had been granted leave to accompany Wilhelmina and Kit down the mountain to explore the cave.

"How soon can we leave?" asked Mina.

"As soon as we have gathered the necessary supplies and equipment," replied the priest.

Wilhelmina translated for Kit, who observed, "We don't need all that much equipment. How long will it take to gather a few torches, some rope, and some drawing paper and pencils?" He thought for a moment, then added, "Can Brother Lazarus get his hands on a camera of any kind? We would need a flash too."

Mina and Lazarus exchanged a word. "He says he thinks Brother Michael at the library might have a camera we can borrow. The rest of the equipment shouldn't take more than a couple hours to scrape together. What kind of weapon are we looking for?"

Kit considered this. "Nothing fancy. A hunting rifle—something like that."

Mina spoke to Brother Lazarus, then said, "We won't be able to get our hands on one of those at the monastery."

"Then we can try in the town," said Kit. He stretched and stood.

"It's nearly eleven," Mina told him. "I've got prayers in an hour, and I am in charge of setting out the service books for vespers this evening."

Kit regarded her with a quizzical look. "What are you saying, Wilhelmina? Are you really a nun?"

"No," she said, dismissing the comment with a laugh. "But I do try to fit in while I'm here. I have duties." She rose and faced Kit. "That said, I do find the daily office very meaningful. I don't like to miss it."

"Okay, but—"

"Listen, let's take the rest of the day, get all the gear together, and then set out tomorrow morning after Matins and breakfast—how's that?"

"Well, if you insist . . ."

"A day of rest won't hurt you." She smiled. "And you can use the time to get to know Brother Lazarus better."

"Fine," agreed Kit, regarding the smiling cleric. "As you know, my Spanish and Italian are every bit as good as my German. We'll have a ball."

CHAPTER 31

In Which a Familial
Connection Is Forged

The journey to China had proved a trial of patience and endurance. Schooners, however luxurious—and they were rarely that—might be strong and reliable, but they were slow. Even the swiftest of the new clipper ships took six months or more to reach Hong Kong from Portsmouth, and there was no faster way to make the journey. At least there was no faster way Charles Flinders-Petrie had ever found. Grandfather Arthur might have discovered a ley line connecting Britain to China, but if he had, that was yet another secret he failed to pass along to anyone. The monumental inconvenience of sea travel was one of the main reasons Charles had never made the journey, and the only reason he was making it now was that cruel necessity had forced him from his beloved London garden.

Now, as the humped back of Hong Kong island slid into view beneath the low clouds hanging over the harbour, it was all Charles could do to refrain from leaping into the sea and swimming the rest of the way to shore. The ship made port a few hours later, and by midday Charles was picking his slow way up the dusty steeps of Wah Fu Road, looking for the house of Xian-Li's sister. Having shunned the clamour of rickshaw drivers at the harbour for the pleasure of feeling solid ground beneath his feet after so many weeks aboard ship, he was enjoying his exotic surroundings as much as the physical exertion was making him sweat.

At the top of the hill he stopped and looked about him. The houses in the neighbourhood were oddly out of place—rambling English-style wooden bungalows with steep roofs, deep eaves, and large wraparound porches—built as they were by European businessmen and bureaucrats for families accustomed to suburban sprawl. They were painted white with red trim, and as a concession to climate and decorum, most of the porches and windows were screened with woven bamboo shades. He had never met Hana-Li, but he had the number of the house and, as the widow of a notable government official, she was well known.

When he had caught his breath he continued on, entering a wide tree-lined boulevard where the houses were larger and set back from the road by green lawns strewn with flower beds and ornamental shrubs tended by barefoot gardeners wearing wide straw hats. At last he came to an iron post at the end of a winding driveway. The post bore a sign with the number forty-three painted in gold. He stood for a moment and gazed at the rambling house, wondering whether he would find a welcome within. There was only one way to find out.

Charles walked up the drive and mounted the steps to the porch. There was a bell pull beside the door, which he employed, once and then again, and waited until he heard the quick patter of sandals on the other side of the heavy wooden door. It opened to reveal a sprightly young girl with long black hair, robed in a plain white shift, with simple sea grass slippers on her feet.

"Hello," said Charles with a smile. "I have come to see Hana-Li. Is she at home?"

If his words made an impression on the girl, she did not show it.

"Do you speak English?" asked Charles.

The girl frowned, then turned away abruptly and pattered off, leaving the door open. Charles stood on the threshold gazing into the dark interior of a spacious vestibule lined with standing porcelain pots in green and blue. He patted the parcel beneath his shirt and waited.

In a moment an old woman appeared. Her dove-grey hair was bound in a topknot beneath which a round face, wrinkled as a walnut, expressed a mild curiosity at what had fetched up on the doorstep. Her robe was threadbare and faded, and she carried a dusting cloth in one hand. Taking her for the housekeeper, Charles replied, "I have come to see Hana-Li. Is the lady at home?"

"She is at home," answered the woman in careful colonial English with a whistling lisp. "Who wishes to see her?"

"My name is Charles Flinders-Petrie," he said. "I am the honourable lady's great-nephew."

"Nephew?" wondered the old woman.

Charles offered a reassuring smile. "My grandmother, Xian-Li, was her sister," he explained. "She is my great-aunt."

The woman paused to consider this, her quick dark eyes wary of this bold *gaijin* stranger.

Charles grew uncomfortable under this scrutiny. "Does Hana-Li live here?" he asked finally. "May I see her?"

As if making up her mind about him, the old woman opened the door and stepped aside. "Please, come in."

"Thank you." Charles entered the foyer. The room was dark; a red silk rug carpeted the floor, and two potted palms stood at the doorway into the sitting room.

The old woman gestured toward the second room. "Sit down, please," she instructed.

From among the chairs available, Charles chose a low-seated rattan model with a red silk cushion. The old woman remained standing in the doorway, studying him as Charles settled himself.

"You like tea?"

"Yes, indeed," said Charles. "I do like a nice cup of tea."

The elderly housekeeper nodded and disappeared into the house. Left alone, Charles gazed around the room. It was light and airy, if cluttered with knickknacks of various kinds large and small—the accumulation, no doubt, of a life in government service. What sort of official Hana-Li's husband had been, Charles did not know—only that he had been involved with the British Board of Trade at some time in the past. He wondered why, after her husband had died, his great-aunt had not moved back to Macau.

Presently the old woman returned with a porcelain pot and two shallow cups and a plate of sugared almonds on a teak tray. "You are far from home," she said.

"Yes, I have come a long way to see Hana-Li," he replied. "Is she coming soon, do you think?"

The woman bunched her wrinkled cheeks. "Yes, very soon." She placed the tray on a table and began pouring it out. She handed Charles a cup and then offered the plate of almonds.

"Thank you," said Charles, selecting a few of the sweets.

"I am sister of Xian-Li," announced the woman, taking a seat in the chair opposite. "My name is Hana-Li." She offered a broad, gap-toothed smile, enjoying her little jest at his expense. "Hello, great-nephew."

Charles sat up so quickly, he almost spilled his tea. "Oh, I am sorry!" he blurted. "I took you for the housekeeper."

She laughed. "I know. Little Tam-Ling is housekeeper."

"Please, forgive me."

She batted away the apology. "You honour me with your presence, nephew."

Charles made a little bow. "The honour is mine, dear aunt."

"Did you know my sister?"

"Indeed I did," replied Charles, remembering. "When I was a little boy, she used to let me feed the chickens on the farm. She was always very proper."

Hana-Li nodded over her tea. "Did she have a happy life?"

"Yes, very happy—quiet, but happy, I think. She was a joy to all who met her."

Hana-Li laughed. "You would not say that if you knew her when she was young. She used to pull my hair and scream like a monkey when we fought." She laughed again. "And we were always fighting."

"I brought you something," said Charles, standing up. He fished in the pocket of his jacket and brought out a small parcel wrapped in blue paper. "I thought you might like this."

The old woman took the present, unwrapped it, and opened the box to reveal a jade brooch skillfully carved to resemble a lotus flower. "Oh!" exclaimed Hana-Li. Tears came to her eyes.

"Do you like it?"

She swallowed hard. "Do you know what this is?"

"Xian-Li wore it often. I expect it was her favourite piece."

"It was our mother's favourite too," explained Hana-Li, dabbing at her eyes. "We were very young when she died, and we were very poor. We had almost nothing from her—but this brooch and a few other small things. Father gave it to Xian-Li when she was married."

"Then I am glad I could return it to you."

"Do you have children?"

"A son. He is grown now. No daughters."

Hana-Li held out the box. "Give it to him to give to his daughter when the time comes."

Charles shook his head lightly. "That is a kindly thought. But I think it means more to you than it ever will to him. I insist you keep it."

"Thank you," she sighed. "You make an old woman very happy."

"I have something else for you," he said. "Excuse me a moment." He turned away and unbuttoned the top three buttons of his shirt to withdraw a cylindrical parcel no bigger than the palm of his hand. It was wrapped in fine suede leather and bound with a leather strap of the same material. He buttoned his shirt and turned, offering the package to his aged relative. "This is also very precious, but for a different reason," he said.

Hana-Li took it and regarded the green suede bundle curiously.

"You may open it," he instructed, "and I will explain."

The old woman gently closed the box containing the brooch and set it on the table beside her chair. Her wrinkled fingers worked at the leather lace and in a moment had unwrapped the package to reveal a tightly wound scroll of semi-translucent parchment. She gently unrolled the scrap and spread it on her lap, her eyes playing over the oddly ornamented surface—a spray of fine blue swirls and lines and tiny dots. She lifted the thin, papery material and held it up against the light from the window to study the richly patterned design more closely.

"Have you seen anything like this before?" asked Charles after a moment.

"These are tattaus," she said. "I have seen them many times, as you must surely know, for my father was a tattau maker."

Charles nodded. "And you know that he created many tattoos—*tattaus*—for my grandfather, Arthur."

The old woman held the parchment across her palms. "That is true. He would have come many times to have his tattaus made. But I met your grandfather only once—when he came to take Xian-Li for his wife. After that, we never saw them again."

"What you hold is a parchment made from Arthur's skin," Charles explained, placing his hand reverently on the map.

The old woman's mouth formed a perfect O of wonder.

"It was made to preserve the marks you see on its surface, and it has been in our family for many, many years."

Charles went on to tell her how his father, Benedict—then only a young boy—had tried to secure a copy of the special map when Arthur had died unexpectedly while on one of their travels. The parchment had been made by well-meaning priests in order to preserve the map. "It has been in the family ever since," concluded Charles. "It has proven its worth many times over."

The old woman nodded, uncertain what to make of this revelation. "Why do you wish me to have it?"

"What you hold in your hands is but one small piece of a larger map. I have divided it up into sections, and I bring this portion to you for safekeeping."

"Why me?"

"Because you are the only surviving member of my grandmother's family," Charles replied. "And because no one will ever think to search for it here." He smiled. "No one knows about you, Hana-Li, but me."

She rolled the scroll once more and rewound it in its leather wrap, then handed it back to Charles. "I will think about it."

"Very well," he agreed, but made no move to take the map from her. "Whatever you think best."

"You will stay here with me, and I will tell cook that tonight we celebrate the good fortune of your arrival," she said lightly. "We will eat together, and you will tell me stories of my sister's life in England."

"I would be delighted."

The old woman rose and crossed the room. She lifted a tiny brass bell from a table and rang. Tam-Ling appeared, and the two exchanged a brief word. "She will take you to the guest room, where you can rest from your journey. I will have hot water brought to you."

"You are most thoughtful, Aunt," he said. Taking her hands in his, he pressed them, and added, "I knew that coming here was the right thing to do."

They enjoyed a sumptuous dinner together, and while Tam-Ling ferried various dishes from the kitchen to the table, Charles regaled his aged relative with stories remembered from his childhood and other family stories passed down through the years: tales of Arthur's daring travel exploits; his mother's winsome, slightly otherworldly ways; his and his father's childhood memories of the farm and country life in rural Oxfordshire; and much else. Hana-Li relished the tales, clapping her hands with pleasure from time to time as a particular story unfolded; she added her own recollections of her and her sister's childhood growing up in Macau. The two went to bed that night sated in body and soul.

Charles arose the next morning to a light rain pattering on the roof tiles; he dressed and went downstairs to find his great-aunt waiting for him in the sitting room. She had the leather roll in her lap and was gazing at it intently. He greeted her with a kiss and then, as she clearly had something on her mind, he stood and waited for her to begin.

"I have been thinking," she said, still gazing at the bundle on her lap. "I am a very old woman, and I will not live many more years."

"You are the very picture of health—"

She raised a hand and cut off his objection. "No, it is true. Therefore, I am not prepared to accept this duty." Before Charles could interrupt, she continued. "However, I understand your desire to keep this . . ." She hesitated. "This *remnant* safe and secure." She raised her eyes to Charles for the first time. "I have a proposal to make to you."

"I am eager to hear it."

"I want you to take me to Macau," she said. "It is many years since I visited my home, and I should like to see it again before I die. There is an old family shrine outside the city—my father's and mother's ashes are there. We will visit the shrine and there, I think, you will find a place to keep this"—she lowered her eyes to the object on her lap—"in all safety."

Charles considered this for a moment. "A splendid idea, Aunt. I think you have devised the perfect solution." Indeed, hiding the pieces in tombs and shrines seemed not only appropriate but inspired. He stooped near and gave her a kiss on the cheek. "It would be my pleasure to escort you to Macau to visit the family shrine. We could also see the old tattoo shop if you would like—I know I would."

"Then I will make arrangements," replied Hana-Li. She took the parcel and offered it to him once more. "We will visit the shrine first, and you will place this inside."

Charles made a little bow and accepted the leather-wrapped scroll. Holding it on the palm of his hand, he said, "That will be a most fitting resting place for this particular piece of family history."

CHAPTER 32

In Which the Newest Member Is Fêted

Chairs had been set up in a neat semi-circle in the genizah to accommodate the small but select group. The centre of the big room had been cleared for the special meeting at which Cassandra Clarke was to be inducted into the Zetetic Society, becoming its newest, and youngest, member. In point of fact, she would become its first new member for over a hundred and twenty-five years—a detail she would have found astonishing, but wholly in keeping with the odd group she was still struggling to embrace.

It had taken five days, Damascus time, to gather the membership and for them to arrive; the last to appear was a blue-haired, bird-like geriatric named Tess; spry as a spring lamb and feisty as a terrier, she wasted no time informing Cass that she was eighty-four years of age in one world and a hundred and twenty-nine in her home world. "How old are you?" she asked bluntly, her voice betraying the remnants of a French accent.

"Twenty-five," admitted Cass.

The little woman's grey eyes narrowed and became piercing in their intensity. "Fascinating," she pronounced. "That's when it usually happens, you see?"

"When what happens?" Cass had asked.

"This!" exclaimed Tess. Regarding Cass's puzzled expression, she leaned close and confided, "Enlightenment, *ma chérie*. Enlightenment. True knowledge of the way the world works, insight into the nature of reality."

"Oh."

The pale-grey eyes grew keen. "Every religious figure in history achieved enlightenment between the ages of twenty-five and thirty-five. That seems to be when human consciousness comes fully into its own and acquires a finer spiritual perception. Perhaps it simply takes that long to develop. In any case, it's a well-documented phenomenon. Look it up sometime."

"I will," agreed Cass. "At first opportunity."

"Knowledge of the hidden engines of the universe and the spiritual foundation of all that exists." She winked. "Most people never tumble to it, poor things. I find it tremendously exciting, don't you?"

"I think I'm beginning to."

Tess grabbed her arm and gave it a squeeze with a bony hand. "You are in for the time of your life, *ma chérie*. You'll never look back." She laughed. "As if one could!"

There were others too—eleven in all, seven ladies and five gentlemen—all of them golden-aged senior citizens who should have been in their dotage, yet all of them full of beans and vinegar and fizzing with rare vitality. It seemed to be the nature of ley travel that not only did it extend life, but those who practised it enjoyed health and vigour beyond any normal expectation. Mrs. Peelstick introduced Cass to the various members one by one as they arrived for the meeting, which would be followed by a gala supper to welcome the new inductee.

After a pleasant tea in the courtyard, Brendan called the group to order, and everyone trooped up to the genizah to observe the ceremony. When the august members had been seated, Brendan, looking dapper in a creamy white suit, took his place beside a raised table on which an unlit candle and Bible had been placed. He welcomed the members and banged his gavel on the table, calling the meeting officially to order. "Before we get to this evening's festivities, I must ask if there is any new business to be discussed."

One of the gentlemen—whom Cass identified as Parton—raised his hand. "I have a question about finance," he said.

"Oh, Dickie," chided the one called Maude, "you always have a question of finance."

"The financial health of the society is important, Maude, darling."

"I agree—which is why I have placed my entire portfolio in Brendan's capable hands." She smiled sweetly. "I have more money than God—more than I will ever need, anyway. It might as well be put to good use by the society."

There were murmurs of "Hear, hear!" and "Most generous" and "Well done" from the other members.

"A full report will appear once I've had a chance to ascertain the value of the Williams portfolio," Brendan continued, "as will an official thank-you from the society."

Maude batted away the idea like a bothersome fly. "Bosh! I do not need a thank-you—official or otherwise—for something I'm only too happy to do. The society has been my passion for more than half my life, and it is only right that I might in some smaller measure give back to the institution that has given so much and meant so much to me."

Again there were affirmations of "Hear, hear!" and "Quite right" and "Maudie, you are a treasure" and the like. Cass was touched by the simple sentiment of the exchange.

The old woman gazed around the ring of faces. "Well, I didn't mean to get up on my high horse and make a speech, but there it is." Suddenly flustered by the attention, she made a shooing motion with her thin hands. "That's enough. Let's get on with the reason we're all here."

"If there is no more business"—Brendan paused and looked around the room, then banged his gavel—"done! We will proceed with the induction of our new member."

He held out his hand and asked Cass to join him before the group. As she took her place beside him, he smiled and placed a fatherly hand on her shoulder. "Fellow members, it gives me the greatest pleasure to introduce to you Miss Cassandra Clarke, late of Sedona, Arizona, in the United States of America. A palaeontologist by training and trade, she brings to our gathering a keen mind, honed in the rigorous cut and thrust of the academy. She brings also a thirst for a more thorough understanding of the universe and its manifold splendours, combined with a healthy scepticism in service to an exacting search for truth."

It made Cass feel self-conscious to hear herself described this way, accurate though the words were. She smoothed the front of the smart blue dress that she and Mrs. Peelstick had bought for the occasion, caught herself fidgeting, and folded her hands in front of her.

"Cassandra," Brendan continued, picking up the Bible, "place your right hand on the Holy Bible and repeat after me . . ." He then led her through a litany of phrases in which she solemnly promised to promote the interests, aims, and objectives of the society; to further the search for knowledge through study and exploration; to use such gifts as she was given and that came to her for the good of her human family; to offer immediate aid to any of her fellow members in need; to provide counsel and contribute to the material welfare of the society and its members; to keep herself in perpetual preparedness to further the quest at every opportunity; to safeguard all that would be placed upon her and expected of her; and, finally, to fight valiantly against evil in all its insidious forms to the glory of the Creator who made and—by perpetual loving care—continually sustains the Omniverse and everything that lives, moves, and has being within it.

With her palm firmly on the Bible, Cass repeated the phrases, mentally agreeing with each one and concluded by saying, "I, Cassandra Clarke, make this vow in good conscience and of my own free will, pledging life, health, and strength to the quest set before me, so help me God."

As she spoke these last words, it really did seem as if she had taken on a new and different dimension to her personality, indeed, to her very soul. The feeling was confirmed when Brendan handed her an unlit candle and asked her to light it from the larger candle on the table. As she held her candle to the flame, he said, "May this light be a symbol of the Great Light on which you may rely as you make passage through the darkness of ignorance, evil, and death towards the never-ending light of eternity."

The unlit wick caught, and the candle flared to life with a bright yellow flame. Cassandra turned to face the gathered members once more.

"Ladies and gentleman of the Zetetic Society," Brendan announced, "please welcome our newest member, Cassandra Clarke." To the accompanying applause, he shook her hand, and then each of the other members came forward to shake hands and welcome her into the fold.

Then it was over—a simple ceremony, but satisfactory in every regard. Cass did feel as if she had joined a band of fellow travellers and friends on whom she could rely in the days ahead. A fine meal of Syrian delicacies followed—flat bread with hummus, baba ganoush, roast lamb with rice, broad beans with tomato and mint, fatoush, and chicken kabobs—which Cass enjoyed, but not as much as the company of her fellow diners, who all made it a point to approach and offer her special words of wisdom for travelling the leys: wear loose clothing and carry a change of underwear; gold is the universal currency, always have a few sovereigns or Krugerands at the ready; a Swiss Army knife with a corkscrew is a lifesaver; a no-nonsense cotton scarf can work wonders; sturdy, high-topped leather shoes won't let you down; secure a broad-brimmed hat . . . and so on.

Each comment was delivered with the best wishes of the giver along with a pledge to help their newest member in any and every way possible. Cass thanked them all for their good advice.

Later, as they were having their coffee out in the courtyard under the stars, Tess sidled up to her. "Smell the jasmine," she said, inhaling the sweet, heady scent. "Absolutely heavenly."

"It's always been one of my favourites," Cass replied, drawing in the perfume-laden night air. "Ever since I was a little girl."

"You seem distracted," Tess observed. "Has someone said something to upset you?"

"No, not at all. On the contrary," replied Cass quickly. "It's just . . ." She hesitated, then confessed, "I feel a little daunted, is all. Overwhelmed. So much has happened all at once, and I know so little about any of it. I feel like I've got a mountain to get over."

The old lady regarded her with a sudden intensity, then announced, "I'm going to adopt you, dear heart. I hope you don't mind."

"Not at all," Cass replied. "But do I look like I need adopting?"

"Not in the least," Tess answered. "I do it for purely selfish reasons. I am far too old to pursue the quest anymore, but I can still be involved in my way. I can uphold you in prayer, for example."

"Prayer is our greatest and most salutary weapon in the eternal battle," put in the man called Schecter, joining them. He took a sip of coffee and continued, "No less than gravity, prayer is one of the elemental forces that moves the world. We underestimate it at our peril."

"Keep your sermons to yourself, Robert," Tess told him. "I saw her first." She took Cass by the arm. "Come, we'll go where we can speak a little more privately."

"You cannot keep her all to yourself," Robert called as Cass was pulled away. "We all hope to get to know her better."

They found chairs in a leafy corner of the courtyard and sat down together. "Robert is right, of course, but he *will* pontificate so," said Tess. They settled themselves, and Tess leaned close. "Are you a believer?" she asked in her forthright way.

"In prayer?" wondered Cass.

"In God—Creator and Sustainer of the Universe."

"Well, yes—ever since I was a little girl." Cass regarded her elderly companion. It was not easy to believe that she was as old as she claimed to be; the vitality radiating from her was almost contagious. "Why do you ask?"

"Because it means there is so much less that one must *unlearn*." She leaned back, and a smile spread across her wrinkled face. "I should know—I was the most obnoxious atheist you ever met. In my unenlightened years I positively relished playing the cat among the pigeons with my God-fearing acquaintances. I thought it great sport to poke holes in their reasoning and rhetoric, to point out all the inconsistencies, and to ridicule their muddled thinking. Although so much religious dogma serves only to buttress power and befuddle the masses, it really deserves to be ridiculed. I mean, you hear these so-called revivalists banging on about heaven and hell and what not— what do any of them *really* know about such things? They claim to know what God wants and what he demands . . . Bosh!" She tapped Cass on the arm. "Anyone who tells you he knows the mind of God is selling something. You can take that to the bank."

She looked at Cass's mildly perplexed expression and sat back. "Good gracious me—I seem to have gotten rather carried away. This is not what I wanted to talk about at all. I want to talk about your assignment. Has Brendan mentioned it yet?"

"He hasn't said anything about any assignment."

"No? Well, in my day all new members were required to undertake a purposeful project—something of material value to the advancement of the society, something we need doing."

"He didn't mention anything like that. If he did, it failed to register."

"Maybe it has gone by the wayside," the old woman sighed. "It has been so very long since we had a new member, you see. Perhaps we don't do that anymore." She passed her gaze around the courtyard. "I wonder what has become of Cosimo? I want to introduce you. I've never known him to miss an induction—or a dinner, for that matter. He is usually the life of the party . . ." Her voice trailed off.

"Cosimo Livingstone?" wondered Cass.

"You know him?"

"Brendan told me about him."

"Well, I should very much like you to meet him. I shall look forward to introducing you personally."

"Are you very good friends?"

"Friends, yes, and something more." Her voice took on a wistful note. "Cosimo and I were once engaged to be married."

Cass raised her eyebrows.

"Oh, it would never have worked out," Tess continued quickly. "We had just come off a particularly harrowing journey together—exploring one of the leys on Cosimo's piece of the map. We had grown very close—extreme danger can do that to you, so take that as a word to the wise." Her voice quavered slightly, taking on a wistful note. "Dear Cosimo and I had made all these grand plans, and then . . ."

The silence stretched. "What happened?" asked Cass at last.

"We came back!" Tess laughed, recovering her former good mood. "That is also much the way of things. Once we had returned, we realised it was all a bit fervid and overwrought—passion of the moment, shipboard romance, or what have you. It was simply not to be."

"Oh, I am sorry," Cass sympathised. "I've never been in love like that, but I can imagine."

"We were very fond of one another, still are. But I had my life and he had his, and that was that. Marriage would have made us both miserable in the end. Besides, it would probably have meant that I would have had to give up questing—which in those days it did, anyway—and I was not about to do that."

"But you did give it up, eventually," considered Cass. "Do you miss it?"

"Sometimes," sighed Tess. "But one gets so *old*, don't you know." She gave Cass a sad smile. "I have my memories, and I still travel a bit—like coming to these society functions. But it is for younger folk to shoulder the burdens now. Still, while there is life and breath, I can help. And that is what I mean to do through you." She reached for Cass' hand. "I want you to know that I pledge every resource at my command to aid you in the quest. Whatever you need—money, advice, a soft place to land, the expertise gathered from a lifetime of questing—it is yours. Do not hesitate to ask."

"Thank you, Tess. That is the best offer I've had in a very long time." Cass turned it over in her mind for a moment. "You said Cosimo had a piece of the map," she continued. "You've seen it?"

Tess nodded slowly. "Seen it, yes, and held it in my hands—a hundred times if once."

"Brendan also told me Cosimo's piece of the map has gone missing."

"Has it now? That is interesting. I had not heard about that." She pursed her wrinkled lips. "I wonder if that is why Cosimo isn't here—he's out searching for his bit of the Skin Map."

"Not exactly," countered Cass gently. "It seems Cosimo has disappeared too."

"No!" The old woman gasped. "Disappeared, you say?"

"That's what I've been given to understand," Cass confirmed. "A man named Sir Henry is thought to be with him—and also someone called Kit, his great-grandson, I think."

Tess made a sour face. "Oh, I don't like that. No, I don't like that at all—not one little bit. Something will have to be done." She leaned forward and took hold of Cass' arm. "Finding them is a matter of highest priority." The old woman leaned close. "I see it now. *This* is why you are here!"

"Pardon?" said Cass. "I don't follow."

"Dear heart, you are here for such a time as this. Someone is needed to find Cosimo and Kit, and someone has been provided."

"Me?"

Tess gave her a solemn nod and released Cass's arm. "There is no such thing as coincidence. All that happens to us happens for a reason."

"I'm happy to help, but I must tell you I don't know very much about Cosimo—or anything else, come to that."

"That is easily remedied," declared Tess. "Cosimo doesn't have a permanent home, but he keeps a flat in London—a little bolt-hole where he has a bed and change of clothes and what not. He spends a lot of time with Sir Henry Fayth at Clarimond House. I would try there first. Brendan can give you the coordinates." She stood abruptly. "Where's Brendan got to? Ah, there he is!" Tess declared, striding briskly across the courtyard. "Come along, there is no time to lose."

Which is how Cassandra Clarke, the newest member of the Zetetic Society, found herself in the hills north of Damascus, walking along a path between two stones, taking her first steps to find Cosimo Livingstone.

CHAPTER 33

In Which Haste Makes Hideous Waste

The French doors of Charles Flinders-Petrie's study were open to the garden, and the drapes pulled back to allow the fresh air into a room that had been sealed all winter whilst its occupant was away on his foreign travels. Those journeys completed, Charles had returned to a London in the midst of a glorious spring, and he revelled in the balmy day. Outside he could hear a steady *snip, snip, snip* as Cumberbatch—his caretaker, gardener, and menial—trimmed the box hedge with his long-bladed shears.

The easy rhythm seemed to give shape to his thoughts as he pored over his ledger. The household had functioned reasonably well in his absence, but there were gaps and oversights to be reconciled and rectified. Had he known he would be so long away, he might have made better arrangements. Still, his plans had come right in the end, and the trifling matter of the accounts was nothing that could not be put right with a visit to the bank and a few letters of apology.

All things considered, he was more than satisfied with the result of his latest, and most demanding, labours. He was ready now, to rest and let nature take its course.

There was a stirring of the drapery, but Charles, fully engrossed in his work, thought nothing of it until he heard a brushing step and the creak of wood on the threshold. Glancing up from his reading, he saw a long, thin shadow on the Persian rug, and raised his eyes as the intruder stepped into the room.

"Douglas!" he gasped. "Good heavens, son, you gave me a start."

"Sorry, Father," replied the young man. "It was not my intention to startle you."

"I daresay." Charles closed his book and stood. "What are you doing creeping around the garden anyway? Why are you here during term?"

"I'm done with Oxford, Father," said Douglas. He crossed to the leather wingback chair across from the desk and slouched into it. "Or perhaps, Oxford is done with me."

"Oh, Douglas." Charles returned to his chair behind the desk. "Do not tell me you have been sent down!"

The young man made a sour face. "I have *not* been sent down. I have left the place."

"We have had this discussion before. You must finish your studies."

"Must I, Father?" he sneered. "Why must I? *You* never did."

"Now, see here!"

"No! You see here." Douglas leapt to his feet and began pacing in front of the desk. "I have been taking orders from you all my life, and I am heartily sick of it. I'm not going back there. I don't care what anybody says."

"Lower your voice, Douglas."

"All those petty potentates swaggering about their tiny fiefdoms—nothing but stuffed shirts, gasbags, and idiots, the lot of them."

"That's unfair—"

"It is a bloody waste of time."

"Mind your language in this house!" Charles regarded his wayward son, struggling to keep his temper in check. "What have you done this time, boy?"

"Don't patronise me!" Douglas stalked in front of the desk, restless, bristling with anger. "I won't have it."

"You cannot expect to live here as a guest. You must have work. What do you intend to do?"

"I am taking up the quest," he replied haughtily. "After all, it is the Flinders-Petrie stock in trade."

"Oh, Douglas," his father sighed. "We've been over this before. We agreed that you would wait until you finished your studies. If you abandon them now, you will be in no way prepared to meet the challenges you will face."

"I am ready now."

Charles studied him for a long moment. "You know that is impossible."

"Why? Because *you* say it is?"

"Do we have to go into this all again?" Charles said. "You know how I feel."

The slender young man stood with his hands at his sides, tight as a coiled spring. "I have come for the map."

"No. It is out of the question."

"I'm not leaving here without it."

"It will do you no good. You do not know how to read it."

"I'll learn."

Charles gave a mirthless laugh. "That I heartily doubt," he scoffed. "It is not like reading a road map, you know. You must know the code."

"Then tell me."

"I will—and gladly—on the day you finish your studies." His father made a dismissive gesture with his hand. "Go back to Oxford. Apply yourself. Show me you can finish something for once in your life."

"I'll show you," Douglas said, lurching for the desk. He snatched up the bronze Etruscan mask his father used as a paperweight. "I'll show you what I can do. The key—"

"Douglas, you may leave now. This conversation is over."

"Give me the key, old man." Douglas hefted the heavy artefact dangerously.

"I don't know what you're talking about."

"The key to the iron chest," he snarled. "I want the map. You think I don't know where you keep it?"

"Don't be hasty, Douglas. Taking the map won't get you anywhere. Sit down, let us talk this out."

"All you ever do is talk. I'm through talking. I want the key to the chest." Douglas, eyes bulging, his long face red with anger, raised his arm to strike.

"Put that down!" shouted Charles.

"I warned you, Father," snarled Douglas. On his smooth forehead a vein throbbed visibly like a purple spear of forked lightning as he swung his arm in a murderous arc.

"Douglas!" Charles put up his hands to ward off the attack. "No!"

The weighty bronze smashed into the elder man's skull. Blood spouted from the gash that opened on the side of his head.

"Douglas, no," Charles moaned. He grabbed his head. "Think . . . think what you're doing. Don't be stupid. I can't—"

But the bronze mask landed a crushing blow to Charles' left temple. Charles lifted himself from his chair. Hands shaking, he beseeched his son in pitiful tones, begging him to stop.

Again and again the brass weight slammed down. The hard bone of the skull cracked under three savage blows. Charles slumped to his knees, his eyes rolling up into their sockets, showing only white. He gave a little groan and toppled slowly to his side. A tremor passed through him, and he lay still.

"Good-bye, Father," muttered Douglas, dropping the paper-weight to the floor beside the body.

Stepping quickly around to the desk, he opened the wide centre drawer and removed the ring of keys he knew would be there. Then, turning to the bookcase in the corner of the room, he pulled out a row of volumes to reveal an iron strongbox, which, though it seemed to rest on the shelf, was instead secured to the wall. He put the first key into the lock and turned; the key met with resistance, and the second key was much too big, so he moved on to the third. The lock gave at once, and he raised the heavy lid.

Inside the strongbox was a gilt-edged leather folder tied with a green ribbon. Douglas snatched up the folder and moved back to the desk. As his fingers fumbled with the satin binding, he heard a sound in the hallway, and there came a knock on the door.

Douglas glanced at once to the body on the floor, his mind racing. How much could be seen from the doorway? What if he were found with the body? Where could he hide?

The knock came again, followed by a voice: "Mr. Flinders-Petrie, sir? There's a rag-and-bone man come to call. Do you have anything for him?"

It was Silas Cumberbatch, the caretaker.

"Send him away," Douglas growled in gruff imitation of his father's tone. "I'm busy."

"Very good, sir."

Douglas waited until he heard the footsteps receding. Then, unwilling to further risk being caught with the murdered corpse of his father, he tucked the gold-edged folder under his coat and moved to the French doors. He stepped outside, cast a swift glance around to make sure he was unobserved, then darted across the lawn to the border hedge and a place he knew behind the holly bush where he used to climb over the garden wall as a lad. Once over the wall, he proceeded down the service alley to the road and hailed a cab to take him to Paddington Station.

He bought a ticket and hurried to the platform where the train was waiting, found an empty compartment in one of the carriages, and let himself in. It was only after the train had left the station and was past Ealing and heading for Slough that Douglas removed the leather folder once more.

Setting it on his knee, he carefully untied the strip of green ribbon and opened the cover. Inside was a single piece of paper with a simple handwritten note. It read:

Forgive me, Douglas. It is for the best.

Your loving Father

The Skin Map was gone.

Epilogue

The three travellers hitched a ride down from Montserrat Abbey in the mail truck that called on the monastery every afternoon. Upon reaching the village of El Bruc at the foot of the mountain, they decided it would be prudent to procure a weapon of some description for the onward journey. In the end, the only thing they could find was a sheathed hunting knife from the little general store on the village square.

"If that's the best we can do, so be it," concluded Kit. "We're wasting time."

Attaching the knife to his belt, Kit led the other two back to the highway and started off along the verge, following the tarmac strip as it wound along the river until, after a mile or two, they came to the place were Kit had been found by the hunters. Happily, there were no gun-toting farmers around this time, so they crossed the little stone bridge and headed up the rising slope towards the cliffs. As they walked, Kit tried to set the scene.

"It is the Stone Age. More primitive than you've ever imagined. No buildings, no machines, no metal, glass, or plastic. Skins, not cloth." He patted his clothes. "It is nature in the raw, and it is man against the elements. That said, it is the middle of winter. At least it was when I left—and that means there are loads of hungry animals around, so we'll have to make contact with the clan pretty sharpish if we want to avoid getting eaten."

"Maybe we should have brought more clothes—something warmer?" wondered Wilhelmina.

"Carrying all that extra stuff would only slow us down. Anyway, I think we'll be okay," he told her. "Once we've rejoined the clan, we can get some skins and furs and whatever else we need if it's really cold. We don't need to spend a whole lot of time faffing about. We get to the Bone House and make the jump to the Spirit Well."

Brother Lazarus said something in German, which Mina translated for Kit. "He is worried that the primitives will be frightened by us—that they might attack us."

Kit stopped walking and turned to his companions. "Look, I can't guarantee anything, as I've already said. But they never showed a trace of violence in my presence. They accepted me straight away, which is fairly amazing when you think about it. And, even if they are a little skittish, they'll remember me—I was adopted by the clan, and you're with me. I don't anticipate any problems, so everyone just relax and follow my lead, okay?" He looked at each of them in turn. "Okay."

A few minutes' hard slog up the hillside brought them to the mouth of a cave.

"This is the place," Kit announced. He glanced at the sun, which had passed midday. "We may have to wait awhile for the portal to become active."

They put down their packs, and Wilhelmina consulted her ley lamp. As expected, the blue indicator lights were dark. "Nothing," she announced. "But it's early yet. I'll keep an eye on it. In the meantime, show us this cave of yours."

Brother Lazarus opened his pack and handed around the flashlights. Kit switched his on and off to check it. "Ready?" asked Kit when they had shouldered their packs once more. "Here we go. Watch your step."

Moving into the mouth of the cave, he switched on his torch and stepped into the interior. The air was still and tepid with the faintly musty smell of mildew and fungus. Among a heap of rocks near the entrance, Kit retrieved his furry shirt—hidden where he had left it a few days earlier.

"You were wearing that?" asked Wilhelmina with a laugh.

"I'll have you know this is the height of fashion," Kit replied. "I made it myself."

"You're lucky the hunters didn't shoot you," she said.

Kit rolled up the shirt and stuffed it into his pack. "This way," he said, and led them into the yawning dark. They followed the tunnel deeper into the mountain, their lights playing on the rough surface of the walls. Brother Lazarus took a keen scientific interest in the tunnel shape and rock formation, pausing now and again to examine a particularly interesting feature.

They reached the place where the winding passageway straightened out. Here Kit stopped and flashed his torch along the path he identified as containing the ley line. He had not previously seen it in such clear light, and it appeared different than he remembered. In his mind he had pictured the cave ley as a corridor of straight lines and right angles. But, although the floor of the tunnel was straight and even enough, the walls bulged and wobbled along a length whose end was quickly lost in the darkness beyond.

"Is this the place?" asked Mina, adding her light to his.

"I think so," replied Kit. "It seems about right." He produced his ley lamp and held it out. Not so much as a flicker of light emanated from the device. "Does your lamp show anything?"

Wilhelmina brought hers out and waved it around. "Still nothing," she said. "What do you want to do now?"

"Wait, I guess," said Kit.

The priest, who had been examining a large crystalline seam in the wall, joined them. "We have to wait a bit," she told him in German. "The ley isn't active yet."

"No?" he asked, gazing at the object in her hand.

Mina glanced down. A faint blue sheen was visible in the tiny openings. Before she could open her mouth to tell Kit, the fickle glint faded and died. She stared at the gizmo, willing it to wake up again. "Come on," she whispered. "Glow."

"What are you doing?" asked Kit.

"Shh!" she said. "Watch."

Even as she spoke, the row of lights flickered to life. Kit dug out his ley lamp and held it up. The device remained dark.

"There is definitely something here," said Mina. "Keep watching."

The indigo gleam deepened, strengthening by the second. Kit's ley lamp, however, remained dead, the carapace a cold lump of metal. Mina's ley lamp grew brighter.

"How are you doing that?" Kit asked.

"I'm not doing anything," she said. "It's just that this new lamp is more powerful than the old one. Upgrades, my friend."

The priest reached out and moved Kit's hand until the two devices were side by side. Slowly, the lights in Kit's ley lamp began to glow— a wavering gleam that gradually took hold and intensified until it matched the brightness of Mina's device.

"Now, *that's* interesting," said Kit. He glanced at Mina's face, her features bathed in the cool blue glow.

Brother Lazarus tapped his temple with a forefinger. *"Sehr interessant."*

"He says yes, it's very interesting," Mina translated.

"I got that," said Kit. "Thanks." He flicked his flashlight down the passage. "Well? This is the place. Let's go."

Wilhelmina held out her hand to him. "And let's try to stay together for once, shall we?"

"Good idea." Kit took her hand, and Brother Lazarus put a hand on her pack and gave Kit a nod.

"Right," said Kit. "Forward, march."

He started off with slow, measured strides; when he judged the others were in step, he increased his pace slightly. After a few metres he felt a flutter in the air, a light exhalation of breeze on his skin as from an unseen vent. At the same time he felt the ley lamp in his hand grow warm, and the lights burned with a fierce intensity. He shoved the device into his pocket and readied himself for the jump.

It came a few paces later, and when it did it was so gentle as to be almost imperceptible. The cavern floor shifted under his feet, and the air shivered—as if someone had closed a door in another room. Suddenly he sensed he was standing in a much larger passageway. The jump was complete.

Kit slowed and then stopped to look around, shining his torch over the grey stone walls. The passage opened up a few metres ahead. He stepped through the opening and found himself in a large gallery, the extent of which his flashlight could not illuminate.

"Everyone okay?" he asked.

"Never better," replied Mina. "You can let go of my hand now."

"Brother Lazarus? You okay?"

"*Molto bene*," came the reply. The priest, lapsing into Italian in his excitement, gazed around the room, shining his torch at a hanging cluster of pale stalactites dripping water like icicles from the roof. "*Fantastico!*"

"We go on," said Kit. "There's a side passage up along here somewhere that leads to another chamber. That's where the paintings are."

Kit led his little team into the gallery, staying close to the wall until they came to a gap where the tunnel branched off; the opening was smaller than he remembered. "I think this is the place," he said. "It's a tight squeeze, but it opens up a little farther on."

"After you," said Wilhelmina.

Kit shrugged through the breach and squeezed along the undulating corridor. As predicted, the channel grew wider by degrees until they could walk without touching either side. They came to a sort of anteroom where Kit paused. "I remember this place. This is where I heard the *clinky-clink* sound. I thought it was water, but it turned out to be the end of Baby's chain."

While Mina explained this to Brother Lazarus, Kit examined the walls with his torchlight. The beam swept the uneven surface of the stone, causing the dips and bulges to leap into sharp relief. "The markings are low down on the wall," he told them, moving farther into the chamber.

Mina and Brother Lazarus likewise began searching, sweeping the walls with their flashlights. Brother Lazarus moved to the other side, shining his light a few feet off the floor. "*Achtung! Sie sind hier!*" he called, waving them over.

"He's found them," said Mina, hurrying to the place where the priest was kneeling.

Kit joined them and quickly confirmed that, sure enough, there they were—a cluster of enigmatic symbols, just as he had seen them on his first visit to the cave. "Am I right, or am I right?" he asked.

"Let's check." Removing her pack, Wilhelmina opened it and brought out a short cardboard tube from which she extracted a roll of paper, which she opened and held up against the nearest symbols. Several seemed to form an identical match, but most, while similar, were entirely different.

"Well," he said after a moment, "what do you think?"

"I think you may have hit the jackpot here," declared Wilhelmina. "It certainly seems to be the real thing. I wonder how they got there?"

"Arthur himself maybe? No way to tell."

"*Bene . . . bene . . .*" sighed Brother Lazarus. He put down his pack and extracted a beautifully crafted Leica. With exaggerated care he removed the lens cap and dusted the lens with a soft cloth, then fitted a flash hood. He directed Mina to train her torch on the nearest symbols, took a light reading, set the aperture, then created a human tripod by turning the camera upside down and bracing the bottom against his forehead as he knelt. He refocused the lens and triggered the shutter. There was a silky click, and the flashbulb popped, illuminating the entire chamber with brilliant white light that seared their eyes, blinding them and causing large purple dots to obscure their field of vision. "*Einen Moment,*" he said. Then, fitting another flashbulb, he counted off three and snapped another picture.

Each section of the wall was duly photographed and the camera stowed before continuing on. The next chamber they visited was larger still, and it contained the animals Kit had seen. "I give you the Hall of Extinct Animals," he announced, shining his torch onto a row of chubby horses. Below them was a grumpy-looking rhinoceros, and farther down a bison with forward-swept horns and a young one protected beneath its mother's belly; a pair of delicate antelope leapt on the adjacent wall, together with a bear on hind legs, its claws extended.

"Oh wow!" cried Wilhelmina, rushing to the wall.

"*Magnifico!*" chimed Brother Lazarus with a clap of his hands. "*Straordinario.*"

"It *is* extraordinary," agreed Kit. "They were working on this one when I was here." He shined his torch on the woolly mammoth, the body of which was now fleshed out in greater detail than when he had last seen it.

Just then his light began to dim. "Uh oh," he said, giving the flashlight a shake. "We'd better move along. We can always come back."

Kit and Mina switched off their torches to preserve the batteries, and the three hurried on. Kit led them to the main passage and from there to the outer entrance of the cave, pausing briefly a few metres from the opening. "Here we are," he said, blinking in the relative brightness of the daylight streaming in through the ragged gap. "Out there is nature in the rough. It is strictly no frills from here on," he told them. "Is everybody still keen to meet the Flintstones?"

Wilhelmina translated for the priest, who nodded his head. "Sole purpose of visit," Mina replied for both of them.

"Right, let's do it." Kit stepped to the outer opening and into the light. "Stay alert and be ready to run at all times."

Kit went first, taking a good look around before climbing through the opening. Wilhelmina came next, followed by the priest, and all three stood on the sloping escarpment shielding their eyes from sunlight as they took in the scene before them: a verdant valley bounded by sheer cliffs of white limestone rising up on every side. The trees and shrubs were in full leaf, and the air was hazy, full of insects, and warm.

"It was winter," he said, raising a hand to the faded greens and ripening golds of early autumn. "Just a couple days ago it was winter."

"A couple of days for *you*," Mina reminded him. "We obviously haven't got the time frame calibrated for a proper match." Seeing the disappointment on his face, she added brightly, "Still, with any luck we're probably not too far off the mark."

"I hope you're right," he said. "In any case, we'll soon find out." He started down to the valley floor, sliding on the loose scree. With a last look around for lurking predators, Kit started towards the slow-flowing river that was now but an oozy trickle at summer's end. They walked along, keeping close to the wall of the gorge, picking their way over the rocks, now in bright sunlight, now in shadow.

Occasionally Kit paused to get his bearings, recognising various landmarks and bends in the river. The sun was dropping behind the towering cliffs by the time they reached the place Kit identified as the winter camp of River City Clan. His heart beat a little faster at the sight, and he bounded up the narrow trail leading to the stony ledge where he had last seen En-Ul and the others.

The ledge was empty now, all signs of habitation—recent or otherwise—completely scoured away. All that was left were a few dried leaves and powdery white dust.

"They're gone," he said, his voice heavy.

Brother Lazarus took a look around, then turned and said, *"Sie kommen im Winter hierher, richtig? Winter wenn sie hier kommen, korrigiert?"*

"Yes," Mina confirmed, "they only come here in winter—that is correct." She turned to Kit. "That's what you said, right?"

Kit nodded. "Then they might be back at the river camp." He thought for a moment. "That's miles from here, and I'm afraid we're going to lose the light. Much as I'd like to make contact right now, that can wait. I think we should press on to the Bone House. First things first."

"Whatever you say, captain," replied Wilhelmina.

Returning to the valley floor, he led them along the river to a nearby trail that climbed up the cliffside and out of the gorge. "This is the way out," he said. "The Bone House is up on high ground in the middle of the forest just beyond the canyon rim."

Kit pushed a relentless pace up and out of the gorge and wasted no time making for the place where he had helped the young clansmen erect the shelter made from the skeletal remains of animals. He had no difficulty finding the place; the crevice where they had gathered the bones was still there, as was the wide circular clearing in the woods.

But the Bone House itself was gone, and in its place was an enormous yew tree with shaggy brown bark and short needles of deepest green. The tree's trunk was gigantic—a half dozen people or more would have been required to link hands to reach around it.

"Well," concluded Kit unhappily, "needless to say, *this* was not here before." He shook his head. "Look at this thing." He indicated the great spreading branches, dark in the gloaming wood. "It's a thousand years old if it's a day!"

Mina and Brother Lazarus gazed at the tree and at the blue patch of sky above. The light was fading fast.

"Dies ist der Ort, sind Sie sicher?" asked the priest.

"He's asking if you're sure this is the place," translated Mina. She started pacing off the distance around the massive yew.

"Yes—I mean, I think so," replied Kit. He gazed around the almost perfect circle of the clearing. "This is it. This is where the Bone House stood. But obviously we're way off course. It looks like we'll have to go back and start over."

"Maybe not," said Mina.

"What do you mean?"

"Check your ley lamp, Kit."

He pulled the device from his pocket to see that it was shining with an intense blue light. "I knew it! The ley is here all right. That hasn't changed."

Mina completed her circuit of the tree and came to stand beside Kit, ley lamp in hand. They held the two gizmos together; the blue lights combined to bathe their faces in a radiant glow.

"*Sehr gut,*" murmured Brother Lazarus, taking his place beside them.

"A very good sign," agreed Mina. "The ley is here and it is highly active."

The electromagnetic force of the ley continued to build, intensifying to an extent they had never witnessed before. The indigo lights pulsed with an ever-increasing strength, and the ring of yellow lights on Wilhelmina's ley lamp flashed and blinked with random bursts, as if tracing the violent surges of power swirling around them.

"Ow!" cried Mina, dropping her lamp and clutching her hand.

"What happened?" said Kit. "Wha—Yikes!" He dropped his device too. The heat had suddenly spiked to an unbearable level.

Mina held out her hand. The palm was red where the flesh was burned. "That's never happened before."

Even as she spoke, there was a faint sizzling sound. Threads of white smoke emanated from the little holes in the brass carapace of

Mina's ley lamp, followed by a soft pop like that of a cork withdrawn from a bottle. Instantly the lamp went dark.

A second later Kit's lamp fizzled out too, and the air carried the distinct whiff of ozone.

"I guess that's that," said Kit.

Brother Lazarus took Mina's hand and examined the burn.

"We know the ley is here—no doubt about that," said Kit, taking in the yew's massive trunk, hard as iron and big as a house growing right in the middle of the ley. "Now all we have to do is figure out what to do about this whacking great tree."

On the Road Again

Human beings are made to travel, it seems. And a lot happens on roads. Most ancient cultures revered the road as a sacred place—the Celts, for example, considered the junction where two roads crossed a holy place. Certainly, the road is a metaphor for change and transformation—originating, perhaps, in tales such as Homer's *Odyssey* and expressed in modern terms in books like *On the Road* by Jack Kerouac.

In Hollywood "the road" is enshrined in a genre all its own: the road movie. From the larky string of Bob Hope and Bing Crosby productions such as *The Road to Rio* all the way to *Thelma and Louise* and extending even to absurdities like *Dumb & Dumber*, the road movie is both a symbol and a celebration of the innate spiritual desire to change, to be transformed. As physicist Werner Heisenberg, a man who knew something about the elusive nature of reality and its effects on the human spirit, put it, "The human race seems to love nothing more than a long detour."

The road and its inherent detours, dangers, and disasters can be a forceful agent of change. Approaching the outskirts of Damascus in the Arab Spring of 2011, I could easily recall the journey of the man who would become known to history as Saint Paul. In the early first century, however, he was still known as Saul, and he was on his way from Jerusalem with a heart full of hate when he was struck down by a flash of light so powerful it could not be ignored; Saul fell to the ground, and God spoke. Ironically, the purpose of his journey was to destroy the men and women who claimed to belong to "The Way"— the name given then to those we now call Christians.

Once in Damascus, Saul was led down what the gospel of Luke terms "the Street called Straight" where, blinded, humbled, and desperate to make sense of what had happened to him, the newest convert to The Way was eventually taken to the house of a man named Ananias. While strolling down that famous Straight Street myself, it became clear to me that my early familiarity with the biblical story of Paul's dramatic journey on the road must have contributed to, if not inspired, my use of ley lines as portals between realms of existence—an impression enhanced, I expect, by my surroundings: Damascus is one of the world's timeless cities, a place where the remnants of successive empires have each left their indelible marks—a place where a traveller could easily believe he or she was two thousand years in the past.

The tale unfolding in the five books of the Bright Empires series has been growing in my mind for over fifteen years. In common with the characters in the tale, and by way of research to enable a more accurate atmosphere in the telling, I have walked down canyoned alleyways in London, strode between parallel ranks of sphinxes in Egypt, descended into the sunken, sacred tufa roads of Tuscany—the current name for old Etruria—and followed the straight path through the Dordogne, Syria, Arizona, Eastern Europe, and most recently, Lebanon. Placing my feet exactly where countless others have placed theirs, often over many millennia, I can easily imagine emerging at the other end of the passage a different person, in a different time.

This is, of course, the imperative and the appeal of pilgrimage: to change over the course of a journey. As the landscape approaches and then disappears, the traveller confronts his hopes and fears, his questions and doubts . . . and then leaves them behind as he walks, it is hoped, into a place of enlightenment and welcome.

Walking on the Camino de Santiago in Spain, the venerable pilgrim route that begins almost anywhere in Europe before finally merging on the French side of the Pyrenees to cross over into Northern Spain, I saw and experienced firsthand the power of the pilgrim path. At the beginning of the journey, many of my fellow pilgrims carried huge rucksacks stacked high and bulging with the necessities of travel, with foam cushions and sleeping bags, teddy bears, tin cups, and extra clothing, flags, and all sorts of bric-a-brac dangling from their massive backpacks.

As the trail wound through mountains and hills, across arid plains and stretches of wilderness to Santiago de Compostela, and as the days bled into weeks, those same overstuffed packs tended to lose their bulk. Near the top of one particularly challenging mountain a day or two from journey's end, I came upon a veritable cairn of T-shirts and waterproofs, paperback books, socks, trousers, bedrolls, and—yes—those teddy bears and tin cups. Labouring up the mountain with my fellow pilgrims, one weary foot in front of another, it was clear that the sense of adventure with which we had all started out had now turned into something else altogether. We were all on the road, *el camino*—but some of us were also, clearly, on The Way.

And the road was growing difficult. Everything unnecessary

had to be jettisoned. Everything that hindered, that held back, that weighed down and encumbered—it all had to go.

Entering Santiago, I observed triumphant pilgrims walking or dragging themselves into the city with flaccid packs, a few carrying only what they had stood up in that morning: a hat, a stick, a bottle of water stuck in a pocket. Everything else had been cast aside in order to complete the journey.

The destination was important, to be sure; the path was not an aimless wandering through the wilds of Spain, after all. Santiago had long gleamed like a city of gold in our imaginations, and that image of safety, rest, and refreshment exerted a mighty pull. But it was the journey itself, the physical act of *going*, that transformed the pilgrims. For if there was to be any transformation in the spiritual orientation of the pilgrim's soul, that change would take place not on arrival as if by magic, but in the long, hard work of The Way.

Acknowledgments

Nabile Mallah was my guide and instructor whilst travelling in Syria during troubled times, and his enthusiasm was inspiring. Adrian Woodford led that trip with skill and wisdom—thanks.

Scott and Kelli Lawhead generously introduced me to the strange beauty of Sedona.

Richard Rodriguez, Hailey Johnson Burgess, Matthew Knell, Daniele Basile, and Sabine Biskup kindly proofed the Spanish, French, Latin, Italian, and German dialogue in this book.

As always, the errors belong to me.

COMING SEPTEMBER 2013

A BRIGHT EMPIRES NOVEL
Quest the Fourth

THE
SHADOW LAMP

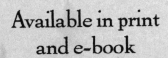

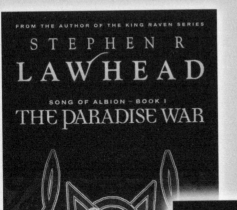

THE Dragon King TRILOGY

Stephen Lawhead's best-selling trilogy is being relaunched for a new generation of young adult readers.

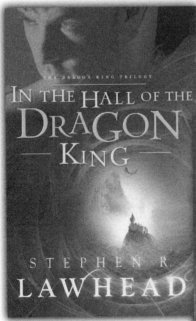

Available in print and e-book

Stephen R. Lawhead is an internationally acclaimed author of mythic history and imaginative fiction. He is the author of such epics as The King Raven, Song of Albion, and Dragon King Trilogies. Lawhead makes his home in Oxford, England, with his wife.

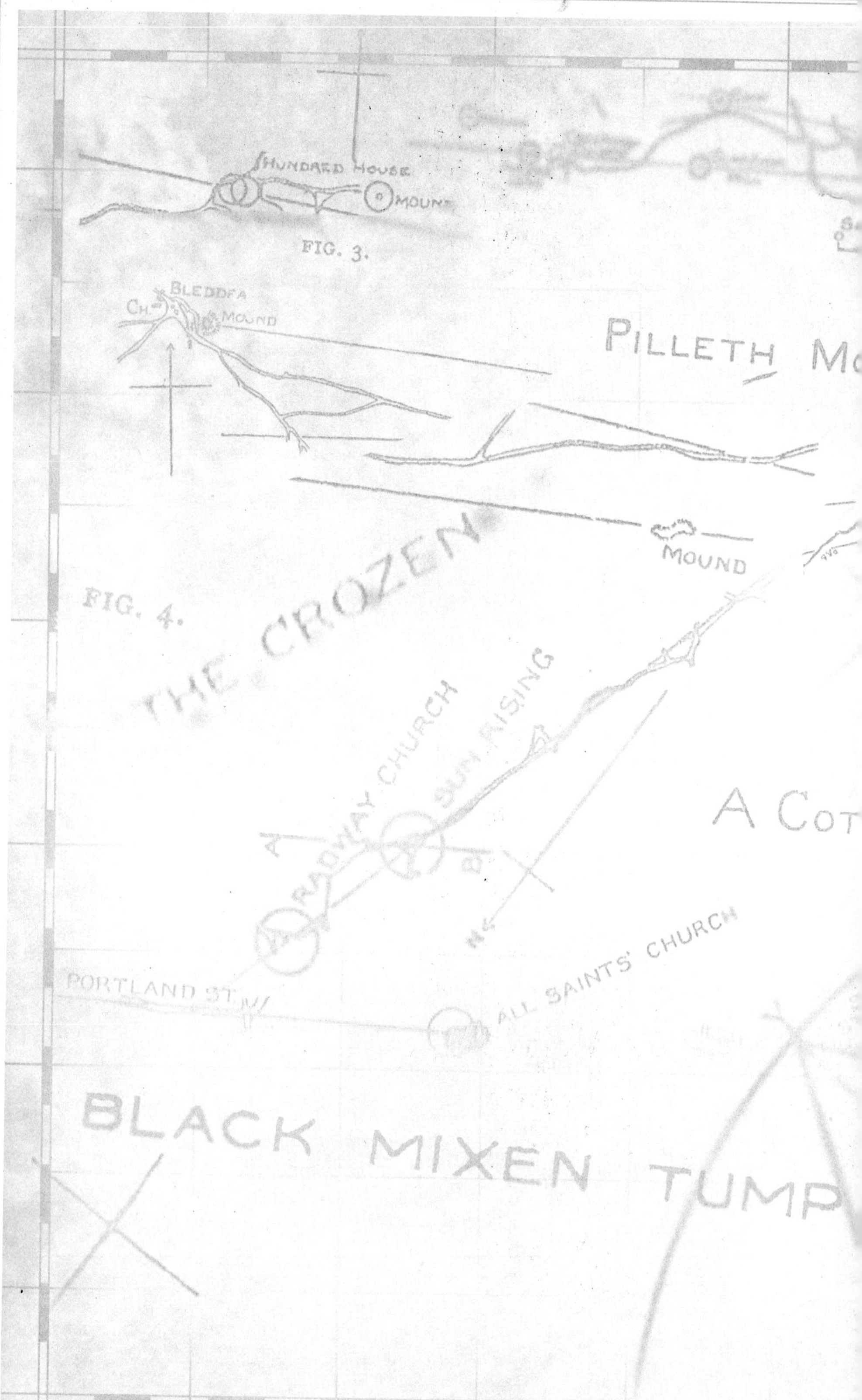

HUNDRED HOUSE

MOUND

FIG. 3.

BLEDDFA

CH.

MOUND

PILLETH Mo

FIG. 4.

THE CROZEN

MOUND

BROADWAY CHURCH

SUN RISING

A COT

PORTLAND ST.

ALL SAINTS' CHURCH

BLACK MIXEN TUMP